To: Ann & Jim
Long time

I, TUTUS

BOOK 1:
THE SON OF HEAVEN

In recognition of your unstinting service (OK, maybe an occasional stint) to our country

By

DON PHILLIPS

Don Phillips
12/10/05

PublishAmerica
Baltimore

© 2005 by Don Phillips
All rights reserved. No part of this book may be reproduced, stored in a retrieval system or transmitted in any form or by any means without the prior written permission of the publishers, except by a reviewer who may quote brief passages in a review to be printed in a newspaper, magazine or journal.

First printing

ISBN: 1-4137-5932-7
PUBLISHED BY PUBLISHAMERICA, LLLP
www.publishamerica.com
Baltimore

Printed in the United States of America

To Amelia, Christine, and Katherine

And, of course, to Chloe and Skye

AUTHOR'S ACKNOWLEDGMENT

~~~

I would like to thank all those who provided support and encouragement as I struggled through this project and who provided many useful suggestions—in particular, Juliet Bender, Robin Bordie, Ernie Grigg, Scott Ki, and Gaye Tawney. I am especially grateful to my wife, Amelia, for her unstinting enthusiasm for the book and her sharp editing skills. Special thanks also to my mother, Eloise, and my daughter, Christine, for their encouragement, careful review, and keen eye for typos and incongruities.

Very special thanks to Lady J (Janice) Shields. But for her hard work, dedication, and indefatigable cheerleading, this book would not have been completed. I also owe a debt of gratitude to the extraordinarily talented Hugh Philipp and Fred Fischer for their indispensable technical assistance in transforming my very crude and inchoate ideas into a polished cover design, creating a map of Tutus' travels, and facilitating the work in a variety of other ways.

I, Tutus is a work of the imagination. But, for this author at least, the imagination thrives only in a rich subsoil of fact. A great many sources provided this nourishment but I would like to acknowledge, in particular: *A History of the Former Han Dynasty* by Pan Ku, translated, with annotations, by Homer H. Dubs; *Everyday Life in Early Imperial China During the Han Period, 202 BC- AD 200* by Michael Loewe; *The Chinese Heritage* by K.C. Wu; *The Essential Confucius* by Thomas Cleary; *The Book of Songs, the Ancient Classic of Chinese Poetry*, translated by Arthur Haley; *Foreign Devils on the Silk Road* by Peter Hopkirk; *Great Thinkers of the Eastern World*, edited by Ian P. McGreal; *The Silk Road* by Judy Bonavia; and *The Hidden Life of Dogs* and *The Social Lives of Dogs* by Elizabeth Marshall Thomas.

I would also like to express my deep appreciation to the University of

California Press for permitting me to enrich the dialogue in Chapters 5, 7 and 8 with four marvelous poems— 'Through Your Window," "A Song of Cherry Time," "The Philanderer," and "A Drinking Bout," translated by Henry Hart in his book *The Hundred Names: A Short Introduction* (Copyright ©1933 The Regents of the University of California.)

I am also grateful to the Library of Congress for the use of their magnificent (both from an aesthetic and a professional point of view) facilities and to the somewhat less sumptuous but very helpful Public Library of Prince Frederick, Md.

We need another and a wiser and perhaps a more mystical concept of animals ...caught like ourselves in the net of life and time, fellow prisoners of the splendour and travail of the earth.

–Henry Beston
The Outermost House

And, to say all in a word, everything which belongs to the body is a stream, and what belongs to the soul is a dream and a vapour, and life is a warfare and a stranger's sojourn, and after-fame is oblivion. What then, is that which is able to conduct a man?

–Marcus Aurelius, A.D. 121-180
In Caruntum, *Meditations*

FOREWORD

Convinced that human urine could be transmuted into gold, the 17th century German chemist/alchemist Hennig Brand uncovered the seemingly magical properties of phosphorous. And as every schoolchild knows (or used to know), it was in seeking the spice-rich Orient that Columbus discovered the vastness of America. The mysterious and beneficent workings of serendipity lie also at the heart of *I, Tutus.*

The seminal event was a long conversation with Professor Wilson Crying Crow Davis of the Department of Parapsychology, San Raphael College. I might note that, in addition to his outstanding academic credentials, Professor Davis is a full-blooded Hoopa on his mother's side and a practicing shaman.

Wilson brought to my attention several fascinating instances where "channelers" had entered into contact with a "spirit" who had lived in the past—instances where they had actually experienced the raw, day-to-day occurrences of these lives. We were particularly excited by the contacts experienced by Rosanna Hofstra. Ms. Hofstra had reported in great detail her "transportment" into the being of a shaman of a little known Potawatomi tribe in Northern Michigan about 300 B.C.E. Her reports had enabled researchers to identify the nature and purpose of a number of puzzling artifacts found in ancient Potawatomi burial sites—artifacts of which Ms. Hofstra could almost certainly have had no prior knowledge. At the end of our conversation, we quickly agreed on an inter-school, interdisciplinary project.

Thus, my voyage began. My goal: to make contact with, and enter into the life of, an adult male or female belonging to one of the Native American hunter-gatherer peoples, well before the arrival of Europeans. Channelers, I might note, almost always have a quite different agenda. They seek contact with "higher spirits" and, from them, messages of inspiration, guidance, or solace. They tend to be fearful of getting "slimed" (to use the parlance of channeling regulars) by contact with low-ranking or unsavory beings.

Upon my arrival in San Francisco, Wilson arranged a meeting with

Gretchen Roskilde, an experienced practitioner of an astonishing range of parapsychological activities—not only channeling but also such areas as reincarnation, re-birthing, and life contract renegotiation. Ms. Roskilde agreed to serve as my guide into the world of channeling (not, however, without a sizeable up-front fee, which I wrangled from our history department with considerable difficulty). I will say little about our collaboration except that it was not successful. I retain the highest regard for Ms. Roskilde's psychic abilities and her skills and virtues—but patience is not one of them (nor does she believe in refunds). There were more futile attempts to "invite" an entity than I care to remember. They would begin with stern commands which would rise slowly but inevitably to shouts:

"Relax... Concentrate..." (which always struck me as somewhat inconsistent)

Then, "You must learn to relax!"

"Empty your mind of the day-to-day!"

"Relax!!...Concentrate!!"

Then, "THIS IS IMPOSSIBLE!!!" and, finally, "YOU ARE JES MOUTING DA WERDZ"—her buried Teutonic accent set free by sheer exasperation. After two weeks, we decided to part ways.

Wilson then arranged a meeting with Tami Watchcroft, the well-known Los Angeles psychic and authoress of several fascinating books on channeling and the spirit world of which probably the best known are: "The Whisperings of the Rainbow: A Guide to Self-Renewal" and "Awakening the Sleeping Chakras: How to Regain Intimacy with Divinity." I met Tami in Monterrey, where she has established the Arraya Ux Ra Center for Psycho Energetic Healing. It took only a few minutes for Tami to gain my full trust and confidence. Not only is she a brilliant, dedicated and serious (though not oppressively so) practitioner of channeling, she is also a genuinely warm, caring and giving human being—with the proverbial patience of a saint. (She also believes in customer satisfaction and without prompting offered a money-back guarantee).

Tami and I first agreed on a radical change of technique. Ms. Roskilde believed firmly and exclusively in conscious channeling. She did not accept as valid, nor would she participate in, any sort of trance channeling. Tami took a more catholic approach to this issue, believing that there is a time and place for the full spectrum of techniques. In my case, given my academic background and training and what she termed my "hyper-techno-materialist upbringing," and the attendant problems I experienced in achieving the necessary degree of relaxation, she suggested that we go immediately to full trance channeling.

I began our session very skeptical of the efficacy of hypnosis, naively believing my mind too strong to succumb to it. Suffice it to say that, within seconds, using only the hoary technique of a swinging pendant, I was in a full hypnotic trance. Unfortunately, this did not result in immediate success.

With Tami's prompting, I "invited" an entity to step into my energy field. I did not specify a particular entity or being, of course, since I sought someone outside known history; nor did I ask for "highest beings of light possible" (a common request). No, I sought someone primitive, whose instincts had not yet been deadened by the heavy hand of advanced civilization, someone in whom the senses still held sway over the artifice of language. I set out a number of other specifications, even suggesting a few peoples or "tribes," by name. Many sessions passed and nothing occurred—though I began to feel, or thought I felt, faint stirrings.

Tami cautioned me not to strain. She assured me that the true channeling experience was quite vivid and unmistakable. I would know it with certainty when it occurred, she told me, flashing her trademark demure and kindly smile. Nonetheless, I grew very discouraged. But Tami was not in the least shaken in her determination and steadfast in her encouragement to persevere.

On the day of the breakthrough I was ready to give up. I remember jogging alone on the beach that morning. It was a cloudy, cool August day, and sea and sky merged into an inseparable, impenetrable gray just beyond the crash of the waves. In the face of such barren results, I could not afford, from either a personal or career perspective, to spend more time on the West Coast. I decided to give it two more days—and if I were still unsuccessful, to leave on the weekend.

When I came out of the trance later that morning, Tami was looking at me strangely. She was clearly upset.

"You were growling," she said in a cold voice, sounding nothing like her usual self.

"Really?" I replied.

"And making some sort of snorting sound. And panting, panting like a dog!"

Sensitive to a fault, Tami thought that I was ridiculing channeling—and her. At that moment, the experience rushed vividly into my memory. I assured Tami that I was not playing the buffoon and spelled out my recollections in great detail. In that first contact I was running about in an immense lacquered

11

room, being pursued by a group of obese, smooth-faced men yelling in frantic, high-pitched voices. Their features and dress suggested, even to my (then) untrained eye, old imperial China.

As you can imagine, after so many weeks of futile effort, we were tremendously excited. Nonetheless, I perceived it as merely a way station to my real goal—contact with a hunter-gatherer. Thus, in accordance with Tami's guidance, at our next session, I asked the "inviting entity" to leave and sought one more satisfactory. This pesky dog spirit proved not so easy to dismiss, however. It would sulk for a day or two, during which I pursued utterly fruitless attempts to summon up another entity—only to return to enmesh me in another scene from its former life. I remember that the second and third contacts took place in what was undeniably ancient Rome.

Two weeks passed: desultory contacts with the dog, otherwise a blank screen. I swallowed hard and reconciled myself to the fact that fate, or the spirit world, had ordained that it was this amazing and amusing creature whose consciousness I should enter. (After some initial confusion, I ascertained the dog to be a female pug—an ancient breed of Chinese origin believed to date at least as far back as 400 B.C.E—and the time period covered by our contacts to be roughly 2-12 C.E., or A.D.)

Only gradually did I realize the full extent of my good fortune—that the cranium of this tiny dog (whom I shall now call by her last, Roman name of Tutus) would provide a sort of camcorder through which I would witness the crushing of innocence by decadence and intrigue in ancient China, experience the incredible hardships of the Silk Road and the savage joys of the vast Eurasian steppes, and unearth a failed and almost unknown conspiracy that could be said to mark the end of the Roman Republic! But Tutus was much more than a camcorder, for I apprehended this ancient world in a most singular way—through the sensory and emotive apparatus of a canine!

I feel it incumbent upon me to state that, at this point, my collaboration with Professor Wilson, for whom I retain the highest regard, ended. Professor Wilson felt strongly that I should continue to hold out for contact with a higher being; communion with a dog, he believed, would demean this new mode of academic inquiry and render it vulnerable to ridicule. We parted ways amicably.

Over the next three months, we worked virtually around the clock. When I was not actually in a trance — usually 5-6 hours a day (although not consecutively), I was furiously transcribing and reviewing my sessions with Tami. To illuminate and provide context for them, I also embarked on a crash course in ancient history, very much neglected in my formal studies which had focused on pre-historical peoples. I sought out, through my network of colleagues in various universities and through the Internet, scholars and experts who could provide advice and assistance. While a great many people have been helpful, I owe a special debt of gratitude to three: Dr. Irwin Ching, Professor of Classical Chinese Studies at the University of Taipei; Dr. Vasily Komodorovich, Professor of Ukrainian and Central Asian Studies at the University of Kiev; and Dr. Norman Feathersworth, Head of the Classical Studies Division of the Department of History, Sioux State University (South Dakota).

Alas, my selfish monopoly on Tami's time and formidable energies could not continue forever. Her lecture tour was scheduled to begin just after Thanksgiving; the dates were inflexible, the commitments ironclad. I, for my part, had bills to pay, the drudgeries of modern life piling up unattended at home, a significant other whose interest seemed to be drifting, and several cats to retrieve from an increasingly irate friend. Tami and I clung to each other for a long time at the airport before I got on the plane to Baltimore. We felt we had achieved, and endured, much together. Something altogether unique.

Enough of this prattling foreplay! The story of Tutus Indomitus Minimus can speak for itself. It begins with Tutus' early life (or rather that of Xiao Ji Long, as she was then called) at the Imperial Palace in Chang'an, the ancient capital of China. This volume recounts those (mostly) happy Palace days and her perilous journey across the Silk Road. A subsequent book will tell the rest of the story—of her life among "barbarian" nomads on the Eurasian steppes and of her arrival, rise and fall in ancient Rome.

Professor Sunny Dayberry
Visiting Scholar
Department of Anthropology
Patuxent State College
St. Leonard's on-the-Cove, Md.

Note: For the convenience of the reader, I have occasionally inserted explanatory notes into the text in brackets.

PART I

少吉龙

**Little Lucky Dragon
(Xiao Ji Long)**

Twinned in times primeval, beyond reach of memory.
Ancient truths and sure instincts long since sundered,
Muddied by cities and kings and gods,
the mad pretense of science.

The dog a steady, dependable moon
About the rushing, wobbling, uncertain orbit of man.

– C. Darlington Gushing
  The Strangest Species: Verse Offerings (1937)

1
My Illustrious, But Difficult, Birth

My sire was Mighty Tiger Slayer, famous for his quickness, his ability to jump and his ferocious manner. He had been brought from the far city of Lin 'An near the sea, a journey of many weeks, which left him frazzled and irritable and in no mood to mate.

My dam was Most Delicate Harmony, renowned for the beautiful shape of her head and ears and the vivid black markings on her face—above all, the perfect black diamond that graced her forehead. She had come from the kingdom of Chung-San, where the Emperor had been made king when he was only three years old. It was said that the Emperor's mother, who had now been made queen of Chung-San, had begun weeping the day Most Delicate Harmony left and had not ceased for two weeks, wailing that Heaven had first called her son from her and now her dearest companion. Despite the reassurances of family and servants, she was unshakeable in her conviction that she would see neither of them again. Most Delicate Harmony was kept hidden in the outskirts of the Commanderie of the Successor to the Magnificence in the North until the red drops began to fall and then she was smuggled into a small building near the palace grounds that had once housed the infamous blind musicians of the Emperor Chengdi.

Both sire and dam traced their ancestry through a long line of champions of the Lo-sze [Pug] breed going back to the early beginnings of the Han dynasty. Thus, expectations ran high for their mating and the stubborn hostility of Mighty Tiger Slayer to my beautiful mother was met with disbelief and consternation. Not only did he refuse to mount her on the first three occasions when they were brought together but he actually attacked her, and these sessions ended in a horrible tangle of shrieks and growls and snapping, bared teeth—and the curses and lamentations of the eunuchs. After that, he became coldly indifferent to her. He would stand rigid and aloof in the corner of the 'bridal chamber' devised for them, a look of horror in his eyes, ignoring the provocative sniffs of my mother, the beguiling twitches of her rump and the derisive encouragement of the eunuchs. It was only on the twelfth, and last, day of her time of fertility that he succumbed to her charms and a successful mating was achieved.

Most Delicate Harmony suffered much during the pregnancy. By her eighth week, she had become very heavy, her belly nearly dragging the floor. Often, in the midst of a slow, waddling, joyless walk about the musicians' building, she would suddenly plop over on her side. Despite the cool autumn air, she would pant and snort as though it was insufferably hot, staring without interest directly ahead of her. While some days she would eat ravenously, other days she would turn from the bowl in disdain and ignore the tasty morsels that the eunuchs would hold just before her muzzle.

Her condition greatly alarmed the eunuchs—for the offspring of two such champions would be much coveted and great plans had already been made for their gifting. The healthiest male would be presented to the Emperor Pingdi himself and a great ceremony was envisaged. The healthiest female was to be given to the Grand Empress Dowager Wang, whose preference for female pugs was well-known, and on whose favor everything depended. If there was a third pup, whether male or female, it was to be presented to the daughter of Wang Mang in the hope that such generosity would thwart objections on his part and lessen the risk of retribution. When Most Delicate entered her ninth week, the eunuchs began to give her warm baths and administer various potions said both to speed and ease birth. The most splendid meals that could be surreptitiously commandeered from the palace cooks were offered to the gods at the Temple of Kao, where the giant stone lion dog stood, in the hope not only of easing the burden on Most Delicate Harmony but also of ensuring birth in the ninth month of the year, which was seen as much more auspicious than the tenth month.

On moushen, the last day of the ninth month, a great commotion arose outside. Bells rang, drums were beaten, and shouts and shrieks rang throughout the palace grounds and blended with the greater din of bells and drums, shouts and shrieks from the city of Chang 'An [modern name: Xian—S.D.] beyond the palace. Though it was mid-day, the sky began to darken and when the blackness had swallowed up the sun, a terrible wail of despair went through palace and city alike. All of the eunuchs threw off their caps and fell to the floor, crawling and writhing and begging Heaven, and whatever gods existed, for mercy. All except Uncle Stupid, who alone remained impervious to this fearful event, and, squatting down at my mother's side, patted her head and neck with a damp cloth, humming and singing those senseless ditties for which he was always ridiculed.

It was then that Most Delicate Harmony began to breathe very fast, then very slowly, then fast again. She shivered and her hind legs twitched and my brother was born. While my mother was occupied biting through the birth cord, licking his damp body clean, and eating the viscous sack that clung to him, a sister came. Too quickly—for Most Delicate Harmony refused to touch her, rolling her head back and closing her eyes. By the time the eunuchs had recovered from their fright and, cursing and screaming at each other, had pushed Uncle Stupid out of the way and torn the sack from my sister's damp, still body, there was no life left in her. Another brother and sister were pushed out quickly afterwards and Most Delicate Harmony made a weak effort to clean them. The eunuchs cursed and coaxed her as she did so and, finally, took my second brother from her and cleaned him themselves with warm, wet cloths.

The sun had long since returned to the sky. The three pups were nestled against the belly of my mother. The eunuchs were swaggering nervously about the room, congratulating themselves on the birth of the three pups and cursing the loss of my sister—and blaming Uncle Stupid for it. As one of them leaned timidly out the doorway seeking reassurance that the sun would remain in the sky, my mother suddenly jumped up and raced past him, pursued by howling eunuchs, and leaving behind the three mewing puppies, who twitched and pawed clumsily in the bed of straw the eunuchs had prepared for them. After they brought Most Delicate back and tucked the puppies against her belly, she rose again, trotted to the far corner of the room, and rolled over on her side. She let out a terrible wail, and I was born. [The mention of the eclipse allows us to place the birth of Xiao Ji Long as probably November 23 of the year 2 B.C. (A.D.)—S.D.]

The year of our birth was that of the sunfire dragon, which the eunuchs deemed the luckiest of years, and the month that of the rainwater monkey, which was also deemed very favorable. But the day was that of the ji har, the sand earth pig, and the eunuchs disagreed violently as to the auspiciousness of that day and whether its interposition with dragon and monkey robbed them of all favorable portent. To resolve the matter, a diviner was snatched from the streets of Chang 'An and, dressed as a low servant, smuggled into the building—for all of the official diviners of the Palace were mere toadies of Wang Mang and could not be trusted. Such was the interest of the eunuchs, who crowded closely around the diviner, and the state of the diviner, who was very drunk when he was led blindfolded into the room, that three tortoise shells were scorched before a clear reading could be obtained. For the crush of the eunuchs kept unsettling the smoking bronze pot in which he sought to heat the tortoise shells to the point where they would begin to crack. Each time this happened, the diviner would jump to his feet, yelling that he could not breathe and struggling to escape, only to be pulled back to his place beside the bronze pot. The diviner refused to begin his fourth attempt until all the eunuchs except Uncle Stupid were kept well clear of the fire.

With Uncle Stupid gazing on in his pleasant, absent-minded manner, the diviner clamped the crackling shell before him between two pestles of bronze and stared hard at it for many long minutes before declaring that the conjuncture of sunfire dragon, rainwater monkey and sand earth pig was indeed harmonious. Setting the shell on the floor, he traced his finger along the deep, bold fissure that ran cross-wise. This dominant crack, he said, represented the earth. Then he pointed to the swirl of tiny, filigreed lines that ran from this deep fissure across the top of the tortoise shell, closely following its existing markings. These lines were those of water and the smooth manner in which they flowed from the dominant crack showed the absence of conflict. Below the deep crack, three straight black fissures slanted back against the grain. These were fire and showed that it had not been extinguished by earth. Uncle Stupid, who sat with his head leaning far over the shoulder of the diviner, confirmed that the lines all ran just as he said.

Shouts of joy and relief filled the room and, amidst much happy, excited laughter, gaily painted wooden cups filled with liquor were passed around. After emptying his cup, the diviner pronounced that all the augurs and portents were greatly favorable and, meshed together as they were, signaled that a great auspicious power was at work within the litter. He drained off another cup and confirmed: Heaven itself was full of favor towards these tiny creatures—or at least one within their midst—and had endowed them—or at least one of them—with wondrous powers. He paused to drink down another cup and with the liquor dribbling out of the corners of his mouth began again: Wondrous powers. Which might yield happiness or unhappiness to man. Powers that would unfold with the ripening of time ...

He was cut short by a piercing, despairing whine from my mother. When they rushed to her side, they found my oldest brother lying on his side, facing away from the nipple, already beginning to stiffen. Most Delicate Harmony pushed him further away with her nose and then her head fell back into the straw.

Five puppies were unheard of for a pug, they all agreed gloomily, resting on their hands and knees and peering down at my mother—and for such a small, slightly built pug as Most Delicate! The cups of liquor were forgotten. The diviner was pushed towards the door, protesting that there was much more that the cracks could reveal and calling for another cup. Then, as they put the blindfold back on him, and bound his hands at his sides, he began to curse them.

"Tail-less dogs!" he shouted. "Nothing so useless as a pan without a handle!"

Outraged by this insulting reference to their deficiency, all the eunuchs, except Uncle Stupid, set upon him and beat and kicked him until he spun around and fell to the floor. Then a gag was stuffed in his mouth and three eunuchs dragged him through the doorway.

The remaining eunuchs then sat down cross-legged in a circle around my mother and the three tiny pups. Uncle Stupid raised Most Delicate Harmony's small head and placed it on his thick ankle, bathing it with a moist cloth throughout the night. The other eunuchs kept an anxious vigil, arguing amongst themselves in faint, whispering voices about the condition of Most Delicate, which pup looked most sickly, and what might be done if things further deteriorated. Their anxiety grew with each passing day, for Most Delicate Harmony remained very weak and was wracked by bouts of heavy panting and tremors that shook her whole body. She tried hard to tend to her maternal duties, licking and nuzzling the pups whenever she had the strength, but she could hardly keep us clean. Uncle Stupid took over much of her duties himself, gently rubbing our gangly, mewing bodies with his moistened fingers and petting our tiny sightless heads with his thumb. We three pups struggled against each other, pushing our front paws hard against her soft belly and sucking desperately for the scarce supply of milk that was all my delicate mother could produce. Although smaller than the other two, the eunuchs said that I was quicker and more tenacious and that I had a sure instinct for finding the fullest nipple.

When my other sister died in the middle of our second week, leaving only my brother and me alive, the eunuchs were completely beside themselves with worry and fear. Only one survivor from the litter could damage—but not destroy—the plans of Wang Yu and the Wei clan. No survivors would be a disaster—and they would surely be blamed—no matter how unjustly—for that disaster! While now the Wei clan could do little to harm them, the situation might be quite different in the future. The Emperor was only a few years shy of attaining his cap of manhood and then his mother, and much of the Wei clan, might install themselves in the Palace. Indeed, that was to be hoped—if only these miserable puppies would live! Wang Yu was a more immediate threat—as the son of Wang Mang, the most powerful man in China, and a favorite of the Grand Empress Dowager Wang, he was already a force to be reckoned with. And if their plan failed, he would seek to stamp out all evidence of his involvement in it, which could mean banishment from the palace—or worse—for them!

In the midst of this fretting, Uncle Stupid came in with an earthen bowl full of sow's milk—for which he was much scorned by the others. Ignoring them, he settled himself down in his familiar place with Most Delicate Harmony's head leaning comfortably against his ankle. After dipping his little finger into the bowl, he thrust it into the mouth first of my brother, and then me, singing to us as we eagerly suckled the thin milk off the tip of his finger. In the next few days, all agreed that we seemed to grow stronger and even my poor mother seemed to improve and her fits of panting and crying diminished.

* * *

These stories of my birth the eunuchs told again and again in the days to come as my brother and I suckled milk from my mother's teats or from the fingers of Uncle Stupid or tumbled over each other in the straw—and told long afterward when I moved into the Palace with Uncle Stupid. The women of the Palace would laugh when they described the thrashing of the drunken diviner but their eyes would fill with tears when they were told of the terrible state of Most Delicate Harmony and the deaths of my brothers and sisters. Then they would cuddle and pet and coo at me with great tenderness.

But I neither saw nor heard these things. For I lived at first in a murky world of darkness and silence—without sight, or hearing, and strangest of all, a world without smell. There was only, in those early days, touch or the absence of touch: the reassuring warmth of my mother's body and the damp, loving lick of her tongue across my head and my flanks and belly, the delicate handling of Uncle Stupid and the pleasant warmth of the damp cloth he dabbed me with, the all-fulfilling contentment of suckling at the nipple—or the terrible loneliness, hunger and cold whenever I somehow strayed from my mother.

Then suddenly my eyes and ears opened up and my nose quickened and I perceived a world of dim shadows and dull noises—and full of strange and tantalizing smells. As the shadows cleared, I saw myself surrounded by the silver tan coat of my mother; saw her dark eyes looking keenly at me from the black mask of her face. Beside me was a silver tan lump from which a tiny black ear dangled. I bit at it. The lump rose and opening its mouth, tumbled on top of me, and we jostled against each other as we struggled back to the nipple.

The days that followed were full of play and discovery. I found I could bark and had a tail that would wag and legs that moved, more or less, at my direction. Whenever my brother and I were not asleep or at the nipple, we would bite weakly at each other's ears and tails and legs and roll and tumble over one another. Sometimes, too, Most Delicate Harmony would play with us, poking us with her flat muzzle or slapping at us with her front paws. I began to hear not only the panting and grumbling of my mother and brother but also the high-pitched mellow voice of Uncle Stupid singing to us amidst the falsetto voices of the other eunuchs. I saw that there was a ring of large pale faces above us, some round and very smooth, others thin and crinkled with age.

Then one day the shrieks of the eunuchs became louder and sharper and Uncle Stupid turned anxious and ceased his singing. Most Delicate Harmony had begun to pant heavily again and shiver with fever. My brother lay listlessly at my side, barely pulling at the nipple. I felt waves of trembling and weakness wash over me. For a long time, Uncle Stupid leaned over us, studying us closely, patting us with a damp, cool cloth, slowly resuming his songs in a strange, tight voice. Then he stood up and announced that he was going in search of medicine. While he was gone, my brother began to sicken and weaken further. He would have nothing more to do with the nipple, although the eunuchs placed his mouth again and again upon it. They then tried to pour sow's milk into his mouth. He lay there on his side, no longer trembling, but very still, a white froth about his mouth and nose, the sow's milk dribbling back into the straw bed. Between my fits of trembling, I could feel a thin, sour smell fill me up, a strange, dizzying sensation that I would later know as the smell of human fear.

My brother was already dead when Uncle Stupid returned and pushed his way through the eunuchs gathered around us on their hands and knees. He thrust a bitter, leafy powder into my mouth and that of my mother. I fell into a deep sleep. I was awakened much later by the gentle prodding finger of Uncle Stupid and the excited wails of the eunuchs. I must be named immediately, they all agreed. The act of naming might in itself invoke some power or magic that would avert further catastrophe.

Thus, because the eclipse had occurred on the day of my birth, which had fallen in the year of the sunfire dragon, in the month of the rainwater monkey, and on the day of the sand earth pig—and no convergence of signs could be more auspicious, because the portents revealed by the cracks in the heated tortoise shell had all been most favorable, and because my brother to whom they had hoped to give this name had died and I alone of the five pups had survived, I was named Xiao Ji Long [pronounced show (as in the first syllable of "shower") jee-lung—S.D.], Little Lucky Dragon, the auspicious beast, the little lucky one.

2
I Am Declared Fit for an Emperor

My mother and I rallied after the powder was given to us. Her bouts of shivering and fever, though still troubling, became less frequent. My trembling ceased but I was at first very weak and almost always asleep, with little zest for the nipple. Whenever I stirred or opened my eyes, I would see the pale, anxious faces of the eunuchs above me. But day by day my strength increased and I was soon brimming with energy—and hungry all the time.

Although I was the only one left to worry her, Most Delicate Harmony often tried to chase me away from my feed, growling and snapping at me. But she remained very weak and I was not easily put off. After a few growls and snaps, she would fall back on her side. I would eagerly resume my suckling though it seemed less and less to satisfy my hunger. Sometimes, too, she would rise up and try to walk away from me, but I would cling to her teat and usually she would go only a few feet away from our bed of straw before she would plop down again, panting and exhausted.

Uncle Stupid was forever pulling me away from her. He would push my muzzle instead into the sow's milk which he now served to me in a small lacquered bowl—although sometimes he would still let me lick it off the tips of his fingers. He also began to give me small bowls of mashed grain with tiny bits of meat in them. They had a more piercing, alluring smell than my sow's milk and I soon became so enamored of them that I would squeal and jump against his leg with impatience and delight whenever he would carry the tiny silver bowl towards me—for he always served the mush in a silver bowl rather than the lacquered one used for sow's milk.

Most Delicate Harmony would no longer play with me. She would only growl and snap at me until I left her alone and then would lie back down on her side, staring indifferently at the empty space in front of her. But Uncle Stupid and the rest of the eunuchs were always ready to indulge me. Although I was now full of vigor, they remained very fearful about my health and I had only to let out a piping squeak of a bark and they would rush to me, eager to give me water or a bit of mush, to pet and massage me, or wipe me clean. Or to chase me about on their hands and knees or run from me if I so desired, jabbing harmlessly at me while I bit at their thumbs and fingers or ran furiously around them in tight looping circles.

At first, the eunuchs had frightened me and I had scampered away whenever they approached. Except for Uncle Stupid, whose smooth, high voice and mild, pleasant scent always filled me with reassurance and delight. They had appeared huge and forbidding in their long gray robes, and I could just barely see to the peaked gray caps atop their heads. Their voices, although high like Uncle Stupid's, startled me, for they seemed always to be shrieking, filled either with anger or grievance. But I soon learned that they were no more to be feared than Uncle Stupid — for when I barked and growled at them, leaning forward on my front paws with my rump in the air, they would beg me to spare them and run from me in those short, mincing steps in which they took such pride, with their shoulders hunched and bent over. Uncle Stupid did not walk at all like them. They made much fun of his broad sloppy stride and rolling shoulders and said he plodded about like a landless peasant of the West.

I spent countless hours exploring the far corners of the room in which we stayed, sniffing and pawing at every object in it, each day discovering new sights and smells, new sounds and tastes. The silk caps of the eunuchs intrigued me most. I would wait until one of them had dozed off on the woven straw mats they had placed about the room. Then I would snatch the cap from his side and shake and snap it from side to side as furiously and as many times as I could, my chest filling with pride and satisfaction, before they could chase me down and, matching the growls from my clenched teeth with their cries of protest, pull it from my teeth.

Upon my return from one such afternoon of fun and discovery, I found Uncle Stupid sitting cross-legged alongside our straw nest. Most Delicate Harmony lay very still in his lap and his head hung over her, almost touching his chest. Suddenly he threw back his head and let out a terrible, frightening cry, which sent me fleeing, my tail between my legs. When I returned, timid and uncertain as to what to do, he rose up, cradling Most Delicate Harmony in the crook of his right arm. "It is not proper for you to see her like this," he said, and I saw tears run very slowly, one after the other, down the sides of his face, as he wrapped my mother in a cloth of blue silk and walked from the room.

In the days that followed, I searched for Most Delicate Harmony throughout the room, gripped by a strange, unsettling feeling of loss and bewilderment, a sad, faint whine rising up from within me. But then the eunuchs began to move about the room excitedly and to gather up all the objects in it and I became curious and alarmed by all this strange and foreboding activity. We must return to our palace duties, they told each other as they worked. The absence of so many eunuchs from the palace is attracting attention—and suspicion. And the diviner has been shouting out strange stories, they muttered angrily—despite the beating and warnings we administered to him—although so drunk and discredited is he that his stories are scarcely understood or believed. Still it would have been better if we had killed him, they agreed. Though some believe it unlucky to kill a diviner, it has been done often enough by Emperors, with seemingly no worse luck than before. Xiao Ji Long must be sent to another hiding place, they declared—with Cheng Sung, whose absence can be conveniently explained, and Uncle Stupid, who is always wandering off and performs no useful duties anyway.

One night the bitter powder was again thrust in my mouth and my muzzle gripped shut until I swallowed it. I was placed in a small bamboo basket covered with a rough dark cloth and then put on a wagon full of the rich, intriguing smells of human excrement. Dimly, I heard the voices of Uncle Stupid and Cheng Sung, complaining about the horrible odor and, a bit farther away, disturbing jingling and neighing sounds. When the wagon began to move, I wanted badly to bark but only a grumble came out when I opened my mouth and sleep overcame me.

When I awakened, I was pulled from the basket and placed in the middle of a large round room with a floor of brown and white pebbles. Many curious things were strewn about. I loped about in little circles for a few moments, barking first at two bamboo poles set upon a stand close by us and then at a hollow log that lay just beyond it—for I had never seen these things before and was not sure what powers they might have to harm me.

Uncle Stupid said that our luck would be better here. We were now far into the Commanderie of the Displayer of Splendor in the South. Good fortune would flow more freely in the South, he said—it was an auspicious place for my training to begin. I looked about and saw men in black hempen trousers that barely covered their knees and black sleeveless coats of the same rough cloth, lounging about the edge of the ring of pebbles. I raced towards them, barking to chase them off and to warn Uncle Stupid and Cheng Sung of their presence. Cheng Sung chased me down and grabbed me from behind as I stood on my toes, my whole body tense from the force of barking. He then picked me up and sought to stare into my eyes. Although much younger than Uncle Stupid, his face had already begun to thin and sag. His lips were a strange reddish color and his eyes singed with black dust.

"These are not to be feared, Xiao Ji Long," he said in a voice even sweeter than Uncle Stupid, "They are only our slaves."

Uncle Stupid talked to me all the time. Whenever he did, Cheng Sung and the eunuchs who visited us, and even the slaves, would gather around with eager, smiling faces, tapping their temples with their forefingers and rolling their eyes, punctuating his stories with laughter and jeers.

"Pugs were not always as small as you, Xiao Ji Long," Uncle Stupid told me. "In ancient times, times even before the reign of the Yellow Lord, they were huge beasts. Much larger than horses. You have not yet seen a horse, I know. But you must have smelt them or heard them from your basket. But those were mere nags. Not the fine horses of the plains or such as the Emperor possesses. Anyway, these ancient pugs were far bigger than horses. So big that they could crush a lamb in the curl of their tails. So big that when they snorted, just as you snort all of the time, Little Lucky One, people a hundred *li* [Chinese measure of distance; about one-third of a mile or 0.5 km—S.D.] away believed that thunderstorms were rolling down on them.*"

"And they traveled in huge herds as numerous as locusts. Herds so large that the trees shook and their roots loosened and rocks began to fall from the mountains when they trotted by. Such was their appetite that they devoured everything in the lands of the northern plains—trees, sheep, cattle, horses, all the other dogs, and even the barbarians who live like savages on these lands. That is why there are no trees there today—though barbarians and livestock have grown up aplenty."

"As they could no longer satisfy their hunger, they began to move south toward the lands of the people of 100 surnames—we Chinese. When they came to his banks, the Guardian Spirit of the Yellow River appeared to them and said: 'You may cross. I shall even still the winds and rein back the strong current for you, and you may eat your fill—of grain, fruits from the trees, fish from the river, cattle, sheep and all manner of animals. But you must spare the trees and the people of 100 surnames.' Then the wind ceased and the vast herd of pugs swam across the river —their huge heads stretching just above the water line, snorting and coughing. But the Spirit's command gave little pause to the Pugs. They regarded it as a recommendation—with far less weight even than an Emperor might give to the memorandum of a junior minister. And, of course, Pugs listen to no one anyway—not even gods or spirits, especially as concerns matters of appetite."

Uncle Stupid paused for a moment, marking the halt in his speech as he always did with a mixed sigh and giggle. I was listening to him intently, cocking my head from side to side to hear him better as he spoke, for, though I could not figure out what, it seemed to me that he wanted me to do something.

"So they paid no attention to the Spirit and whenever a Chinese appeared, they ate him. In fact, they preferred the Chinese to barbarians, because of their better diet most likely."

"The Spirit of the Yellow River appeared to them and said, 'You have betrayed my trust. For every delectable Chinese you eat, you will grow that much smaller.' This meant nothing to the Pugs and they continued to eat as they pleased. Soon they found themselves no bigger than a man, then much smaller, finally smaller even than all the other dogs—not much bigger than a good-sized rat. Then things became upside down and the people of one hundred surnames began to eat the pugs. Before that, the Chinese had no taste for dogs, but the Spirit invaded their dreams and showed them all sorts of delicious recipes for the preparation of dogs—pug roasted in garlic and pepper, pug cutlets, and many more. They could not get enough of these delicacies and soon the vast herd of pugs was gone and the pugs had all but disappeared—only a few were left, hiding in thickets and pig sties, and other obscure places."

"The Spirit of the Yellow River took pity on them and said, 'I will flatten your faces even more (for these giant pugs of old had a longer muzzle than today, though not so long as a wolf; no, more like a chow-chow). And make your eyes round and limpid as a child's so you will be too cute to eat.' One day the Emperor saw one who had been thus transformed and he took it under his protection. Then he ordered all the few remaining pugs to be gathered up and delivered to him. He strictly forbade the eating of pugs—although it is, of course, allowed to eat other dogs—and decided that only the Imperial family and those few grandees who had been granted this special privilege by the Son of Heaven would be allowed to keep pugs. And so it is today!"

"A poor tale that not even a pug would find amusing," said Cheng Sung, with a pained look on his face, pointing at me. I was no longer paying attention to Uncle Stupid but instead playing with a silk slipper Cheng Sung had tossed at me, slapping at it with my paw, then seizing it in my teeth and shaking my head from side to side as hard as I could.

"Perhaps you did not understand it," Uncle Stupid said and began to repeat the story. Cheng Sung wandered off in disgust. The slaves drifted away as well, seeking a comfortable place on the floor where they could lie down and sleep. But, as Uncle Stupid gave me a tiny piece of ham hock at the end of his story, I sat and watched him intently as he retold it.

One day Uncle Stupid said to me, "It is time to tell you of the glorious funeral of your mother, Little Dragon." As he began to speak, Cheng Sung winked and motioned to the two eunuchs who were visiting to come over to us. The slaves saw this and also began to gather around us.

"When the Queen, the Emperor's mother, heard of the tragic death of your poor mother, Most Delicate Harmony…" I recognized the name when he spoke it and let out a sharp bark which first startled and then amused them. "When she heard of the death, she let out a terrible scream and shut herself in her room. She ordered that a magician be employed to treat Most Delicate Harmony with medicaments and potions so as to preserve her body and then she spoke to no one until the body was brought to her a week later. When she saw Most Delicate Harmony before her, she fell on her knees, sobbing and wailing, clutching at your mother's poor, lifeless body. It took four servants to drag her back into bed and administer a sleeping potion."

"When she awoke, she was a changed woman, very calm, her voice steady, her eyes dry and clear. The Queen then set about … It seems odd to call her 'The Queen' for I knew her when she was the beautiful Imperial Concubine Wei – a far more prestigious title I might add, for Queens are as common as lice these days, with no more power than the great scholar Li Huan who serves now as the Minister of Nothing-in-Particular, and far less power than a clever eunuch like Cheng Sung." They all laughed at this, even Cheng Sung, who blushed deeply and looked at the ground.

"So the Queen—and I'm sure she was also much happier in those long ago days for they say that even before the death of Most Delicate she cried every night that her son had been taken from her to become the Son of Heaven. The Queen devoted herself entirely to the preparations for the funeral of dear Most Delicate Harmony. First, she ordered that a jacket of red jade squares be strung together for her—for jade, as is well known, prevents all decay. Then, that everything she would need in her afterlife be assembled—a silver bowl for her food, a red and green lacquered bowl for water, the wooden ball she had played with as a puppy and many other toys—anything that came to the Queen's mind or was whispered in her ear by some maidservant or eunuch. Wooden replicas of other dogs and of her unfortunate puppies—all but you, Auspicious One—grain cakes, dried meat, bones, and the sugary bean curds that Most Delicate Harmony especially liked—all these were provided in abundance. Then a retinue of one hundred men and women was put together: maidservants, eunuchs, slaves, a few favored commoners. She even insisted that a few low-ranking black-ribboned officials attend. All dressed up in fine silk! All the other members of the Wei family were quite horrified by this extravagance and disregard for seemliness. Since their involvement in the witchcraft scandal, they have observed the proprieties with the greatest strictness. And now this…irregularity! But the Queen would have none of their objections."

"So your dear mother, Little Dragon, was taken outside Chung-san, facing the warm sun of the Red Bird of the South, where the force of Yang is strongest—as befits such a beautiful, feminine creature as your mother. She was placed in a mausoleum of beautiful white stone touched with brown—much like her beautiful coat, and like yours Xiao Ji Long—such stone as they find only in the West, inlaid with gold. Her mausoleum was covered over with earth to twice the height of a man. A cypress tree will be planted atop it and two stone lion dogs are now being crafted to stand guard over the tomb."

Uncle Stupid paused and leaned his head back and scratched at his smooth chin with both hands. "I am indeed honored to be in the presence of a noble, rare, exalted creature such as yourself, Xiao Ji Long," he said to the snickering of the men gathered about him. "Other than the imperial household itself, I believe there are not more than a dozen families in the Central Kingdom—that is to say in all the world—who possess such creatures, and I daresay none of them can match the nobility and beauty of your visage and bearing. Let me see, there is the queen, the Marquis of Chengdu, the Marquis of An-Yang, of Hung-Yuan, and, of course, the Marquis of Lin 'An, the master of Mighty Tiger Slayer, if a pug can be said to have a master. And I hope you will not be offended, Little Lucky One, if I say that your father's ferocity seems much exaggerated to me. Certainly he did not live up to his reputation in the bridal room—where he showed all the vigor of overcooked cabbage." Laughter shook the group and I attacked the right foot of Cheng Sung who was stamping it up and down as he laughed.

"Ai-ya! Xiao Ji Long does take offense," shouted Cheng Sung, and shook his foot to push me away.

"I wonder what sort of funeral the Marquis will undertake for Mighty Tiger Slayer when his time comes," Uncle Stupid continued. "They say Marquis' wealth is exceeded only by his bad temper and his anxiety about his own immortality. That each time he has fallen ill, he has had a new jade suit prepared for his journey to the next life. Already I hear he has three jade suits—one of green, one of brown and white, and one of a pale golden hue."

"I should like to be buried in a jade suit," Uncle Stupid said after a thoughtful pause. The eunuchs and slaves roared with laughter. "Yes, but mine must be white. Because I am pure from birth, like Cheng Sung. The knifer visited us when we were but infants and so we have never known the rough temptations of the Red Dust. Yes, my funerary suit should be of the finest, purest white jade. And the vase containing my pao [the severed male organs of a eunuch—S.D.]—the treasures taken from me when I was a baby—should be inlaid with the same pure white jade and placed in the coffin beside me. I shall speak to the Grand Empress Dowager about it."

Cheng Sung and the two visiting eunuchs—and even the slaves—found these notions hilarious and almost danced with laughter. But Uncle Stupid ignored them. Suddenly, he began to sing in a loud, dramatic voice, more high-pitched even than normal:

> *He's everybody's uncle.*
> *So stupid they all say.*
> *But Xiao Ji Long prefers him*
> *So Luck will mark his days*
> *And when they're lying, grim-faced*
> *With naught but earthworm vests*
> *Old Uncle'll be in his suit of jade*
> *In smiling, peaceful rest.*

The song drew much laughter and many appreciative comments were made about his voice, which was compared to the singer Golden Moon, found wherever men drank and caroused, and about the 'earthworm' line. So Uncle Stupid sang it again to weaker laughter and then continued singing it until Cheng Sung and the other eunuchs left the room and the slaves walked away and laid down on the pebble floor to sleep.

* * *

My nights were spent with Uncle Stupid, snuggled tight against his back or curled up in the crook of his arm. But my days were given over to Cheng Sung, to whom the two visiting eunuchs gave the assignment of training me for presentation to the Emperor. Once Cheng Sung had secured this assignment, everything about him changed. His slouching shoulders straightened and his mincing steps lengthened into a prideful stride. His voice, which had been even sweeter than Uncle Stupid's, took on the aggrieved shriek of the other eunuchs. He complained endlessly—about me, about the poorness of the meals served to him, about the laziness of the slaves, which he blamed on the fact that one no longer had the power to put them to death. Harsh, acrid smells of anger and command radiated from him and he looked at everything about him with scorn.

The first day of my training he fastened a rope around my neck. After letting me bite and scratch at it for a few moments, he shook the end of it a few times and commanded me to walk. I froze my body and dug my front paws into the pebbles, not at all liking the strange feel of the rope tightening about my neck. Cheng Sung tugged gently on the leash for a long time, speaking softly to me in the sweet voice he had possessed before becoming my trainer. But as I still would not budge, the tugs became harder and Cheng Sung's voice rose to a painful screech.

"Mud-wallowing pig. Mongrel spotted with sores. I will teach you!" he yelled and then he began to drag me across the floor, sweeping a path through the pebbles as I growled and whined until the rope squeezed my throat so tight that I could only cough and choke. It was only when I was wracked by hacking, choking sounds that Cheng Sung would stop. And then, after a brief rest, he would begin again. Many hours passed this way—my stiff, resisting body dragged through the pebbles, Cheng Sung's curses ringing in my ears, my body wracked by gagging and coughing.

Whenever Cheng Sung would free me from the leash, I would snarl at his feet and then run to the other end of the room, zigzagging to and fro to avoid the slaves he ordered after me, scattering the pebbles with my swirls and arcs—much to the delight of Uncle Stupid, who likened the spring and lightness of my sideways jumps to that of a flea and my ability to change directions instantly to that of a squirrel. When finally I was caught and returned to him, Cheng Sung would put the rope on me again, giving it a short, painful pull and screaming in my ear that I could expect no respite from my pain and none of the treats I loved so well until I accepted him as master. After several such long, wretched days, I decided that it was easier to obey Cheng Sung and walk beside him on his hateful leash than to endure such torments. I was rewarded with many treats—bits of chicken and pork and sugary bean curd.

Soon I realized that Cheng Sung wanted only a very few things from me—to sit or stay when he shouted "Zuo Xia!" or "Bie Dong!"; to come to him when he shrieked "Lai!"; to lie down when he commanded "Tang Xia!"; to walk alongside him without pulling on the leash; and, above all, whether on or off the leash, to trot about in a proud and jaunty manner with my tail in a tight double curl and my head held high, carrying my ears in a straight line with only the black tips folded over. This last demand caused me no difficulty, for it was natural for me to strut about in such a manner, and I loved to hear the shouts and murmurs of appreciation from Uncle Stupid, the slaves and even from Cheng Sung as I trotted proudly about the wide circle of pebbles.

To achieve my compliance with his wishes, Cheng Sung made free use of the choking rope, a small bamboo switch that he held close to his chest, upright and quivering, and lavish treats whenever I did something that pleased him. And he cut back on my meals so that I would be all the more desirous of these treats. Although I paid little attention to his shrieking and cursing, I greatly feared the strangling noose of the rope and the swish of the bamboo stick as it rushed to my rump—and I yearned for his treats—though, unless he held me tight by the leash, I always took them far from him and gobbled them down as quickly as I could.

Uncle Stupid would shake his head as he watched these training sessions, rubbing his arms and tugging at his ears irritably. "Such training is more suited to a donkey than the offspring of great champions," he would sometimes shout. But he never interfered unless Cheng Sung became too zealous with the rope or stick. Then he would stand up and take one step towards Cheng Sung, who was much smaller than him, and Cheng Sung would loosen the rope or spring the stick back to his chest, and pace back and forth, cursing me.

Eventually, we reached a truce. I would sit, stay, and come when commanded. I would walk unhesitatingly beside him on the leash, adapting my pace to his, or trot about the ring in a long circle, haughty and perfectly composed. Cheng Sung and Uncle Stupid were also delighted when, with almost no prodding, I jumped the small hurdles of bamboo and the hollow log they placed before me, barely touching them as I flew by. When I crawled through the hollow log without any urging they jumped and shouted with delight. But I did these things not because of any threats from Cheng Sung, but because they gave me pleasure.

As days went by, Cheng Sung made less and less use of his choking rope or stick and treats were bestowed on me in abundance. But still I hated Cheng Sung and growled and snapped at him whenever he put the leash on me. This did not matter to Cheng Sung. Nor did he care that I growled and chased the slaves, nipping at their feet and ankles, or that I greeted each visiting eunuch with unrestrained barking—long after I recognized their scent, or that I squealed and whined and turned in circles and threw my body against the legs of the slaves whenever my meal was served. Cheng Sung did not even care where I relieved myself; slaves were immediately summoned to clean up my mess, cursing and grumbling and arguing amongst themselves as to who should undertake this hated task. I was much praised and petted, kneaded and massaged by Uncle Stupid and the slaves in those days. Treats were mine to be had with only the smallest hint of a whine or whimper. No objections were raised when I growled and clawed at their feet or bit at their hands. All that I did was regarded as great fun. Even Cheng Sung praised and petted me, though my tail dropped and I froze at his touch. I cared nothing for his praise and had no desire to play with him. I wished only to avoid the stick and the rope. I never refused his treats, however.

One day, five eunuchs came to visit us. Although I knew all but one of them, and soon recognized their scents, they looked strange and threatening to me as they stood at the entrance. I barked at them quite furiously until Cheng Sung managed to place the rope around my neck and give it a sharp tug. The eunuch I had neither seen nor smelt before was very old, with dry wrinkled skin that fell from his face and arms, and a weak, dusty scent. He was very stooped, and his head hung down as though he feared a beating. He walked with such slow, tiny steps that he appeared almost not to move and spoke in a voice so soft that the others had to stretch their necks and tilt their heads to hear him. Still, the others arranged themselves about him in submissive postures and I could smell wisps of human fear as they crowded and swarmed around him, smiling and nodding whenever he turned his low hung head and fixed his bright black eyes on one of them. Except for Uncle Stupid—who did not move towards the old eunuch but stood still, looking upon him with great happiness.

"How are you, my old friend?" the old eunuch asked when he noticed

Uncle Stupid. "And how is it that you remain so smooth of skin and so fat while all the rest of us turn to bone and ashes?"

"I am very happy," replied Uncle Stupid, "for I have been thinking much about my death and the splendid funeral I shall have."

Everyone laughed and the old eunuch himself breathed a dry chuckle. "Yes, I think often of such things myself these days."

A low bamboo stool was produced for the old eunuch and, after he had settled himself comfortably, he said: "Wang Yu is anxious that this auspicious beast be presented to the Emperor as quickly as possible. His father Wang Mang will return from this business of drought and locusts in the South in just a few days. Wang Mang's spies and snoops have grown lax in his absence but he will soon frighten them into diligence. Some rumor of our plan will surely reach him soon and he will do all that he can to upset it."

He paused and took a sip from the cup of barley water one of the eunuchs held out to him, bowing as he did so. "So we must act quickly. Wang Yu has already spoken to the Grand Empress Dowager and she is agreeable. She is much moved by the devotion of the Emperor's mother to the Son of Heaven. But, given time, Wang Mang will change her mind with his ingenious arguments and incessant scheming. Did he not talk the Empress Dowager—over her many, many objections—into finally agreeing to the exile of Wang Li, her favorite nephew? A decision that gave Wang Li no choice but suicide? Like a termite happily ensconced in the innards of a mighty palace, he does not cease his wheedling, and gnawing, and scheming until the edifice collapses!"

"I think you will see, esteemed master, that Xiao Ji Long is quite ready and has all the virtues and attributes of the greatest champions of her race," Cheng Sung said proudly, lowering his head in respect only after he finished his sentence. "Her color, coat and markings are all superb. Her proportions perfect, the forequarters and hindquarters equally balanced. Though still a pup, her neck is thick and full of muscle, her chest deep, her thighs and rump full and compact."

"Yes," said Uncle Stupid, suddenly coming alive with enthusiasm. He had been standing outside the group, examining his fingers as though they were something just bestowed on him, new and curious to behold. "Her legs are neither too short nor too long—but just right. Her paws land square, one after the other. Just like this." He rolled his hands about each other. "And her tail! Such a tight double curl has not been seen since the days of the Yellow Lord when pugs ruled the northern plain!"

"Her markings are exceptional. She has the perfect black diamond—so rarely found—on her forehead," Cheng Sung resumed quickly when Uncle Stupid paused to look again at his thick fingers. "And just the right amount of black running through her trace from neck to tail to set off the silver in her coat. Her head is not too large and perfectly smooth from the brow to the back of her neck. The jowls are ample but the face still square and pleasing. All in all, quite unlike that fat, odious, sad-looking thing that drags himself wheezing at the side of the Emperor."

"You should not speak of Wang Mang's gift to the Son of Heaven in such terms," said the old eunuch with a chuckle.

Uncle Stupid suddenly scooped me up and held me before the old eunuch, my front paws sticking out in front of me, and my hind legs crossed and dangling. "Look at that face: perfectly poised between ruggedness and delicacy. Tough as a soldier. Comely as a flower. A muzzle as black as a moonless night with deep, voluptuous folds that confuse the eye. Two black moles in perfect symmetry on her jowls. And regard this: thin, delicate eyebrows, that any fine lady of the court could envy, that appear only when she frowns and disappear, as if by magic, when Xiao Ji Long is at rest."

Cheng Sung started to speak but Uncle Stupid silenced him with a further rush of words. "A mason could set his stone by the line that runs straight from ear to ear. And each delicate velvet fold of ear is as perfectly balanced as weights on a scale. And her eyes. Dark, bold, lustrous. Dreamy as a poet when content. As full of fire as a soldier when aroused. Such powers of expression as I have seen only once—when I had the honor to see a performance of the great actor Ting Mao."

Uncle Stupid leaned over and dropped me to the ground. "But you must see her walk and trot about," he continued, oblivious to all about him. Cheng Sung rubbed his thighs and frowned.

"A strong, sure walk, feisty as a rooster, full of purpose and free of doubt, each paw landing square and straight, with that coquettish roll of the hindquarters that is so much admired in pugs. To see her run is to feel your heart soar as when a crane flies low over the still mirror of a pond."

All remained silent for a moment when Uncle Stupid ceased speaking, exchanging looks of astonishment.

"Such carrying on about a dog, Uncle," said the old eunuch softly, "and has this dog quickened some sleeping poet's soul within you?"

Everyone snickered but Uncle Stupid seemed not to notice.

"I have always loved dogs and found them far superior to men. I believe only dogs and other animals are worthy of serious thought or passion," he said without expression.

"A strange line of thinking," said the old eunuch. "But for those who have lived as long and seen as much as you and I, Uncle, one that may be difficult to refute convincingly. But enough talk, let us see this wonder perform."

Cheng Sung called me to come to him. Then to stay and sit and lie down. He did this many times, giving me a small treat each time I complied with his commands, thrusting it into my mouth and holding me by the back of the neck so I would not run off. Then he put me on the leash and we circled around the eunuchs: first in a brisk trot, then a slow stroll, basking in appreciative murmurs and sighs. Cheng Sung removed the leash and I ran about the circle several times by myself. Then he led me to the hurdles and log and at his command I jumped easily over them, hearing applause from the eunuchs and loud shouts from Uncle Stupid as I did so.

"A marvelous athlete," said the old eunuch.

"Yes, her father was a famous jumper," said Cheng Sung, happy to be again at the center of attention, "but a timid lover."

They all laughed and the old eunuch rose to his feet and said they must return to the Palace. After they had bowed and said their goodbyes to each other many times, the old eunuch looked again at me and said, "You have done well, Cheng Sung, and of course, you too, Uncle, but I know you neither need nor care for praise."

He fixed his bright, black eyes on me: "Yes, it is as though every feature and motion has been created not only to summon up the yearnings and affection that lie deep within even the dullest and coarsest human heart, but also to pleasure the finicky appetites and lust for niceties of the most demanding aesthete. She will indeed be a fit companion for the Son of Heaven."

3
The Son of Heaven

As soon as Uncle Stupid opened his eyes, I growled at him and charged his hands, for I had been awake for some time and was eager to play. But he rose quickly and, tucking me under his arm, yelled loudly to the slaves to prepare a bath for me. "We have no time for nonsense today, Xiao Ji Long. We must devote ourselves to your preparations."

The slaves placed me in a large bronze basin, doused me with water and an oily, bitter smelling liquid and began scrubbing me thoroughly, ignoring my snarling, wriggling protests. I liked the drying off even less and tried to bite the hands that were thrust at me from every direction, pressing and rubbing me from behind the rough hempen cloths. When they had finished, droplets of perfume were shaken on me and I walked about the floor, sneezing, shaking my head and pawing at my eyes, while Uncle Stupid and the slaves laughed at me. Finally, a scarlet and black ribbon, which Uncle Stupid said were the preferred colors of the Wei Clan, was tied about my neck so cleverly that I could not dislodge it.

I was placed in a closely bound bamboo cage, carried into a horse-drawn carriage and put beside Uncle Stupid. As we drove through the city of Chang 'An, I heard the clatter and thud of the horses and around us the chatter and shouts of hundreds of voices and many, many other noises that were frightening and unfamiliar to me. Through the thin lines of the bamboo cage, I could make out nothing but changing shapes and colors and bits of the white silk robe Uncle Stupid had worn today instead of his usual gray one. But no other smells could find their way through the cloying aroma of the perfume with which not only I but the bamboo cage was drenched.

"I was not much older than you, Little Lucky One, when I first came to the

Palace," Uncle Stupid said. "It was much grander then. And very, very grand to me as I was not born an aristocrat like you, Little Dragon, but the son of a poor farmer. Pure from birth, as I have told you, for my father thought to get a better price for me that way. But I had first to undergo many years of training before I was sent to the Palace—though I do not recall exactly what I was trained for."

"When I came to the Palace, all said that I looked like an angel and the ladies of the harem begged the Emperor to assign me to their quarters—and there I was sent—and have stayed forever, except when I have been entrusted with special tasks such as your care, Auspicious One. I arrived when the great Emperor Xuandi was the Son of Heaven—at least all say he was great—I cannot judge these things for I care nothing about expenses and taxes, lands and armies, laws and edicts—all those things by which greatness is judged."

"I remember most his exceptional skill at 'playing the drums.' Nothing else in the palace pleased him so much as that—and I was his only serious rival. I will show you how it is played some time—we go to the highest balcony in the palace and from there we drop bronze pellets at a bulls-eye painted far below on a large drum. When the Son of Heaven and I were locked in such a contest all else was unimportant to him—officials and emissaries, generals and governors. None could disturb him then."

"But we must wait until Wang Mang is gone from the Palace. He and his gang of officials disapprove of this game and have forbidden its practice within the Palace—for fear of corrupting our new Emperor. Anyway, it was when Xuandi was Emperor that I became the confidant of the Grand Empress Dowager Wang, who was then the beautiful Concubine Wang, and somewhat later, I became the confidant of your dear mother's mistress, the queen, who was then the even more beautiful concubine Wei – or was it the other way around? I can no longer remember who was the most beautiful – and would tell no one but you even if I did."

"The Grand Empress Dowager's son, whom we called Chengdi — the Accomplished Emperor— although all say privately that he accomplished nothing, was a most unusual Emperor, for he cared no more for taxes and titles and conquests than I do. He was cruel and foolish and impulsive—and exhilarated all by his presence. To be near him was like being on a ship in high seas—or, so I am told, for I have never been on such a ship. When he first became the Son of Heaven, a wild youth of 19, he would sneak into the city each night, disguised as one with only two or three orders of rank, or even as a commoner. A group of eunuchs would accompany him —and I was always among them. For I was very big and strong then (while now I am only big) and I daresay, I saved the Son of Heaven from getting many a lump on the head. For although dressed low, he behaved high—as though he still expected rivers to part before him—and such conduct did not always find favor amongst the rough crowds in which we traveled."

"We caroused away the night at cockfights, and gambling halls, and houses of drink. I did not like the cockfights, of course, for even then I loved animals, but I was fond of gambling and have never turned away from liquor. And just before crawling back to the Palace at dawn, we would stop at some low brothel—though the Emperor had the most beautiful and refined women in the world at his disposition, he seemed to prefer coarse and ugly women who were unaware of his divine nature."

Uncle Stupid tapped on my bamboo cage. "An ugly story is it not, Xiao Ji Long? You must keep it to yourself."

"In any case, after he became besotted with Flying Swallow—who cast a spell on him through her sublime dances, such trips ceased and I saw much less of him. Flying Swallow never cared for me. I do not mind being called Uncle Stupid—most say it inoffensively and even with affection—and those who are rich in years and honors, usually shorten it to just 'Uncle.' But the way Flying Swallow used to say 'Uncle Stupid' was very unpleasant."

"We will soon be at the gates of the Palace, Little Dragon, so you must be on your best behavior. You will encounter many important people today. People so important that they can hardly be said to be mere human beings any longer. The Emperor, of course, is truly no longer a mere human being but divine—the Son of Heaven! He was human once—although a king almost since he could walk (but kings are nothing). How such transformations occur, I do not know. Perhaps that is why they call me Stupid. But who can know the reasons for such things?"

"The Grand Empress Dowager will be in attendance. As will the Marquisa of Ping-O who pretends to represent the interests of the Wei Clan, although she is joined to them only by remote marriage and her blood and loyalties are of the Wang clan. You will see Ministers galore—more 'Caps and Belts' [high-ranking officials—S.D.] than there are ticks on a dog—an uncouth mongrel I mean, of course, not one such as yourself. For Wang Mang has insisted that there be a big turnout of officials—though that would seem to make no sense. I am told that the Grand Minister of the Multitudes will be there as well the Grand Minister of Works and the Grand Controller of Agriculture. The Keeper of the Imperial Purse. The Grand Herald. The

Bearer of the Gilded Mace. Also, the Superintendent of Imperial Horses—perhaps they believe you to be a horse, Xiao Long. And the grand Augur and the Gentleman of the Household."

"I suppose that the Minister of Nothing-in-Particular, Li Huan, who is venerated and ignored for his great learning and firm principles, whom no one and nothing can quite please, will also be there. For he is always doddering about the palace these days making a nuisance of himself and has succeeded in antagonizing the Grand Empress Dowager, Wang Mang, Wang Yu, and even the young and mild Son of Heaven himself. None of the Ministers can abide his ceaseless criticism anymore. The eunuchs, of course, all despise him and he, them—but that is to be expected since, like earth and fire, officials and eunuchs do not accord. But as he is as stupid in his own way as I am in mine, I am rather fond of him—though he is seized with horror every time I call him 'my good friend' or, if I have the pretext of drink, try to clap my arm about him."

"The General of Chariots and Cavalry will be there. And the General of the Left, the General of the Right, and the General of the Van but our rear will be unprotected because the General of the Rear is at his ancestral home attending to the funeral of his father."

"You shall see Wang Mang himself and his son Wang Yu, restless as a monkey on a chain in his father's presence. How can one describe Wang Mang? A fortune teller, who has since been chopped in half, described him thus: 'the eyes of an owl, the jowl of a tiger, and the bark of a jackal,' then he added, 'certainly capable of devouring others, but the chances are that he will be devoured himself.'"

"I believe the fortune teller's death to be a suicide, for how could one capable of foretelling the future say such a thing about Wang Mang, who respects and fears only magic, and expect to live?!"

For good luck we entered the East Gate of the Palace. At the gateway, a group of soldiers stopped the carriage. I felt the cage being prodded and shaken. "Very well," said Uncle Stupid and unfastened the top of my cage. I looked up and saw a high tower of stone with green pennants flying atop it and in the midst of them a huge white flag with a green dragon on it. Beyond was a sky so bright that it hurt my eyes and made me blink. A soldier tipped the cage slightly towards him with his spear and when I saw him peering into the cage, with his padded tunic studded with iron, his stern, suspicious face, and, most startling, the huge, fearsome topknot that stuck out from the side of his head, I leaped against the side of the cage, thrusting my head out, and barked as ferociously as I could, a prickly sensation spreading down my back as my fur thickened. The soldier jumped back in surprise and the others laughed at him, and waved our carriage forward.

Uncle Stupid did not replace the top even after my cage was removed from the carriage and placed on a litter carried by four servants. Thus, I was marched into the palace grounds with my front paws resting on the front of the cage, my head sticking out well above it. Uncle Stupid walked at my side, as we moved along broad paths of white stone, taking care to avoid the raised stone path in the middle which he said was reserved solely for the use of the Emperor.

Grand buildings, painted white and scarlet, stretched out before us on all sides, their long, curving tile roofs the color of baked golden earth, each row of tile ending in a circle inscribed with symbols or lettering. Below the tiles stood sturdy wooden pillars and pavilions with garlands of flowers and brightly colored tapestries. Courtyards of stone and brick opened on all sides of us and hills of white stone bridges rose before us. And, alarmingly, new smells began to seep through the cloud of perfume in which I had been drenched—the sour smells of the servants who flanked me, wisps of flower smells and the dull, dry smells of stone and tile, and far off human scents. Uncle Stupid tried to shush me by explaining all that surrounded me—for I barked at everything that approached my litter and when there was nothing moving toward me, I barked at the four servants, silent and dull-faced, who carried my litter.

"That is the Hall of Fragrant Blossoms, where the Imperial Concubines are enrolled into the service of the Emperor. Quiet, Xiao, it is only a few harmless servants scrubbing stone."

"And that large two-storied building is the Hall of Everlasting Harmony, where the ceremonies by which ranks are bestowed are conducted."

"And there, the Hall of Celestial and Terrestrial Union where the tedious business of the Emperor is conducted, endless matters of taxes and grants, edicts and petitions. I have entered it only once – from sheer curiosity. I have sought all my life, with much success, to stay clear of such dreary business…. Shush, little lucky one, they are only eunuchs on their way to fulfill their duties at the Shrine."

"Here we pass the Hall of Flourishing Teaching, where scholars while away their time disputing all day the meaning of some word or phrase while waiting for promotions and appointments." A group of men wearing black robes headed toward us from the courtyard of this building, running at a slow, shuffling pace. All had wispy beards that waved beneath their chins as they ran and wore black square hats with a band of ribbon flowing to the side. A few old men at the front of the procession wore purple or blue ribbons; behind them were the ranks of yellow-ribboned men; and then a larger group of the black-ribboned. Sashes of matching color, inscribed with gold lettering, were pulled tightly about their waists. This strange apparition incensed me and I barked so hard that I nearly upset the cage.

"Look, there is old Li Huan himself," Uncle Stupid said with a chuckle, pointing to a very old, thin man, with a few spare wisps of grey hair dangling from his chin and two purple ribbons hanging from his square hat. The others passed by us and continued down the road but Li Huan struggled, barely keeping pace with us. "Because of his age and learning, he has been excused from the 'scholar's trot,' at which all other officials, whether high in rank or fresh from their examinations, must run whenever they are on the palace grounds. But he is too stubborn to accept the privilege."

"Hello, old friend," Uncle Stupid called out to him, but Li Huan ignored him, his head bent and thrust out in front of his slowly rolling fists. "Take care not to stumble into the Emperor's lane, old friend, for I share your belief in strict adherence to custom," Uncle Stupid shouted again.

Li Huan gave no sign that he either heard or saw us. As we began to climb up the incline that led to Emperor's quarters in the innermost part of the Palace, he fell behind the litter. Uncle Stupid turned his head and yelled back at him. "We must have a drink together." Then he sang: "Life hurries by us too quickly. A cup of wine together will make us glad."

"Were I anyone else he would have me flogged for my insolence. But should he complain about me, they would say, 'Oh, that stupid eunuch: never mind him, he's a simpleton.'"

Finally, we reached a great building, larger and grander than all the others and festooned with yellow wall hangings and pennants. Uncle Stupid said it was the Palace of Celestial Purity and reserved for the use of the Emperor and any audiences he might choose to conduct—or really, at present, for the Grand Empress Dowager, since she would act as regent until the Emperor received his cap of manhood. The litter was placed on the ground and before he could explain it further to me, I leaped out of the cage and raced to a bronze turtle about twice my size that had caught my eye. I circled it warily, for it gave off little scent, testing its mettle with low growls, and when it did not respond I tapped its outstretched neck with my paw.

Cheng Sung suddenly appeared and ran to us in a state of great agitation;

the old eunuch trailed behind him, a weary, annoyed look on his face. "Why is Xiao Ji Long not in her cage," Cheng Sung shouted at Uncle Stupid

"Because I wished her to see the sights of this marvelous Palace, where she will live out her days as I have," Uncle Stupid replied indifferently.

The old eunuch sighed and Cheng Sung muttered "imbecile" as he pulled the hated rope from within the folds of his robe and, before I thought to evade him, placed it around my neck. He snapped the rope and led me into a tree-covered garden whose twisting paths stretched far into the hills beyond, beckoning three servants to follow us.

"You must do your business here," Cheng Sung shrieked at me.

But there were so many new smells and sights that I could give no thought to my "business" but instead walked from bush to bush and flower to flower and tree to tree, sniffing in the strange and fascinating and ever-different smells that arose from each of them. Cheng Sung became more and more infuriated and began jerking the leash, cursing me between clenched teeth in a tight, hissing voice, and even giving me two short kicks in the rump. Finally, a servant ran up to us.

"The master says you must return now," he said to Cheng Sung, who bent over and pulled me close to him by the scruff of my neck. Thrusting his twisted, red face an inch away from mine, he snarled, "Wretched refuse of a turtle and a bitch overrun with mange, do not disgrace me or my gentle switch will grow thorns."

I was carried into the Hall of Celestial Purity on the litter, my cage closed tight. Through the thin cracks between the bamboo, I spied the old eunuch walking very slowly in front of me with Cheng Sung and Uncle Stupid on each side of him. Doors opened before us and the smell of many humans penetrated the veil of perfume that had begun to fade from my cage, scents of fear and submission, and of challenge and assertion. I could hear all about me the rustle of silk robes and the shuffle of silk slippers.

"Yes, we are aware of your views on the irregularity of the ceremony, Li Huan," said a tired, old woman's voice, "and on much, much else with which you find fault."

The litter was placed on the floor. The old eunuch got down on his knees with great difficulty, as did Cheng Sung and Uncle Stupid, and they began bowing.

"Arise," said a high, piping voice.

"Arise, old one," echoed the old woman's voice. "I am sure your ancient knees balk at such reverence. And you, Uncle, you may stop bowing now."

"Greatest and most beautiful and benevolent of Empress Dowagers," Uncle Stupid said, continuing to bow. "As I am twice as stupid as other men, I am twice as unworthy of being in the presence of the Son of Heaven. So my head must touch the floor not nine but eighteen times."

"Another of your bits of clever foolishness," the Empress Dowager said with a dry laugh.

The old eunuch had by now struggled to his feet. "Divine Son of Heaven, great and generous Ruler of All Domains," he intoned, "Splendid Center of All Elements, and Forces and Things of this Earth, who alone can dispense the will of Heaven and bring harmony, Chain-string of all lands, Model to all men, whom all spirits serve and all men love."

"Divine Son of Heaven, your earthly mother, the queen, bids this lowly servant to express her sorrow that she could not attend the celebration of your eleventh year. Through me, she wishes to tell you that she has invoked prayers and made offerings in one hundred shrines and fifty temples that all happiness be granted to our lord, that his rule shall stand always—like a scepter of white jade—lofty and exalted, that his time of rest be pleasant and diverting, that his life be prolonged and blessings limitless come to him, that he doff soon the cap of manhood and beget sons and grandsons in the thousands, and that deep bliss be his forever."

"By way of me, your mother sends you a gift, the sole issue of the dear womb of her own dearly beloved Most Delicate Harmony with whom you played as a child. Through me, she expresses the hope that this gift will greatly please you and comfort you in times of distress, that it will preserve the memory of those happy childhood times, before you were called by Heaven, when your family enclosed comfortably about you as the nest of an oriole encloses its young in peace and security, and that it bring you good luck in such abundance as the full-throated river brings to the crops in spring, for all signs and augurs tell us that this little one, Xiao Ji Long, like the Auspicious Beast of ancient times, has been endowed by Heaven with the gift of good fortune."

The old eunuch signaled to Cheng Sung and he crawled sideways, still on his knees, to the cage. I huddled back as far as I could into the corner of the cage as he released the latch and swung the door open. I could see his bent head peering into the cage as he cooed to me to come to him in a soft, tiny voice. But all these strange goings-on frightened me and I drew back even further into the dark safety of my corner. Cheng Sung gave up his cooing and, sticking his head half into the cage, he reached back with one arm to grab me.

I could hear him grunting and see his lips moving soundlessly as finally he got a firm hold on me and pulled me, growling and biting, out of the cage.

I shook myself and ran in tight circles for a few moments to get my bearings. Then I looked up and saw far above me a great mass of shining yellow, glittering with jewels and precious stones. Then, looking more closely, I saw enclosed within that mass of yellow folds and flowing robe, the small, pale, nervous face of a boy. Seated next to him was a tiny old woman surrounded by a huge silk dress of deep green, her brow, neck and wrists glittering with jewels. On the step below them stood a chubby, round-shouldered man wearing a square-cornered black cap and a gaily colored robe covered with twisting red and green dragons.

"A very comely creature," said the Grand Empress Dowager.

"Yes, bring her closer to me," said the Emperor Pingdi in a squeaky voice, craning his face out of his yellow cocoon.

"Yes. Very comely. But quite wild, it seems," said Wang Mang gravely, and his fat jowls quivered atop the fleshy rings of his neck when he spoke. His dark eyes were set deep and shifted subtly but constantly about the room. "And its name? What proof do we have that he [the inattention to Tutus' sex pervaded her adventures—S.D.] merits such a name? It would be wise to first determine whether this creature is suitable for an Emperor before allowing any intimacy."

I had kept the company only of eunuchs and slaves (who were allowed to speak only in mumbles and murmurs and whose heads and faces were shaved bald) and was not used to the deep voices of men or the hair that covered their chins and lips. Although he moved with great delicacy, the harsh snap of Wang Mang's voice and the menacing wave of his beard and mustache greatly startled me. I fled, racing along what seemed an endless line of men, seeking a way around them. They towered above me, some in black, some in brightly colored robes, each stooped so that he stood just shorter than the man before him. Beyond the men, silk paintings hung from ceiling to floor, covered with birds and mountains and trees or huge black letters as big as I. And in front of the paintings stood soldiers with spears and fearsome topknots. I wheeled and raced back behind the cage, going through the legs of the old man Uncle Stupid called Li Huan, who stood apart from the line of men.

Cheng Sung and the servants ran close behind me, crouched over, in pursuit. All about me were men kneeling, startled faces tightened with suppressed laughter, smells of fear and excitement. Twisting and turning

49

among them, I became ever more frightened, searching desperately for an exit from this crush of strange sights and sounds and smells.

I was caught at last between a servant and Cheng Sung, who fastened the rope around my neck and led me back. Tranquility and order settled again over the room as he walked me slowly back and forth directly below the Son of Heaven while the old eunuch touted my virtues. I walked well enough: my head high, my tail wound tightly and my paws full of bounce, hitting squarely but lightly on the floor. The Grand Empress Dowager made clucking sounds of appreciation. My race about the room had quickened the Emperor Pingdi's bearing and flushed his face and he leaned far forward in his throne to see me better.

"But its head is a bit small, is it not?" said Wang Mang. Then: "Let us see how she obeys you."

Cheng Sung removed the leash and squatted down, calling out his commands to me. Although I could hear them clearly, I was so overwhelmed by the profusion of smells and the subtle sounds and movements of the dozens of people spread throughout the room that I could neither concentrate on, nor understand, them. Either I sat when he called, "Come," or trotted over to him when he called, "Stay," or I did nothing at all at his command but stare at him and turn my head from side to side. Huge whiffs of rage poured off Cheng Sung, and his fists clenched and unclenched as they always did when he cursed me. But he said nothing. I could hear Li Huan, who had moved close behind us, snorting in disgust. The old eunuch let out a great sigh.

"Why, he understands nothing!" Wang Mang said, as though amazed.

Cheng Sung abandoned his commands and signaled to me to run around the circle that had been cleared about him and the old eunuch. I did my circles very well, beginning now to feel proud and self-assured. I did not even let myself get distracted by the servants who were placing small bamboo hurdles within the circle. The Empress Dowager again made her clucking sounds of appreciation and Pingdi uttered a small cry of delight.

I saw Wang Mang brusquely stroke his beard between his thumb and forefinger and suddenly the air was filled with painful noise. I shook my head first side to side, then up and down as I continued, though with a broken stride, around the circle. My ears throbbed and ached as the noise cut a path from behind my eyes to the base of my neck and I felt as though my head would burst if it could not be stopped. I saw Cheng Sung's lips moving, and those of the old eunuch too, but I could hear nothing and feel nothing beyond the rising pressure of the noise. I threw myself to the floor, rolling over and batting at my ears with both paws. Then I leaped suddenly to my feet and ran through the circle, leaping a hurdle as I did so, not knowing where I was going, seeking only to escape the noise. Soldiers moved toward me from the far end of the room. I turned and ran amidst a group of serving girls, raising screams of delight and alarm.

Still there was no relief from the noise! Others seemed not to hear it. I turned again and raced up the steps to the platform on which the Emperor and the Empress Dowager were enthroned, biting and snarling at the hands of Wang Mang who stooped to grab me as I brushed by him. Cheng Sung and a host of servants and eunuchs, even the old eunuch and Uncle Stupid, chased up the steps after me, as I slipped and scrambled and tumbled through the yellow skirts that spread out about the Emperor. It was only after I looked over my shoulder and saw them chasing after me, down on their hands and knees so as to stay as far as possible below the Emperor, that I realized the noise had stopped. But by then I was surrounded by a mob of crawling, panting servants and eunuchs, Cheng Sung at their lead, his eyes burning with rage. I shuddered with relief, and fear of Cheng Sung, and squatted down. A puddle of pale yellow spread on the polished red wood of the floor below me.

"This is most indecorous," said Wang Mang, tugging at the ends of his moustache, as Cheng Sung leaned on his right hand and crawled across the platform to the steps, pressing me tightly to his body with his left arm.

"Most unfitting. Dreadful," Wang Mang continued. "Is the dog just poorly trained—or might it be possessed by demons?"

"Demons! Poorly trained!" Li Huan erupted in a loud, croaking voice. "Why the dog has no knowledge of the rules of right conduct—much less its practice! So how can it be expected to attain proper character? In that, she reflects the times, and her unmastered masters, to whom the Li—all those proprieties through which one demonstrates and cultivates right feelings— are unknown or practiced falsely, with contempt. [The Li is a difficult-to-translate ethical concept. It refers to both a complicated set of rules of conduct, an etiquette if you will, and to the inner state of right conduct or righteousness that the practice of these rules is supposed to cultivate—S.D.]

"This creature is in truth no worse disciplined than the typical youth of today—or a courtier!" A tremor of laughter started round the room but was abruptly quelled by a stern glance from Wang Mang.

Cheng Sung hurled me to the back of the cage, but so anxious was he to prostrate himself that he did not fasten the latch. The door swung back open and before me I could see Cheng Sung, the old eunuch, and Uncle Stupid bend over and knock their foreheads against the floor, a jumble of apologies and self-chastisement pouring from their lips.

"Blessed Son of Heaven, forgive me," the Old Eunuch said and the others chanted with him.

"Most Benevolent Grand Empress Dowager, forgive us," they pleaded.

"May I fall into the sea and be swallowed by a turtle," said Uncle Stupid.

"May I be trampled by a hundred feet," said the Old Eunuch.

"May my heart be pierced by ten thousand arrows," said Cheng Sung.

"May my cheeks be burnt with hot iron," said one.

"May all deities and demons persecute me and my body be invaded by chronic sores," said another.

Uncle Stupid reared back on his knees and began slapping his cheeks, first with one hand, then the other, without ceasing to plead and to curse himself. Spying him from the corner of his eye, Cheng Sung rose to his knees and followed suit.

Wang Mang paid little attention to this display. He paced back and forth on the step below the Emperor and the Grand Empress Dowager, stroking his beard. "It is clear that the Emperor cannot accept this gift," he declared in a loud voice, and the lamentations of the eunuchs dropped to a murmur.

Pingdi shifted in his throne as though he were about to say something but Wang Mang hurried on, "Beloved Son of Heaven, you are not like other men. You can accept only what is perfect, only that in which the forces of this universe are brought into balance so that exquisite harmony is attained. Your honor, and the unbounded reverence which all men feel for you, demands it."

"Ah, but she is a beauty, Wang Mang!" said the grand Empress Dowager. "Don't you think so, Li, er, I mean, Son of Heaven? I could see the color begin to return to your face—which has been so pale since your recent illness—when she came out from her cage. I have always envied the Concubine Wei, er, the Queen of Chung-san, her Most Delicate Harmony. And this one is her very likeness. Though much more spry. Too spry, perhaps," she said with a cackle. "But it would be a shame to lose such a beauty!"

"Yes, it is just as you say, beloved Grand Empress. I had no thought of losing such a beauty. The fault is not in the dog—though I do not rule out entirely the possibility of demons— but in her preparations—of which, strange to say, though I am Commander-in-Chief, I had no knowledge." Wang Mang turned and stared at the line of officials below him.

"You were away on more pressing matters," the Grand Empress Dowager said sharply. 'We had no need to trouble you."

"I believe there is much in what Li Huan said," Wang Mang said, with an air of great thoughtfulness. "Li Huan, do you believe this Xiao Ji Long can be returned to right conduct?"

"Though the rules of right conduct vary for dogs and men, the principles underlying right conduct are the same throughout the universe. All things in this universe that are shaped by cultivation have within them the potential to achieve the right conduct appropriate to them. A dog as well as a man. Or a fruit tree or a horse for that matter."

"And how do 'all things' realize this potential?" Wang Mang asked with an amused air. The Grand Empress Dowager let out a sigh. "How does a dog attain right conduct?"

"A man attains right conduct," replied Li Huan, "and through right conduct awakens the inner righteousness and proper feeling that rests dormant in all men, through the study of the Masters and through self-cultivation in accordance with their precepts. Were there no Masters, The Way would be lost to us – or at least to all of us except those uniquely blessed. A dog attains right conduct through the observation of its Master—and his guidance. For as right feelings and conduct travel from the works of the Masters to the hearts of men by touching and illuminating our minds, so they travel from the heart of Master to the heart of the dog through the quality of his voice and the beneficent tugs of his leash."

"So a dog can attain right conduct only if trained by a man who has already ascertained the principles of right conduct and awakened his own sleeping righteousness?"

"I believe that is evident," replied Li Huan.

"What if the dog has already wandered from The Way? Can it be restored?"

"As a man can be returned to The Way, through study and discipline and re-awakening of proper feelings, so can a dog."

"Then a man such as yourself, who is revered above all of us for his study of the Masters and his self-cultivation, would be best-suited to bring Xiao Ji Long into balance and harmony and establish in him right conduct and feelings… And would you be prepared to undertake this task on behalf of the Son of Heaven?"

I could see the slippers of the line of officials shuffle back and forth as they do before men laugh, but no laughter ensued.

"I believe that my dear cousin, the Son of Heaven's earthly mother, would be very pleased with such an arrangement." A sugary yet somehow menacing voice addressed the Grand Empress Dowager. "For she is most anxious that the Son of Heaven accept this gift. And she holds Li Huan, whom she knows well from the old days, in the highest esteem."

"Is that you speaking Marquisa? I find it difficult to hear with all this carrying on. But, yes, Li Huan, do accept," said the Grand Empress Dowager. "The business of the Court has made you quite testy lately. Such a task might freshen your temperament."

I saw a pair of slippers step forward far down the line of officials and heard one cough and then another. Wang Mang turned in that direction: "You may speak."

"There is also the matter of Waking Bear, the Emperor's favorite, who has grown very attached to the Son of Heaven. He is known to be very fierce and full of vinegar concerning any competition for the affections of the Emperor. Thus, it would be best if he could become accustomed to this newcomer so that he will not do her harm in the future."

The Grand Empress Dowager leaned back and looked heavenward, and let out a great sigh of impatience.

"Very well," Wang Mang said and glanced hurriedly at her.

"I think we can dispense with this matter. You must draw up a memorandum for approval by the Grand Empress," he said, fixing a stare on the official who had raised the matter of Waking Bear, "outlining your recommendations as to the arrangements by which Li Huan shall assume charge of the creature." I could hear Li Huan snorting behind me but he said nothing. "And, include such other suggestions as may be appropriate. Include as well recommendations for appropriate punishments for those who have so badly bungled Xiao Ji Long's first training."

With that remark, Wang Mang turned his gaze on the eunuchs. Cheng Sung and Uncle Stupid were still bowing and slapping their faces, their lamentations faded to whispers. But the old eunuch was bent far over, balanced precariously on his forehead, and not even a whisper came from his lips. Wang Mang stared down at him quizzically and a deep quiet spread through the room.

"Wake him!" Wang Mang commanded but when Cheng Sung and two servants hastened to do so, the old eunuch toppled stiffly over, his mouth half open, a dry white crust on his lips, his pupils rolled back into his head.

"What indecent, unhappy omen is this?!" Wang Mang bellowed. "Son of Heaven, Grand Empress, you must leave immediately lest you be tainted before the purifiers can be brought in!"

As dozens of servants and attendants surrounded the Emperor and the Empress Dowager and began to hurry them from the room, Wang Mang fell to his knees, wringing his hands: "Supreme One! Spirit of Heaven and Spirit of Earth! Whatever deities or demons have knowledge of or are involved in this foul occurrence! If there is any ill-luck loosed by this unhappy omen which must be borne, let it fall on my head. Let the Son of Heaven and Grand Empress Dowager be free of it. Let the mighty dynasty of Han, which has been shaken by ill-omens and auguries of decline and disaster—by eclipses, by drought and locusts, by earthquakes, and streams which run the wrong way, remain free of it. Let the full burden fall crushing instead on their humble servant Wang Mang, so that their noble line may continue for ten thousand years!"

4
I Am Brought into Balance

Uncle Stupid opened the bamboo cage as soon as we left the palace grounds. As he drew the curtain, he called to me to sit on his lap in the carriage.

"This shall be our last evening together, Little Dragon. But only for awhile. The Grand Empress Dowager believes that life with Li Huan would be far too boring for you. She has promised to reunite us as soon as right conduct is restored to you—should such a feat be possible. In the meantime, I must settle the Imperial Concubines into the East Lateral Courts of the Palace. For all eleven have now been selected. It will not be easy work, but no one is the match of Uncle Stupid in making them feel comfortable and disarming disputes—in keeping fresh the sweet wine of girlish friendships and forestalling its souring into the vinegar of womanly jealousy."

"The West Lateral Courts will, of course, be solely occupied by the Empress-to-be and those who attend her. When she arrives, that is, for the marriage will not occur until next year. I do not think I will be allowed often into the West Palace."

"You should know that the Empress-to-be is Wang Mang's very own daughter. She has been chosen from among the most beautiful and refined young ladies of all the most prestigious families of the Middle Kingdom—as have the eleven concubines, of course. Her selection was very difficult— almost as difficult as your birth, Xiao Long. For Wang Mang withdrew her from consideration and very strongly opposed her reinstatement. He believed that such a high honor was not due him. Thousands enrolled in petitions asking that Wang Mang's unfortunate decision be overruled and that his daughter be considered. Thousands more appeared before the gateways to the

56

Palace each day pleading that this be done. Each day, too, the waiting rooms of the Grand Empress Dowager were filled with marquises and marquisas, barons and baronesses, officials, and all sorts of prominent men seeking audiences to urge consideration of Wang Mang's daughter. The Empress Dowager grew so weary of it that at last she ordered Wang Mang to allow his daughter to be considered. That was very wise—for strangely enough, she was in fact selected."

"Wang Mang is a very unlucky man, for he objects to all honors, gifts, titles and privileges—and is always very firm and persistent in his objections. But somehow they always find their way to him. There are not many who are cursed with such bad luck as that."

Uncle Stupid rubbed the top of my ear between his thumb and forefinger.

"Your former master, Cheng Sung, is a broken man. He would have killed himself had I not otherwise persuaded him. For I told him that only by living longer could he ensure that his *pao* will accompany him into the afterlife where he will be made complete again. If he were to die now, I told him, his *pao* would be 'lost' as has happened with the *pao* of my ancient and unfortunate friend who did not survive your presentation to the Emperor. His wealth and titles have all been stripped from him as well—for Wang Mang believes in vengeance not only against the living but the dead, and severe punishment not just for great crimes but also for the smallest slights or circumventions of his will."

"I believe it was the prayer that the Son of Heaven 'soon doff his cap of manhood' that most incensed Wang Mang. For even in the midst of my bowing, I could see his knee tremble as it was uttered. Of all things, he fears most that when Pingdi reaches manhood he will avenge the cruelty to his family—and to his mother in particular. For she cries constantly, as she is not permitted to come to Chang 'An to see the Son of Heaven."

"Cheng Sung has been expelled from the palace and sent to the salt mines, where he will be despised by all and worked, starved and beaten to boot. As have all the other eunuchs who took part in your birth and preparation for the Emperor. All except your old Uncle. For it seems as though it is as I foretold in my little song—your good luck has conveyed only to me. Although I had in mind only average bad luck for the others, nothing so catastrophic."

"It was not the recommendation of that flunky—excuse me, I mean the Prefect of the Masters of Writing (for Wang Mang never recommends anything himself), that I be allowed to stay in the Palace. No, he had much the same fate in mind for me. But the Empress Dowager would not allow it. The Prefect is very upset about this and is thinking hard about whether he should resign. But I think he will stay. After all, he has ruined all but one of us. His staying will be a great relief to me—for I would hate to think that the fate of a mere simpleton would bring an end to a career so hard bought with tedium and toadying."

"In truth, I do not believe the Empress Dowager wished any of these punishments. But she did not wish to weary herself arguing with Wang Mang—except in my case. For I believe she regards me like a twist of hair cut long ago or some broken amulet, an ancient and useless memento of her youth that memory has made dear to her. There are some, too, who believe I am immortal because I have not aged as have the other eunuchs. This theory has yet to be proven, although I feel quite well. In any case, I am not like those great persons—and Wang Mang himself—who are forever seeking after some new potion or incantation that will confer immortality. I do not wish to live more than another hundred years or so."

Uncles Stupid fell silent for just a moment and we listened to the rain which had begun to strike hard against the top of the carriage. "Wang Yu has not abandoned his plans, however shattered they may now be. He hopes by keeping alive the love between Pingdi and his mother, of which you, small emissary, are a token, to effect the restoration of the Wei clan to honor and power, with himself as their champion. Whenever he is full of liquor, he swears he will outwit and outmaneuver his father yet."

"His face was something to behold at the Hall of Celestial Purity, for I could see it well each time I slapped my face to the right. His blood boiling with anger one moment, draining away in fear the next, and all the while his eyes and mouth fixed in a careless smirk of indifference."

"There is no doubt that he is an unfilial son and as such an abomination to all those who revere the Li—whose numbers you will soon be among, Little Dragon. But is it possible that there are circumstances where it is permissible to be unfilial? The question is too complex for me. Perhaps Li Huan can find an answer for you in his classics."

"Ah, feel those bumps, Little Lucky One, we have turned off the main boulevard now and will soon be in the lane where Li Huan lives. Let us hope he is in a fit mood to receive you. For all of Chang 'An regards it as a great joke that Wang Mang tricked him into accepting you as his pupil. The great Li Huan, who has ever aspired to tutor an Emperor! I do not share their scorn. To me, the tutoring of a great pug—as you aspire to be, I am sure—is to be preferred to the tutoring of a Great Emperor. And the likelihood of establishing true greatness much better!"

The carriage came to a halt and Uncle Stupid placed me back in my cage and carried me to the door. A hard rain was falling and I licked the water as it trickled through the bamboo. An old servant woman was already waiting at the door and she pulled the cage from Uncle Stupid without speaking and sought to close the door. Uncle Stupid thrust his head and shoulders inside. "Let us have a cup together, old friend," he yelled. "Drinking wine is very lucky." But then I heard him no more.

Li Huan sat on a low stool by a table littered with bundles of wooden sticks, a dim lamp deepening the many wrinkles in his long, thin face. He wore no hat now and his old head was streaked with wisps of gray hair, as thin and sparse as his beard. The darkness and closeness of the room intimidated me, for it was very small and the stacks of bundled wood were piled everywhere and filled every wall and corner with strange shadows. I sat very still while he stared silently at me.

"I have long thought on this," he said finally. His voice was calm and level—with none of the harsh, irritated tones that tightened his words when he spoke to Wang Mang. "I am no longer dissatisfied."

He stared again at me for a long time. "We must begin," he said suddenly. "I am sure that that fool of a eunuch gave no thought to that which is necessary to your health." He reached down and fastened a leather strip about my neck, which was attached to the very long, very thin cord of rope which lay on the floor beside him. Unlike Cheng Sung's rope, it did not tighten and choke me when I pulled against it.

Next to the room of wooden bundles was an even smaller room with only a cot and several square chests, lacquered deep black, and in its far corner a pile of white fleece. There were no bundles of wooden slats in this tiny room and only a crossbow adorned the wall, a quiver with five arrows beside it. Li Huan pulled a patchwork hempen cloak, smelling richly of animal fat, off a peg by the door and we went outside into a cramped courtyard covered with damp pebbles. It was enclosed by high walls and filled with tiny trees and bushes and pots of flowers, all dripping with rain. The wetness of the raindrops and pebbles was very unpleasant and I lurched back towards the doorway of the house. Li Huan halted me with a brisk snap of the leash.

"You must do that which is necessary to your health," he said in a calm, steady voice. He began to walk me around the walls of the garden—four steps, a turn, four more steps, a turn, again and again. I had no idea why he continued this unpleasant, monotonous exercise and I looked up at him frequently for some sign that would explain it to me. "For health," he would say each time I caught his eye. Round and round we went, as I grew wetter and wetter and more uncomfortable and Li Huan's cloak turned black with rain. "For health," he said, over and over again. I began to shiver from the dampness and chill of the night air and my insides began to tremble with a desire to relieve myself. But this unfamiliar, damp courtyard, unmarked by my smells, hardly seemed suitable for such a purpose and I struggled on, turning now and then in a circle to see if I was wrong and that in fact there might be a place in the courtyard that was appropriate. "For health," Li Huan would say each time I turned a circle, "For health."

Rainwater clung to my coat and coursed down my flanks and dripped from my chin. Li Huan began to cough and sneeze and shake huge droplets off his cloak. Still we continued around the courtyard. A deep shiver ran through my innards. I turned round under a tree half the size of Li Huan, then turned again, then a third, fourth, fifth time—at last the feel of it seemed just right to me. I squatted down and relieved myself.

"For health," Li Huan said, his calm voice inflated by a hint of excitement. "Most excellent."

Then we went into the house. Li Huan rubbed me dry with rags of hempen cloth and then massaged my back and legs and stroked my head and tail. But he did not give me a treat. "We must sleep now," he said, placing me atop the pile of fleece. I did not much care to sleep alone, and whimpered for a moment, thinking of the warmth of Uncle Stupid's ample body, but so exhausted was I by the rain and the endless rounds of the courtyard that I quickly fell asleep.

"You will not find me harsh, Xiao Ji Long," Li Huan said the next morning, after we had finished our walk on the still damp pebbles of the courtyard. The old servant woman placed before me wooden bowls of water and warm grain mush flecked with chicken fat and then retreated to her tiny room at the front of the house.

"A man who knows only the harsh strictures of law and punishment can know nothing of honor or shame and will act rightly only when the fear of mutilation or death weighs upon him. Just so, a dog who yearns only to escape the stinging switch and the choking rope will act rightly only when these are vivid in its mind. True and unerring right conduct can be attained only by the inner cultivation of right feeling, the spring from which all principles and rules of right conduct flow—and that can only be achieved by study and repetition of the practice of right conduct and the gentle correction of faults by one whose intentions are pure. In that way, one does not merely learn and practice the Li but absorbs it into the essence of one's being."

"Nor will you need to learn fancy tricks, Xiao Ji Long, for simplicity of manner should be no less valued in a dog than in a man. And fancy tricks are as empty of value and as unconducive to right conduct in a dog as tricks of rhetoric are to a man. Did not Master K'Ung [Confucius—S.D.] himself say that such things disrupt virtue?"

Li Huan rose and walked to the door of the old servant's room. He seemed to be listening for something, but I heard nothing. "But all of life cannot be study and discipline and self denial. Natural exuberance and passions will and must find their outlet. One cannot keep a bow forever stretched taut – still less can one leave it loose and not stretched at all. To stretch it and to loosen it, and then to stretch it and then loosen it again. It is in this manner that one begins to find the Way."

I heard the rattle of a carriage and the neigh of a horse outside and began to bark. Li Huan gave the leash a quick tug. "Quiet, Xiao Ji Long, it is time now to loosen the bow."

After we had settled in the carriage, Li Huan told the driver to proceed to the North Gate of the Palace. He looked down at me and patted my head. "I have been given many privileges, such as the daily use of this carriage, in undertaking to train you, Xiao Ji Long. By elaborating these niceties, the clever men of the Palace sought to make even greater the ridiculousness of my position. But that is of no consequence. Though I have refused many privileges, I will accept these—for the people of Chang'An have only rarely seen such as you, and to take you about in the city would cause an excitement and a distraction to your training—and perhaps a danger. There are always those who covet the rare!"

"I will use this time to clarify my thoughts. It is indeed as the Empress Dowager said: I have given way to anger and bitterness. And anger causes confusion."

"Since I was old enough to think, the world has moved further and further down the cycle into decay. Lost in dreams of ancient god-kings, when virtue and right thinking wielded the jade scepter, I have foolishly thought, again and again, that I could halt this by teaching and example. That the cycle must in any event turn of its own in accordance with the fundamental laws of the universe. And turn it must, I am sure – but I believe now that my time will then be long past. Only anger—and confusion—comes from fruitless efforts to change what cannot be changed. One must recognize that rotten wood cannot be sculpted. But these things are not pertinent to you, Xiao Ji Long."

Li Huan remained silent until we came within sight of the fluttering black pennants of the North Gate of the Palace. A bronze snake, entwined about a plodding tortoise with one foot outstretched as though to take the next step, stood at the base of the tower. "Weak though it is these days, the force of Yin is strongest here. This will be good for you since as yet you have little within you of the mettle of Yin, and far too much of the female and the capricious child. Beyond this gate, a park of great beauty stretches for as far as we can see. It is here that we will take our relaxation."

Paths of chipped white stones twisted endlessly up and down the hills of the park, which Li Huan called the Park of Verdant Radiance. The hills were covered with thick green grass, criss-crossed with tiny streams of water, and dotted with trees and shrubs of all sizes and shapes, each with its own beguiling smell. Here and there, I smelt too the powerful, unmistakable odor of other dogs, the musky odors of other animals, and the weaker traces of humans. Li Huan kept the leash fastened about my neck but he let the rope run out to a very great length so that it proved no hindrance to my explorations. Li Huan did not speak until he saw me turning in a circle to relieve myself. "For health," he shouted. When afterwards I ran to him, he bent over and patted my head and gently seized and shook the loose skin of my jowls.

"With efforts such as these, right conduct will soon be yours," he said and I raced off happily to explore an odd-shaped tree that stood just at the ridge of the hill before us.

Li Huan did not speak again until I was well tired of running and content to walk close by his side as we headed back toward the North Gate. "I had thought to take such walks as these with the Emperor Pingdi. For like you, there is little of the force of Yin in him—though on rare occasions I have seen its fire flash and the light of benevolence shine in his eyes. It was enough to make me believe that, sickly and fearful as he is, and so surrounded by ill intentions, he might still be brought to the kingly way. For, if he lives, which is by no means certain, he need not always be imprisoned within the web Wang Mang has spun about him. The cap of manhood might be for him no mere symbol."

"But after each walk, and there were not many, he fell ill. And then it was either too hot or too cold or too damp or too dry for the Son of Heaven's frail constitution. But one fair day, with which not even Wang Mang could find fault, we went again for a long walk and the lightest and most refreshing of summer showers fell briefly on us. But Pingdi was again afflicted by a mysterious fever upon his return and lay in bed writhing and trembling for days. Wang Mang worked the Great Empress Dowager into a fury.

"'Though as ancient as the Four Immortals, the old fool has gone quite mad with his fixation on walks and exercise. He will kill the boy!'—I am told that she said. And the walks were no more. Nor was I even allowed to serve as tutor to our unfortunate Son of Heaven, who now finds himself totally immured within the prison Wang Mang has built around him."

Soldiers awaited us at the North Gate and I began to bark furiously at them. "Shush," said Li Huan, and after a few moments had passed he spoke a sharp "No!" and gave my leash a forceful tug, repeating this again and again until I fell silent. He bent over and rubbed my head and back, and his eyes became soft as he looked at me. "It is well to bark, and sound alarms, at any new strange occurrence. But to continue barking after you are assured that there is no danger is mere foolishness and indulgence."

He sat with his right hand clasping his chin, looking through a thin opening in the curtains as our carriage barely moved through the crowds of carriages and carts and people walking in all directions. As I dozed beside him, he scratched the top of my head with his left hand. "Wang Mang fears the force of Yin—as indeed he fears all powers and influences that are not within his control, whether they are elemental forces, or spirits, or the mere thoughts of men. He is the very essence of the ignoble man that the Master described: worrying ceaselessly about getting and once he has got it, worrying only about losing it, and in worrying about losing, there is nothing he will not do."

"But he is also very clever—and as cautious and stealthy as a thief. He mutes his intimidation with great dissembling. It is curious: all know him to be insincere. At least all who truly know him—for he has built great allegiance across the land among the ignorant who know only his gift giving and the humility he wears always—like the mask of a mediocre actor who has learned but one role. And yet they greet his insincere declarations with relief and gratitude. Yes, men are strange creatures, Xiao Ji Long, as you yourself have no doubt discovered already. It is as the Emperor Shu has said: The heart of a man is ever so dangerous. The core of truth is ever so small."

"'There is much in what Li Huan says,' so Wang Mang would begin after my every utterance and then he would proceed to twist my words to his own purposes. He turns everything upside down! Indulging the Son of Heaven in all that is harmful, while reining in tightly all that should be allowed to run free."

Li Huan packed me again into the bamboo cage when we were almost at his house. "Despite his caution, I believe that great and evil deeds rumble within him. He discovers everywhere auguries and omens which foretell the end of the dynasty of Han—while pretending that his every thought and effort aim only at averting this terrible fate!"

"In this one thing, I believe he may be correct. Just as the centipede dies but does not fall down so it may be already with the House of Han—so far are we into the cycle of decay. But these things are not pertinent to you, Xiao Ji Long."

My days with Li Huan followed a regular and unvarying pattern. After my walk in the courtyard, I was given my morning meal of grain mush and chicken fat. We would take our relaxation in the Imperial Park. A large meal of grain mush with sometimes bits of chicken and pork would await my return and after another trip to the courtyard, I would take a long nap. In the afternoon we would practice commands and obedience and Li Huan would lecture me. Li Huan would then roll before me brightly colored wooden balls, in which I did not take great interest and hand me a large dried pig's ear, which I very much enjoyed gnawing.

Li Huan himself would spend the rest of the evening with his wooden sticks, running his fingers along the letters that covered them and muttering to himself. Sometimes he would jump up from his sticks and pace about the room, talking aloud to himself, or to me, as he did so. I was given a light evening meal of mush and goat's milk and after a brisk walk in the darkness of the courtyard, taken to my bed of fleece to sleep. Except when he placed me in this bed (which was surrounded by a crisscross fence of bamboo for I sought in these first few nights to leave it and climb into his cot), Li Huan kept me always on a leash, which he tied about his waist when he did not wish to hold it in his hand.

Although I sometimes yearned, especially at night, for the warm and gently heaving body of Uncle Stupid beside me, and for his sudden bursts of song and our wild chases and battles, and above all, for the treats that had been lavishly given to me, the sameness and predictability of these days filled me with great assurance and contentment. Then too, our walks in the park became ever longer and more interesting. Except when we returned to the gate and I was very tired, I would always walk ahead of Li Huan, happily snorting and grumbling as I trotted along, stopping to investigate any flower, or shrub or bench that attracted my interest—for we were never in any hurry. When I would feel the leash slacken, I would turn my head to make sure Li

Huan was still behind me. And I would always find him with the leash tied round his waist, moving his arms forward, and backwards and sideways, and rolling and shaking his neck and shoulders in slow, exaggerated motions. As he did all this, his sleeves would fall back, exposing arms that seemed no bigger than twigs.

"You look at me strangely, Xiao Ji Long, but such movements are excellent for health and circulation. Much like those long stretches that you take each morning upon awakening."

Li Huan would also cough and spit quite often as we walked along, which he also claimed to be excellent for health. "Perhaps you think that I spit, as others do, to cast off evil spirits and influences," he said when I ran one day to investigate his spittle, pulling hard against the leash. "No, that is mere childishness, as is most prattle about spirits and the other world. One should follow the ceremonies and sacrifices set forth in the classics. That is quite enough for the gods, as the Master himself has told us. Too much interest in them is as unseemly as your interest in my spittle."

After Li Huan was satisfied with my conduct in these daily walks, he began to take me to the Garden of Ever Present Breezes because, he said, I must become accustomed to the presence of such people as I would encounter during my future life in the Palace. The twisting, tree-shaded paths were always bustling with fine ladies and gentleman of the court, startling me with their flashing silk robes and tinkling jades as they walked by, with groups of chattering eunuchs in their gray robes and caps, and with dark-robed scholars and officials, locked in earnest debate, the ribbons of their square hats floating behind them. At first, the sight of each new human filled me with alarm and I barked and lunged at them. But each time I did so, Li Huan would snap his leash, and speak his crisp and stern "No!" Soon I learned that I was allowed only a low growl upon the approach of a new person and the pressure on the leash warned me not to persist beyond that.

Li Huan took me next to the Park of All the Beasts of the World where tigers, lions, bears, deer, antelope, pheasants, peacocks and animals of every kind were kept chained behind bamboo fences or in iron-barred cages or low pits surrounded by high walls. The sight and smells of these beasts, and the growls and roars with which they greeted our approach, both terrified and incensed me, and I pulled on the leash with such force, first lunging forward, then backward, that Li Huan could hardly hold onto the leash. His claps and commands went unheeded, buried under the roar of beasts and of my own frenzied barking which so consumed me that my whole body bounced up and down. But Li Huan brought me back again and again to this park and after many, many trips I learned to walk beside him calmly, impervious to the cries and taunts and threatening smells of these caged animals. Li Huan then began to practice the commands in front of the cages of lions and leopards—and I learned to perform them without hesitation in spite of the glaring eyes, and ominous pacing, and occasional roar of these beasts.

"You have conducted yourself in a most exemplary manner today, Xiao Ji Long," Li Huan said after one of these trips, pulling from the folds of his robe a small piece of dried beef. At first I was not sure what it was because he had never before given me a treat, but I ate it with eager delight. "As men of righteous character, whose inner minds are just and harmonious, do not deviate from right conduct at any time—even in the midst of turmoil—so you must learn to obey your commands even in the midst of the howling of beasts."

Later we walked along the shore of Sea-Like Lake, which sat in the hollow below the hills of the Garden of Ever Present Breezes. In the center of the lake, a long paddle wheel turned endlessly, sending thin, lapping waves shoreward.

"Let us sit here and listen to these gentle waves and think, Xiao Ji Long."

Li Huan sat down on the stone bench that overlooked the lake while I occupied myself digging pebbles out of the sand that lined the shore. "Your path is not too difficult, Xiao Ji Long. You have but to master four commands: To come, to sit, to lie down, to stay. And five attainments: to do your necessaries always outside, never in the house, and if possible when and where directed by our master; to walk and to run with dignity, which is as natural to you as breathing; to bark an alarm upon the approach of some strange, unexpected person or event, but to refrain from senseless barking once your task is completed; to follow the lead of your master and not to pull or lurch on the leash; and to cease from harmful or foolish activity upon direction of your master. That seems to me not so difficult. And once you have accomplished the Four and the Five, right conduct and superior character are yours."

"The path of a man who aspires to cultivate proper feelings and to think and act rightly in all circumstances, and thereby to achieve righteous character, is much more difficult. Each day I must do the Three by Three: I must examine myself three times against the three questions. I must seek to rid myself of Four evils and honor Five refinements. I must remember that there are Three kinds of friends that are beneficial and Three that are harmful—though all those beneficial have long since died and there are very few left even that are harmful. I must practice Five things to achieve righteous character—which are similar but not identical to the Five refinements. And to cultivate right feelings, I must cultivate the Nine thoughts and maintain the Three disciplines—though I need no longer concern myself with the discipline of sexuality and, though I am old, I do not need, and have never needed, discipline in matters of gain. So here I must concern myself only with discipline in matters of contention."

"I must keep in mind always that there are Three great aims and Eight steps for achieving them. I must study and restudy the Five Classics, for each reading reveals a new facet of meaning. I must abide by the rules and proprieties that are precisely described in the Twelve Chronicles of the Spring and Autumn Annals of Master Lu and the Book of Rites—and do my best to ensure that all those about me abide by them. For these books prescribe what needs be done in each season and each month of the year as well how we must treat others in all social situations, how we must mourn, how music is to be performed and, most importantly, how we must demonstrate filial piety. All these I must do and learn and remember if I am to attain righteous character. For it is by the rigorous and unfailing practice of such rules and rites that one establishes right character and cultivates the proper feelings from which all right conduct flows. Thus it is that you become fit to act in accordance with the Way and to so instruct others."

"I confess to you alone, Xiao Ji Long, that I sometimes feel weighted down by all these numbers, that I sometimes fear that proper feeling and righteous character, which is indeed the goal for which all right conduct is practiced, may smother under so much thinking and so many rules. Sometimes I think to study again the philosopher Mozi, whom I was taught to despise, and have always despised, for his foolish disdain for proper rites and rituals."

I began to feel the need to relieve myself and I turned in circles, here and there, along the shore of the lake, looking up at Li Huan as I did so; I was not certain whether it was seemly to do my necessaries in such a place. Finally, he awoke from his thoughts and led me under a nearby tree.

"Why do you strut about so after your necessaries," he said with a faint smile after I had finished. "Kicking back in that stiff-legged, odd manner, tossing leaves, and grass and dust in the air." He coughed and spat. "And with such force and defiance! and such a look of self-satisfaction! What could be the meaning of such strange behavior? Sometimes you are very amusing, Xiao Ji Long."

As our walks became longer and began to extend into midday, so too the days themselves became longer and hotter. Sometimes the heat would rush up through my paws, run along my heaving flanks and fill my head with such panting and snorting, that I could not stand it. Then, I would plop down in the nearest patch of cool shaded grass, oblivious to the doings of Li Huan. "Like all pugs, you do not fare well in hot weather," Li Huan would say, dousing me with the water he carried in a leather sack around his waist and cupping some water in his hands so that I might drink it. "You must better develop your resistance to the elements. But for now we shall return to the cool of the courtyard. "

"What have you done to this baby?" The old servant woman would exclaim whenever we returned from our walks on such days, and Li Huan would carry me into the house, panting and snorting, with my tongue hanging far out. Then she would bathe my head and back with a damp cloth. She had become quite fond of me and on those rare occasions when Li Huan left us alone, she would take me from behind my bamboo fence and arrange pieces of cloth into tiny caps or scarves on my head and put necklaces of shell and stone around my neck, laughing as I struggled to free myself of them. As payment for the amusement my struggles gave her, she would give me tiny bits of fat.

Long after I had been placed in my bed, Li Huan would stay in the other room among his sticks and letters, looking at them by lamplight. Sometimes, too, he would rise in the middle of the night or very early in the morning. I would hear him padding about the floor, even though he walked more softly than he usually did so as not to wake me, and fumbling with his lamp, then muttering and exclaiming as he became lost in his thoughts. One night I saw the lamp go out and listened as Li Huan walked back very slowly into our room. He sat himself down with great deliberateness on the side of his cot. I could see him in the dim light, his hands hanging over his knees, the moonlight catching a few wisps of gray hair that stuck up from the top of his head. He stared straight ahead for a long time.

"I can no longer even summon up a dream of Master K'ung, so far have I deteriorated," he exclaimed, in such a harsh, taut voice that I stood up in my bed and growled. "At fifteen, the Master set his heart on learning—as did I when I was nearly twenty. At thirty, he had established right character —as had I. At forty, he was unwavering—as was I. At fifty, he knew the Order of Heaven—as, so I thought, did I. At sixty, he listened receptively—but I could no longer abide the thoughts and speech of those who did not know the Way.

At seventy, he followed his heart. But my heart is filled with confusion. My anger has thinned in this last month but confusion has thickened. I know better the way of proper feeling and righteous character for a dog than that for a man."

"I am not a worthy disciple of Master K'ung" he cried out in a voice of such pain that I turned about in my fleece and whimpered. "That is why he has deserted my dreams." Then he lay back in his cot and spoke no more that night. But I could see his lips moving in the dim light and hear the twisting of the coverlet in his fingers.

That next morning the rain beat heavy on the tile and thunder shook the house. The sky barely lightened and the courtyard filled with puddles. Streams of water washed the pebbles across the stepping stones. When the carriage came, and I rushed eagerly to the door, Li Huan pulled back on the leash and bade the old servant woman to send it away. So great was my disappointment that I jumped against the door, bouncing off it again and again long after the carriage had left.

"One cannot take a walk on such a day, Xiao Ji Long. Things cannot always be as you desire. Today you must take your relaxation with your ball and ear," he said, tossing these toward me.

Li Huan pulled a bundle of sticks from a shelf and spread them out on his table and quickly became engrossed in them. I had no interest in the ball, sniffing it once and pushing it away with my paw. Nor did chewing the pig's ear give me much satisfaction and I soon abandoned it and began to wander about the room. In one corner of the room a bundle of Li Huan's sticks had fallen and spread out fan-like against the wall. I moved toward the sticks cautiously, for their unusual slope held some hint of excitement, and perhaps danger. I uttered a low growl and slapped at them with my paw, retreating quickly when they moved. After I had done this several times, I decided they offered no danger—and no more excitement—and that it would be more pleasing to chew on them.

Tiny bits of stick had begun to come off in my mouth and the end of the stick was riddled with teeth-marks before Li Huan noticed me. He gave a sharp pull on the leash and shouted "no" and then said "this is most unworthy of you" as he examined the stick with great displeasure and placed it on a shelf. Li Huan went back to his reading but when he spied me, eyeing a bundle of sticks that stood leaning against the edge of the doorway, he yanked again on his leash, shouted no, and sought to distract me, as he often did, by cupping his hands and wriggling his fingers. But I had grown used to this trick and today it only bored me; I merely stared at him a moment before wandering to the other side of the room.

Li Huan again became lost in his thoughts and, after a few moments, I noticed a bundle of sticks that stuck out just over the edge of a shelf. Standing on my hind legs, I could just reach it with my front paws and pull it ever closer to me with tiny taps of my paws. Suddenly, it fell to the floor with a great clatter.

Another jerk of the leash and an admonition. Li Huan, looking very cross, rose and replaced the bundle. I sat at his feet for a long while when suddenly I felt an irresistible urge to run—and I raced across the room first to the door of the servant's room and then back all the way to the doorway to the courtyard, stopping only when my leash became so entangled in the legs of Li Huan's table and stool that I could no longer move.

"This is most unseemly," Li Huan said angrily, and led me to the darkest corner of the room and commanded me to sit and then to stay. Which I did for a very long time—but then the urge to run possessed me once again and I raced zigzag across the room under the stool of Li Huan and from there into our bedroom, again brought to a halt by the tangled leash.

Li Huan grunted and muttered as he unfastened and untangled the leash and led me back to the corner. "You have behaved as though the rules of right conduct were unknown to you," he scolded, shaking his finger at me. But I could no longer endure the boredom of this day and growled a shrill, squeaky growl of playful impatience and snapped at his shaking finger, then leaned forward on my front paws and raised my rump in the air, wagging not just my tail but my whole rump back and forth and growling and snapping at him.

His eyes brightened and he gave off that thin, unpredictable human scent that sometimes promises play and sometimes portends aggression. "Ah, so you wish to challenge Old Li do you? You think I am just a dried-up, feeble scholar whose appetites are whetted only by the fragrance of books!"

"But your assumptions are quite wrong!" Li Huan lunged at me and I scampered away from him, unhindered now by the leash, running first to the one side of the room, then the other, leaping onto Li Huan's stool and jumping off and racing into our bedroom.

"Yes, in taunting Li Huan you taunt a man who has known war and combat." He followed me into the bedroom and lunged at me again. Again I scampered crazily away from him, and this time I bounded from his stool onto the table and ran over his out-spread bundle of sticks and jumped down, coming to a halt before the old servant's doorway. Aroused by the commotion, she peered out at us.

70

"Now you have done the unforgivable!" he declared, "you have trampled on *The Great Learning*—a book that is sacred to me. Such a deed must be punished severely!"

He walked into the bedroom and when he returned the crossbow was in his hands. "I was not always a scholar, Xiao Ji Long, but in my youth served as a soldier with the great Duke of Chou," he declared, as he loaded an arrow into the crossbow. "Bowman Huan they called me in those days for there was no surer shot in our company. And many a barbarian fell before my unerring aim."

The old servant woman emerged a step or two inside the doorway. "Ai-ya, honorable sir, you cannot do this!" she screamed.

"You are quite right" he shouted in reply. "It would make too much of a mess inside. I must execute Xiao Ji Long in the courtyard."

He propped open the door and chased me about until I ran into the courtyard. Then he followed me out, holding his crossbow before him, training it on me as I ran from side to side, ignoring the pelting rain that streaked his face and the screams of the old servant woman at the doorway. As I dashed past him back toward the house, he let out a great laugh and pulled the trigger. The arrow hit with a thud square into the trunk of the pear tree at the end of the courtyard. The servant and I stood watching him from the doorway as he danced about the garden for a long time in the pouring rain, waving the crossbow above his head, his shoulders shaking with laughter.

Many days later, Li Huan and I walked along Sea-Like Lake. It was a clear, cloudless morning and still pleasantly warm. "You must return to the Palace in two days, Xiao Ji Long" he said. "It is my earnest hope that you do not fall back into foolish and incorrect ways." He sat down on a bench and unfastened my leash, for he often let me run free now, so sure was he of the efficacy of his commands.

"I have something for you." He pulled from the folds of his robe a hard, chewy piece of flesh with a pungent and delicious smell. I squealed with delight as I took it from his hand and gobbled it down. "Yes," he said, "I thought you would like it. It is cured venison—from the deer deep in our forests."

Li Huan sat watching me as I walked along the shore of Sea-Like Lake and among the trees and shrubs that covered the base of the hill that led to the Garden of Ever-Present Breezes. "When I see you thus, Xiao Ji Long," he said in a voice so mild that I could hardly hear him. "So jaunty and eager and self-assured in your walk, so full of life and hope and curiosity, undisturbed by any care...."

"When I see you thus, Xiao Ji Long, a feeling of joy leaps from my heart and flies out of my face." Then Li Huan rose from the bench and walked to the edge of the lake. His shoulders shook with an enormous cough and he spat into the water.

5
Palace Days

As soon as he saw me, Uncle Stupid picked me up and, cradling me in his arms like a baby, twirled around in circles. "Ah, Little Lucky One, you have returned to me. But, despite your absence, much good fortune has come to me anyway. Perhaps a carryover from our early days together—'and luck will mark his days'—as I sang in my excellent song." I detested being held in this manner, with my belly turned to the ceiling, so I wriggled and struggled until he turned me over and tucked me under his arm.

"Yes, much good fortune, Little Dragon, for the palace is filled with beautiful, refined and wondrously enchanting girls—who are all quite in love with me. You will find here your pick of jades and fragrances and other precious things. I have told them much about you and they are all quite eager to meet you. A palace becomes quickly dull without ever-fresh diversions. But my tongue should be pulled from my head for not first congratulating you. I am told that you performed superbly at your examination—that even Wang Mang could not find fault with you."

"Li Huan has been very much praised for his effort and, as a reward, he is being sent, with an imperial escort, to visit the village of his ancestors—something that has not been possible for twenty years, owing to the press of business and his loathing for his own kinsmen." Uncle Stupid chuckled. "And as a special mark of favor, the escort procession will include a half-dozen of our most prominent eunuchs. Well, you can imagine how this has delighted Li Huan. But for once he held his tongue since it was the Grand Empress Dowager herself who bestowed this great favor on him. Were I not occupied with the entertainment and education and comfort of so many beautiful girls, I would have begged the empress Dowager to assign me to the escort party."

"But you must be worn out from your journey and your examination. Let me show you our room."

The room was just beyond the entrance to the East Lateral Courts, which was flanked by fierce, grimacing wooden creatures, taller even than Uncle Stupid. Remembering the teachings of Li Huan, I obeyed the summons of Uncle Stupid and walked calmly past them with only a bit of hurry in my step. The walls of the room were a dark brownish red, shiny with lacquer. Long strips of cloth hung from the walls, depicting cranes flying or walking in shallow green water, tree branches full of colorful birds and blossoms, and steep hillsides from which elaborately curved and twisted trees protruded. I rose on my hind legs and sniffed the fringes of these hangings. Silk—just like the robes of Uncle Stupid and all the men and ladies of the court. I felt an urge to pull at it with my teeth but did not do so.

A huge silk screen stood at the far end of the room, covered with hundreds of men and women engaged in every sort of activity—walking about in every direction, drinking, eating, playing music, dancing, practicing with the bow—over a vast expanse of courtyards and buildings and gardens. Just below it was a huge thick rug, piled and bunched atop a mat of bamboo poles.

"That is your bed of yak's hair, which the Grand Empress Dowager had made especially for you, for it is her belief that this material is most suitable and comfortable for an imperial dog," said Uncle Stupid. "But, as I know you well, I am certain you will prefer the comfort of my own bed unless you are angry with me or in a contrary mood." He pointed to the large bed at the other corner of the room, which was littered with pillows of every color, and bordered by posts and a headboard of intricately carved yellowish wood, inlaid with red and brown jade and other precious stones. An orangish-red canopy floated above it.

"This bed belonged once to the former Empress Fu, whom we can no longer call an Empress as she was stripped of this rank and all other honors after she was long deceased. Indeed her tomb was opened and her seals taken and destroyed and her body removed and re-buried in a simple coffin. To perfect the injury, the mound covering her tomb was leveled and thorns planted on top in the freshly dug earth."

"Since she was already dead, she could not be killed, but many of the Fu clan were executed or forced to commit suicide. And that of their possessions that could be got at were confiscated. Alas, the same fate befell the former Empress Ting and her clan. She had not so nice a bed as former Empress Fu although that beautiful silk screen behind your yak's hair bed once belonged to her. But you should not feel sorry for them, Xiao Ji Long. Their fates were well deserved—much earlier they had conspired against Wang Mang and once actually succeeded in having him removed from office."

"There is a lesson to be learned here, Little Dragon. One must not offend Wang Mang and always speak respectfully of him—as I do. For he does not forget an injury." He plumped some pillows and leaned back in the bed. "No one else will have this bed for they believe it to be unlucky. But I believe the luck you have bestowed on me will more than counter any such ill-luck, will it not?"

Two straw baskets cluttered with bright-colored objects lay beyond the huge black lacquered chest at the foot of the bed. I began to approach them cautiously. "Ah, you have discovered the toys I have collected for you," said Uncle Stupid, but I was distracted then by eager, girlish voices, giggling and chirping. The doorway was suddenly crowded with young women in beautiful silk garments of every color and the fragrances of their perfumes filled the room as they pressed against each other to get a better look at me.

Uncle Stupid jumped up. "Come in, impatient ones, since you cannot wait for me to bring our prize to you. Xiao Ji Long, here are your new mistresses. Have all of them come? Let me see," he said as they filed into the room and arranged themselves in a half-circle about us. I leaned my head forward and uttered a low growl. "Ah, Xiao Ji Long is quite overcome by such a profusion of beauty and exquisiteness—as indeed I was myself when I first beheld them."

"But cease your growling, Little Dragon. Although beauty can kill, it is such a death as we should embrace."

The young women giggled and cooed at me, some of them leaning over and beckoning me to come to them. One of them, her tightly wound black hair glittering with jewels, stepped forward and bent far over, extending her hand toward the top of my head. I turned my head to the side to avoid her touch and growled again.

Uncle Stupid squatted down on his haunches and stroked my back. "Shush, Little Dragon, this lovely, high born lady is Splendid Moon. And just behind her are Lovely Jade, Snowy Jade, and Adorable Jade. Have I not told you before that it is indecorous for all the jades to be grouped together?" They laughed and moved closer to me for I had stopped growling now and bestowed a few tentative licks on Splendid Moon's hand.

"See how Lotus Blossom and Floating Petal stay one to each side. That makes for much better composition. And beside them are Blossoming Spring and Enchanting Fragrance…and Golden Bracelet. And just a bit behind them is Swaying Oriole. See how she holds herself with such grace, as though perched amidst cherry blossoms in the mildest of summer breezes." Swaying Oriole blushed and brought her hands to her face.

"But who is missing? Of course," said Uncle Stupid as another young woman entered the room. "Precious Wisdom. Always the least hurried. I implore you again to change your name. It conjures up in my mind the dreadful wisps of an old scholar's beard. A strange name indeed for one so lovely—and for one who aspires to be Highest Lady. Do you not know that wisdom in a woman inspires only fear in a man?"

"But is it not also true that men only trifle with beauty," replied Precious Wisdom, unperturbed, "and are ruled by fear?"

The others laughed, their eyes wide with amazement and delight at the brazenness of Precious Wisdom. "Ah, yes," replied Uncle Stupid, "but one should keep wisdom—and fear— tucked up one's sleeve like an assassin's dagger. Not displayed for all to see like a jeweled diadem."

"Tinkling Jade, perhaps," suggested Uncle Stupid scratching his temple. "But no, we have already too many jades. Graceful Instep, perhaps. Something that will subtly excite a man."

"Adorable Toes. Would that be to your liking?" Precious Wisdom said in a wry, determined voice and the other young women shook with laughter.

"Excellent. Shall I submit a petition?" Uncle Stupid then bade each of the women to pet me briefly and take their leave, saying that I must eat and that he and I, being old friends long separated, had much to catch up on.

"But before we part, I will tell you a little joke—one that seems simple and straightforward but contains complex and subtle flavors, like the simmering quails that were prepared for us last night."

"In the town of Ping-O there lived a horribly crippled hunchback. Whom all the town pitied—and avoided. For people like cripples no more than they like eunuchs. One day a magician, never seen before, came to town. After selling potions for immortality and making coins and jewels disappear—all the usual things that magicians do, he spied the hunchback and proposed a wager. 'I will bet any man 1,000 shu that I can straighten this hunchback.'"

"The people of Ping-O, like all the people of the One Hundred Surnames, very much like a gamble—and this seemed a sure thing. So money poured in to match the magician's wager. The hunchback was not at first very enthusiastic—for he had little reason to believe the townspeople or the magician wished to do any good deed for him. His reaction was much the same as mine might be if a magician suddenly appeared at the Palace and promised to make me whole—and Wang Mang bet against him." Uncle Stupid paused and looked about as the girls blushed and covered their faces and tittered with delight. "But the townspeople eventually persuaded him— mentioning that they would throw him in the river if he did not at least attempt the treatment proposed by the magician."

"On the day chosen, the hunchback was brought to the center of the market place. Two assistants to the magician laid him on a wooden slab and stretched him out—in so far as they could for he was so crooked that he stood not more than 3 feet high from head to toe. Then they placed a heavy board on top him, and stretched his arms and legs, then added heavy rocks, and then stretched him again. Then more heavy rocks, more stretching. All during this, the townspeople watched with great curiosity, and I am sure there were several scholars there debating the merits of this treatment."

"The hunchback, of course, screamed and groaned in pain. Although as the rocks grew heavier and heavier, his groans became duller and duller. Finally, the magician and his assistants removed the rocks, very slowly and carefully—and then the board. The hunchback lay there quite straight! From head to toe he measured as tall as one of our barbarian cavalrymen. But he was also quite dead!"

"'You have killed him!' the townspeople of Ping-O shouted in unison.

"'I only said that I would straighten him,' said the magician as though insulted. 'I did not promise to keep him alive.'" Uncle Stupid let out a loud cackle and, with a self-satisfied grin, surveyed the faces of the young women, who quivered with uncertain laughter. Only Precious Wisdom did not react.

"Though I am only 14 years of age," Precious Wisdom burst out. "I have heard that joke some 10,000 times!"

"I am the eldest at fifteen years of age," said Snowy Jade, "so I have heard it 10 thousand one hundred times."

Uncle Stupid ignored their quips. "Beware of promises," he said, talking as he did when he imitated Li Huan, "for the efforts of men end most often as do those of the magicians. Unless, of course, they are undertaken by men of undisputed quality—such as Wang Mang."

"What happened to the magician?" asked Lotus Blossom, who seemed very much taken with the joke.

"The townspeople of Ping-O were not fools. He was charged with murder and chopped in half. They might have let him go but they owed him too much money."

"It does not always pay to be too clever," Uncle Stupid said, exchanging looks with Precious Wisdom and Snowy Jade as, giggling, the girls filed out of the room.

That first night, and the second, I stayed aloof from Uncle Stupid in my bed of yak's hair, ignoring his calls to come and join him. But in the middle of the third night, I awoke with a chill and, intrigued by the soft snores of Uncle Stupid, I leapt into the bed and curled up by his back. Thereafter, I slept each night with him, except when he gave off too much heat and I moved to the smooth coolness of the floor. My yak's hair bed I used only occasionally for afternoon naps.

During the day I spent little time in our room. My meals, which consisted of rice or barley with large chunks of chicken or pork or duck, were served to me twice a day by a serving woman who ladled them out of a silver bowl into my bright red and green bowl. My water was replenished by a different servant, who regularly emptied and cleaned my blue and gold water bowl, and poured in fresh, cool water from a silver pitcher.

The toys were, at first, of great interest to me, both forbidding and beguiling in their strangeness. I approached them cautiously, pawing at the edge of the basket and retreating quickly, feinting and running in a half circle or jumping sideways when they moved. Then I would cry and whine until Uncle Stupid grabbed the basket and spilled the toys—balls of all sizes and colors, wooden horses on wheels, rabbits and mice made of gold and silver cloth—onto the floor for me. It was only after many approaches and retreats and the stubborn refusal of Uncle Stupid to get up any more from his bed that I discovered that I could, without danger, tip the basket over and snatch one of the toys in my jaws and race away to the corner of the room. But, even then, I continued to approach the basket with the utmost care and ceremony— pawing timidly at first, warning it with low growls and a few squeaky cries, retreating quickly and cleverly with feints and circles and sideway leaps — the excitement and pleasure of this ceremony being greater than that of the toys themselves.

These pleasures paled, however, in comparison to those I experienced outside our room. For I was allowed to wander as I saw fit through the numberless corridors and rooms of the East Lateral Courts, which overflowed with the bright, dazzling robes, the light, sweet sounds and the thousands of delightful smells of women, with here and there the dull gray robe and shriek of a eunuch. Everywhere women sat before mirrors or reclined on pillows, lounged in their baths, amused themselves with song or poetry or lilting conversation, worked at their embroidery or practiced with the harp or the erhu. Or busied themselves in sweeping and adjusting and perfecting clothing and hair or running about with trays of food or pots of hot barley water—for each concubine had several maids and many servants to attend to her. Everywhere I was met with great interest and kindness and amusement—and offers of treats and play.

"Auspicious Beast, Little Lucky One: shall I throw the sticks today? Which color will be lucky for me?" They would ask me.

"Xiao-Xiao, Little Dragon," the women would coo at me, "Come lie with me."

"Why do you grumble so when you walk about, Xiao-Xiao, are you unhappy?"

"Come join my bath."

"Come, I will play a song for you on my harp, a song of pugs."

I would stop at each doorway and cock my head from side to side to better assess the sounds from within, a movement that always drew laughter and praise. Sometimes I would enter and, sometimes for no particular reason, I would continue to the next room. This made them laugh all the more and they would shout behind me. "You are a haughty one, Xiao-Xiao. You will get no more treats from us." But they always gave me some anyway whenever I next entered their rooms: bits of meat, or minced fish, pickles and water chestnuts, tiny bones of quail that they held while I licked them clean.

I was most fond of visiting Precious Wisdom and Splendid Moon, who lived side by side in Evening Breeze Court and who seemed always together. Indeed only these two, and Uncle Stupid, inspired in me a relentless craving to be always near them.

Precious Wisdom and Splendid Moon spent much time in competing to see who could make me talk the most. Precious Wisdom in particular was convinced that I could be taught to speak a few words.

"You were born to talk, Xiao Ji Long. For why else would you go about mumbling and grumbling and snorting and humming your little songs all day long? And such sad, warbling whines and sighs. Whenever did a dog make such sounds?" She would make a humming noise in imitation of my own and, after we had traded sounds for some time, she would say "P-p-precious. Say it! P-p-precious!"

"No, say: Moon," the other would say. "M-m-moon. That is much easier—M-m-moon. Yes, did you hear it? Moon. She said it. She loves me more dearly than you."

Splendid Moon would then grab me up and dance around the room with me, ignoring the objections of Precious Wisdom that she heard no such sound. But Splendid Moon had less patience for this exercise and would soon abandon it after a few attempts. Precious Wisdom, however, would continue to talk to me and try to coax words out of me long after Splendid Moon had become bored and returned to her own rooms.

One day, Splendid Moon called to me as I stuck my head around the corner of the doorway to Evening Breeze Court. She held her cupped hands close to her face and, smacking her lips together, uttered great sighs of delight. Precious Wisdom sat to her side, a maid combing her hair and fastening it with clasps of shell. Snowy Jade stood gazing out into the courtyard. "Xiao-Xiao, come to me. I have something I am sure you will like," Splendid Moon said and, as I approached her, I picked up a food scent that filled me with a desire more compelling than any I had experienced before. I rushed to her and jumped against her knee.

"It is from very far away," she said, holding the tantalizing bit of food just above my head. "From the great ocean itself." She placed it against my lips and, after one brief curious sniff, I gobbled it down in one swallow. "Dried cuttlefish, such as we have every day in my homeland. But all too rare here in Chang'An. But I have more of it," she said and went over to a black and gold lacquered chest, spattered with white and pink shells. When she opened the chest, the smell of dried cuttlefish rushed out and filled the room, exciting me so that I jumped against her legs, yelping and whining, turning in circles.

"But you cannot have another bit of it until you say Moon. M-m-moon." She held the cuttlefish, which was wrapped in cloth, high above her head and twirled about the room, as I chased after her. Precious Wisdom and Snowy Jade, and the maid too, bent over with laughter. "M-m-moon. I do not hear it. One cannot expect such a rare tidbit just for yelping. M-m-moon," she continued, twirling from one side of the room to the other, as my jumps and whines became more and more furious.

"I suppose I shall just have to put it away." She approached the chest and made as though she were going to put the cloth-covered cuttlefish back into it.

So maddening was her taunting and so overpowering my desire for the cuttlefish that a kind of blackness came over me and I let out a horrible, ear-splitting scream. Splendid Moon threw her head back in laughter when she heard this while Snowy Jade and Precious Wisdom jumped up and put their fingers in their ears.

The clasps dropped from the maid's hands, "Ai-ya! It is the sound of a child being murdered by demons," she exclaimed, spitting on the floor to ward off these demons. "May a thousand deities swarm down and protect us."

"Very well. I shall give you another little bit," Splendid Moon said after I screamed again. "But let us take her around and show the others." She ran from Evening Breeze Court, with me trotting close at her heels and Snowy Jade and Precious Wisdom chasing behind us, to Watching Pines and Appreciating Paintings Studio where we found Lovely Jade and Adorable Jade practicing calligraphy. Then to Autumn Sky Pavilion where Blossoming Spring and Enchanting Fragrance were practicing a dance. And so we continued until my screams had been demonstrated to all the women of the East Lateral Courts of the Palace. For each time we stopped, Splendid Moon would dance around with the cuttlefish held high above her until her taunts would drive me to screaming and then the others would stick their fingers in their ears and run about yelling in delighted horror.

Finally, we encountered Uncle Stupid in the corridor.

"Ah, so Xiao Ji Long has the gift of the scream," he said somberly. "It does not surprise me, though there are only a very few pugs who have this gift. The mother of the mother of our Little Dragon was one such. And this gift is always coupled with other strange powers. But Xiao Ji Long has from the start been touched and favored by the gods."

"Have I yet told you the story of the ancient race of pugs and how they came to be so small?"

"Yes, far too many times, Uncle" said Precious Wisdom, and she and Splendid Moon skipped down the corridor, laughing, with the remains of the cuttlefish.

Later that night, Uncle Stupid said, "It is telling, Little Auspicious One, that you have been most drawn to Splendid Moon and Precious Wisdom—and they to each other. Splendid Moon is the most beautiful of all the concubines, but with a wild and unripened spirit. Precious Wisdom is the most clever and her sallies of playful wit disguise a hard will. The question of Empress is settled—for the moment, though such things are not unchangeable and Empresses may rise and fall even while one Son of Heaven remains. And, of course, one may bear a future Son of Heaven and be assured of the title. So such secret ambitions need not be abandoned. But who is to be Favorite Beauty and who, Highest Ladies? These questions are to be answered soon, when the Son of Heaven receives his cap of manhood. All eleven aspire to be such. All, that is, except Splendid Moon, but that is a secret we must keep to ourselves, Little Lucky One."

Many days later, Uncle Stupid took me with him to the Courtyard of Heavenly Bamboo. All were there except Lovely Jade and Floating Petal, who were being instructed in court etiquette, and Blossoming Spring and Golden Bracelet, who were scheduled to practice their embroidery at that time. Uncle Stupid always said that he was too stupid for such dreary chores and suited only for the more serious task of frivolity.

He brought with him small squares of white silk on which were sewn black characters that he concealed from the women with exaggerated care.

"These represent the names of famous personages in the history of the Central Kingdom," he explained as he attached a square to the back of each of the concubines by looping a string around their necks. "You are to determine who you are by asking questions of the others—for all will know this but you. However, you may answer only yes or no to any questions. The winner shall receive a pin of the purest gold representing her birth month."

As soon as the last square was tied, the girls began to rush eagerly at each other.

"Stop!" shouted Uncle Stupid. "To all personages that are part of our play, I swear that no offense is intended. Let me be trampled by 10,000 feet if this is not so. To ensure against any offense, I have arranged that an extra meal be offered at their ancestral shrines." He paused and looked dramatically into the face of each contestant. "Now you may begin!"

The girls again rushed eagerly at each other, talking rapidly and excitedly, pushing to obtain an audience, rubbing their faces and clasping their hands as they pondered the answers, rushing to another when the answers were unsatisfactory or when those they were questioning deserted them to pursue their own questions. This strange, frenzied behavior confused and unnerved me and I retreated under a bench at the edge of the courtyard, watching them apprehensively.

"You look so disapproving, Xiao Ji Long," Lotus Blossom said, suddenly noticing me as she searched for someone to ask questions. "Do not be such a spoilsport."

"Yes, our Little Dragon is very serious-minded" said Uncle Stupid. "You must remember that she has been educated by the great scholar Li Huan and disapproves of all frivolity, but hurry along or you will be left out. Look, there is Precious Wisdom, talk to her."

The game ended in tears and bad feelings. Snowy Jade quickly guessed that she was the Yellow Lord and although Precious Wisdom finished close behind her, guessing that she was the Duke of Chou, she was quite angry with herself for not winning. Splendid Moon was jealous that Adorable Jade wore the name of the great beauty, Flying Swallow, and had shed tears when she discovered that she was the ancient ruler Shen Nong, whom she thought quite dull since he had merely invented agriculture and, based on the representations she had seen, very homely. Lotus Blossom was unable to guess her identity even after all others had succeeded and, as they stood around her laughing at her questions, broke into sobs.

Uncle Stupid suddenly pointed at the sky above: rays of sunlight shot out from behind a cloud of black and silver that covered half the sky. "I propose that we discuss now the question of which is more beautiful—a sun-fringed cloud or a moon-fringed cloud. Splendid Moon shall, of course, speak in favor of a moon-fringed cloud."

She had just begun to do so when a lopsided feeling gripped my head, spreading pain from behind my ears to the base of my neck. The darkness came over me, as it had when Splendid Moon taunted me, and I ran out from under the bench, screaming and turning in circles. Splendid Moon stopped talking and she—and all the others—looked at me in amazement. "Has some cuttlefish been hidden...," she started to say but then the earth began to shake and pieces of pottery fell from the niches that lined the courtyard. The women ran from the courtyard and Uncle Stupid chased me down with great difficulty, finally succeeding in folding his arms around me. Struggling and screaming, I was rushed inside as cracks began to run up the white stucco wall at the far side of the courtyard.

I experienced this intense, lopsided pain twice more—and at each of these times a great thunderstorm rolled suddenly across the grounds of the Palace. Just after the second storm had cleared, I stood at the side of Splendid Moon, looking out the window of Evening Breeze Court. Splendid Moon leaned forward with her elbows on the sill of the window, her chin on her cupped hands. I had hopped onto the bench under the window, resting my paws on the sill. I uttered a low growl—for the branches of the tree below us shook as a squirrel moved along them. The sky was now clear and moonless, filled with stars. Puffs of mist rose up from the hot earth, set loose by the thunderstorm.

"Why must the Emperor be so plain?" she said. "And such a baby? Like a tiny trembling leaf, already withered, in the midst of all his yellow finery." Splendid Moon looked down at me and tugged at my jowls. "And Wang Yu is so beautiful! So brave!"

"His eyes are so languid and melting, but full of fire when angered or when he speaks of his passion. When first we met, before my selection to the Palace, he whispered to me: 'a moon rising in splendor.' His finger grazed my cheek as he spoke these words, light as a feather, unseen by anyone."

"My fate is worse even than that of the girl from Hopeh whom the Emperor Yuandi saw in a dream. So enthralled was he that he ordered that the whole realm be searched for her. But in the likeness that was sent to the Emperor her face was rendered hideous with ugly blemishes by a painter bribed by her rivals. So the Emperor gave up his search and she was given to the Khan of the Mongol Tribes. And when the Emperor visited the Khan and saw her many years later, he realized his mistake and henceforth never ceased mourning her loss. And she, she died of grief. In the dry, windswept desert, her grave remains always green—even in winter."

"But my fate is worse because my beloved is near. Within reach but unreachable. I can speak of my sorrow only to you, Xiao-Xiao. Not even to Precious Wisdom, who would in any case just stick her fingers in her ears. Nor to Uncle Stupid, who would only counsel me that one cannot think irreverent thoughts concerning the Son of Heaven."

* * *

"You have become quite famous," Uncle Stupid said as we sauntered through the courtyard after my morning meal. Two servant women trailed behind us ready to collect any droppings I might leave and I kept looking back at one of them who wore a long red kerchief that fluttered in the breeze in a manner that intrigued and disturbed me.

"All the court is talking of your powers. Which some regard as demonic, and others argue are more of a benevolent nature. Wang Mang himself has asked that any further screaming or unusual behavior be reported to him immediately. And for some reason everyone in the palace now craves dried cuttlefish. There is not a bit to be had in all of Chang 'An. Although several wagon-loads are said to be on their way."

"But you must not allow such things to make you pompous and discourteous. For this morning you begin your visits to the Emperor Pingdi. So you must be respectful. And you must remember the excellent training of Li Huan."

The Emperor sat in a simple chair of camel wool in the middle of a small antechamber adjoining the Hall of Celestial Purity. Instead of his enormous yellow robe, he wore a simple black robe and tunic, and a black skull cap, all fringed with gold. A host of servants and eunuchs hovered about him, taking care to keep their heads lower than his.

Uncle Stupid led me toward him, keeping the leash tight against my neck, walking, stern-faced and stiff, as he did when he imitated Li Huan.

"There she is, Son of Heaven, and dearest nephew," said the Marquisa of Ping-O in her sugary voice, kneeling next to the Emperor. Raising my head, I caught the heavy scent of her perfume and, beneath it, something malicious. I began to growl but Uncle Stupid yanked on my leash quickly and I ceased. To the right of the Son of Heaven, I saw a huge pile of tan fur and when I was half-way to the Emperor the pile began to stir and coughed out several growls of warning. Then it rose up and thrust forward its black mask, shaking its head from side to side barking, and I saw clearly the enormous bulk of Waking Bear, the Imperial Pug. He was at least three times my size with a huge head framed by great folds of sagging jowls and a belly that swayed just above the floor. The ferocity of his barking increased as I came closer and a servant crawled along the floor beside him, trying to fasten a jewel-studded leather leash on him. Once this was done, he went wild with fury, leaping against the leash so that the servant had to scramble to his knees to regain his balance.

Both terrified and provoked by this display, I first lurched forward snapping, then lurched backward to flee, and when the leash caught me, I pulled wildly from side to side. Uncle Stupid halted and pulled the leash close in and commanded me to sit. After twisting my head left to right in an unsuccessful effort to free myself from the constraint of the leash, I came to my senses and obeyed this command.

Uncle Stupid waited until Waking Bear had been dragged through a doorway behind the Emperor, still barking furiously, his paws spinning and scratching wildly on the polished wood as he struggled against his removal. Then we walked several steps closer to the Emperor and Uncle Stupid stopped, commanded me to sit, and fell to his knees and brought his forehead to the floor his customary 18 times. But he said nothing because the new chief eunuch, who had met us before we entered the Hall, had strictly ordered him to hold his tongue and forego all his usual foolishness.

The Emperor Pingdi leaned forward in his chair. The row that Waking Bear had started had piqued his interest and he looked at me with eager anticipation.

"Come here," he said in his piping voice, seeming to be annoyed that I did nothing but sit there. "Come here!" he said again, louder this time, trying to force the pitch of his voice lower. "Do you not know that I am the Son of Heaven? All must obey me!"

It had taken me some time to learn to listen to the commands of Uncle Stupid as though he were Li Huan. Even now, I responded only haphazardly to them. But the circumstances of my audience with Pingdi confused me and I felt now that it was safest to listen only to Uncle Stupid.

"Do something!" Pingdi said, falling back in his chair in disappointment and annoyance. "He is as dull as Waking Bear."

"But see how well-behaved she is, Son of Heaven" said the Marquisa. "It is only that she has become timid in the presence of such magnificence, dearest nephew." I started to mumble with vexation when I heard her voice again but Uncle Stupid, who had completed his bows, heard me and jerked the leash.

"I am sure you will find her an excellent source of amusement in due time," the Marquisa said and seized Pingdi's hand in both of her hands and, after kissing it, pressed it to her bosom. Pingdi's eyes darted about nervously.

"Let him off the leash," said Pingdi, "and command him to approach me." Uncle Stupid crawled about on his knees, fumbling with the knot of my leash, then he put his hand on my rump and pushed me towards the Son of Heaven.

I walked forward very cautiously, my tail down, for all this was very strange and frightening and the scents emanating from the Emperor told me that he meant me no good. The Son of Heaven suddenly pulled a wooden ball from behind his back and, with a scream of delight, hurled it at me as hard as he could. It sailed harmlessly past me. I turned and followed it until it stopped, pawed at it once or twice, and, finding it of no interest, turned away from it.

"Too dull and stupid even to play with a ball," Pingdi said disgustedly. Then he clapped his hands with sudden enthusiasm. "Let us put her in the Chamber of Celestial Waters with Waking Bear. We can watch them from above and see how they get on."

Uncle Stupid started to object but a signal from the chief eunuch cut him short. "Yes, they must get to know each other," said the Marquisa, again kissing Pingdi's hand. "Only let a servant go with them, nephew, so that Waking Bear does not get too rough with her."

In the center of the Chamber of Celestial Waters was a large round fountain, and inside the lip of the fountain stood many bronze animals—a horse, a rat, a pig, a rooster and many more, water gushing from their mouths. In the corners of the chamber stood huge stone bowls of water, their surface thick with floating flower petals. The Son of Heaven, the Marquisa, and their retinue of servants were assembled on the balcony of polished red wood that looked down on the fountain.

But I hardly noticed their presence for as I entered the chamber, Waking Bear, who had been stretched out sleeping against the wall of the fountain, struggled to his feet and charged at me, once again growling and barking, shaking with indignation at my presence. I ran as fast as I could, my tail down in terror, and hid behind one of the petal-strewn bowls at the far side of the room. Waking Bear followed me only half-way, contenting himself with a great bombast of barking and growling, sticking his head high into the air as he did so, the force of his efforts bouncing his head up and down. He did not move until I emerged timidly from my hiding place and then he charged again, baring his teeth and yelping at me. And again I fled, hiding this time behind a different bowl. But again Waking Bear pursued me only half-way.

This happened again and again and I began to think that Waking Bear really wished to play and so I began to emerge more and more quickly from my hiding places and to turn and run only when he was almost upon me. And instead of running always to the stone bowls I began to run around the circle of the fountain. Waking Bear ran half-heartedly after me, his tongue hanging far out, panting and snorting now more than he was barking. However, I was much faster than him and after a few laps around the fountain, I found myself in pursuit of Waking Bear, almost at his rump. When he turned and saw me thus, his tail fell and his eyes widened with terror. He let out a horrible squeal and ran faster, a thick, prickly stand of hair rising up the center of his back. But he could not match my speed and I chased him round and round the fountain, pawing and biting playfully at his tail, until finally the servant took pity on him and, with a great grunt, lifted him up and carried him off. Above us, I could hear the shrill laughter of Pingdi and the approving chirps of the Marquisa.

* * *

I was sitting on Precious Wisdom's lap in Pear Fragrance Court and Snowy Jade, Blossoming Spring and Golden Bracelet were clustered about us. They were singing about the months of the year and all that must be done in them. Sometimes they reached such high notes that it caused me to sneeze and bat at my ears and they would stop singing and burst into laughter. Then they would begin again and try to sing even higher. Splendid Moon danced gracefully about in the center of the floor, and I followed with rapt attention the movement of the silken scarves floating about her and the swoop of her long sleeves as they lightly grazed the floor. They were singing about the eight month and threads and dyes and the making of robes when Uncle Stupid rushed excitedly into the room.

"I have most extraordinary and excellent news!" declared Uncle Stupid. "Wang Mang has been given the title 'Duke Giving Tranquility to the Han Dynasty.' Is that not excellent? Who can doubt that the dynasty will now last ten thousand minutes?" The young women giggled and Precious Wisdom stuck her fingers in her ears.

"Years, of course," he corrected. "I have become so stupid. I meant to say years."

"As part of this great honor, he has also been enfeoffed with an additional 28,000 households in Shao-Long and Hsi-Hsi, and the same title and estate as the founder of the house of Wang—and all manner of other honors and titles too complicated for my poor mind to remember. Except that he has also been granted a meal from the Imperial Cuisine twenty days out of each month. That is such an honor as I could savor. But it seems wasted on Wang Mang. All know he eats little more than barley. Though he seems to thrive on it. For he gets ever more plump."

"Wang Mang refused all these honors, of course, as is his custom. It was only after a decree, which he had not authorized, was signed by the Grand Empress Dowager herself that he reluctantly accepted these overdue rewards. 'Only when the people have a sufficiency in their households, should I be given any awards,' he said at first. 'Any awards should first be given to the nobles and commoners.' No man is more humble or generous than Wang Mang. Though I am disappointed that he did not mention eunuchs in his statement."

"Shall I tell you again the story of Wang Mang and how, though an orphan and in humble circumstances, he rose to high position?"

"No," shouted Precious Wisdom, and, laughing and giggling, the girls began to sing loudly about the tenth month and the hunting of foxes and wildcats.

"But there is also news for Xiao Ji Long," Uncle Stupid said loudly and the song died away. "Li Huan is back. Yes, and he has already spied you from afar. He says that you have become fat. And also that you were behaving foolishly, jumping about and yelping for a treat. He has entreated the Grand Empress Dowager to resume his walks with you and this permission has been granted."

Splendid Moon snatched me from the lap of Precious Wisdom and, lifting me over her head, began to spin me around.

"Ooh, I can hardly lift her, so fat has she become," she said as the others laughed and clapped their hands. "Your fat and lazy days are soon to end, Xiao-Xiao."

* * *

Li Huan stood before me at the entrance to the Park of Verdant Radiance, looking very stern and even more ancient and spindly than I remembered. He commanded me to sit after I had dragged the servant to him, wagging not just my tail but my whole rump with the joy of seeing him again. After he had taken the leash from the servant, he leaned over and patted my head, then poked my ribs and made a disapproving grunt. After we had walked a little way, he removed the leash and commenced his own peculiar exercises, accompanying them as before with much coughing and spitting.

"My visit to my homeland has quite freshened me, Xiao Ji Long," he said finally. "I find that goodness, and simplicity, and right conduct still exist outside the gates of the Palace, beyond the corruption and falseness of Chang 'An."

"I have come to doubt this business of courts and nobles and great scholars and Sons of Heaven. My heart is carried now towards the people, as by a rushing, clean mountain stream that would carry me far away from Chang 'An. One cannot hurry the cycles. Did not Master K'ung himself tell us that when the way does not prevail, it is useless to aspire to public position? In such a place as we are now, have I any choice but to remove myself from public life?"

"In such a place!" Li Huan said bitterly, "where fine gentleman and ladies regal themselves with dish after dish at banquets—without regard to season or cost. And would think it a disgrace to drink from a cup not inlaid with silver or without golden handles. While all about them, the poor of our cities and peasants chew on leeks and grass and gnaw at the discarded bones of their meals to survive. Where dogs and horses go about bejeweled and bedecked in gold and silk, while commoners wear rags full of holes. Where poetry and heavenly music are neglected so that time can be made for cockfights and tigerfights and screeching foreign girls and dancing bears and monkeys. Where the classics are ignored and people give way to the beseeching of spirits and strange powers!"

Li Huan cleared his throat with a tremendous cough and spat into the grass as he wandered off the path up a steep grassy hill. He paid no attention to me even though I ran about his feet in short, tight circles in the hope of getting him to play with me.

"Wang Mang!" he grunted. "Only in such a land could this furtive spirit who guides the hand of every Minister be regarded as an exemplar of the teachings of Master K'ung. Praised and wheedled by scholars, who care only that Wang Mang expands the Imperial University, and creates three positions of Erudites where only one existed before, and establishes their pet texts as authoritative subjects for university study for the examinations. So low is the state to which the disciples of the Master have fallen!"

Li Huan continued determinedly up the hill, ignoring the heavy dew that soaked his slippers and dripped from the ends of his robe. "And now that he has been made this Duke of Tranquility, they make much of the white pheasant given him long ago by ignorant barbarians from the South—and liken him to the Duke of Chou!"

"'How amazing,' they say, 'that these barbarians gave him this gift without any knowledge that it was a symbol of the great Duke of Chou' and they talk about how the barbarians made a long speech that no one could understand. But I was there and I understood their speech, which was not made in some foreign unknown tongue but only in very poor Chinese. And the barbarians said 'Is this not the gift you sought, O great lord of this and that.' And no one but me, with my fading hearing, could understand this?!"

"To liken Wang Mang to the noble Duke of Chou! A man who seeks not justice but intimidation. Who would shoot roosting birds and call it sport. It is as though one should liken a toad to a man—and not just any man. But a man ennobled by every virtue, and enriched by the cultivation of every quality!"

Li Huan stopped speaking and looked about him, seeming surprised that he was on this high hill overlooking the winding paths of the Park of Verdant Radiance. He reached down and stroked my flanks. "How have you become so wet, Xiao Ji Long? Have you been wading in some pond?" He held my head gently in his hand and looked into my eyes.

"I have said nothing about your flaws, Xiao Ji Long. Your behavior today shows still a core of proper conduct. But I fear you are falling into decadence and unseemly conduct. We must walk more often."

As we walked back to the carriage, Li Huan said, "I must learn not to trouble myself with such bitter thoughts, Xiao Ji Long, for they lead only to anger and confusion. Some sprouts do not send up shoots; some fields are forever barren. One must learn to reconcile oneself to what cannot be changed."

After that, Li Huan took me for a walk every other morning and on those mornings I would sit waiting by the entrance to the East Lateral Courts fidgeting and whimpering with impatience and enthusiasm. He made no more long speeches but instead took great interest in rehearsing my commands, after which we would walk silently for a long time as I explored the ever fresh smells of the park and he attended to his exercises and his coughing and spitting.

"Phew!" Uncle Stupid said upon my return one morning from such a walk. "You are smelly as a eunuch, Little Dragon." He paused and watched as Floating Petal, Lotus Blossom and their maids, who passed us in the corridor, blushed and averted their eyes at this indelicacy. "I must look into this matter and determine if Li Huan is not overtaxing you."

The next morning Uncle Stupid accompanied me in the carriage. Li Huan watched in surprise and disgust as he led me to him. "The Grand Empress Dowager has ordered me to accompany you and Xiao Ji Long on this walk," Uncle Stupid said, wrinkling the corners of his eyes as he did when he told one of his jokes.

Li Huan took the leash from him, then he cleared his throat and spat. He began walking quickly down the path without speaking. Uncle Stupid hurried after him and began to talk as he always did, speaking of the lovely and enchanting girls of the East Lateral Courts, their various talents and characters. He talked also of the games they played and the many amusing incidents that had occurred since the eleven lovelies had been installed in the Palace, punctuating his remarks with broad chuckles and half swallowed giggles. Li Huan walked rapidly forward, silent except for his coughing and spitting. He did not let me off the leash nor did he do his exercises.

Uncle Stupid began to talk of the arduous preparations that were underway even now for the wedding of the Son of Heaven and Wang Mang's daughter. Still, Li Huan plodded on without speaking. Uncle Stupid looked sideways at me, wrinkling his eyes, and then began to speak glowingly of Wang Mang's new title of Duke Giving Tranquility to the Han Dynasty.

"The decree said that Wang Mang may indeed be said to be perfect and encompasses in entirety the one pervading principle. That his upright character is a model for the empire. I believe that to be an understatement, Li Huan, don't you? But tell me, what is the one pervading principle?! There are many teachings of Master K'ung that I do not fully understand."

Li Huan merely sighed and walked faster.

"I am very fond, in particular, of the teaching of the Master," Uncle

Stupid continued, "in which he says something like: 'Once I determined to go without food and drink so as to think better. It did me no good. Better just to study.' I believe that to be perhaps his finest saying. Although I do not much care for study."

"This is impossible! Am I to discuss the Master with you?!" Li Huan threw my leash at Uncle Stupid and ran stiffly towards a clump of mulberry trees that stood far to the left of the path. "I can bear it no longer," we heard him shout as he moved across the field.

* * *

Every other morning the carriage still took me to the Park of Verdant Radiance, but Li Huan was no longer waiting for me. Splendid Moon had volunteered to assume the responsibility for my walk. Uncle Stupid had said that this would be very irregular, for the concubines were normally allowed to walk only in the Garden of Ever-Present Breezes and then only during certain hours when all but the eunuchs were forbidden to enter its grounds. But the chief eunuch had acquiesced to Splendid Moon's proposal on condition that she would be accompanied at all times by a eunuch and that the park be closed to all but eunuchs during any such walks. Uncle Stupid surmised that he had done this in deference to the very great affection the Grand Empress Dowager had for me, her concerns about my health, and indeed her desire to someday get a female puppy from my first litter.

Uncle Stupid said that he had far too much to do to accompany Splendid Moon on these walks and, in any case, that he could not show so much favor to one concubine, especially the most beautiful one. Instead, a short, obese eunuch, whom Uncle Stupid and everyone else called Minced Meat because of his extravagant fondness for that dish, was chosen for this task. Minced Meat, whose black eyes hid in the puffy fat of his face, said little and left Splendid Moon and I very much alone.

Whenever we would wander off the path—and Splendid Moon loved to leave the path and run up and down the hills of the park—he would remain behind, finding a bench on which to sit and eat the small pies of minced meat and flour paste that he always carried with him, never offering me even the smallest particle as a treat.

Splendid Moon would walk quite ceremoniously up the hill, humming in a soft voice that only I could hear. But as soon as we were out of sight of Minced Meat, she would unfasten my leash and snatch me up from behind and, holding me far out in front of her, she would run shouting through the grass. I would squirm and wiggle and try to bite her hands—though I dearly loved these romps. When she would finally put me down, she would begin to sing in a playful, naughty voice, and to dance to the right and then the left, holding her palms together in front of her, swaying and dipping her head close to the ground, and flashing her dark brown eyes seductively at me. I would growl and yelp and bite at her feet until she would suddenly stop her dance and scold me, saying I was a very bad dog, a mean, hateful little dog who would bring no good luck to anyone. Then she would pick up a branch or stick and chase after me and I would run around her in wide, frantic circles, changing directions whenever she came close to me, using every feint and twist at my command.

Sometimes I would tire myself out so completely with these exertions that I could run no more. I would plop down in the grass, snorting and panting and wheezing, my tongue hanging far out of my mouth. Then Splendid Moon would pick me up and carry me to a pleasant grassy spot under a tree or to the stone pier that extended into Water Lily Pond, where we would sit down in the shade of the peaked bamboo roof that stood in the middle of the pier.

"I fear you will not live, Xiao-Xiao," she would say to me. "But you must, you must," and she would pinch my jowls. "For if you died in my charge, I could not bear the disgrace and would kill myself."

When my breathing had steadied, Splendid Moon would begin to sing her songs of cherry blossoms and the shadows made by the moon, of throbbing hearts and longing, of wives who thought only of their husbands far away in the wars. Sometimes, Splendid Moon would go to the end of the pier and lean over on her knee and look at her reflection. When I followed her and peered over the edge, I would growl and jump back in alarm, for there looking up at me was the flat-faced black mask of a dog that looked much like my mother but gave off no scent.

"Ah, Xiao-Xiao, you are right to be afraid. For that is the demon dog of the lake, so ugly, not at all pretty like you."

One day as we sat on the pier, she pulled a piece of silk, folded many times, from deep within her robe, looking about nervously as she did so. "It is a love poem, Xiao-Xiao," she said in a whisper, "that Wang Yu has smuggled to me."

"'*I watched your red lips move in song,*'" she said very softly, not even looking at the letters on the silk, seeming to hold each word on her lips before releasing it.

93

And your jade-like fingers pluck the stringed lute
Love urged me on to enter
Take you in my arms
Make you my own
But I blushed, I trembled
I dared not move
And now
It is too late!

"Ah, he still loves me, Xiao-Xiao," she exclaimed, picking me up and pressing my jowl to her cheek in a way that was most annoying. "Wang Yu. So handsome, so brave," Splendid Moon squeezed me even tighter against her. "Oh, my beloved, how I long for you!"

* * *

"Do not think, Xiao Ji Long, that I have not come to see you because of that idiot of a eunuch who, to your great misfortune, is always about you," Li Huan said as he walked me to the nearby Courtyard of Morning Sun-Warmed Reflection. He had shown up unannounced at the entrance to East Lateral Courts and asked that I be brought to him. "Though he is harder to bear than a thousand bedbugs, I have endured worse."

Instead of his black silk robe and hat, Li Huan wore a tunic and trousers of rough hemp and the cloth cap of a peasant. "I am going away. I have lived too long among the privileged ten thousand. I must go out now to the 60 million, the gentle folk who shape our land."

"All say I am too old for such a journey. But who knows how long life will last or whether the spirit will go on or perish. It is not for to us to know. We should not tarry with such thoughts, but focus only on the Way."

"I tell you I have become happy, Xiao Ji Long. I have become like Master K'ung: so enthusiastic that I forget to eat, so happy that I forget all worries and am utterly unaware of ever-impending death."

Li Huan slid behind a large shrubbery cut in the shape of a phoenix and called me to him. "You must be quiet, Xiao Ji Long," he said in a whisper, "and follow me through the corridors."

We went through an entranceway behind a stand of poplar trees, so low that Li Huan had to stoop over. Then we walked along the narrow corridors of the building, making many turns, until we came at last to a tiny room, empty except for the musical instruments strewn about the floor. "It is here that the Imperial Orchestra practices. Such music is to be heard only by the Son of Heaven and his most esteemed guests—and those whom he has specially designated as worthy of such honor. But as I know I shall never hear it again, I shall permit myself this transgression."

As we started I could hear music coming from beyond the far wall. I started to growl but Li Huan raised his finger sternly and silenced me. Then he opened the door just a crack and my ears filled up with the dense, solemn variegated sounds of the orchestra and, in their center, the slow, plodding thump of drums. Li Huan backed quietly away from the door. He stretched out his arms towards the music and closed his eyes, swaying slightly from side to side. When finally the music stopped, and the sound of voices came through the cracks in the door, Li Huan tiptoed forward and gently shut the door, then signaled for me to follow him out of the room.

"Such music rises like a flock of birds," Li Huan whispered to me after we had passed through the corridors and re-entered the courtyard, "carrying us away from impurities, falseness and doubts—but only for those who know how to listen."

"Who has need of food, or companionship, or even study, when there exists such music as this?"

Li Huan spoke no more until we stood by the huge, fierce creatures that guarded the East Lateral Courts. "I have come to say goodbye to you, Xiao Ji Long. The leaving of you—and perhaps my old housekeeper who cries each time she sees me, though I have arranged for her to live very well—is my only regret."

Li Huan bent down and squatted beside me and stroked my head, then reached down with both hands and massaged my neck and back and legs as he used to do when I stayed with him.

"I have brought you something. As you know, I do not approve of treats, but as this is an unusual occurrence..." He pulled a piece of cloth from his tunic and unwrapped it. "It is not cuttlefish, the scent of which, I am told, makes you behave like an unreasoning beast. But I will not speak of your flaws today, Xiao Ji Long." He lay the treat on the floor before me "It is simple, wholesome fish from the river—very nutritious."

As I bit off pieces of fish and swallowed them, a woman servant came through the doorway and took the leash from him.

"Our classics teach us that our people were created by Heaven, Xiao Ji Long, and, unlike barbarians, had from the earliest days rules for right behavior."

"You should try to be worthy of such a people, Xiao Ji Long, even if they are but a dream from our ancient past." He turned from us then and I let out a pulsing whine of unease and displeasure as I watched him walk away.

*   *   *

Splendid Moon was full of excitement as our carriage rambled to the park one chilly autumn morning. She talked restlessly throughout our journey—of the game of chance she had learned and played last night with Precious Wisdom and Snowy Jade, and of Lotus Blossom, who had not been able to master the game; of the crisp, cool weather that had suddenly come on us; of Li Huan's strange appearance and behavior (for she and Snowy Jade had been on a pavilion high above the courtyard and had spied Li Huan and me as we dashed behind the Phoenix bush). And every garden and building and person that we passed seemed to her fresh and worthy of comment. She talked not only to me but also to Minced Meat whom she usually ignored. I raised my head and sniffed the air curiously, for beneath her giddiness was a smell new and strange to me, something intense and implacable.

We walked rapidly along the paths and up and down the hills of the Park of Verdant Radiance, the crispness of the air and the crunch of Splendid Moon's feet on the frost-covered grass filling me with pleasure and making me eager to go even faster. Although Splendid Moon sang her songs, she would break them off suddenly and then walk silently straight ahead, ignoring my growling and play-biting at her feet. And she neither danced nor chased me with a stick.

After we had walked over one tall hill into a cluster of pine trees, Splendid Moon stopped suddenly. "*Love urged me on,*" she said in a loud whisper. Then she walked further into the pine trees, her feet swooshing through the red-brown pine needles that covered the ground. I raced around in circles at her feet, enjoying very much the feel of the pine needles as they flew out from under me. Then I caught a strong scent, the musty and menacing scent of some human or large animal, and I pressed my nose to the ground and followed it through the needles. Splendid Moon stopped again. "*Love urged me on,*" she repeated.

"*I dared not move,*" a man's voice answered softly and Wang Yu stepped out from behind a large pine tree. He wore a silk robe of reddish brown criss-crossed with boughs of green, and was without a hat—instead his hair was fixed in a knot atop his head like a soldier. He took a few careful steps towards

Splendid Moon, then stopped, tilting his head to one side and looking at her with cloudy eyes.

Although his movements were relaxed and graceful, his smell and everything about him —the straggly wisps of beard on his chin and below his lip, his cloudy eyes and soldier's topknot, the way his robe emerged and then faded into the needles and tree behind him—greatly disturbed me and I rushed towards him barking and snarling. When he bent over and tried to touch me, my rage increased all the more and I jumped backward out of his reach, barking and growling even louder, the hackles rising on my back. Each time he approached me I backed away so that he could not touch me, but when he moved away I chased after him and stayed just beyond him, bouncing up and down on the pine needles in fury.

The cloudiness disappeared from Wang Yu's eyes. "You must quiet that miserable rodent," he said angrily, "or it will give us away."

Splendid Moon tried to grab and calm me but I would not be appeased nor cease my barking. Finally, she managed to get the leash on me and dragged me out of the pine trees and down the hill as I twisted and pulled behind her, still barking at Wang Yu. She thrust the leash into Minced Meat's hands and, for a moment, I occupied myself with the bits of meat and flour paste that fell off him when he stood up. But when I saw her walking back up the hill, I resumed my barking. She stopped half-way up the hill, raised her hand as though to wave but instead pressed it to her eyes, and stood there with her head bent over. Finally, she walked back.

Splendid Moon did not speak during the rest of our walk or during the carriage ride back. When I tried to climb into her lap in the carriage she pushed me away and two days later, when our next walk was scheduled, she declined to go, saying she had a headache. This churlish behavior infected me as well and, during this time, I did not seek out Splendid Moon nor go to her room and indeed avoided her company as much as possible.

But soon our walks resumed and she was as carefree and exuberant as ever—although she paid little attention to me until after she visited the hill of pines. As we approached them, she would leave me on the leash with Minced Meat, who would immediately pull a piece of dried cuttlefish from the sack in which he carried his pies. Minced Meat did not taunt me as did Splendid Moon. As soon as she had disappeared over the hill, he would lay out before me a large portion of dried cuttlefish. He would pay no attention to me as I gobbled it down, being entirely occupied with eating his pies of flour paste and minced meat with his right hand while holding my leash with his left. I would stare at him after I had eaten the cuttlefish and, although he would never offer me any portion of his pies, many tasty crumbs would fall from him.

After she came back from the hill of pines, Splendid Moon would brush the flakes of cuttlefish from my muzzle and forehead and call me a pig. She would swear that I would eat cuttlefish until my belly swelled up and I fell over dead. Then she would pick me up and call me her dearest Xiao-Xiao and we would race up and down the hills and she would sing and dance and chase me with a stick as before.

When we returned from those walks, she would race from room to room, pulling at the hair of the other girls or snatching a piece of embroidery they were working on, and they would chase after her laughing. I would run along with them through the corridors, much delighted with this madcap behavior, although I often became sick and threw up from having eaten so much during our walks. But that would halt me only for a moment and I would dash by the servants who swooped down to wipe my mouth and clean up my mess and catch up with Splendid Moon and the others.

In the evenings, Splendid Moon would call me to her as she sat looking out her window at the bright, yellow moon of autumn. I would stand on the bench beside her, my front paws against the window sill. Then she would press my jowl to her cheek in that way that annoyed me and call me her beloved.

She would sing:

> Love urged me on to enter
> Take you in my arms
> Make you my own
> But I blushed, I trembled
> I dared not move

"Oh, Xiao-Xiao, it cannot be too late!"

* * *

There were but few things that distressed me during these Palace days: my frequent baths, during which I was always sprinkled with rosewater and other repugnant substances; the even more frequent dousing with all manner of perfumes and fragrances, for all of the concubines liked to try out their favorites on me and very much enjoyed my sneezes and the disgusted faces I would make when these were applied; then too, like Li Huan's old servant, they were forever putting necklaces on me and tying bits of cloth around my head and neck and back (of much finer quality, of course, than those of the old woman), and laughing as I struggled to rid myself of them. But, in truth, the perfect happiness of these days was marred only by my visits every third day to the Emperor Pingdi.

These visits took place in a small room to the side of the antechamber that led to the Emperor's bedroom. The ceiling was covered with dark blue silk studded with the bright gold stars of the constellations. Scrolls of silk were stacked about the shelved walls and the tables. The floor was littered with wooden and clay soldiers—almost as big as me—of all ranks and description, several of them on horseback. Pingdi dismissed all but two servants whenever I arrived and these stayed with their backs pressed against the wall and never spoke.

"Someday I myself will command large armies," Pingdi bragged as he watched me sniffing tentatively at these curious soldiers. "I will conquer the Xiongnu, [ancestors of the Huns—S.D.] which no Emperor before me has ever been able to do. Thousands will die before the might of my armies."

The soldiers were something new and very interesting to me and I crouched down before them growling, stretching out my front paws and thrusting my rump into the air. When I jumped from side to side to confuse them, I knocked one of them to the floor. Pingdi screamed and ran at me and I darted quickly away from him through a field of soldiers, knocking more spinning soldiers to the floor. Pingdi rushed to his soldiers, and cursing me in a loud wail as a toad-eating mongrel, he put them back into position.

Pingdi mostly ignored me during my first visits to him. He would toss a ball or piece of wood to the other end of the room and, after I followed it to the end of its course, and sniffed it, and walked back towards him, he would complain, "Can you not even fetch a stick? You are so boring." Then, commanding me to sit, he would walk into the midst of his soldiers and move them about, sometimes crashing them together, all the while making mock sounds of battle.

But one day as I was sniffing and pawing at a soldier, he came upon me from behind and, seizing me by the scruff of the neck, swung me high off the floor. I wriggled and yelped with pain and humiliation, but still he would not release me, gripping me tightly with outstretched arms, watching gleefully as I struggled. Suddenly, he let me go and when I hit the floor the breath went out of me and I lay still for a moment before flipping up and racing away from him. The Emperor found this to be a great amusement and, on my following visits, he would chase me about the room, not caring how many soldiers we knocked over, until he was able to trap me in a corner. Then he would lift me up as before until my wriggling and struggling wearied his arms and suddenly pull his hands away—and I would crash to the floor.

But after many days of this, Pingdi became ill. When I visited him, I found him sitting in a chair, shivering and wracked with coughs, with silk coverlets pulled up close around his throat.

"Come to me, Xiao Ji Long," he said in a weak and kindly voice. "I will not hurt you." Although I came closer to him out of curiosity, I stayed well out of his reach. He signaled to one of the servants, who picked me up and put me on his lap.

"I shall be a real ruler, Xiao Ji Long, after I have received my cap of manhood," he said after he stroked my head and fondled my ears, his eyes glistening with fever. "I shall lead my own armies into battle, and I myself shall make all the decisions of state and appoint my own ministers. Those who dare thwart my will shall be dismissed. I shall be strong and fearless and merciless to my enemies. But I shall be just. For the most serious crimes only shall they be beheaded or chopped in half. For lesser transgressions, I will merely enslave them or exile them to remote parts of the Central Kingdom. I shall be the wind that blows across the land, and the people as the grass that bows before it."

"Wang Mang says that to be magnificent alone is a heavy enough burden and sufficient for the Son of Heaven. That I need not trouble myself with the petty details of government, which lowly persons such as he can attend to. But I do not believe this is the proper course for a ruler. And after I have received my cap of manhood, I need not follow his guidance."

"I shall bring my mother to Chang 'An and install her in the Palace. Wang Mang says that to do so would show weakness. That an Emperor should remain aloof from such ties and that it would be seen as unmanly. That I should be suspected of being one who 'cuts the sleeve.' But I believe none of this. And so I will rule according to my own judgment." [I found the expression "cuts the sleeve" quite puzzling. I am indebted to Professor Ching for explaining that it is a euphemism for homosexual behavior. Its origin is apparently an anecdote about the Emperor Aidi, who is said to have cut off his sleeve when summoned to court rather than disturb his (male) lover who slumbered beside him—S.D.]

"I regret the dropping of you, Xiao Ji Long," he said, his eyes half-closed as sleep began to overtake him. "I will no longer do this."

After Pingdi recovered, he never again picked me up and dropped me. But after several visits, he took to hurling a small wooden ball at me with all his might, waiting until I was preoccupied sniffing a toy soldier or otherwise unaware. Although the ball was very light and his aim not very good, I felt more than once the sharp, stinging smack of the ball against my ribs or ear.

After one such stinging hit, Pingdi kneeled down on the floor and began to play with his soldiers. The servants put a silk rug underneath him and placed many pillows on it and, presently, Pingdi fell asleep, the spear of one of his soldiers still clutched in his outstretched left arm. I crept slowly upon him from behind, retreating several times to assure myself that it was not a trick. Leaning over the dark hair that spread out from under his black and gold cap, I stared down at his face and became fascinated by the soft, pink flesh inside his nose. Very slowly and stealthily, as though plucking some delicate treat from the corner of a plate, I placed my teeth, which, undulled by age, were as sharp and spiny as needles, on his nose.

Pingdi jumped up with a tremendous howl, so quickly that my teeth stuck inside his nose, and the force of his movement threw me over his shoulder. Blood dripped from the nose of the Son of Heaven as he turned and ran, screaming at the top of his lungs, into the antechamber. One servant ran through the doorway after Pingdi and was met there by a distraught mob of servants closing round the bleeding Emperor. The other servant threw a silk coverlet over me and, bundling me up, ran out the door after them.

When at last I was tossed out of this blanket, I was in a room enclosed by bare stone walls and surrounded by a dozen servants and half that many soldiers. Wang Mang then appeared, making his way through this crowd at the head of a troop of scholars, their black and blue and yellow ribbons dangling limply in the still damp air.

"We must ascertain whether this creature has some disease, such as distemper, or is mad, or whether this is the work of some demon," Wang Mang said, his jowls quivering with authority and determination.

A dozen hands seized me and I was carried off and pushed down on the stone table in the corner of the room. My eyes and mouth were pried open and the flaps of my ears pulled back. Ropes were tied about my legs and chest so that I could scarcely move and I felt fingers poking my ribs and probing into my mouth and anus. Two hands stretched my mouth open and I could feel the leafy powder being sprinkled into it and then they held my mouth shut tight and stroked my throat until I could not help but swallow it. Colors and light began to ooze into darkness and the shouts and scuffling and jostling sounds of the men about me melted into the sounds of tinkling bells and I fell into the deepest of sleeps.

When, much, much later, my eyes half-opened, I could see figures wavering before me like the shadows made by candlelight. Voices floated slowly and soothingly about me. My body seemed unable to move but I felt no alarm—for I had no desire to move. I wanted only to lie there, half opening my eyes from time to time, peaceful and content. A tall, thin-faced man with a square-cornered silver hat leaned over and peered in my face. "We find no evidence of any disease," he said to Wang Mang, who peered at me from just behind the tall man's shoulder.

"The powders have lessened its strength and caused its spirit to slumber," said Wang Mang. "Can you now cure its madness and rid it of all demonic powers?"

The tall man ran his fingers down the long wisps of beard that fell almost to his waist. "One can never be certain in such cases," he signaled to his assistants who carried over a leather trunk and placed it on the wooden table that had been set up beside him. "But we shall try."

The physician began to pull long, slender silver needles from his trunk, the largest nearly as long as me, the smallest no longer than my hind paws. He held each one of them for a moment, studying them very closely, then shaking them very softly in his hand as though weighing them. He tilted his head back slightly and looked up to the ceiling quizzically.

"Let us begin with this one," he said, and he picked up a needle about as long as one of his long, slender fingers and, with an air of great precision, pressed it into the place where my spine and tail met. I followed his movements sleepily, with no alarm and no great interest, and the needle slid painlessly into place. A longer needle was inserted into the curve of my back, centered between my neck and tail, and then shorter ones into the haunch of each leg. A final needle, which I could not see, was pressed into the thick muscle of my neck just behind my ear.

The physician then stepped back and sighed. Wang Mang looked apprehensive and seemed about to speak but the physician silenced everyone with a wave. He drew several lettered sticks from the trunk and began to read an incantation.

He had read no more than a few words when the silence was broken by the irate cackle of an old woman's voice, and the clatter and thud of bodies dropping to the floor. The Grand Empress Dowager suddenly appeared in the blaze of torches that three servants, crouched and stumbling, carried before her. She was surrounded by a large entourage of agitated servants and maids. In lieu of her fine silk robes, she wore strange garments of lace, hastily covered by a silk cape, and a lace covering lay askew on her gray hair.

"Ai-ya!" she screamed when she saw me. "What is this nonsense? You have turned Xiao Ji Long into a pin cushion!"

"Remove them!"she commanded. "Release her immediately!"

Wang Mang, who had fallen to his knees, began to object.

"I have seen the Son of Heaven!" the Empress Dowager shouted, cutting him short. "It is a mere scratch!"

"Release her!" The Empress Dowager's shrieks reverberated against the stone walls of the room. "Release her!"

* * *

"The story has spread throughout the Palace," said Uncle Stupid as he carried me through the corridors of the East Lateral Courts, "of how you entered into the dreams of the Grand Empress Dowager and summoned her to your rescue. And how she awoke all aflutter and went straight as an arrow to parts of the palace grounds she had not before even known about."

"We shall do nothing to discourage such tales of your marvelous powers, you and I. But you should know that your good Uncle has repaid in some small part the luck you bestow on him. But let us not talk of unpleasant matters. I have planned a celebration in honor of your return. A poetry contest for which you and Snowy Jade will be the judges. All await you at the Courtyard of Heavenly Bamboo."

All eleven of the concubines were indeed in the courtyard smiling and clapping their hands gleefully as Uncle Stupid carried me through the entranceway. Splendid Moon danced before me after I had been placed on the ground and taunted me with her floating scarves and swooping sleeves until I growled and lunged at her.

"The Little Lucky one is restored to us," Uncle Stupid declared. "Let the contest commence."

Precious Wisdom began with a long and graceful poem about the calendar plant that gains one new leaf each day for the first fifteen days of the month, and loses one leaf each day for the remaining fifteen days, which gained sighs of appreciation and envy and much polite applause. Golden

Bracelet recited a very short poem praising the Duke of Chou. Lovely Jade then recited a poem about the curative powers of jade and Adorable Jade, one about the beauty of jade, and Uncle Stupid chastised them for their vanity. Lotus Blossom tried to recite a poem about Springtime but the words did not fit the meter and she began to stammer and could not remember the concluding lines and finally sat down in confusion.

I became bored with all this sitting and talking and wandered about the courtyard, biting at the slippers of the concubines in an effort to get them to play with me. As that failed, for they were all very much absorbed in the poetry contest, I sat down in front of one after another, whining in a squeaky, chirping manner that quite annoyed Uncle Stupid, who declared that I was disqualified from the judgeship because of my rude behavior.

Splendid Moon was the last to make her presentation. As Splendid Moon prefaced her poem with a dance, I became interested again and rushed up to her. After I had chased her about the courtyard and very nearly seized one of her scarves in my teeth, she grabbed me by the front paws and continued to dance about the courtyard dragging me with her, as shouts and laughter broke out on all sides of us.

Uncle Stupid pulled me away from her and held me on his lap while she delivered her poem—a long and complex one about a young woman imprisoned in a fortress far out on the frontier, who pines day and night for her courageous lover, who crosses the desert, outwits demons, and slays bandits and tigers and other strange beasts to find his way to her. But at last he does find her and steals into the fortress and they speak to each other of their love as they stand before the bright yellow moon of autumn. But then soldiers burst in on them and though he slays ten of them, he is himself slain. And she leaps from the high wall of the fortress to share his fate. As she said that last line, Splendid Moon twisted her body slowly and gracefully and leaned so far over that her sleeves and long black hair trailed gently along the stone floor of the courtyard.

There was a great burst of applause for Splendid Moon's performance and Precious Wisdom shouted: "Never have I heard such a tale of Breeze and Moonlight!" The women then crowded around Snowy Jade and implored her to decide the contest.

"But wait," shouted Uncle Stupid, "I have not yet presented my own poem." He pushed his way into the center of the courtyard and, after they had settled down, he began. "My poem is not about spring or jade, nor Breeze and Moonlight, nor plants that grow according to the whim of mankind. It is a didactic one concerning the perils of drink, which has savaged at some time or another all gentlemen and not a few fine ladies. Therefore, it merits your careful attention."

Uncle Stupid first described the dignified manner of guests when they first arrive, taking mincing steps back and forth across the floor while reciting these lines, his head held high and a prissy look on his face.

But then he sang of how their manner changed when more wine was drunk. Pulling his gray eunuch's cap so that it hung precariously over one ear, he interspersed his lines with lurching, staggering walks and sudden yelps and howls. I watched his behavior curiously, cocking my head from side to side as the courtyard shook with the laughter and applause of the young women.

He concluded his poem by stumbling into a table, knocking to the floor several straw baskets that he had placed there before his presentation began. He then bowed with great ceremony and, after straightening himself, cried out in a trembling, piteous voice: "Pray, drunken Sir, do not drink more!"

After the applause had died down, Precious Wisdom charged into the center of the courtyard towards him.

"That is not an original composition at all!" she announced, "but taken from the Shih Ching!" [*The Book of Songs*, an ancient Chinese Classic—S.D.]

"Yes," said Uncle Stupid, not in the least unsettled, "but done with such freshness and feeling as to make it new. Besides, I have made a few edits and improvements. So I believe it should count as a new poem and thus be eligible for consideration."

The matter was referred to Snowy Jade, who ruled that it was not in fact an original composition and thus did not meet the requirements of the contest. With that issue resolved, everyone began to clamor once again for Snowy Jade to announce the winner. She retreated to a corner of the courtyard and deliberated for a long time before returning to announce that Precious Wisdom's poem was the winner, citing its intricacy and the perfection and beauty of its imagery. She praised Splendid Moon for the force and originality of her poem and awarded it second place.

Uncle Stupid called for the servants to bring in the prizes. Precious Wisdom was given a small piece of creamy jade wrought in the shape of a sheep, to represent her birth year. Splendid Moon was given a silver hair pin topped with a red stone. But all of the participants received prizes, even Uncle Stupid, who awarded himself a small vial of liquor which he drank with one swallow.

The excitement attending the end of the contest had riled me and, as the women rushed about comparing gifts, I ran from one to the other, biting at their slippers and jumping against them to try to steal their gifts. My antics angered even Uncle Stupid, who several times chased me out of the courtyard. Later I knocked over a tray of delicacies that one of the servants lowered so that Floating Petal and Blossoming Spring, who were seated, might select one. Finally, my behavior proved so intolerable that Uncle Stupid had one of the servants carry me back to our room. All the disciplines I had learned from Li Huan had faded. Except for one—after Li Huan's training, I could never again abide the thought of relieving myself inside a building.

6
I Become a Hero

After I bit the Son of Heaven on the nose, he seemed to become more fond of me. Instead of my scheduled visits, I was summoned often to his quarters, especially when he was not feeling well, and I usually stayed with him for many hours. Sometimes Waking Bear would be with him, kept on a leash held by a servant in the corner of the room. Although he always created a great ruckus when he first saw me, he would soon tire of it and fall back asleep, leaving Pingdi and I undisturbed. Pingdi no longer dropped me or threw the ball at me. But he would sometimes chase me about the room with a small spear he had taken from one of his soldiers and threaten to disembowel me— a game which I joined enthusiastically. Most of the time, however, he felt too ill for such exertions and would lie back on his pillows, talking to me as he stroked my head and fondled my ear or watching me as I stalked about his bed, pouncing on his hands and toes as he moved them under the coverlets.

"I have talked to the Grand Empress Dowager," Pingdi said one day, "and she agrees that I should be given my cap of manhood very soon. The ceremony shall be scheduled next year just after my twelfth birthday and just before my marriage to the Empress-to-be Wang. She agrees also that I should begin to attend court with her on some occasions so as to familiarize myself with various ceremonies and procedures. Though she will continue to act as Regent until the cap of manhood is bestowed on me."

"She says that I should also begin to acquaint myself with the concubines." Pingdi's voice tightened as he said this and he looked at me strangely as though expecting some reaction. "So that I might begin to think about who shall be Favorite Beauty and who Highest Ladies. I have watched them many times from windows and balconies as they strolled about the courtyards and gardens. I believe Splendid Moon is the most beautiful, don't you? Once I saw her dancing by herself in the garden. But Lotus Blossom is also very beautiful and seems more kindly and demure."

"There is, of course, no question of sexual relations until I receive my cap of manhood," he added after a pause, fidgeting under the covers as he did so.

One afternoon, as Uncle Stupid walked me back from a visit to Pingdi, we saw a huge dog trotting towards us, his muzzle and ears as black as my mother's but with a tawny coat streaked with faint black stripes. Far behind him, a very fat eunuch ran and walked, puffed and yelled. Uncle Stupid bent down and put on my leash just as I was about to charge.

"Ah, that must be Shih Yu's dog, Prince, about which I have heard much. A very dull name for a dog. But then Prince is a mastiff and thus tends towards a very sober disposition. And Shih Yu is a dullard whose imagination is stimulated only by his complaints."

"Shih Yu is an excellent man to know. He is the quartermaster of food supplies for the palace. So I am always very polite and courteous to him and listen to all his complaints with great attentiveness and keen interest. Though he is a terrible bore."

Prince trotted past us, his head held high, a large stick clinched in his teeth, the powerful muscles of his jaws and neck, his shoulders and haunches, rippling effortlessly. A rope was draped about his neck and trailed behind him. Though I lunged and snapped at him, he paid no attention to us, not even altering his stride. I ran yelping after him and Uncle Stupid pulled tight on the leash, raising my front paws off the ground. A few feet past us, he paused and began sniffing the shrubbery, raising his leg from time to time, as high as he could, and urinating on it.

Shih Yu then came up to us, wheezing and shouting at Prince. When he reached us, he stopped and leaned forward with his hands on his knees, breathing heavily. "He has escaped from me again," he said to Uncle Stupid when he had caught his breath. "Turd-eating mongrel," he shouted at Prince, who turned his head and looked back at him for a second, then looked away and resumed urinating. "I will give you such a beating as you will remember when I get hold of you!"

"He has the brains of a flea and the stubbornness of a mule," Shih Yu complained, "and the strength of an ox—for he is always breaking loose from his rope. I don't know why I put up with him—though I do admit that the mere sight of him helps to keep servants and indeed my fellow eunuchs from pilfering my stocks. Still, he is too much trouble. I should have served him up for dinner long ago."

"Yes," agreed Uncle Stupid, wrinkling his eyes at me. "There is nothing so tasty as a good dog cutlet. Though they say the flesh of a pug is much tastier than that of a mastiff."

"I do not know, for it is forbidden to eat pug," he said humorlessly, then added with a great sigh. "I cannot keep chasing after this monster all the time. At my age and as hard as I must work to feed ten thousand hungry mouths each day."

"Yes," agreed Uncle Stupid, "you work far too hard." He wrapped my leash around the trunk of a small cherry tree and he and Shih Yu began advancing on Prince. But as soon as they came close to him, he would trot further down the path, the stick still in his mouth, pausing only when he discovered another shrub worthy of urination. I pulled against my leash, yelping and whining, watching this scene repeat itself again and again as they pursued Prince down the path, until finally they disappeared from my view.

When at last Uncle Stupid returned, I was stretched out in the dirt under the cherry tree, feeling very distraught at having been left alone so long.

"Prince is re-captured, at least for the moment," Uncle Stupid said as I rushed to greet him, wagging my rump and turning in circles, so great was my pleasure and relief at seeing him again. "Shih Yu is very happy! I have offered to have Prince taken along on your walks. This exercise should make him less of a burden to poor Shih Yu, and I have yearned for some time to make the acquaintance of Prince in case I should chance to visit the storehouse. And it will be good for you as well, Xiao Ji Long, for you should know the companionship not just of emperors, concubines and eunuchs but also of your own kind. Something other than that loathsome creature, Waking Bear, whose horrid breath alone makes him unfit to be a comrade."

"And it will provide an occasion for me to accompany you and Splendid Moon on these walks," he added, rubbing his smooth chin between his forefinger and thumb. "I do not believe Minced Meat can bear up under this harsh burden much longer. He has already grown so fat as to be hardly able to walk."

"Yes, I believe Prince will be a perfect match for you. For just as you will not leave people alone, he will have nothing to do with them—but cares only for sticks and balls and other trifles."

The next morning when Uncle Stupid announced that he would accompany Splendid Moon and me on our walks a look of shock spread across her face and just as quickly disappeared.

"Oh, that would be wonderful, Uncle," she said and clapped her hands in delight. Minced Meat said it was far too generous for such a busy man to undertake such a chore and objected that, in good conscience, he could not accept such a great favor. But Uncle Stupid insisted: as he himself had promised Shih Yu to include Prince in our walks, he must assume this duty. At length, Minced Meat gave up his objections and walked away with a glum look on his face.

Splendid Moon held herself with great calm and self-possession as we drove out to the park, conversing in a very facile way with Uncle Stupid and showing great interest in his account of his discussion with Shih Yu, who had told him in detail of the food preferences of all the eminent persons of the Palace. But the carriage was filled with a strange, itchy scent that felt like sunlight tickling my nose and Splendid Moon's eyes would frequently steal away from Uncle Stupid and fix themselves on something far outside the carriage.

A servant of Shih Yu's was waiting for us when we reached the Park of Verdant Radiance, holding Prince on a leash with some difficulty. We walked side by side along the paths of the park, Splendid Moon holding my leash while Prince was held by Uncle Stupid. Prince gave off a penetrating scent of supremacy and prerogative that greatly perturbed me. He walked straight ahead with nonchalant dignity, completely ignoring my existence— and my efforts to jostle against his foreleg or to cut in front of him, efforts which resulted in my getting the leash tangled again and again around the legs of Splendid Moon or the leash held by Uncle Stupid. As we approached the hill of pines, Uncle Stupid suggested that they should walk up there and free the dogs for it was clear that Prince badly needed a good run. But Splendid Moon demurred, saying that the recent rains had made it too muddy and that we should continue on to Water Lily Pond.

When at last we were released, Prince started across the field in a proud, unhurried trot and, though I growled and squealed and darted in front of him and thrust my head against his chest, he still paid no attention to me. Nor did he change his pace at all, but merely altered his direction ever so slightly so as to avoid me, acting as though he had intended to make such a change anyway. Or he walked right through me as though brushing aside a stalk of grass.

Suddenly, with a bound, he took off up the slope of a hill and, though I ran as fast as I could, I saw him move farther and farther away from me. When I reached the top of the hill, I could see him no longer. I looked back at Uncle Stupid and Splendid Moon, who were seated on a bench far below me, oblivious to my heavy panting and whines of displeasure. Then I caught the scent of Prince on the ground and followed it into the woods that stretched out behind the hill. I had not gone very far when I lost the scent of Prince in the profusion of new smells that beset me from all sides of this dark forest. Still, I trotted on, hoping to discover some sign of Prince. When at last I gave up this hope and sought to return, I found I did not know where to go and I ran anxiously in one direction and then another, smelling and seeing nothing that was familiar to me.

I heard noises in the stand of pine trees just beyond me and ran towards them. Then, as I got closer, I heard a low, growling voice followed by a thumping sound. The sharp, acrid smells of violence flooded my nostrils and, badly frightened, I crawled into muddy reeds that lay at the base of a knoll of pine trees. Before me stood Wang Yu, his topknot loosened and strands of hair falling over his face. He held Minced Meat by the collar of his robe with one hand and with the other he pounded his back and face.

"Money?! You fail me and dare ask for money?!" he shouted in a strangled voice, his teeth biting into his lip so hard that a trickle of blood ran down his chin. He struck Minced Meat full in the face. "And to speak to me of 'your poems.' Why, they are nothing more than copies of the pinings of some lovesick scribbler."

"But I put myself in great danger—"

"There, you are right," Wang Yu shouted. "To speak to me with such insolence!"

He silenced Minced Meat with a volley of blows that drove him to his hands and knees in the deep, squishy mud that lay just beyond them. Then he grabbed the gray eunuch's cap that now hung from Minced Meat's ear and threw it even further into the mud.

"One thing you must know: after so much effort, that tasty plum must not be denied me! You must find another way." Wang Yu grabbed him by the hair and dragged him back from the mud. He walked around Minced Meat's outstretched body, kicking those parts that were least muddy. Minced Meat covered his head with his arms and cried for mercy.

"Ah, pie-eating sow," Wang Yu said with sullen glee. "Where is it?" He bent over and tugged at the sash around Minced Meat waist, then pulled out the crumpled remains of his pie of flour paste and meat, looking at the mud on his hands in disgust. Wang Yu threw the pie into the mud.

"Eat that pie, swine, and I may let you live".

"No, please, I will come up with something," Minced Meat begged.

Wang Yu picked up a thick, broken branch of pine that lay near by and began to beat Minced Meat on the back with it. "Eat it," he commanded and Minced Meat crawled after the pie and began picking pieces of it from the mud and putting them in his mouth. When he began vomiting, Wang Yu threw the stick at him.

"You are too filthy to kill. Do not fail me next time," he said, smacking his hands together to shake off the mud. As he turned to walk away, he spied me among the reeds. "So the gods have delivered up this little rodent to me as well," he shouted and began to move toward me. I turned and ran, my body quivering with fear, my tail hanging far down. I kept running even after the shouts of Wang Yu and the sounds of his body crashing through the woods had long since ended, ran until I was well out of the woods, and had gone up and down a long, grassy hill. I heard then the voices of Uncle Stupid and Splendid Moon above me, walking with Prince along the ridge of a hill, calling my name in loud, anxious voices.

"You are covered with mud," Uncle Stupid said angrily when he saw me. He handed Prince's leash to Splendid Moon. "Where have you been, insufferable pest? You have filled us with worry." He began scraping the mud from me with a small branch, holding me by the neck so that I could not jump against him.

"This old head holds many secrets, Splendid Moon," he said as he continued scraping the mud from me, wrinkling his nose in disgust. "Do not expect, Xiao Ji Long, to sit on my lap in the carriage."

"There is no safer place for you to entrust your secrets," he said without looking at Splendid Moon who did not look at him either but kept her eyes fixed on the woods beyond. "For all think I am indiscreet and believe that I leave nothing unsaid. But I have taken into the depths of my heart the saying: a scratch on a sceptre of white jade can be polished away, but a slip of the tongue cannot ever be repaired."

But Splendid Moon said nothing.

* * *

After that day, Splendid Moon showed less interest in our walks. She rarely danced or chased after me with a stick anymore and I was given no cuttlefish. Often she was too ill to accompany us and Precious Wisdom volunteered to take her place. Precious Wisdom was very curious about the plants and shrubs that lined the paths of the Park of Verdant Radiance and always asked Uncle Stupid where they came from and many other questions which he could seldom answer.

"You have made me feel even stupider than before," he said, and the next day another eunuch appeared, whom Uncle Stupid called the Imperial Botanist. He and Precious Wisdom walked behind us, stopping at every tree and shrub, while Uncle Stupid staggered up and down the path with outstretched arms, as Prince and I pulled him along on our leashes.

On our next outing, Precious Wisdom persuaded Uncle Stupid to take us to the Park of All the Beasts of the World, where they were amazed by the calm manner in which I trotted past these roaring, taunting beasts and by the crisp boom of Prince's full-throated bark and the unflappable dignity of his bearing. At the park, a huge procession suddenly appeared all clad in yellow, preceded by eunuchs running and beating drums. As it began to bear down on us, Uncle Stupid ran to investigate.

"It is the Son of Heaven," he said excitedly when he returned. "There is to be a tiger fight in Chang 'An this evening and He himself has come here to preside over the anointments of the beasts."

Precious Wisdom and Uncle Stupid fell to their knees and looked down at the ground as the procession came near us but I could see the eyelids of Precious Wisdom fluttering up to meet the Emperor as he passed us. Pingdi signaled the procession to halt and leaned out from his litter to look at me, stealing a glance at Precious Wisdom as he did so.

"Have Xiao Ji Long brought to me," he commanded, forcing his voice into a lower key. The procession started up again and a servant raced over and picked me up, carrying me into the yellow whirl of marching bodies and drums and bells, my leash dragging on the ground behind us.

The rigors of the procession seemed to greatly tire and weaken Pingdi and he was urged, upon his return to the Inner Palace, to retire to his chamber and take his dinner there. Pingdi lay back against his many bright-colored pillows, his eyes half-closed, paying little attention to me as I roamed about the room. Having made his usual fuss at my arrival, Waking Bear lay sleeping beside the bed on his leash.

Although Pingdi said he was not hungry, his attendants insisted that he must eat to regain his strength. I was chased from the bed and he was propped up on his pillows and a bamboo stand set before him. Soon a huge golden tray was brought in and the warm, inviting smells of dozens of foods wafted down on me. In the midst of them, I detected the indescribably delicious smell of dried cuttlefish. I rushed to the side of the bed and propped myself up against it with one paw, whimpering in anticipation as I tried to peer into the tray the servant extended toward Pingdi so that he might choose the dishes that pleased him.

"What is it that has so excited him?" Pingdi said, taking an interest in the increasing urgency of my whimpering and the trembling that had overtaken my body, for I had not eaten cuttlefish in many days now.

"They say that she goes quite mad at the sight of dried cuttlefish, Great Son of Heaven", replied the attendant.

"Indeed," said Pingdi, and his weary eyes lit up as he signaled for the bowl of cuttlefish and several other dishes to be placed on his bamboo stand.

"Hmmm, this looks quite scrumptious," he said, waving a small piece of cuttlefish before him with his silver chopsticks. He placed the cuttlefish in his mouth and moved his lips up and down and from side to side, making great smacking noises and grunting with pleasure as he did so.

This was more than I could bear. The darkness came over me and I began to scream and run in circles at the side of the bed, nearly treading on the slumbering Imperial Pug, who raised one eye and scrunched up further into his corner. Pingdi was greatly amused by these antics and seized another piece of cuttlefish in his chopsticks and waved it before him. In desperation I leapt onto the bed, striking the bamboo stand as I tripped and rolled on the coverlets, and bowls of food were hurled to the floor. Pingdi screamed with delight as servants chased me off the bed and pursued me about the room. As they did so, Waking Bear sprang from his corner and began gobbling down the food strewn about the floor.

The servants trapped me in the far corner of the room and one of them picked me up and squeezed me to his chest while the other fastened a leash about my neck.

"Bring him to me," said Pingdi, laughing, "so that I might beat him myself." At that moment, Waking Bear let out a horrible wail and raced around in circles. Foam began to fly from the corners of his mouth and he fell over on his side. For a few moments his legs twitched and his head jerked and then he ceased all movement.

Shouts of alarm and horror rang out on all sides and people began to run in and out of the room. Several attendants grabbed hold of Pingdi and threw him over the side of the bed, sticking their fingers down his throat and forcing him to vomit. Then potions were rubbed on his neck and chest and held under his nose. A steaming bowl was brought in and he was made to drink it and vomit again. At length the Son of Heaven lay back on his pillows, looking very confused and much more weary than before.

"Xiao Ji Long has saved me," he said as servants dabbed his face and neck with warm cloths and pulled off the vomit-stained coverlets and replaced them with fresh, shiny ones.

Wang Mang burst suddenly into the room and threw himself down on his knees at the side of the Son of Heaven. An attendant hurried after him, carrying wooden slats and brushes, and squatted down beside him.

"Gods and deities, I beg that you spare the life of the Son of Heaven," he declared in a booming voice. "O Supreme One, who rules all things, and who alone has the power to change fate, I declare unto you that it is my wish that my life be taken in place of that of the noble and wise and compassionate Son of Heaven." He tore the jade circlet from around his neck and, placing it on the floor, crushed it with a stone the attendant handed to him. "If my words be not true and of utmost sincerity, let me be as these pieces of jade."

"To legalize this oath, I command that my words be written down and placed, along with these pieces of jade, in an indestructible coffer in the Front Hall of the Palace."

"O Supreme One," he continued, "show me the way to combat these evil powers and malevolent auguries that threaten again and again the glorious Dynasty of the Han. I swear that, even if it cost my life, I will overcome them."

Wang Mang then stood, ran to me, and grabbed me from the servant so quickly and forcefully that I was hardly able to utter a growl of dislike. "It is indeed as they say," he boomed, as he dangled me before him, "you have saved our most cherished Son of Heaven!" Then he threw me roughly back to the servant and rushed back to the bed, falling to his knees and repeating his oath to the Supreme One.

Several officials warily approached him and leaned over to speak to him. "Do not presume to speak to me about such matters," he said in a loud, teary voice. "How can I concentrate on the business of government when the Emperor lies so ill?"

* * *

After my heroic act, I spent most of my time with the Son of Heaven, who was very eager to surround himself with the good fortune that emanated from me. Pingdi would send for me immediately after I completed my morning walk and I would not return to the East Lateral Courts until the evening. Only then would I be able to wander through its corridor and rooms, which was

115

much more pleasurable and exciting than my visits with the Son of Heaven. Before I returned late at night to Uncle Stupid's room, I would sometimes take a nap with Splendid Moon, who had become very pale and now spent much time lying in bed. When we were alone, despite her frailty, she would often steal from her bed and go to the window and stare into the sky for a long time. Then she would recite her poem about the lover who had braved deserts and demons and slain ten men before being himself slain.

Prince often accompanied me on my tours of the East Lateral Court—or rather I accompanied him, for I stayed forever close to him as he stalked about, sniffing his rump, pushing my head against his shoulder, cutting in front of him, or swatting at him to get his attention. But except for a cursory sniff of my rump and a tight, menacing growl when I became too annoying, he paid me no mind. Prince did not care what I did as long as I did not disturb "his" toys, for he took ownership of all my toys whenever he came to visit. He would pluck my red and green ball from the basket and stretch himself out pleasantly and chew it, utterly ignoring my whines of protest. But then, if I were to pull my silver mouse from the basket, he would take that from me too, and shield it between his two paws along with the ball. And if I were then to pull out my wooden horse, he would take that too and pile it with the others.

Prince cared only for toys and balls and sticks. He did not care to be petted except by Precious Wisdom for whom he had taken a liking. He had always a toy or ball or stick in his mouth and, if it were taken from him and put on a chest or some high place where he could not reach it, he would sit before it for hours, making a strange clucking noise and shivering, until it was returned to him. Precious Wisdom sometimes did this to amuse the other concubines whom she would call from their rooms and who would laugh at and taunt him. But this did not affect him in the least and he remained steadfast in his watch, staring fixedly at the toy or ball until Precious Wisdom wearied of his shivering and clucking and returned it to him.

Prince chewed and gnawed incessantly on my toys until, one by one, they were all destroyed or so drenched in his saliva that they were thrown away. This greatly annoyed Uncle Stupid. "You are even a greater nuisance than Xiao Ji Long," he would say. "I can see now why Shih Yu is so happy to be rid of you for these hours. Let us hope his gratitude is great—and tangible. For if not, I shall have to kill both him and you."

Pingdi not only had me brought to his chambers but taken along with him wherever he went—on walks within the Palace, in processions, and even to the proceedings of the court. And, as he had agreed with the Grand Empress

Dowager, he now attended many such sessions. He had ordered a small yellow jacket marked with the insignia of the Han made for me, with holes for my legs and tail, and hoops and buttons across my belly to fix it in place, and a matching cap which was fixed to my head by tiny straps that sunk into the fur across the back of my neck and under my chin. He also had made for me a thick and heavy collar of black leather embossed with sparkling stones of blue and red and green and mother-of-pearl. To my great annoyance, these articles were placed on me whenever we left his chambers despite my vigorous struggle with the servants as they fastened them on me. I could do little about the jacket and collar but—unless I was very tired—I always managed to get the cap off my head within minutes.

Whenever we left his chambers, I was carried, body upright, legs dangling, facing straight ahead, by a special attendant who wore a blue tunic with the yellow figure of a pug, as large as I was, on the chest; below this figure, Lo-Tze was spelled out in large yellow characters. Alone among men, this attendant was allowed to stand as high as the Son of Heaven, for Pingdi wished that I should be able to look about. Thus, on these walks I saw the world as an Emperor does, a sea of gentleman and ladies parting and falling before me, the rustle of silk as they fell to their knees and touched their foreheads to the floor, the scramble of crouching servants seeking to stay close to us yet out of the way, and behind us people rising again like lightly trampled grass springing slowly upright.

For my appearances at the court, Pingdi had ordered that a small squat replica of his throne be constructed and placed between him and the Grand Empress Dowager, wide enough so that I could stretch out and assume what the Grand Empress Dowager called my "Imperial Pose"—my head held erect, my right hind leg tucked under me, and the left one curved behind; my right foreleg extended all the way forward with my left paw tucked in. Pingdi decreed that no one should be allowed to strike or curse me, or even to speak to me in an unpleasant voice and, in those first few days, I was given free run of the court.

During that brief period, I most enjoyed the commencement of the court proceedings when the floor was strewn with kneeling bodies, their rumps in the air, arms outstretched, foreheads touching the floor. I would race through these columns, inhaling everywhere scents of compressed anger and cringing fear, pawing and biting at their silk-covered slippers or leaning on their rumps as I looked over them at the Son of Heaven and the Empress Dowager. These two looked quite different and somewhat menacing to me at this distance and often I would let out a long, ululating howl at the sight of them, quite reveling in the sound of it. I had a particular fondness for the rump of the Grand Minister of the Multitudes, which was soft and fleshy, and one day I leapt on his back, balancing myself with difficulty along the length of his spine, as I watched the Son of Heaven chastise me.

Complaints had been welling up, however, about the unseemliness of my behavior and, after that day, I was put on a leash and held near or at my small throne by the special attendant, who knelt down behind me.

Sitting on the dais at these sessions of the court was very taxing. It was at once boring— for I could not run about and no one stroked or petted or played with me and no treats were given to me; and unsettling—for the smells of fear and anxiety from the fine gentlemen and ladies and the officials and eunuchs below us continually ebbed and flowed and swirled about me. The smells of fear would become greater each time Wang Mang spoke or gestured or the Grand Empress Dowager spoke or sighed and would recede whenever attention shifted to the Son of Heaven, even though all displayed the utmost deference and submission to him. I noticed too that whenever I growled or barked—and I did this very often, until I got used to the proceedings and spent most of the time sleeping—fresh smells of fear and worry would be unleashed.

"You are very much feared, Little Dragon," Uncle Stupid said to me one night. "For stories of your powers have multiplied since you saved the life of the Son of Heaven. Already dozens have been executed for that crime. The tasters—because they themselves did not fall ill that day although one sought to fake illness after he heard what had happened. Several cooks and servants, who have been judged negligent and a few eunuchs and a marquis or two that were already out of favor. But no one has confessed convincingly. And everyone is suspected! You are believed to have the power to read minds and to identify those involved in the conspiracy against the Emperor. So your growls might send a guilty man—or an innocent one—to the executioner."

"The Son of Heaven has somehow got it into his head," Uncle Stupid continued, rubbing his face with both hands in exasperation, "that you should be honored for your services to our Great Kingdom and to Him personally. All oppose this notion except for the Grand Empress Dowager, who is not feeling well these days and who says she will not be bothered with such nonsense. But the Son of Heaven persists. Even Wang Mang has failed to dissuade him. Though I have my doubts as to the forcefulness of his arguments—for I do not believe that anything can really happen without Wang Mang's assent."

"I believe the Son of Heaven, since he is still just a child, had in mind a very great honor. An honorary Marquisa perhaps, or even an honorary kingship—er, queenship. But after having been badgered ceaselessly, he has settled on your being honored as possessing Abundant Talents of Unusual Degree. Although this award is only of middling importance, and already in the possession of many thousand of petty officials, some not nearly as smart or capable as you, you can be sure it will cause great consternation. For the yokels in the distant commanderies and provinces who receive these awards take them very seriously and will be greatly insulted when…" Uncle Stupid wrinkled his nose at me in disgust, "…they find out a mere dog has received such an award."

The ceremony bestowing on me the medal for Abundant Talents of Unusual Degree took place, despite the chilliness of the day, in a field of frost-covered grass alongside Sea-Like Lake. The Emperor had encouraged all nobles and high officials and even the eunuchs to bring their pet dogs with them, for he wished me to be honored not only by the court and all mankind, but by my own kind as well. The special attendant led me down the path that wound through the hills of the Garden of Ever-Present Breezes, resplendent in my jeweled collar and yellow cap and jacket, and very much annoyed that, for some reason, I could not paw the cap off my head this morning.

When at last we rounded a hill and the field came into full sight, I saw such numbers and sizes and shapes of dogs as I had not known existed in the world. For, except for Prince and Waking Bear and the shadowy remembrances of my infancy, I knew of my own kind only the distant occasional sight of some ragged, skulking creature spied from Li Huan's carriage or of some ribbon-bedecked pile of hair on the silk leash of a fine lady.

Stretched out now before me, was a pulsing, barking, howling, whining, yapping mob of dogs, wearing jackets and robes and caps and hats of all colors and designs, adorned with pendants and muzzles of jewels and silver and even gold. Short bucked-toothed creatures covered with blond hair, huge black or gray hounds with enormous long heads and paws, pointy-nosed dogs with thick fur of reddish gold or white or brown. All of them straining at the leashes of silk or embroidered rope or leather held by their masters or by servants whose costumes were specially designed to match their own. I reared back on my leash, my nose drinking in an intoxicating, dizzying profusion of smells, far more raw and powerful and uncomplicated than anything I had ever experienced with humans. I did not know whether to charge or flee and pulled this way and that, growling with menace at one moment, yelping with terror at the next, until finally the special attendant had to pick me up and carry me, struggling wildly in his arms, onto the platform constructed at the head of the field.

Wang Mang then came to the platform, walking very slowly and submissively, and stood at my side, looking troubled and downcast. Bells and drums announced the procession of the Emperor, and clouds of yellow robes and banners began to cross the field, the Son of Heaven held high in the center of them in his jeweled litter. And this seemed to increase the level of agitation and distress even further as the din of barks and yelps and howls grew louder and everywhere you saw the arms of masters and servants jerked forward as they struggled to keep their balance.

After the Son of Heaven was installed in a makeshift throne of bamboo, Wang Mang was handed a scroll of silk covered with lettering and while I lurched this way and that at his feet, whining and growling and moaning, very much troubled by all these smells and sounds and sights, he began to read a short speech honoring me. He read not in the booming voice with which he customarily made such pronouncements but in a weak, half-hearted drone—at one point apologizing for his performance to the Son of Heaven, and the most honored and esteemed nobles assembled there, saying that he had just that morning been afflicted by a most unfortunate cold. Then a servant handed him a large round copper medallion, inscribed with lettering on one side and with a lean, elongated dragon on the other, and he handed it to another servant, who placed it around my neck to a smattering of applause—and growls and barks and yelps. After the Son of Heaven had been placed back on his litter and the procession had departed, I was led down from the platform, tripping and pawing at the heavy copper medal, which was so cumbersome and annoying that I forgot for a moment the ruckus all about me.

"I do not at all like this business of honors, Little Lucky One," Uncle Stupid said to me several days later. "As I predicted, officials and scholars have been trooping in from all over the country to pester the Grand Empress Dowager with complaints about the ceremony honoring you. From places that she did not even know existed. She is most exasperated. And all officials, everyone indeed except for the eunuchs, tell her that the Son of Heaven is immature and still far from ripe in judgment. They say that to talk now of the cap of manhood, which she had promised him next year, is folly. That it should be put off indefinitely."

"Wang Mang has offered to resign but this, of course, has been refused."

Uncle Stupid looked at me slyly out of the corner of his eye. "Since all know he is blameless, having tried his best to prevent the ceremony, And the most terrible and ridiculous rumors have begun to spread —as to how the Son of Heaven has corrupted ancient and revered rites in his foolish desire to honor you and coddle your favor. There is even a story that he plans to build a shrine to you on Mount T'ai, the holiest of sites."

Uncle Stupid again cast his sly look at me. "Where do such stories come from? Wang Mang has done his best to squelch them. He has such a sad and weary look in his eye when he tells everyone, again and again, that all such rumors are false."

"I tell you again, Xiao Ji Long, I do not like this business of honors. In my experience, honors always precede tragedy. I have sought all my life, with remarkable success, to avoid honors."

"Although once," Uncle Stupid's face suddenly brightened, "once, in the time of the Emperor Chengdi, when palace life was very lively indeed, I received an award for composing a model letter of apology for drunkenness. It was one of my most excellent ideas and a very useful invention indeed."

"For when one is shaking off a bad hangover, worsened by the slowly spreading realization that one has grievously offended one's host and made a complete ass of oneself in the bargain, who has the energy or composure to write a letter of apology. Much better to have a polished piece of work already in hand!"

"'Yesterday, Sir!' My letter began, 'I was so intoxicated as to completely lose myself and have no recollection of what I did or said. But when others told me of my abominable behavior I became sick with shame,' and so forth and so on."

"The Emperor himself gave me the award while we were in a house of pleasure. He was in disguise, of course. I also wrote a suitable reply for the offended host. Very useful also, for it is very unpleasant to deal with such matters: who wants to take such trouble for a drunkard? Especially, if you are not really ready for true forgiveness. 'Yesterday, sir,' it began 'you did indeed behave in a truly abominable manner, such that I vowed to have no further contact with you, but now that you have tendered your sincere regrets....'"

7
Love and Its Consequences

One evening as I sauntered by Evening Breeze Court, Precious Wisdom raced out and pulled me into her room. Then she swung me around her by the forelegs, which was very disagreeable.

"Today I have been presented to the Son of Heaven, Xiao-Xiao," she said, as she set me back on the floor, her eyes full of force and bright with happiness. "I believe he was very much taken with me," she continued, grabbing my forepaws and walking me about the room while I bit at her knuckles in irritation.

"Insensitive beast," she scolded, letting my paws drop to the floor, "do you not care about my happiness?" But she immediately fell again into her story:

"When first I rose up from my deep and trembling bow, as graceful as a swan, I looked upon him like this." She fluttered her eyes and assumed a timid and fearful look.

"No, you must be up high to see it correctly." She picked me up and placed me on her black lacquered chest, which pleased me for I found it gratifying to be in high places where I could look directly into the eyes of, or down on, humans. Then she fell to her knees before me. "See," she said fluttering her eyes again and tilting her head slightly to the side. "I looked upon him as though I had never seen such a wondrous, dazzling being."

"When he told me that he would crush the Xiongnu and force them to pay tribute, I recoiled in horror at his boldness and asked him how he would accomplish this. And when he mumbled something about stealth and allies, I told him that I could see that he had studied well the maxims of Sun Tzu and showed deep understanding of the art of emptying one's opponents and filling oneself. And when he told me about you, evil one, and how you had once bitten his nose, I winced and said I could not imagine such pain. But he said it was a mere scratch and told the story again, laughing as he did so, and I joined in laughing with him." She sent forth a light, feathery, musical laugh which was very curious and pleasant indeed and I cocked my head to hear it better.

"Then the Son of Heaven mentioned that he liked dates and I told him that the best of all dates were the red dates of Lanzhou which were dried in the sun and then doused with white wine and stored in wine pots, and that nothing so lightened the monotony of a winter's day as one of these delicious dates. I told him I would direct my family to send him several pots."

Precious Wisdom rose and stood in front of me. "Then the Son of Heaven tensed up and his eyes darted about, and his leg twitched and he became very confused, as boys and even men do when they wish to do something to you but do not know how to go about it, and he mumbled something about 'being delighted' and our audience was ended."

Precious Wisdom clapped her hands and began to pace about the room. "I am not so beautiful as Splendid Moon nor even as that dimwit Lotus Blossom. But I am not dull nor do I fritter away my gifts in foolish daydreams of things that can never be. My father says that beauty without the knowledge to use it is like a beautifully crafted bow—without arrows! And one with both beauty and guile but without will, like an archer who has not the strength to draw his string and make the arrow fly straight."

Precious Wisdom halted, then suddenly whirled about and fixed her eyes on me, startling me with the abruptness of this movement. "Dearest Son of Heaven, you must try one of these delicious grapes which come from special orchards planted with vines from the kingdom of Bokhara," she said, plucking a cloudy blue grape from the bunch that lie on her table, and carrying it to my lips with a gentle, flowing motion.

"Ah, you are weary, most exalted Son of Heaven," she said as I felt the strange, delicate smoothness of the grape with my tongue and then swallowed it. "Let my fingers remove the tenseness from your back." She pressed her thumbs between my shoulder blades and rubbed my back in a way that was very soothing.

"I believe that I am destined to rise above the rest, to become Consort and then Highest Lady, and indeed, one day, Empress. For I am determined to bear the Emperor a son. And any son I bear shall stand out far above the rest. He will be taught all things—but, above all, self-discipline and astuteness—

just as my father taught me. For my father has no sons—he does not count my brother as a son for he does nothing but drink and gamble and is as stupid as Lotus Blossom. So he has placed all his hopes in me. And once I have attached myself to the Emperor, I shall bring my father to Chang 'An to be Grand Minister, for he badly wants to return here, not for the luxuries that surround us, but to bring discipline and wisdom and order to the rule of government."

There was a great commotion in the corridor. Snowy Jade stuck her head in the doorway. "You must come see him!" she cried. We ran down the corridor after her into the Courtyard of Heavenly Bamboo. A ceiling of felt had been placed over the courtyard for the winter and it was warmed by the iron pots full of hot coals that stood in every corner. All of the concubines and their maids were gathered there except for Splendid Moon, who was not feeling well and had stayed in bed, and Blossoming Spring, who, accompanied by Uncle Stupid, had returned to the home of her family for her father's funeral. In their center was a strange, very short man, guarded by four eunuchs, with a large head and a big, knobby nose and thick, stubby arms and legs. He wore only a limp red cap that dangled down his back and a short red tunic that extended only to his knees and left his hairy forearms and much of his hair-streaked chest bare.

"I am Xiao Hu Hu, the most famous dwarf in all the world," he said in a croaking voice in strangely accented Chinese. I did not like the sight of him at all nor the pungent smell he gave off, much stronger than that of the humans of the Palace. I began to bark and growl, but my objections were lost among the murmurs and shouts of amazement and surprise.

"My performance here is a gift to all the beautiful ladies of the East Lateral Courts with special wishes to the most beautiful lady," he said, pulling five balls out of a sack and placing them on the table before him, then throwing two of them in the air.

"And who might that be?" asked Precious Moon, and everyone laughed.

"That is not for me to say," the dwarf said with a grunt, tossing the third ball into orbit.

"And who is our benefactor for this wonder?" asked Snowy Jade.

"The most desperate man in Chang 'An," the dwarf replied in a tight voice, for he had now put the fourth ball in orbit. Everyone laughed and cheered and I barked even louder but no one paid any attention to me.

After the dwarf had juggled the balls, he threw many sticks into the air and kept them revolving in a circle, then let them fall and did handsprings about the courtyard, almost knocking into Enchanting Fragrance. He then picked up a long bamboo pole and placing a large spinning ball on top of it, he raised it above him and placed in on his forehead, and, after finishing that trick, did more handsprings. Then he placed a board on his forehead and a ball atop that and ran about the room as the ball rolled to one end, then the other, always about to fall off but never falling.

Each act that he performed was met with greater cheers and applause and giggles of wonder and delight and I felt very much aggrieved, as I paced about the courtyard, barking and growling over my shoulder at him, my alarm at his strange appearance augmented by the dismay of being so completely ignored. I saw the dwarf look at me as he removed the ball from the board and spun it round on his finger. Then he tossed the ball over his shoulder and ran at me. I got away from him easily, dashing behind Floating Petal and Adorable Jade, but the women joined in the chase and I was soon caught by Golden Bracelet. The dwarf had again placed the board on his forehead and signaled that I should be placed in the center of it. When Golden Bracelet had done so, he staggered about with his arms outstretched for a few seconds, while I whimpered and cringed in terror. When, in desperation, I jumped off, he caught me and, after flipping the board behind him with a quick jerk of his head, he threw me above his head and spun me around like one of his sticks.

When he placed me on the ground, to wild applause and laughter, he grabbed hold of my ear and pulled a gold coin from it, holding it up for all to see. Lotus Blossom came over to console me and, as I growled and fretted, the dwarf went to each of the concubines, the eunuchs crowding closely about him as he did so to make sure that this deformed barbarian did not touch them improperly. He began to pull coins from their hair, and pieces of silk from their sleeves, to discover Adorable Jade's hairpin in the hair of Blossoming Spring and that of Golden Bracelet under the slipper of Swaying Oriole, and many other tricks.

"But where is Splendid Moon?" Lotus Blossom cried suddenly, "She should see this too." And she led the juggler and all the rest to Evening Breeze Court, where Splendid Moon was lying in bed, though wearing a fine robe. Although the room was too small for the dwarf to do all his tricks, he cheered her up very much and when he pulled a gold coin from her sleeve, she clapped and screamed with delight. As he did so, I saw him slip into her sleeve a crumpled piece of cloth and, thinking there might be a morsel of food in it, I moved toward her. But the dwarf ran at me again and I fled in terror to the laughter and delight of all about me.

Very late that night I left my room and began to wander down the corridor. A few days earlier, Uncle Stupid had appeared in a white robe of mourning and told me that he had been commanded by the chief eunuch to join the delegation of eunuchs accompanying Blossoming Spring to her father's funeral. But I understood nothing of this and each night I would wait for him to return. When finally I grew weary of the wait, I would search through the corridors until I found a door that could be pushed open and settle myself in the bed of one of the concubines.

That night as I approached Evening Breeze Court, I saw the light of a candle falling on the floor of the corridor and then the voice of Splendid Moon humming softly. "Ah, Xiao-Xiao, come to me," she said as I pushed the door with my shoulder and entered. She was bent over her table, a piece of wrinkled silk stretched out before her on which she made careful strokes with her brush. After she had finished, she held the cloth before her with both hands and blew on it. I leapt onto her lap and pushed my nose under the floating end of the cloth. "There, I believe I have gotten it down correctly," she said and began to read in a whispery voice:

> *My heart is stirred to its depth by the gift you have given me*
> *To remind me of your love.*
> *Come to my chamber when you will, my lord*
> *I await you with a longing*
> *As ardent as your own.*

She stood up suddenly, hurling me off her lap, and carefully folded the cloth into a tiny square. "I will call for Minced Meat tomorrow," she said decisively, "and have him send for some more cuttlefish for you."

* * *

After the visit of the dwarf, Splendid Moon's illness went away. She became very lively and once again took great interest in playing with me. I no longer went to the rooms of the other concubines but each night I would come to her room after I had waited for Uncle Stupid to return. If she were already asleep, I would leap into her bed and twist and turn about until I had found a suitable spot in which to lie down close to her. But, often, when I pushed open the door, she would still be awake and I would join her at the window as she sang and hummed.

One night when I went to her room, I found the door fixed so that I could not enter. This greatly vexed me and I pawed fretfully at the door, making a loud scraping noise, and whimpering to be let in. After a few moments, I heard Splendid Moon whispering on the other side of the door, "Xiao-Xiao, go away. You will awaken everyone." This only increased my desire to get into the room. I threw myself against the door with my paws flailing, whimpering even more loudly. When Splendid Moon opened the door very slightly and made as if to strike me, I raced past her into the room.

"Very well," she said crossly, "But you must be quiet. Here, I will give you something." She walked toward the black lacquered chest, and I followed her eagerly, greatly excited—for I associated the black chest always with treats of cuttlefish. But then I noticed, at the far end of the room, the black cloak of a common servant seated on a bench with her back to me. This inappropriate and unexpected sight distracted me and I took a few steps in that direction and uttered a loud growl of alarm.

Splendid Moon called to me, dangling a piece of cuttlefish before her, and then tossed it to me as I ran back to her. "Be quiet and I will give you some more," she said, pulling another piece from the folds of cloth she held. Though the delectable smell of cuttlefish enveloped me, I began to pick up another, and very disturbing, scent in the room, strange and yet somehow familiar to me. The black cloak stirred impatiently and the smell, signaling anger but something else as well, became stronger. I growled louder, watching intently as the black cloak shifted on the bench. Splendid Moon threw another piece of cuttlefish to me but as soon as I had gobbled it down, I turned my attention again to the black cloak. My growl turned into a bark and I felt the fur on my back begin to rise.

"Give the little rodent the white powder, or, by Heaven and Earth and Sun and Moon, I will throw it out the window," the figure in the black cloak said in a hoarse whisper. It stood up and faced me and I knew now that it was Wang Yu. The scarf that he had pulled tight about his face fell open when he stood and I could see his black hair hanging loose at the sides of his face and his beard smeared back against his chin and neck with grease. Splendid Moon caught me from behind as I began to slide backward from the force of my barking at the approach of Wang Yu. As I struggled in her arms she pressed a piece of cuttlefish, coated on one end with white powder, against my mouth and I gobbled it down as fast as I could, ceasing my barking only just long enough to do so, and keeping my eyes fixed on Wang Yu. But as I began to bark again my fury suddenly abated, and I felt pleasantly weak and sleepy, and I offered no resistance as Wang Yu took me from Splendid Moon and laid me on my side on the rug.

"Let us hope the monster has not awakened half the palace," Wang Yu said in a faint whisper.

"It will not hurt her?" Splendid Moon whispered back.

"Let us be still for a few moments and listen for any sounds," Wang Yu said in a still, small voice. "No, it will not harm the rodent."

When no sounds were heard, Wang Yu took Splendid Moon by the hand and led her to the couch, strewn with black and silver and pink pillows that sat in front of a black silk screen across which flew silvery, pink-eyed cranes. I lay on the floor watching them with half-open eyes unable to move or cry out and indeed with no desire to do so.

"I have told you all this only because I trust you with my life," Wang Yu whispered, playing with Splendid Moon fingers as he sat by her side.

"But the risk is very great. One cannot reason with my father, for he thinks himself much cleverer than anyone else and surer in judgment. Nor can I attain to any greatness, nor indeed have any sort of life at all, as long as he holds the Central Kingdom in his grip."

"No, the only way to move him is to confound him with magic. It is that alone which he fears and respects. One must make him believe that the gods, and spirits, or demons or whatever forces exist, dictate that a certain path must be followed—only then will he move. And it is to that end that we have put all our effort," he said with a sudden, throaty, quiet laugh. "We have begun to set him trembling."

"But is it not impious to deal in such a way with one's father?" asked Splendid Moon, looking upon him with large, bright eyes.

Wang Yu pulled her close to him and brought her hand to his mouth. "Which is to be preferred? To be a son or slave?" he said angrily though still in a whisper. "A father may kill a son if he displeases him—for whatever reason—and no one will challenge him. But to kill a slave is more complicated—one must pursue legal procedures. And a slave need not twist his innards into knots of filial piety. No one expects a slave to love his master!"

Both of them fell silent. "*Love urged me on,*" Wang Yu whispered, leaning over and licking at Splendid Moon's ear. A rancid, buttery smell like that of overripe fruit fallen from the ginko tree began to fill the room.

"*I dared not move,*" she said in a faint musical whisper, drawing him closer.

"*I watched your red lips move in song*," Wang Yu whispered in a tight, urgent voice and with a quick, violent motion that caused Splendid Moon's hair to fall along the back of her neck, he seized Splendid Moon's shoulders and forced her beneath him.

"I cannot be denied any longer," he grunted between clenched teeth, pulling at her robe. Splendid Moon struggled against him, calling out beloved, and tried to speak of longings and throbbing hearts and sleepless nights of yearning. But Wang Yu said no more and pulled and yanked at her clothing and his own all the harder and pushed her back against the couch when she sought to rise.

Groggy as I was, I raised my head to see better these strange goings-on. I felt as though I should bark or growl but no sound came from me. A pleasurable languor coursed through me and my head felt so heavy that I dropped it back to the carpet, watching and listening as they thrashed about on the couch amidst grunts and sighs and sobs. Finally, they became still and Wang Yu lay as though lifeless atop her for several moments. Then he rose up suddenly and began to straighten his clothing.

"We must clean up the blood," he said in an anxious whisper. "Give me everything that has blood on it and I will carry it away under my cloak." Splendid Moon wept very softly as they searched the lounge and her clothing for blood stains.

"A fine jade can extinguish tears and sorrow," Wang Yu said and placed an oval-shaped piece of green jade in Splendid Moon's hand. "Keep this in remembrance until I return to you again," he said hurriedly. Then he gathered the clothing up under his cloak and crept out the door.

Splendid Moon held me tight against her in the bed that night. "It was not as I had thought, dearest Xiao-Xiao. But still I love him," she said defiantly. "I yearn already to see him again." After that night, I slept no more with Splendid Moon. For a eunuch was posted to keep me in my room all night, and I slept by myself on the rug of yaks' hair until Uncle Stupid returned.

* * *

Red drops began to fall behind me as I wandered up and down the corridors of the East Lateral Courts, which I seemed to do all the time now. For I no longer felt comfortable staying in one room or another very long and would soon take my leave and wander back into the corridors, ignoring calls to stay longer and cries that I was again being haughty. Also, I was very thirsty now and drank water constantly. Again and again each day, I would need to run towards the doorway and whine and scratch at a door or wall so that someone would take me out into a courtyard or garden where I could relieve myself.

Prince began to take a great interest in me. After I had squatted down and urinated in the grass, he would rush to that spot and examine it meticulously with quick eager sniffs. Then he would raise his head and stare off in the distance as though lost in some deep reverie. Now, too, he always wished to sniff my rump, and this infuriated me. Each time he attempted to do so, I would snarl and growl and bite at him and, once or twice, I even succeeded in putting him to flight. But if he persisted, as he usually did, I would run from him, or if I could not escape him I would sit down on my rump when he approached and refuse to budge.

Uncle Stupid observed this one day. "Ai-ya, Xiao Ji Long! I must send Prince back to Shih Yu for some time," he said. "I have seen you snapping and biting at him. I fear you will harm him," he added, with a broad, knowing smile.

Whenever I walked down the corridor, with the red drops falling behind me and the servants rushing to mop them up, concubines and maids would come to their doorways and call out to me, wearing broad smiles like that of Uncle Stupid.

"Ah, Xiao-Xiao, your days of being a child are over."

"Xiao-Xiao, you are a woman now."

"Ah, you will soon know the secrets of Clouds and Rain, Little Lucky One. Yes, the Grand Empress Dowager will make sure of that."

Then they would gossip about how intent the Grand Empress Dowager was on securing a female from my litter and though she had let me go unmated during my first time of ripeness, she was said to be determined this time that I should be mated with the best-blooded pug in all the Central Kingdom. They said also that she would not let the birthing be handled by clumsy eunuchs, whom she blamed for the loss of Most Delicate Harmony and all but one of her pups, but rather would assign it to the most skilled physicians of the palace.

After a few days, I began to bleed more heavily and it was decided that a cloth should be clasped about my rump in such a way as to catch the blood but leave my tail and legs free. An old woman servant was assigned to follow me about and take me outside and undo the clasp whenever I needed to do my necessaries, which was very often for I felt as though I had to urinate all the time. And this she did with many bitter complaints and much grunting, wailing that to be put upon to do such a distasteful task was another sign from heaven that she had lived past her time.

One afternoon as the old woman was unfastening my cloth in the small garden in front of the East Lateral Courts, I heard in the distance the sound of paws striking hard on the pebbled path. In the next instant, I saw Prince racing towards us, a broken rope hanging from his neck. The old woman, who was cursing and fumbling with my cloth, did not see him until he leapt over the shrubs into the garden. Then she flung the cloth into the air, and, screaming in terror, ran from the garden. Prince approached me cautiously, sniffing the ground all about me and then losing himself in the scents of the cloth, which had hung itself on the lower branches of a small peach tree. Before I thought to attack him, Precious Wisdom, who was studying the red blossoms of a bush at the end of the garden, rushed over, seized me in her arms, and ran towards the entrance to the East Lateral Courts. Prince at first paid no attention to this but stayed where he was, sniffing, and then looking dreamily into the air, then sniffing again.

"We will be safe here, Xiao-Xiao," Precious Wisdom said between breaths as we ran past the guards at the entrance way. Then she slowed to a walk and put me down by her side, fastening a leash on me and looking disgustedly at the dark red stain on the sleeve of her green robe. "Come, I must go to my room and change my clothing immediately."

Precious Wisdom's maid greeted her with sympathetic looks of dismay when she entered Evening Breeze Court. The green robe was soon discarded and another robe of glittery silver put on her and, just as the maid finished adjusting it, we heard screams and shouts and the sound of many feet striking the floor. Running to the door, we saw the huge figure of Prince, dark against the dim light of the corridor, bounding towards us, the rope dangling across his shoulder, pursued by a host of shouting guards and eunuchs and servants. Precious Wisdom pulled me back into the room and latched the door. Then, as we heard Prince throw himself against the door, Precious Wisdom gathered us behind the silk screen that stood by her bed.

The door slammed to the floor with a loud crash as Prince burst into the room. We heard him bolting about the room, sniffing deeply and, between sniffs, sobbing in great keening gulps. The shouts and clatter of the crowd came closer. As he came near the screen, I was invaded by the strong scent of supremacy and prerogative that he always carried about him, thickened now by some imperious frenzy. I realized then that he no longer infuriated me and

I lunged toward the bottom of the screen. I knew now that what I really wanted to do was run at him and have him chase me and I suddenly ached with the desire to sniff at him more closely.

Prince threw his front paws on the screen and it began to collapse. The servants and maids and Precious Wisdom ran screaming out from under it and pulled me behind them, struggling against my leash and dragging my feet as I sought to run back to Prince. As we rounded the doorway, the mob of guards and eunuchs and servants swarmed into the room. Still running down the corridor, we heard behind us heightened shouts and screams and sounds of great struggle. Then Prince emerged from the room and began loping down the corridor towards us, the broken rope dragging behind him on one side, and on the other, a boy eunuch, who had succeeded in placing another rope round his neck, sliding and running and at last falling and dragging on the floor.

Precious Wisdom marshaled us into the room of Lotus Blossom, who stood in her doorway, her maids and servants gathered round her. They fled before us, their screams magnifying those of Precious Wisdom and her maids and servants. Prince soon bounded in the room after us and Precious Wisdom picked me up and held me over her head with outstretched arms and ran to the far corner of the room. The whole pursuing mob then poured into the room and, with much screaming and shouting and cursing, more ropes were fastened on Prince, and prodded and beset by sticks and shouts and menaced by the spears of two guards, he was finally dragged from the room and down the corridor, protesting with howls and great sorrowful, gulping sobs.

* * *

That night the servants were moved out of the room next to the one I shared with Uncle Stupid and a pen of bamboo poles was set up. When the old servant woman came with clasps and a fresh cloth, Uncle Stupid said to her, "That will not be needed, old one." He pointed to the pinkish, watery drops beside me. "There is little blood now. These can be cleaned up easily. But I will get someone else to do it, old one. I believe your hair is two degrees whiter than when first you were given this chore."

The old woman grunted a grudging thank you and quickly left the room. "You cause everywhere too much excitement, Xiao Ji Long," Uncle Stupid said to me, pretending to wipe sweat from his brow. "I am an old man. I must find an old dog for a companion."

The next morning, after I had eaten and done my necessaries, Uncle

Stupid placed me in the bamboo pen. "A very highbrow gentleman is coming to visit you this morning. I have not yet myself had the pleasure of meeting this gentleman." Several eunuchs had gathered round the pen and they laughed as Uncle Stupid spoke to me.

"But he is said to be a great champion. He is called Charging Lion and is descended from many great champions and the sire of many more. The unfortunate Waking Bear was one of his sons. You should be honored. The Grand Empress Dowager herself has selected him to be your husband. Or perhaps I should call him your paramour. He is said to be a bit of a rogue and greatly adverse to the settled life."

Charging Lion seemed to me twice as large as Waking Bear. His jowls descended into thick rolls of flesh around his neck and these widened into a great mane of silvery tan fur. His mask and whiskers had whitened with age and his face was without a trace of refinement. One of his eyes was half-closed as though about to fall asleep and, when he trotted about the pen, his left rear leg jumped out oddly every third or fourth step. Nonetheless, he showed great interest in me and, after rounding the pen, he rushed to me and begin sniffing my nose in great, snorting draughts. Then he moved to my rump and began sniffing even more eagerly.

I took only a few cautious sniffs of him, and, finding them quite repellent, I ran from him. He chased after me, still sniffing eagerly behind me. We went round and round the ring for quite some time until finally I wearied of it and turned on him, snapping and snarling. Charging Lion recoiled and looked at me for a long time as though perplexed. Then he resumed his chase, and so it went, round and round the pen, snaps and snarls, and a momentary pause. Then, again and again, around the pen. Sometimes Charging Lion would grow tired and lay down on the floor heavily, panting and drooling. But then he would rise again and resume his chase. Sometimes I would weary of running in circles and sit down on my rump so that he could not sniff me. But he would pester and nudge me until I could maintain this posture no longer and I would growl and snort and resume my run once more.

The eunuchs grew impatient. "Do not be such a prude, Little Lucky One," they began to complain to me.

"It is well past lunch, we are hungry."

"Come, give Charging Lion a chance, Little Dragon. Do not resist so much the secrets of Clouds and Rain." Once the eunuchs tried to hold me still but I squirmed and bit and snarled with such vehemence that they let go of me.

"Come, Xiao Ji Long, do your duty," Uncle Stupid said sharply. "He is, after all, no uglier than a Minister!"

Later in the afternoon, as I ran from Charging Lion, thinking only of the second meal that was very late in being served to me, there was clamor and bustling in the corridor and, in the next instant, as all the eunuchs fell to their knees and touched their foreheads to the ground, the Grand Empress Dowager was carried into the room on a litter, a dozen servants crowding through the door behind her. After the litter was sat down, the servants disengaged her from it with great care and she walked to the edge of the pen. She was wearing a fine robe and headdress of red silk and an enormous necklace of green jade that hung down almost to the top of the pen as she leaned forward. She studied us for a few moments, scrunching up her face in irritation as Charging Lion chased me, rather slowly now, about the pen.

"Hold her still, nitwits!" she shouted in a voice of exasperation and the eunuchs stumbled over each other in trying to get hold of me. I squirmed and snarled and struggled and was able to get free of them at first.

"Is she some mighty dragon from North of Mount Wu Tai that you cannot control her?" screeched the Empress Dowager.

This time I was gripped firmly by four pairs of hands, one of which made sure I could not push my rump to the ground. I felt Charging Lion's paws and then his chest on my back and his rear haunches thrusting first alongside me, then banging against the back of my legs.

"Push him to the right," commanded the Empress Dowager, "no, no, not so much."

Then I felt something enter into me. Charging Lion began to thrust harder, rocking from side to side, and I felt his heavy head at my neck, the breath coming out of him in great puffs. He kept at this for some time and I began to grow used to it, and all at once I felt a jolt and we were somehow locked together. Charging Lion made a few more thrusts and then he pushed softly off my back and his front legs landed beside me.

"Must I do everything!" the Grand Empress Dowager muttered as she was helped back to her litter. The eunuchs fell to their knees again and touched their foreheads to the floor while Charging Lion and I struggled for a few moments until he was able to get himself turned around and facing in the opposite direction from me.

After the Empress Dowager left, the eunuchs began to disassemble the pen and bowls of food and water were brought to us, but Charging Lion and I were still joined together. Although three times my size, he seemed very much spent by his efforts and let me lead him backwards about the room, and into the corridor, and then into my own room. I was very confused by this bizarre arrangement, and feared that this huge lump of flesh and fur would stay glued to me forever. I looked over my shoulder again and again—but still he was there, his head hanging down, his paws plodding slowly backward.

Golden Bracelet looked into the room and saw us. "Ai-ya, there is a two-headed beast in the Palace!" she yelled and ran down the corridor, shouting it again and again. The room was soon crowded with pointing, giggling, blushing concubines and maids as, glum and discomfited, I walked Charging Lion up and down the room, hoping that he would somehow fall off me.

* * *

Day by day, I grew heavier and more sluggish. My belly began to sway when I walked and sometimes I would feel within it strange twists and wiggles. While food had always been uppermost in my mind, now I thought of nothing else—except sleep. And I much preferred sleep now to my wanderings in the East Lateral Court. My outings with Pingdi had also ceased since the Grand Empress Dowager feared they would be too taxing for me. I was now given four meals a day, but still this did not satisfy me. No sooner had I finished my meal than I began to think about the next meal or treat.

One day Uncle Stupid approached me with my yellow jacket and cap. "You must dress yourself up, little mother," he said, as a servant began to fasten on me this dreaded apparel—although I did not now mind the jacket so much as it had gotten very cold. The Palace was everywhere filled with steaming cisterns of hot water and smoking iron pots filled with hot coals.

"The buttons and loops of your jacket have been abundantly expanded—so as to accommodate the unusual expansion of your abundant talents." Uncle Stupid said in a formal tone as the servant giggled. "So you should be quite comfortable. If you do not object, however, I will hold on to your copper metal for I believe you already carry enough weight."

Uncle Stupid then packed my bowls and some of my favorite toys in a sack and instructed the servant to gather up my yak's hair rug. I waddled from the room behind them to a waiting carriage, stopping for a moment to brush the cap off my head so that it hung down under my chin.

"The Grand Empress Dowager has had a birthing room prepared for you in the Court of Blissful Renewal—only a few moments from her own quarters by litter," Uncle Stupid said as I snuggled next to him in the carriage. "And, happily, she has consented that I may go with you though I am not to interfere with the physicians. I am to obey them in all things," he added, mimicking the voice of the Grand Empress Dowager and twisting his face into a look of great severity.

My room at the Court of Blissful Renewal was enclosed by screens of golden, lacquered wood and covered with a bed of straw, on which were strewn silk rags of many colors. After Uncle Stupid arranged my toys and bowls and fluffed up my yak's hair rug in the corner, three physicians came to examine me. They wore the same black robes and hats as did the scholars and officials but, instead of colored ribbons, epaulets and sashes hung from them. Although I did not like their presence, I felt so weary that I hardly growled as they gently probed my belly, and looked into my mouth, and widened my eyes between their thumbs and forefingers. After they had finished with me, a diviner entered the room. He bent down over me, pulling at the pale green stalk of a plant he held in his hand and bringing its tattered strips very close to his eyes.

Afterwards, all of them stood for a few moments clustered together, murmuring amongst themselves and nodding approvingly, and then Uncle Stupid and I were left alone. He led me to my yak's hair rug and, patting my head, sang a song to me. Then he left and went to sleep in the cot which lay just outside my room.

In the next few days, nothing seemed so necessary to me or gave me so much pleasure as digging into the straw that covered the room. Whenever I was not eating or sleeping or lying still and watching, with upraised eyes, the comings and goings of the physicians, the diviner, and Uncle Stupid, I would dig frantically into the straw with my forepaws. The floor was soon covered with holes and mounds of straw. But none of this quite satisfied me and no sooner had I finished than I would set myself again to this task, digging into these mounds and covering the holes.

Then one morning before it was light, I awoke with an overpowering desire to tear up the silk rags that lay about the straw floor. I went from rag to rag, ripping and shredding each of them as best I could. Then I spied my jacket and cap folded on top of a stool in the corner and, leaning against the stool with my front paws, and stretching my neck as far as I could, I was just able to catch a piece of the jacket in my teeth and pull both jacket and cap to the floor. They were well stitched and hard to rend, but I was very determined and soon they lay shredded and torn among the other rags.

When the physicians and diviners came, I became very upset and went after them with such rage when they sought to enter my room that they soon retreated and watched me from over top the screens. I could only bear Uncle

Stupid to be near me. When he brought me my meal and I turned my head from it disgustedly, he said, "Ah, the time is very near, little mother." And he moved close to the entrance and squatted down to watch me. I walked away from the bowl and lay down on my side at the far end of the room, watching the entrance to make sure no physician or diviner would enter.

As I lay there, breathing very fast, then slower, then again faster and slower, my mind and body seemed to escape from me. I began shivering and my leg twitched. A tiny, gooey lump pushed out of me. And without thinking, I licked it clean, bit off the cord that fastened it to me, ate the goo that lay all about it, and nudged it toward me. I lay there panting, a feeling of weary contentment and relief spreading through me. Then the fast breathing started again. And soon another lump pushed out of me. And I licked it clean and nudged it to me as I had with the first and lay there, panting and content, while Uncle Stupid squatted before me with a happy look on his face and the physicians peered silently over the screen.

"Unlike your poor mother, I believe you have but two, Little Lucky One," Uncle Stupid said after watching me for a long time.

"Yes, two, two is quite enough for such a small dog," one of the physicians said from over the screen and I growled at him so that he would not think to enter my room.

For many days thereafter, I remained all the day in my room, leaving only to attend to my necessaries. Except for my meals—and my food bowl was always kept full, I cared for nothing but licking and cleaning the two pups, for the push of their paws against my belly, and their reassuring tugs on my nipples. A strange, hysterical protectiveness came over me and I wished no one to come near us except Uncle Stupid—and even him I barely tolerated, growling if he made as if to touch the puppies. And during this time, as the puppies nuzzled and suckled me, I was filled with a feeling of great happiness and gratification. This narrow life seemed perfectly complete to me and I felt as though I should never want anything more than to lie on my side in this bed of straw and torn silk rags.

But, as the days passed, I began to feel restless and, more and more frequently, I felt a rush of desire to leave these ever needy pups and look for treats or food outside my room—even though a bowlful of food lay next to me. When I would return from these leave-takings, the thought of lying down once again and having these two increasingly heavy and rambunctious creatures clambering over me no longer seemed so pleasurable. The male pup was particularly annoying: always he pushed and pulled to be first to the teat.

But then he was never satisfied with the teat he was suckling! Wanting always then the teat on which his sister had settled. I began to stand up when they approached and when still they ran at me and tried to hang onto my nipples as I walked about, I would growl and snap at them. More and more I welcomed those times when Uncle Stupid, and even the physicians, would take them from me and pet and clean them and place before them small bowls of milk and a watery, unappealing mush.

One day, after the Grand Empress Dowager had come to the room and, with much cooing and sighing, had petted and fondled each of the puppies, the physicians took them and did not bring them back. I had entirely ceased to nurse them by then and was not in the least troubled by their disappearance. Uncle Stupid said that Wang Mang had intrigued to have the male given as a gift to the khan of a northern barbarian tribe whose more active assistance against the Xiongnu he hoped to secure. The female, of course, was promised to the Grand Empress Dowager, said Uncle Stupid, and not even Wang Mang could contrive to have her sent away.

I never saw either of them again—nor did I ever think of them. For the strange feelings of protectiveness, fulfillment and selflessness, which had so firmly seized hold of me, had entirely disappeared and I longed to return to my old life of play and treats, romps in the park, and unfettered meanderings through the endless corridors and rooms and courtyards of the East Lateral Courts.

At last, I was ready to leave the Court of Blissful Renewal. My room was cleaned of straw and silk rags, my jacket and cap discarded as useless and Uncle Stupid had just placed the last of my bowls and toys in the sack. But the physicians then came into the room and looked at me with stern, serious faces and probed my belly and forced open my mouth. They said that I was quite ill and must go with them. And Uncle Stupid was left holding the sack of toys, a look of puzzlement and foreboding on his face as they carried me off.

* * *

The entranceway to the East Lateral Courts seemed very quiet as I stood waiting, looking apprehensively at the two ferocious wooden demons who guarded it. After so many weeks away, they seemed somehow different to me. I raised my head and sniffed. There was a strange, still, sullen scent in the air. Precious Wisdom and Snowy Jade ran to me and greeted me enthusiastically, but there was something odd and different in their manner.

Precious Wisdom picked me up and pressed my face to her cheek and I yelped when she did so for my belly was still very sore. They each placed a finger on the shaved skin of my belly and ran it delicately along the thickened ridge of skin that ran through the middle of the shaved spot, shaking their heads sadly and murmuring endearments to me.

They carried me to Uncle Stupid's room, placing me on the floor and nudging me very gently through the doorway. But they themselves did not stay. Uncle Stupid sat cross-legged with his back to the door. A small pot full of sticks that glowed and smoked, filling the room with a sweet, greasy fragrance, sat in front of him. He barely turned as he heard me trot across the floor.

"Ah, you are back, Little Dragon. Come to me." Although it hurt me to do so, I jumped up weakly against his shoulder and licked his cheek. Uncle Stupid brushed his eyes with his fingers and then sat me down on his lap.

"They said you were ill, Xiao Ji Long, but I do not believe this.

"They said that the ruins of a pup were rotting in your womb. But I do not believe this either. I do not believe anything that is said in the Palace—for all is the opposite of what is said." He raised me up by my forelegs, causing me to wince and yelp, and looked at my stomach.

"We have much in common now," he said gloomily, then lay me back down on his lap and began to stroke my head.

"Did you know that ten days ago the sky thundered though they were no clouds in the sky? And though we are still deep into winter. There are hundreds who swear to this. And that the rumor has spread through Chang 'An that a thundering sky without clouds is like a baby kept from his mother and promises disaster?

"Did you know that endless rains due north of Chang 'An, have pried loose landslides that have washed away whole towns, killing many thousands? But, that above the town of Yungang, the rocks and mud were halted by a huge rise of copper and iron that was pushed up from out of the mountains. An official from Yungang solemnly attests to this. The diviners are now pondering this strange occurrence. But many believe that this now means that the house of Wei must be restored, for they are of the element metal, and that the house of Wang, which is of earth, can no longer protect the Han Dynasty from decline."

Uncle Stupid's peculiar manner and the dull timbre of his voice perplexed me and I cocked my head and stared hard at his face. "You look skeptical, Xiao Long," he said, looking down at me. "But do you not realize, as the proverb tells us, that though there are things which cannot be imagined, there is nothing that cannot happen.

"Two nights ago a madman appeared at a banquet attended by Wang Mang and all high officials and many nobles. He appeared suddenly, no one knows from where, whirling about before the banquet table, the rags of his clothing spinning through the air. He sang praises of Wang Mang's generosity and humility, speaking of him as though he were deceased. Then he fell to his knees, and beat his chest, and shrieked that had Wang Mang accomplished reconciliation he would have been honored by the gods with immortality. When at last two guards got hold of him and wrestled him out of the banquet hall, he disappeared as though he were a spirit! All say that this is yet another sign that Wei and Wang must be reconciled and equalized. Wei must be lifted up and Wang taken down.

"They say that Wang Mang is very distressed by all this and that he cannot sleep nor think clearly. But I do not believe this either—at least the last, for devils do not need sleep anyway."

Uncle Stupid fell silent and pulled two sticks from the pot. He blew on them and placed them again in the pot, then spread the sticks evenly about the sides of the pot.

"Splendid Moon is dead," he said in a heavy, flat voice and a tear squeezed out of his eye and ran down his cheek. "She died while you were nursing your pups. It is said she died of a fever. But this is not true. 'Small evils are recorded. Great evils are not mentioned!' And what has befallen Splendid Moon, so young, so full of the sweetness of life, so perfect in her beauty, is a great evil!" Although I understood nothing of what he said, Uncle Stupid paused as he finished each thought until I raised my eyes and met his gaze, as though he needed my reaction before he could continue.

"Splendid Moon became pregnant. And though the pregnancy was ended, it was greatly feared that secrets would get out. The secret of the pregnancy itself. And the secret of the father. But Splendid Moon herself did not ever reveal the father.

"It was, in any case, now impossible that she could pass the examinations that are required after the Son of Heaven receives his cap of manhood.

"She could not be returned to her family. The disgrace of a concubine sent back after being chosen from many hundreds for the Son of Heaven would be too great, even if the pregnancy remained unknown. They told her that she could only live as a commoner in some far city. But that was just to frighten her further—for they had no intention of letting her live and risking disclosure of so many secrets. So each day the eunuchs and those relatives of hers that lived in Chang 'An would gather round her to try to persuade her to commit suicide.

"After many days of pleadings and threats she consented. But when they brought the poison, she could not go through with it and threw the poison to the floor and ran crying from her room. The relatives could not bear her sorrow any longer and did not come any more to persuade her. But the eunuchs redoubled their efforts.

"They had become very afraid themselves. For there was not only the secret of pregnancy, and that of the violation of the sanctity of the harem—which clearly required the transgressions of many, not just one. It was feared also that her lover, in his boastfulness, might have told her other secrets. Secrets which would have placed many lives in danger.

"Splendid Moon again consented but again when the poison was brought, she could not do it and broke away weeping. But my brother eunuchs could not give up—too much was at risk—and they started on her again. And this time they brought to her a special potion. And Splendid Moon became very happy and, singing her stupid poem about the lover who braves deserts and demons and slays ten men, she took the poison mixed in with still more of the potion.

"I believe that it was the intention of these devils that you too should die—from 'infections' resulting from your surgery. But when the Grand Empress Dowager began to inquire into your sudden illness, fear of her wrath shattered their resolve."

Uncle Stupid fell silent for a long time, stirring the sticks in the pot, one way and then another, and I dozed off in his lap.

"What do you suppose Wang Yu was doing during this time?" he said suddenly, a snap in his voice.

"Someone has told me that he was very upset. For they said he was very fond of Splendid Moon and very sorry to hear of her illness. This someone told me that his temper became shorter than ever. And that in his nervous and agitated state, he began to drink and gamble even more than usual, and to spend the whole night, not just an hour or so, in houses of pleasure."

Uncle Stupid brought one of the sticks close to his lips and blew on it, watching it glow and fade. He began to sing a song about a rat in such a soft, humming voice that I could hardly hear him.

"Wang Yu is like the drunkard who kills a man when he is wild with liquor," he said, no longer looking at me. "But when his crime is not found out his shame quickly leaves him and he soon fills his cup again."

He paused and sang again of the rat, who deserved to die yet sought to evade death.

"Having escaped from reaping disaster from his folly and indulgence, he must move on to some greater folly and indulgence, some new foul and reckless deed.

"Wang Yu is like the gambler who has suffered heavy losses. But upon awakening and finding that he can still obtain money, he must risk it again. He cannot stop playing until he has lost all. It should be our great hope and duty to help him towards his appointed end."

He pulled two sticks from the pot and crossed them. "Let us take an oath of revenge, Little Lucky Dragon, on all those who caused the death of Splendid Moon. And pray that just as air turns wine into vinegar, the luck that the gods have bestowed on you shall be transformed by justice into their misfortune and agony."

Uncle Stupid stirred the sticks again, and, seeming very pleased, resumed his humming.

8
Pugnapped!

After I returned to the East Lateral Courts, Pingdi began once again to summon me almost daily to the Inner Palace. He looked and smelt even sicklier than before and an air of despondency hung about him. Once he mentioned the unfortunate death of Splendid Moon and looked sad for a moment. But each day he complained that the exact date of the ceremony to bestow his cap of manhood had still not been set, and that the Grand Empress Dowager grew very annoyed with him whenever he sought to raise the subject. He no longer played at all with his soldiers but spent much time in his bed, his thumbs locked and forefingers tapping against each other, seemingly deep in thought.

But he also had sudden bursts of energy and would call unexpectedly for his fine robes and litter and persist on being taken to the Lateral Courts or the Hall of Celestial Purity or even, despite the still severe cold, to the Park of all the Beasts of the World. Often, he would descend from the litter, and the special attendant would carry me, or, if we were at the Park, walk me beside him. While we were in his chambers, Pingdi confided that he wanted to show that neither was he too ill for the duties of Emperorship nor had he been driven to hide himself from his subjects by criticism of his immaturity.

I also accompanied him once again to sessions of the Court. Because my belly was still sore and it was perceived that it was uncomfortable for me to lie in one place very long, I was once again allowed to roam freely about the Court. But, also because my belly was sore, I did not now frolic about the court; my demeanor was very subdued and correct.

I could see everywhere a tenseness in the gestures and bearing of the men and ladies of the court. Great clouds of fear and hatred and apprehension wafted into my nostrils from every side. There was much whispering about

143

those who were, or might be, newly implicated in the failed assassination of the Son of Heaven and of the landslides, the madman, the cloudless thunder, and other strange events. But when I wandered too close to the men and ladies of the court, they would fall silent and watch my approach with sidelong glances of fear and malice.

One morning, before the announcement of the Son of Heaven and the Grand Empress Dowager, the whispering was replaced by an excited clamor. Everyone spoke with horror and indignation of the rebellion that had broken out in the east, where the spring floods had spoiled much of the harvest; of the corrupt official who had sold for his own gain the grain that had been dispatched to alleviate the famine; of the ragtag army of peasants that had risen up and killed the official and all his assistants. Most appalling, the peasant army was said to be still growing in strength and murderousness and swarming through the land, killing not only petty officials—but even nobles—as they went. It was another omen, all agreed. Some said it foretold of the decline of the Han that Wang Mang was always struggling so untiringly to prevent. Others that it was another warning, like that of the madman, of the need for reconciliation with the House of Wei and reunification of the Son of Heaven with his mother.

After the Son of Heaven and the Grand Empress Dowager had been installed in their thrones, and Wang Mang had taken his place below them, the nobles rose from their bows, and abandoning decorum, shouted questions at Wang Mang about the rebellion. Wang Mang endured this onslaught for a few moments, his arms folded in front of him; then, in a pleasing, calming voice, he informed them that the General of the Right was already on the march to engage this 'army', which was nothing more than a mob. The rebellion would soon be crushed and all the ringleaders executed. Wagonloads of grain were now on their way to the famine-stricken area to replace those stolen by the corrupt official, Wang Mang proclaimed, and, as an example, the members of his family who had not been slain by the rebels would be executed. He ended his speech with a tepid shout of "Ten Thousand Years to the Han" and this was echoed unenthusiastically throughout the room. No one should doubt, Wang Mang asserted, that the beneficial rule of the Han, which was ordained by heaven, remained secure. A few more questions were hurled at Wang Mang, who answered them in the same pleasant, patient manner but with increasingly hard looks at the questioners, and the shouts died away to scattered grumblings.

A petitioner was then announced. He was a barbarian from the South and dressed very strangely, with a high-waisted robe and painted slippers. I had trotted back to the dais by this time and was curled up in front of my small throne. As he fell to his knees before us, and bent his back again and again to touch his forehead to the floor, I rose up, and, uttering a low growl, stalked to the edge of the dais. He wore a large round hat that looked much like one of the pillows on Splendid Moon's couch and the sight of this strange hat bobbing up and down very much provoked me. Despite the pain in my belly, I broke into a fit of barking, turning sideways towards him in disdain as I did so. I could see his knees quaking as he got to his feet and, with false and fleeting smiles, sputtered benedictions for the Son of Heaven and declared his affection for the new Imperial Pug, Xiao Ji Long.

I thought for a moment to run down the steps at him but suddenly felt something twist in my head and then the painful, lop-sided feeling in my ears. The darkness closed in quickly on me and I let out one of my screams. All movement and sound in the great hall ceased. Everyone stared at me. Then the whole world shook and trembled beneath and about us. Just as suddenly the trembling stopped. An empty cup fell from the stand beside the Empress Dowager and rolled with a whirring sound on the floor. In a somber and sonorous voice, Wang Mang declared that the proceedings were ended. As the special attendant carried me through the kneeling nobles and officials and eunuchs, I smelt waves of fear rising up and washing over me.

* * *

Uncle Stupid sat on a low stool, basking in the heat of the iron pot, when I returned. On the floor beside him was a nearly empty cup and a glazed, earthenware jug. He was in a very merry mood, singing to himself as he pulled and toyed with something red that was hidden in his hands.

"Drink up, dearest Xiao-Xiao," he shouted, as I began to investigate his cup, "for a droplet is all that is left. Drink quickly, or you will miss your chance."

"A pretty thing , is it not?" he said, as I licked the tiny bit of wine left in his cup, holding up a doll with a red headdress and a red silk robe that was not yet attached to it.

"A few stitches and it will be quite perfect." He began to sing again: *"How long lying here on this fragrant grass? My jug and wine cup overturned! And my guest long departed!"*

"But it is not for you, Little Lucky One," he said as I leaned my forepaws on his knees and sniffed at the doll.

"Another earthquake! Though a mild one." He turned from his doll and fixed a severe look on me, with his eyebrow arched and his head slightly wobbling. "I am sure that you screamed an appropriate warning. That will set them even more aflutter with tales of your unnatural powers and unseemly influence over the Son of Heaven. Even now they still march in to the Empress Dowager to complain about your medal."

"Abundant Talents of Unusual Degree!" he said with a snort. "Could one write a song or a poem about such an honor? I do not think so."

"Ah, the Grand Empress Dowager is very weary of this parade of whiners and belly achers, I can assure you. Last week she threw a cup of boiling water at one of them—who had a particularly offensive, wheedling tone of voice. Or so I am told. But she has now, at least, your daughter to console her."

"I cannot remember picking flowers." He took up his song once more, clutching the tiny robe in one hand and doll in the other and stretching both hands out before him, looking as though he were astonished to find them there. *"Yet my hands are quite full! How ever did they come?"*

He pulled back the doll and twisted it about in his hands. "There, that is good enough. Now only a few pins are needed." He stuck a small silver pin into the chest of the doll and another into its head, then one each into all the elbows and knees of the doll. "There is one left, Xiao Ji Long." He raised one eyebrow and fixed a questioning look on me.

"Ai- ya, Little Dragon, you are very naughty." He took the last pin and thrust it into the rump of the doll.

Uncle Stupid then stood up and carried the doll over to his chest. He moved many things about and then with slow and unsteady but very careful motions placed it far into the bottom of his chest. "Let us see what else I have that will amuse you," he said, lingering over his chest. He pulled out a clump of silk cloth. "This was found in the rooms of Lotus Blossom. I do not think she even realizes that it is missing."

He looked at me knowingly and stretched out the cloth, which was covered with lettering. "I have become very diligent."

"This cloth speaks of sleepless nights and tossing and turning, and fond but painful thoughts of first meetings, and eating the bitter herbs of heartbreak and neglect. A poor meal indeed—though not without flavor. What tender heart might send such a message?" Uncle Stupid crumpled the cloth, tossed it back, then locked the chest.

"Come!" he shouted loudly, clapping his hands together. "Let us arrange a contest." He grabbed a handful of lettered sticks and charged into the corridor, walking rapidly and erratically from room to room, clapping his hands and shouting for the concubines to come out. And soon there was a crowd of concubines and maids gathered about him, very much amused at the state he was in.

"Let us have a contest to measure and improve elocution and proper speaking," he shouted. "Lotus Blossom, you have a beautiful voice. You shall begin by reciting this verse."

Uncle Stupid fumbled a bit with the sticks and then handed one to Lotus Blossom, who had come up beside him looking both fearful and eager, pleased that she had been chosen. She held out the stick before her and began bravely, her voice vibrant and cheerful.

> *When I gather herbs in the land of Mei*
> *Do you know on whom my thoughts dwell?*
> *On beautiful Meng*
> *Of the House of Ch'i*
> *Who promised in Sang Chung*
> *To meet me in Shang Kung*
> *And go with me to Ch'i Shang*

But when she began to recite the second verse, the first line of which was "*When I gather wheat in the north of Mei,*" all cheerfulness left her. Her voice faltered and dropped to a whisper when she read of "*Of beautiful Meng of the House of I.*" And when she came to the third verse, which sang of gathering seed in the east of Mei and beautiful Meng of the House of Yung, her voice cracked and halted and with sniffling sobs, she ran from the room. [These verses are from the poem "the Philanderer", written sometime before 200 B.C., poet unknown—S.D.]

* * *

On the fifteenth day of the month, as was customary, a diviner was summoned to the Court. He was wearing a robe of crimson and bright stippled silver with an enormous crimson sash. A square hat of crimson stood high on his head. He carried a whitened turtle shell and a bamboo stick with a tip of red jade, which he laid alongside him as he made his bows. As he did so, a servant carried in first a tripod and a pair of wooden-handled iron tongs and then, slung on a sturdy wooden pole, an iron pot, the air curving and wavering above it. I started to move towards it for I thought that it might be used to prepare some food, but the special attendant quickly caught me from behind and looped the leash around my neck.

The diviner held the shell in the pot for a long time without speaking and except for the rustle of silk, the occasional shuffle of a slipper, and the labored breathing of the Grand Empress Dowager above and beside me, I could hear no sound within the hall. Finally, he pulled the shell from the pot and held it before him, gripped in the tongs.

"Such fissures are small and harmless," he said in a matter-of-fact, pleasant voice. He pointed with his jade-tipped stick at the tiny cracks in the shell. "In the absence of contravening marks, all would agree that they provide assurance that, despite minor incursions of barbarians, the borders are secure."

He placed the shell back into the pot and waited a while longer. Then he held it before him again and pointed to a long crack that ran parallel to the edge of the shell. "Such a crack foretells, in most cases, ample rain this year to feed the great rivers of the Central Kingdom. This has been established by Book of Divination itself and confirmed by long observation. But we must pay careful attention that further signs do not emerge that might signal the likelihood of too much rain."

He repeated the process again and again, discerning signs concerning the crops in the South, the orchards in the West, the sheep and goats in the North, the winds that might strike the faraway lands by the coast of the sea, the likelihood of sons being born in this new year. It was clear now that no food would be prepared in the pot and, lulled by the stillness of the room and the smooth cadence of the diviner's voice, I dozed off.

A sharp pop awakened me. The diviner pulled the shell before him and examined it with a look of deep concern. At the apex of the round shell, the squares were deeply buckled and at their very center, a charred, ragged hole showed through. "Tumult and discord at the center," he mused. "But there may also be signs here as to how harmony can be restored." He turned the shell about with the tongs and ran the jade tip along it.

"Ah, here! Such tracks have been determined to symbolize the tie of family. And since it begins near the tail, southwards, it speaks of the female line. See, it starts to the center but then runs from it and dips back to the edge."

He traced its path with his stick. "The fissure, however, is very slight when it turns away from the center—so this anomaly can be corrected. This may tell us that the family of the Son of Heaven can still, and must be, restored."

Wang Mang went down the steps and moved towards the diviner. "Are we not all the family of the Son of Heaven?" he said in a polite and thoughtful voice. "His children, as it were?" The diviner at first did not respond.

"And where in the Book of Divination does it speak of such a crack as indicating the tie of family?" Wang Mang asked. "I recall no such reference."

"But in the Third Chronicle of the Annals and again in the Fifth Commentary there are ..." The diviner started to argue but Wang Mang silenced him with a mild wave of his hand.

"Bring that shell to me." A servant seized the tongs from the diviner and held the shell in front of Wang Mang, who turned the servant's hand so that he could look at the inside of the shell. "Has it not been filed down and hollowed at the center?" he asked with an air of sincere curiosity.

"Seize him!" Wang Mang commanded suddenly, and before the stricken diviner could respond, soldiers rushed at him and gripped his arms.

"What is this?" snapped the Grand Empress Dowager, who was very fond of divination, though like me she had began to doze until the sharp pop of the bursting shell was heard.

"Most honored Grand Empress and wondrous Son of Heaven, it is my burden to tell you that we are in the midst of a plot," Wang Mang said in a mild, sad voice. Then his voice hardened as he turned on the diviner. "Admit now, wretch, that you have been bribed by traitors for this false prophesizing and you may yet live."

The diviner sought again to argue about the Third Chronicle and the Fifth Commentary but Wang Mang waved and the soldiers tightened their hold on him. "Place these tongs again in the fire and we may get some truth out of them yet—by squeezing this wretch's face. And you, fool, count your heads while we are waiting for it to heat. For if you do not speak the truth, you are soon to lose one!"

When the tongs were brought close to his face, the diviner cried out that he had, in truth, been paid a bribe by Wei Cheng, the uncle of the Queen of Chung-San, the mother of the divine Son of Heaven. But it was not for the money that he had corrupted his divination—he had feared that his family would be harmed by the Wei clan who were well known to be skilled in the practice of black magic. Wang Mang gave a signal and the soldiers dragged away the diviner, his legs dangling and crimson sash trailing behind him.

"There is far, far worse," Wang Mang said, shaking his head sadly, with a catch in his throat as though it injured him to say the words. He called the Marquisa of Ping-O forward and she threw herself on the floor before the

Grand Empress Dowager, shaking and sobbing as she rose to her knees and touched her forehead to the floor. The Grand Empress stared at her in amazement, seeming both annoyed and intrigued by this performance.

The first sounds out of the Marquisa's mouth were such a mixture of sighs and sobs and half-choked words that no one could understand her.

"Am I to understand such gibberish?" The Empress Dowager snorted. "Calm yourself, my dear."

With that, the Marquisa regained her sugary voice, which I so much disliked. She said that she had been entertaining, at her apartments in Chang 'An, the Marquis of An-Yang, the brother-in-law of the Queen of Chung-San, and his wife Wei Zhang, the sister of the Queen. As was well known, they were in Chang 'An in the hope of arranging an appointment with the Son of Heaven and, as the appointed representative of the house of Wei, she felt it her duty both to entertain them and to seek to facilitate an appointment. She could see no harm in it. But—and at that point, although still on her knees she doubled over sobbing and could not continue to speak. Silently, she held before her, in a trembling hand, a doll dressed in red silk impaled with quivering pins.

The Grand Empress Dowager leaned forward, squinting, and I jumped to my feet and pulled to the end of my leash to get a better look at it.

"What is it?" asked the Empress Dowager.

"It is an effigy … of you!" The Marquisa cried with a sob. "Stuck through with pins. Which I found hidden under the bed in the room in which the Marquis of An-Yang and his wife were staying!" and, sobbing, she collapsed again on the floor.

"Such can only be expected from the House of Wei!" Wang Mang said, shaking his head sadly again, looking as though he were greatly pained by the revelation. "Who have never abandoned their devotion to witchcraft and black magic. Most dear and beloved Grand Empress Dowager and beloved Son of Heaven, whose devotion to the Grand Empress Dowager is, as all know, unbounded, be assured that I will not cease my efforts until I have rooted out all those who have conspired in these crimes—and that their punishment will be of the utmost harshness!"

* * *

A few nights later as I slept curled in the crook of Uncle Stupid's leg, I was disturbed by a rustling and fumbling near the doorway to our room. I raised my head, let out a kind of grunt (for I was not sure this disturbance merited a bark), and stared into the darkness of the room, straining to determine what was there.

"I must talk to you, Uncle," a voice whispered and I recognized the sound and scent of Minced Meat, who stood just inside the doorway. Startled and offended by his visit at this inappropriate and inconvenient hour, I began to bark at him, but Uncle Stupid quickly gathered me up in his arms and shushed me. Then he groped in the darkness for the lantern, and after lighting it, placed it on the floor beside a low bench. Minced Meat made his way to him and they sat down side by side on the bench.

"I have expected your visit," Uncle Stupid whispered.

"Save me, Uncle," Minced Meat whispered back, his face white in the light of the lantern and his eyes darting about in desperation.

"You cannot be saved," Uncle Stupid said quietly, and he said no more until Minced Meat stirred on the bench and let out a moan.

"You cannot be saved," Uncle Stupid repeated. "You must think now of the afterlife and how to ensure that you will then be made whole again. For Wang Mang will not permit you even that small bit of mercy if he can prevent it."

"And you must consider who has beaten and abused and ill-used you, and not just you, and whether he shall go free while all others pay with their lives." Minced Meat listened and nodded his head in understanding. "Will you do it? There must be some justice in this world."

"I will do it," Minced Meat said weakly.

"Very well, then. We must move quickly to protect your treasures." Uncle Stupid went to his chest, rummaged in it for a moment, and returned to the bench. "Take this jar. Sealed within is nothing but the giblets of a chicken. Place it where your pao is now kept. You must bring your own pao to me as quickly as possible. There is very little time."

They walked to the doorway and whispered together for a few moments. "Your pao will be held in safety," Uncle Stupid said in a quiet, reassuring voice, "and secreted into your tomb when the time is right. Even should I, myself, die it shall be arranged that it will be done."

After Minced Meat had gone, Uncle Stupid carried the lantern to the corner of the room and found his jug. He blew out the lantern and poured himself a cup of wine in the darkness. "The rat has been flushed from his hiding place," he said, raising his cup to me. "But still he scurries from corner to corner. Still he does not wish to die. Ah, but now the tunnels are all flooded or filled with stones!"

* * *

As I was being taken to visit Pingdi that morning, I noticed for the first time in many months a touch of warmth in the air. The corridors of the Hall of Celestial Purity were full of nobles and officials and their attendants and servants and the air was thick with the excited buzz of many voices.

The special attendant led me into a spacious antechamber alongside the grand hall itself. The Son of Heaven was already there, looking very small and troubled in the huge wicker chair. Wang Mang was at his side, stooped over and whispering in his ear.

"It cannot be!" Pingdi exclaimed in a frail, reedy voice. But Wang Mang, looking again sad and much wearied by his duties, nodded his head reluctantly. The Emperor became very pale and his head fell back. Then he reared forward, gulping at the air as though he were suffocating. Attendants and servants swarmed about him, patting his hands and pressing his back. A physician arrived and fought his way through the crowd and began applying a lotion to Pingdi's chest and throat. Then Pingdi was raised up and placed in his litter and carried off in the midst of the anxious crowd.

Only Wang Mang and I were left in the antechamber, for my special attendant had been swept up in the crowd that had taken Pingdi away.

Wang Mang looked at me searchingly. "You seem nothing but a little dog. A useless pet. But there have been too many strange occurrences . . . to be mere chance." He paused and stared at me. I met his eyes for a few moments but I did not care for this game and looked away. Nor did I care for the curious, bitter scent he gave off, like that of an old, corroded drainpipe.

"And what is chance, anyway? I do not believe in it. There are always forces at work."

"No, I believe you to be a demon—or guided or empowered by some demon or spirit." He walked toward me and stared at me again.

"But beware, demon," he said to me in a disinterested voice, as though he were reading a memorandum. "Just as men can be outwitted and overpowered by other men and demons, so it is that demons can be overpowered by men and other spirits."

"I too have powers," he said, as he walked away from me, his eyes probing the room. "Mind and will are not to be scoffed at. But such powers do not come easily." He no longer looked at me and seemed to be speaking to someone else.

"To gain them one must work and think, calculate and calibrate every

word, every move and gesture and nuance. And then, like a thunderbolt..."
He clapped his hands together. "...before people can turn around, before the
sun has time to move on the sundial, to set in motion the grinding,
unstoppable mechanism of government. And great things are accomplished
and enemies broken!"

"Still, mind and diligence do not always carry the day," he said, stroking
his beard. "So I must be always watchful of these other forces. These slippery
and unpredictable magics and tricks of demons and spirits, so easy in their
execution but so elusive in their source. Tricks and magics that can upend all
preparation and scheming."

Wang Mang turned his gaze on me again, but I ignored it and began to
sniff cautiously at the bronze crane that stood near the door looking out over
my head.

"To devour enemies as a silkworm devours a mulberry leaf. That is my
magic, demon," he said softly and then left the room. I was glad that he was
gone as his strange way of looking at and speaking to me made me uneasy.
But I did not like being in this big room alone. I wandered about for a few
moments, whimpering half-heartedly. Finding nothing of interest, I laid
down by the door.

Inside the grand hall I could see Wang Mang speaking to the anxious
throng of nobles and officials crowded about him. The Grand Empress
Dowager sat above him with an unhappy look on her face but Pingdi's throne
and my small throne beside it were empty. "The plot has sunk its toxic roots
deep into this court and spread them wide throughout the Empire." Wang
Mang said gravely, shaping each phrase with great care and deliberation.
"None of us are untouched by this poison."

"My love for my son, Wang Yu, is very deep." Here, a sob caught in
Wang Mang's throat. "But we cannot always transplant our own good into
the hearts of our offspring. And I cannot presume to consider my private
interests against the interests of the Imperial House. So it is that Wang Yu
must be arrested and punished with the rest." There was a stir in the crowd
and a faint cry of protest as the soldiers moved to seize Wang Yu.

"Neither can the Grand Empress Dowager presume at such an unhappy
time to impose on our beloved Son of Heaven the heavy burdens of high
office. Thus, she has decreed that the bestowal of his cap of manhood be
postponed until such time as corruptions are eliminated and the court has
again become peaceful."

"We have found that the Marquisa of Ping-O, whose hospitality and kindness have been so ill-used, is innocent of all wrongdoing." The Marquisa let out a loud shriek and all the court could hear her sobs of joyful relief. "And it is the wish of the Grand Empress Dowager and the Son of Heaven that the Queen of Chung-san , the mother of the Son of Heaven, whether guilty or innocent, be spared."

"But all others…" So unpleasant did Wang Mang's words now seem to be to him that he seemed to pull away from them as he spoke, "…and owing to the power and dark magic of the Wei Clan, the list of names goes far beyond the treasonous House of Wei… All others will be arrested and justly punished for their crimes."

Wang Mang then began to read the list, pausing after each name so as to allow the gasps and cries from the crowd to settle and the soldiers to remove them if they were in the hall.

> Wei Chang
> Wei Li
> Wei Yu
> Wei Feng
> The Princess of Ching-wu
> The King of Liang
> The eunuch Luo Li
> Wei Hu
> Wei Gao
> The Marquis of Hung-Yuan
> Wang Li
> Wei Jen
> The eunuch Wang Jen…

The special attendant came back into the room, placed the leash on me, and led me into the corridor. The calling of names and gasps and moans followed us down the corridor. Then we walked out into the bright sunlight and I could hear these sounds no longer.

* * *

In the weeks that followed, Uncle Stupid always kept a dagger close by. In the day, he would hide it in the folds of his robe and at night he would place it carefully under the pillow on which he laid his right arm. Often he would run his thumb across the blade.

"I can expect no thanks from Wang Mang," he would say when he did so. "The loss of his son is a great blow to him."

Then he would laugh and drink again from his wine cup. But despite his songs and laughter, I sensed within him a great sadness and a knowledge that something final and terrible was going to happen—and this made me also sad and apprehensive. Each night he took his jug and wine cup to bed with him, for he said that with so much death about him, he could no longer sleep unless drunk, and often after he had fallen asleep I would lick the sticky stain of wine that spread on the pillows or coverlets from his overturned cup or jug until all the flavor was gone from it.

He began to keep Prince all the time now for Shih Yu and to let him stay all night in our room—something that had never been done before. Prince liked very much my yak's hair rug and would fall asleep on it each night—with all my toys gathered within his two huge forelegs. Things were as they were before: he took no interest in me but would spend the whole day walking about with my silk mouse or cat or one of my balls in his mouth or chewing contentedly on them in a corner—ignoring my protests and chasing me away should I try to take any of the toys for myself.

One night Uncle Stupid carried two jugs of wine to bed with him. One, he placed between his thighs and the other he pressed against his hip with his left hand. He rolled me over with his right hand and ran his fingers along my belly, pleased that I showed no sign of pain. Gradually, the soreness in my belly had diminished. It no longer bothered me at all on bright and sunny days but on gray days, when the rain and snow flurries carried a damp chill, I sometimes felt an ache.

Uncle Stupid then busied himself with his wine jugs. "We must drink a toast to Wang Mang, Little Dragon. For his daughter has now become Empress. But more important: he has completed his composition."

He drank his wine cup almost dry but left a tiny bit that I could lick from the rim when he turned his cup toward me.

"It is in eight separate volumes and is to warn posterity of the dangers of an arrant son. A noble work, a brilliant work, I am sure. Though I do not believe I shall have time to read it."

"We should drink also to the Marquisa," he said and swallowed the entire contents of his cup, not giving me even a lick. "Were the acting profession not beneath so fine a lady, she would be the greatest actress in Chang 'An." He looked at me smugly. "I myself gave her that pretty doll that has brought so much blood and madness to the land."

155

"Let us drink also to the imprisonment—and death—of so many traitors. There are hundreds of them, you know, and many, surprisingly, were those who had spoken out against Wang Mang previously. Tortured and taunted by guards until they committed suicide. All of them."

Uncle Stupid clinked both jugs together and took a drink from each of them, leaving the cup on its side so that I could lick up the little that remained in it. He looked up at the ceiling above him.

"So many already dead . . . and many too of my brother eunuchs—for eunuchs can never resist the temptations of an intrigue, especially with a wastrel like Wang Yu . . . With so many dead, what does one fat, old eunuch matter?"

Suddenly, his face brightened. "Wang Mang's composition is to be published in all the Commanderies and Kingdoms. School officials will be obliged to teach it and those who can recite and explain it will have it recorded favorably on the official register of Meritorious Persons Preferred for Official Positions. It is to be a literary classic!"

"But I will get no thanks for my help in spurring the creation of this literary classic."

I had licked the wine cup clean but Uncle Stupid gave me no more to drink. Nor did he refill the cup, but continued to drink directly from each jug, first from one, then the other.

"Wang Mang will have his revenge. I do not believe the loss of Wang Yu is any more to him than the riddance of a great nuisance—although possibly since I am a eunuch I do not fully understand these things. But though he has made the best of it, to lose a son under such circumstances is an embarrassment."

"Those who embarrass Wang Mang do not live long, dear Xiao-Xiao." He took another drink from each jug.

"Ah, but why think!" he said after a pause and began to sing his song about the man who awakes in a field of fragrant grass, with his wine cup overturned and his guest departed, and his hands full of unremembered flowers. He kept singing until both jugs were finished and then he cradled one under each arm and fell asleep.

Much later, I was awakened by a deep menacing growl and I saw Prince standing above the toys and rug, bristling. The sour smell of a coiled, impending violence drifted to my nostrils and I heard tiny, scratching noises about the door. I also began to growl and, when I did so, the door burst open and men clad from head to toe in black rushed into the room, their spears and swords also black against the dim light of the corridor.

Prince charged them and knocked the first to the ground. I heard grunts and thumps and slashes and Prince fell with a mournful yelp to the floor. Uncle Stupid had just begun to stir when they were upon him, striking him in the chest and throat with their knives. He fell back with a moan and black stains began to spill out over his gray shirt. I leaped off the bed but before I could run to the corner I was swept up in a net and hurled roughly into a pitch-dark sack. I jumbled about helplessly in the sack as they ran down corridor after corridor, tossing the sack from one hand to another. Then I heard the neigh of a horse and breathed in its strong, sweaty smell and the sack was thrown into the back of a lurching, bumping carriage.

Struggling wildly within the sack, I managed for a moment to get my head free of it. I saw for just an instant the mist rising off Sea-Like Lake and beyond it the white walls of the East Lateral Courts gleaming in the moonlight. The windows and corridors were full of the light of lanterns and torches but I could hear no sound. A black clad man then saw me and with a curse pushed my head back into the sack and drew it tight.

I had no sense of it then, but this was the last time I was ever to see the Imperial Palace with its familiar but still endlessly intriguing rooms and corridors, its Garden of Ever-Present Breezes and Park of Verdant Radiance. And never again would I hear the delicate bird-like voices of Splendid Moon and Precious Wisdom and all the other concubines and maids—or the rough, laughing songs of Uncle Stupid.

PART II

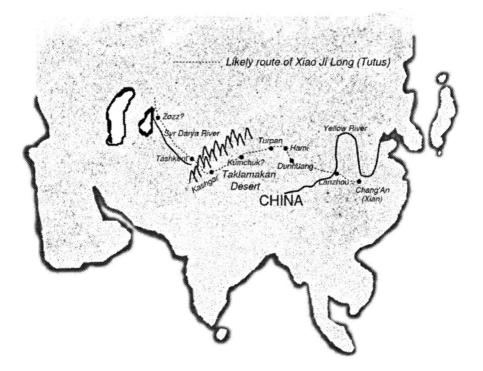

Likely route of Xiao Ji Long (Tutus)

Zozz?

Syr Darya River

Tashkent

Turpan

Hami

Yellow River

Kumchuk?

Dunhuang

Kashgar

Taklamakan
Desert

Lanzhou

Chang'An
(Xian)

CHINA

The Silk Road

...the splendour, squalor, suffering, and accomplishment
of travel older than history...

-Langdon Warner
  The Long Old Road in China

Cuteness is actually a survival factor [in evolution].

-Stanley Aren, psychologist, University of British Columbia,
  as quoted in the Article "Fido Has Lots to Tell You," *Mysteries of*
  History, Special Collector's Edition, U.S. News and World Report.

Note to Reader:

The contacts experienced during this part of Xiao Ji Long's (or Tutus') story were more fragmentary than those covering Part I. This situation was aggravated by the vast territory traversed, through regions and cultures only dimly recorded by history. Put simply, it was not always possible to ascertain exactly where our heroine was during this journey, nor was it entirely clear how long she lingered in the oasis towns of the Silk Road. There are, moreover, substantial gaps both of time and place in the contacts experienced. To better reflect the immediacy and lack of context of these contacts, I have employed the use of the present tense in Chapters 12, 13, and in the first section of Chapter 14.

Despite the difficulties cited above, I have sketched out in the preceding map my best guess as to the route followed by Xiao Ji Long along the Silk Road during the period covered by Book One. I hope the reader, while taking cognizance of these caveats, will find it helpful.

A word about the Silk Road: To avoid confusion, I have used the term "The Silk Road" although, as many have advised me, this name was coined only in the 1870's by the German geographer Ferdinand von Richthofen. This ancient route was actually called by many names in the course of Xiao Ji Long's travels—from the West Road (or East Road as you get closer to Kashgar) to more dramatic monikers such as the Road of Death, the Road of Fire and Ice, and, at least by one interlocutor, the Road of Silk and Death. S.D

9
Paradise Lost

The sack changed hands many times that night. I felt that I would be imprisoned forever in its darkness—drenched in the sharp smells of sweating horses and men in haste, in the midst of which faint scents of Uncle Stupid and Prince still lingered. Again and again, I heard the neigh of a horse and shouts of recognition. I would feel myself thrust through the air until the sack was snatched by the next rider. Then, once again, the rumble and clatter of saddles and hooves and the flanks of horses beating against me as the new rider raced off and I struggled to right myself.

When at last I was pulled from the sack, I found myself face to face with a squatting man in a coarse black cloak. His black eyes rolled from side to side as he appraised me, his mouth agape, two long, discolored, jagged teeth fixed before me. Although he held me by the scruff of the neck, I was so disoriented and jumbled by the rough handling of my rides that I hardly resisted and, when he put me on the floor and fastened a thick, prickly rope around my neck, I uttered only a squeaky bark of protest.

"So this is the famous beast of Abundant Talents," he said in a merry but menacing voice. The rope tightened when pulled—something that he demonstrated three times by running the knot deep into the flesh of my neck, a beam of satisfaction lighting up his eyes.

He then left me and ambled through the flaps of animal hide that covered the opening in front of me. The floor groaned and creaked and rolled about me and I could smell, stronger than all the other strange new scents that crowded in on me, the thick, monotonous smell of oxen, a disagreeable odor I had first discovered on my carriage rides with Li Huan through the streets of Chang 'An. Huge insensible beasts they seemed to me then, badly in need of chastising. I uttered a set of perfunctory barks in protest.

I could move only a few feet in any direction in the back of the wagon. Still, I could see and smell all about me sacks of grains and spices and dried fruits and meats, piles of rough cloth and mats, pieces of earthenware and bronze and ironwork of all shapes and sizes. From one of the sacks came a sweet, perfumy smell such as Splendid Moon possessed and I stretched the rope as far as it would go in that direction and raised my head to drink in this scent. I settled down in that spot and let out a low pulsing whimper.

Nowhere else did I detect the fine, delicate aromas of the Palace or of those with which I belonged. Not even those faint scents of Uncle Stupid or Prince—for the sack had been taken away and I could no longer catch even a whiff of it. I stretched out and began to whimper more loudly, flattening my belly against the floor as much as I could and planting my head between my paws, thinking of nothing except that I did not wish to be in this wagon.

From the front of the wagon, I smelt the oily, malevolent scent of the snaggle-toothed man and, very much like it, the smell of another man. Then the scent of smoking food drifted back to me and I realized that I was very hungry. I ran towards the front of the wagon but the pinch of the rope brought me to an abrupt halt and I began to yelp and bark and whine to let it be known that I wanted to be fed. The snaggle-toothed man stumbled finally into the back of the wagon. But he did not seem to know the rules of the Palace for he began to curse me in a harsh, swaggering way, smacking his hand with a bamboo switch, and then to beat me with the switch, his plump nose twitching with delight, as I lurched this way and that to avoid its sting.

Neither did the other one, a small, emaciated man who filled the air with the smell of sickness when he came close, know the rules of the Palace. He had a huge lump on the side of his thin neck—a sight so riveting and abhorrent that, even his savage flailings with the switch could not quell my ferocious barking at his approach. But he rarely took the trouble to come back to abuse me since my barking so enraged him that he would be quickly disabled by a fit of coughing and forced to return to the front of the wagon. Instead, whenever I barked or somehow incurred his displeasure, he would lean through the flaps and hurl blocks of wood at me, yelping with pleasure whenever he managed to hit me.

The snaggle-toothed one, however, did not hesitate to come back and beat me and I soon learned to keep my silence and rarely advanced even to the end of my rope. Besides, I found that, hateful as they were towards me, they did not stint on my food. The snaggle-toothed one brought to me steaming bowls of porridge flecked sometimes with chicken, sometimes with pork. He would watch me approvingly, urging me on as I gobbled them down. After I had finished, he liked to poke me in the ribs with his thick fingers.

"Did Your Excellency enjoy his meal?" he would say as he did so. This I disliked very much, but when I growled, he would strike me with the bamboo switch. After this happened several times, although I would always turn my head with displeasure when he poked my ribs, I made no sound.

"Prince Flatface has begun to learn a thing or two," he said as he stumbled back through the flaps after one such visit.

"Yes, this Xiao Ji Long will soon learn that he is no high-born prince, and not so lucky. And no dragon to be feared," I heard the sickly one respond in his shrill voice, ending his words with a coughing laugh.

"We should not say the name Xiao Ji Long."

"As if that would help us if the soldiers of the Emperor found us. As though every poor merchant takes a pug about in his wagon!" The sickly one said with a sneer, then a laugh and a cough. "I say we rid ourselves of the beast as we were paid to do. Each day's delay adds to our risk. We should strew its bones and flesh in tiny bits along the road. One li between each chunk."

"Ah, but we were paid to slaughter the little monster far to the West. For it is said to possess, or be possessed by, demonic powers that can only be extinguished in the West, where the power of the Dragon is weak."

"Who believes such nonsense? The danger is not from demons but from the Imperial Soldiers. Wang Mang has said he will make utmost efforts to find this creature. He is said to be overcome with grief and rage. First, the sorcerers of the House of Wei bewitched his son and led him into treason and execution. Now, he says, they have taken from the Son of Heaven his dear pet, the beloved pet of the Imperial Court."

"But has he not killed off the whole House of Wei by now—except for the old queen?"

"Wang Mang says that not all of the Wei Clan and their traitorous allies have been found out yet. He blames the theft of Xiao Ji Long on some old eunuch who has lived forever in the Palace and was supposed by everyone to be simple-minded. He is said to have used his black arts to cast the guards into a deathlike sleep and thus allow the bandits to steal into the Palace. And then, as though seized by a whirlwind, bandits, pug, and this old eunuch disappeared."

"Do you mean that old fool, Ting something or other, that everyone called Uncle Stupid? I used to see him many years ago at the gambling halls during the time of the Emperor Chengdi."

"Yes, that is the one."

"But, I thought he was killed that night."

"No, they say it was he who plotted the whole thing and then disappeared with the bandits."

"Well, I know nothing of this. But what does it matter to us? Someone has paid us well to get rid of the little beast. But only far to the West, mind you. At least as far as Lanzhou, and that we shall do," The snaggle-toothed one said in a firm voice.

"I always do exactly what is agreed… Unless there is some greater profit to be made by a different arrangement," he added slyly.

"The rule of the Empire is weak in the West," he mused after falling silent for a few moments. "But their desire to emulate Chang'An and the grand cities of the East is very great. I would wager that some wealthy family of nitwits could readily be found that would pay a fortune for such a rare creature, so esteemed by our nobility."

"To speak of selling the pug in such a manner is madness," said the sickly one, coughing with worry. "To be caught with this creature would mean ten thousand excruciating deaths. It is not only the soldiers one must fear. There is the reward, two catties of gold. For such a reward…" His voice trailed off into an anxious cough and they both fell silent for a few minutes.

"Perhaps you are right," the snaggle-toothed one said. "Still, it seems poor business to destroy such valuable merchandise."

"With each hour we keep this creature, the risk of discovery by soldiers grows greater and greater."

"Ah, but the route I shall take is little known and few soldiers would wish to venture there. At its end, just outside Lanzhou, is a place where we will find keen interest of a different sort in Prince Flatface."

"Ai-ya, now you would have us lose all to bandits!" the sickly one said, quite beside himself with coughing and alarm. "For I know the route you speak of and it is as thick with thieves as the markets of Chang 'An."

"You have become like an old village woman. The risk is small compared to those we have already run. And this way we can get good recompense for our trouble. For, as the Emperor has strictly forbidden the eating of pugs, this one will fetch a mountain of coin from those who will pay any price to do that which is forbidden. And the beast will vanish, leaving behind only a few well-gnawed bones."

He crawled back, stuck his head through the flaps and looked at me. "This one is already quite plump. By the time we get there, I will have it as fat and juicy as a six-month hog."

He said no more for a few moments and I heard only the clink of cups from their compartment as the wagon rattled forward. "How did you come to hear of the reward?" he asked the sickly one in a quiet voice.

"Only a deaf man could not have heard it. Criers have been running the streets of Chang'An ever since the dog was stolen," the sickly one said, trying to hide accents of fear within a loud, shrill voice and much coughing.

"But I thought you left Chang'An, as I did, on that very night."

"Well… of course, but such news travels like a fire in dry grass. It had spread far into the countryside even before the light of the torches from the great city had faded from sight."

"Hmmm, strange I had not heard of it," the snaggle-toothed one said, talking again in his quiet voice. "That is a great deal of money. Many a man would sell his son for far less than that—would indeed sell his sons and daughters for such a sum!" They both fell silent and I heard only the scraping of bowls, the smacking of lips, and the clink and jangle of cups.

I understood none of their words, but I knew, as they had showed again and again, that they meant me no good. The scents of fear and cunning and the shifting mix of hushed tones and false heartiness that came from the front of the wagon further unsettled me. When the snaggle-toothed one came through the flaps, even though he carried a large, aromatic bowl of porridge and chicken, I shrank away from him.

"Don't be afraid, Your Excellency," he said, setting the bowl before me and showing me a big smile as he watched me with hard, determined eyes.

"Eat well, Little Lucky One. Eat as much as you want." He reached towards me as though to pinch the flesh along my ribs and only laughed when I squirmed to avoid him. I could not bring myself to eat as long as he was before me but, after he had tired of watching me and returned to the front of the wagon, I stuck my head in the bowl and ate every last bit of porridge and chicken, licking the bowl long after everything was gone.

Late that night, I was awakened by the loud coughs of the sickly one and then a muffled cry. The carriage stopped and I heard something being dragged across the floor of the front compartment. Despite my fear of the switch, I uttered a low growl and then a quick, short bark, as I heard a thud beside the wagon and the murmured curses and grunting of the big, snaggle-toothed one, and the raspy sound of something being dragged through the dirt outside.

Then the wagon began to move again. I heard only the tiresome clatter of oxen and wagon and the snores of the snaggle-toothed one and I fell back asleep. I heard then the voice of Li Huan, alternately querulous and emphatic, as he walked about his room late in the night arguing with himself. Then the sweet delicate voice of Splendid Moon as she gazed out the window and sang to me. Then I heard her calling me and Uncle Stupid began calling me too but I could not see them for I had followed Prince into the woods and gotten lost. I ran frantically this way then that but I could catch neither sight nor scent of them, nor of Prince who had disappeared far into the woods.

I was on my side and my legs were still circling through the air when I was startled awake by the stumble of Snaggle-Tooth into my compartment. "Wake up, Prince Flatface, wake up and eat, Little Lucky One," he said in a merry voice. Smells of chicken and porridge fell off him along with dark, anguished odors that seemed to come from the sickly one. "Yes, perhaps, you do bring luck. For if money is the best form of luck, then, overnight my luck has doubled."

I did not wait for him to leave this time before diving into the bowl he placed before me, for as soon as I had awakened I felt as though I were starving. "Yes, snort away, Prince Dogchop," he said, mimicking the grumbling sound of my breathing. He looked dreamily at the top of the carriage, rubbing the switch between his hands, bouncing a bit with the bounce of the carriage.

"Perhaps you think, as foolish young women say, that you are too cute to eat. A false assumption! You are not nearly so pretty as a lamb—although indeed you do resemble one a bit—yet who troubles themselves about slitting their throats."

"No, you will provide many a fine—and very dear—dog cutlet to some lucky—and very wealthy—customer." He reached over and pinched my shoulder, then my ribs and haunch. Seeing the switch quivering in his other hand, I did not resist.

Many days passed; each one like the last. Four times a day, big bowls of porridge were brought to me—most of the time mixed with bits of pork or chicken. I gobbled down each meal eagerly, for food was the only thing of interest to me on this dismal wagon. Snaggle-Tooth was always very happy when I licked my bowl clean and would shower me with praise. But I cared nothing for his praise and only wished he would go away as had the sickly one. He did not always tie me up now for he disliked adjusting and readjusting the knot of the rope, which became ever tighter around my neck. And he would let me out of the wagon to do my necessaries whenever he stopped to stretch or relieve himself. Bare yellow-brown hills seemed always to surround us whenever I looked about during these stops or peered through the tears in the hides that covered the wagon. The sky and the road about us were filled with the same yellow-brown dust, as was the wagon and everything in it. And except for the smell of this dust, the only smells were the familiar, boring smells of the oxen and the wagon.

He did not often beat me with the switch now but sometimes, unpredictably, he would stumble, laughing, into the back of the wagon and flail it about, indifferent as to whether he hit me or the sacks about me. Then, too, several times the road led us past a tangle of caves in the brown bare hillside, outside of which stood humans, dirty and gaunt, wearing rags that barely covered them. This excited me and even the thought of the switch could not restrain me from barking at them. When I did so, Snaggle-Tooth would rush into the back, twisting his face and raking his tongue over his jagged teeth, and pull the rope tight and smack me hard with the switch.

I yearned for the company of those with whom I belonged: for Uncle Stupid, and Precious Wisdom and Splendid Moon, for old Li Huan whom I had almost forgotten, and sometimes even for the Son of Heaven. As I faded into sleep, I would think of them and wonder why they had not come to get me. I would then see Uncle Stupid as he fell back in his bed with spreading black stains on his white gown. A feeling of dread would fill me and the thoughts of those with whom I belonged would fade into blankness. It seemed proper that I should just eat and sleep and do nothing more until I could return to them. Each time I awoke I felt ravenously hungry and after I had eaten I felt immediately very drowsy. Thus it was that I became chubbily and sleepily accustomed to this life on the wagon, neither happy nor unhappy, merely existing.

One evening Snaggle-Tooth came through the flaps, merrier than ever. He twirled about awkwardly in the cramped quarters of the wagon, doing a kind of dance, holding my fourth meal—I could smell that it was not porridge this time—ceremoniously out before him.

"Here you are, Your Excellency," he sang out. "Something special for you tonight, Prince Flatface. Salted mutton and flatbread. Ah, yes, a most auspicious feast. For me, that is! Eat up, eat up, my plump little dragon." He placed the bowl in front of me, then patted my head and pinched my jowl. "Only one more day on this miserable, dusty road. Then I shall go my way and you shall go yours," he said happily, squatting down in front of me and watching me eat, which I did eagerly, despite his presence, for the smell of the mutton was much more exciting than my usual fare.

"I shall go to a fine inn and eat and drink to bursting—not this rubbish of porridge and chicken specks, porridge and bits of pork that you—despite your Imperial airs—love so well. No, a sumptuous feast shall be laid out for me! With a dozen or so young beauties as my companions. And you, you shall go to the dinner plate. I do not think they will wait too long. For certainly, they could fatten you up no more. You have already eaten more porridge than a whole village of starving peasants."

I paid no attention to his ranting, but gobbled down my food and continued to lick my bowl until he got up and went back through the flaps. I felt enormously heavy and drowsy after my meal, as I always did now, and plopped down on my side. I heard him stumbling about in the front of the wagon, clinking his cup, and singing loudly. After a while he settled down and began to sing in a soft, slow tearful voice. I stretched out my head and legs and was once again overpowered by the urge to sleep and dream.

When later I was awakened by the far off squeak of saddles, Snaggle-Tooth was still singing his mournful songs. The squeaking grew louder and I soon heard the snorting of horses and the padding of hooves in the dust. Snaggle-Tooth stopped his song and I heard him scrambling about the front of the wagon. Suddenly, the soft muted sounds of the horses erupted into the pounding of hooves and shouting voices and the rustle and clatter of saddles and swords. Outside the wagon, the sky lit up with torches. I jumped to my feet and ran to the side of the wagon, barking with every fiber of my being. Then, remembering the switch, I fell silent for a moment.

But Snaggle-Tooth did not come through the flaps. Instead, he screamed into the torch-lit night that he was a special emissary of the Son of Heaven and any who obstructed his journey would bring down the wrath of the Emperor upon themselves. A roar of laughter rose up outside and the wagon was shaken by the beating and slapping of swords against its ribs.

"These oxen were granted me by order of the Son of Heaven. You are forbidden to take them," Snaggle-Tooth shouted defiantly, but I smelt waves of fear washing off him.

"They seem quite ordinary, not at all Imperial," one of the bandits shouted back in the midst of another roar of laughter. He, and all the other bandits, spoke in harsh, rasping tones, such as I had never heard at the Palace, as though gargling some bitter and distasteful liquid.

"And you, Exalted One, show yourself so that we may pay homage to you and receive the gifts the Son of Heaven has sent you to give us."

Snaggle-Tooth made no reply and I heard him moving frantically about in front. I stared through a tear in the hide and saw all about us strange beings on horseback, covered with furs and rags, their faces blackened with dust and grime. But they smelt as men do and their eyes, bright and fierce, in the light of the torches were like those of men.

"Come out, Exalted One," the bandits shouted. "Do not insult us by your unfriendly manner."

Snaggle-tooth burst into the rear of the carriage. He ran wildly about the compartment, stuffing things into the pockets sewn both inside and outside his cloak. Then he swooped me under his cloak and climbed out the dark side of the wagon. I heard him panting and wheezing as I bounced along, pinned tight against his chest.

"Do not run off, Celestial One," the voice of the bandit sounded close behind us. I heard the slow deliberate stepping of his horse and sniffed, even from under the coat, a sour smell of violent intention like that Wang Yu had given off before beating Minced Meat.

Snaggle-Tooth ran faster. "You will regret your incivility," he stuttered, each word broken in two by a pant. "The Son of Heaven is not to be trifled with." I felt the jolt of his body as he turned and began to run downhill. Then I heard the quick rustle of a saddle and a whooshing sound. Snaggle-Tooth let out a short yell and released me and I fell, tumbling down the hill alongside his tumbling head, as his body ran a few more steps before lunging to the ground.

I came to a stop in a muddy marsh, a thin chilly stream running over my paws. Snaggle-Tooth's head was a few feet away from me, his eyes and mouth open, gaping into the black night. I could see the shadowy figures of the bandits on the ravine above me, cursing and grumbling as they pawed through his cloak, shouting with delight whenever they pulled something from one of the pockets. I crawled deep into the tall reeds of the marsh and pressed myself down into the cold mud.

After they had finished with the coat, one of the bandits came down to the marsh and, grabbing the head by its hair, pulled it from the mud. He pushed down on the teeth with two fingers and looked into the mouth. Then he raised the head above him and looked at it for a moment before tossing it carelessly back into the mud and walked up the hill.

I sat as still as I could, shivering in the cold, damp mud, and waited until all the sounds of the bandits—shouts and curses, things thrown about and out of the wagon, and, finally, the sounds of horses and oxen retreating into the distance—had stopped. Then I waited until at last the rising sun began to lighten the marsh. Only then did I crawl out from my hiding place. The head lay just in front of me, one eye looking at me out of the mud. Beyond it, I could see the stream widen into a small pool of water. I moved along the side of the ravine with my tail hung down, uttering a low, fearful growl, breaking into a run as I passed the head.

I drank thirstily from the pool of water and rolled in the grass along the bank to clean the still cold mud off my coat. Already I was hungry again, but I saw no bowls of food anywhere about me. I hesitated and looked about for Uncle Stupid, who always seemed to know what to do. Then, since I could think of nothing else to do, I began to walk along the sides of the stream, following the trickle of water that coursed slowly through the dry brown stalks of marsh grass.

10
I Become a Barbarian

At first, I could not walk very far. My limbs quickly became heavy and sluggish and I would begin to pant so hard that I became dizzy. Although the air was cool and dry, the sun seemed merciless. My journey was broken by many stops, when I would plop down in a cool bit of mud or in the shade of one of the rare stunted trees that grew along the creek until my panting slowed and the pounding sensation behind my eyes eased. Still, I rested in one place no longer than necessary, for I had found the world to be full of danger and, though I did not know why, I felt that I must continue along this stream until night began to fall. Then, I would find the thickest and driest clump of marsh grass and burrow into it, sleeping restlessly, my ears pricking up at each sigh of the wind, each rustle of grass.

As soon as I awakened, the rumblings and yearnings of my belly would begin and grow stronger with each moment. But still I could find no bowls, nor even any bits of food about. Nor did I see any humans, which seemed unnatural to me, for I had thought that they were everywhere in the world. There was only the slow, insistent trickle of the water before me, the waving of marsh grass when the wind blew and, here and there, a small bird that clung twittering to a stalk before flying off at my advance. Hunger gnawed at me incessantly throughout the day and even more so at night whenever some small noise stirred me to wakefulness. But, strangely, as the stream itself imperceptibly widened and its current became faster, I began to feel stronger, my head lighter, my pace quicker.

Such was my craving to eat that I began finally to tear and chew at the marsh grass. But it only caused me to gag and retch and did nothing to appease my hunger. Then one day, as I rounded a small bend in the stream, my nostrils filled suddenly with the pungent smell of ripening flesh. I began to run, following the scent up the slope of the bank. As I came closer, I heard the rustling of wings, and, mingling with the smell of ripe flesh, a sour and unfamiliar smell. In the stony ravine that stretched above me a brown and white antelope of the kind I had seen in the Park Of All the Beasts of the World lay crumpled. Its head was twisted to one side, its eyes gazing out with the same still look as the eye of the snaggle-toothed one. Red, rubbery coils spilled out from the white fur of its belly and a semi-circle of large black birds with hooded gray heads stood guard over it, looking on patiently as four of their kind tore at the flesh of the antelope with their hooked gray beaks, hissing and grunting.

I stayed for a long time at the base of the ravine, my body taut, my head stretched high, sniffing the air. Long ago, I had seen the head of such a beast, with its long, spiraling horns, on the huge platters brought before the Son of Heaven, and I remembered the juicy morsels of meat he had thrown to me, laughing as I caught them in midair. Despite the fear I felt, I moved slowly up the ravine, ready to flee at any moment. Wings flapped in annoyance and the vultures erupted in louder hisses and grunts. But they stayed their ground. I crept closer still, almost to the black hooves of the outstretched front legs of the antelope. One of the four vultures reared up from the carcass and tottered quickly toward me, widening its wings and sticking out its gray wrinkled neck in a way that made it look enormous. The curved, whitened point of its beak waved menacingly before me. I turned and ran down the ravine, stopping when I saw that it had not pursued me.

From below, I watched intently as the vultures tore at the antelope's flesh and pulled the red rubbery coils still farther from its belly, fear and desire welling up within me, the rumblings of my stomach urging me to action. I rushed up the hill barking and growling. Several vultures took flight but two of them rose from the carcass and waddled toward me, their hooked beaks stretched far forward, their black eyes glaring at me. I stopped short of them but sent up such a show of snarling and snapping, jumping from side to side in front of them, that they came no closer. This standoff continued for some time until finally they waddled back to the belly of the antelope and I was ceded a place at the raw, red haunch of its front leg.

The meat was tough and stringy, not at all like the tender delicacies of the Palace, and I had to work hard at it with my jaws before I succeeded in tearing off even a tiny bit. But to be immersed in the flesh of this animal was deeply satisfying. I felt too a determined ownership of this haunch: I would let nothing drive me away from it. I gobbled down a tiny piece of meat and then another just a bit bigger. I was tearing hard at another piece, my muzzle deep into the red flesh of the antelope, when there was a great flapping of wings and the vultures flew off. I lifted my head, smeared now with blood and fat and bits of flesh, and only then did I catch the scent. It was both like and unlike the rich smells of Prince and the other dogs who gathered around me when I received my award—the scent of a dog surely but thinner and more penetrating than I had smelt before. I heard a low snarl and saw him far above me in the ravine, picking his way through the rocks with an easy, confident step, headed directly toward me. His coat was rough and torn, with large bald patches, and his ribs stuck out of his lean flanks. He bared his teeth menacingly as he came closer to me.

My tail collapsed and my ears flattened with fear but still I could not bear to give up my place. I kept tearing at the antelope, growling back at this dog-like creature, my eyes fixed on him. His snarl became louder and more savage and I could see flecks of spittle flying from his long snout. Suddenly, he leaped over the antelope and I felt a sharp pain in my rear haunch as I abandoned my piece of flesh and fled zigzag down the ravine, barely keeping my footing on the rocks. At the bottom, I feinted to one direction, then another and ran in a tight circle into the marsh grass. But he had not pursued me. I saw him waving his head up and down above the antelope and then he settled down beside it, thrusting his snout deep into its innards.

I watched him sadly from my hiding place in the marsh grass, hoping he would go away. But as the moon began to rise, two more such beasts joined him, just as thin, mangy, and savage and giving off the same penetrating scent. After much snarling and waving of heads, they reached agreement on their places about the antelope. I rose from my hiding place, knowing that I would have no more chances at the antelope, and ran farther along the stream bed. Night was coming on; my stomach was still growling despite the few chunks of meat I had managed to gobble down. My haunch ached and was matted with blood. I sought out a thick clump of marsh grass and burrowed into it and there I stayed until dawn, licking and nursing the wound on my haunch, snatching only a bit of fitful sleep now and then when utter weariness overcame me.

Late in the afternoon of the next day, I came to a place where the stream turned down sharply over a steep hill. Below, it joined another stream and spread out into a large black swamp covered with marsh grass and tangled bushes and brambles. Beyond the swamp on the rise of a hill stood small dust-covered huts of mud and stick and, beyond them, yellow-brown cliffs riddled with caves.

I nestled in between two large rocks, nicely warmed by the sun, and studied the scene before me. Three large black and white hogs rooted in the black soil of the slope that ran down from the village into the swamp. Above them, on the dusty paths, I saw what looked like humans walking about, though they were too far away to be seen clearly and the dense, overpowering smell of the swamp swallowed up all other smells. This both excited and alarmed me because, though I craved the company of humans like those with which I belonged, I could no longer be sure that any of them would bear me goodwill. And I did not wish to leave these rocks, so comfortably warm and soothing to the ache in my haunch. I sat there for along time, watching the village, thinking of very little. When, at last, the sky above the cliffs began to turn red and the rays of the sun weaken, I got up from the rocks and started down into the swamp.

Darkness descended quickly on the swamp and hampered my search for a new resting place. I wandered at random, dripping with black mud, taking care to keep well away from the hogs I could still hear rooting and snorting along the slope. It was only when the light of the moon had begun to creep over the steep hill behind me that I spied a kind of tunnel in the thickets of briar and vine that covered the far side of the swamp. Hardly able to fit into it, I went down on my haunches and worked my way through it, finding at the end that it widened into a patch of solid earth, covered with crushed, dry marsh grass and overhung by an outcrop of rock. I turned around in a circle, once, twice, then another time, pawing and kicking up the grass. Then I started to lie down but rose again and turned once more in a circle. At last it felt right to me. I lay down with a big sigh, and fell quickly asleep, sleeping better than I had since I left the wagon of the snaggle-toothed one.

When morning came, I crawled back through the tunnel and began to pick my way through the swamp, heading for the black slope that led to the village, badly wanting some food and vaguely hoping that there might be one there who was friendly and wanted to play. The black and white hogs were already there, snorting and grunting, their legs sunk deep in the black mire and their sides covered with filth and sores and flies. Just above them, on the dusty path that ran along the edge of the slope, a group of scrawny, uneasy dogs skulked about, their fur rough and patchy like that of my assailant, one of them with thin teats that almost dragged the ground. The dogs no sooner got a whiff of me than they sent up a thunderous racket of barking and howling. But they did not venture down the slope, and only milled about, inciting each other to louder and louder barks and howls of protests. In response to this uproar, the men, women and children ran out from the village and began to beat them with sticks and switches.

These humans were like those I had seen from the wagon, standing before their caves. Their dust-covered legs and arms were thin as sticks and their clothing nothing but rags. Their faces were gaunt and hollow-eyed, and only their knobby cheekbones, shiny in the morning sun, seemed free of the ever-present brown dust. Many of them walked strangely with their heads thrown back, revealing lumps on their necks like that of the sickly one on the wagon. The dogs ran off yelping and squealing, only to re-establish themselves at the end of the path and resume their barking.

Then someone saw me and all the humans began to shout and jump about with excitement. Some of them called and waved as if to summon me while other hurled stones and sticks at me. A few children began to run down the hill but were called back by the others. Badly frightened, I began to run along the side of the hill but when I came near several of the hogs, they abandoned their slop and, with a chorus of fierce squeals and grunts, charged at me. I tumbled down the hill trying to evade them and when I reached the bottom of the slope, I fled back into the swamp, not stopping until I had reached the very end of my tunnel.

That night, and each night thereafter, I crept out of my tunnel and made my way through the swamp onto the black slope. In the day, I stayed curled in my lair or in the brambles outside it as I did not choose to risk another encounter with the hogs, the dogs or the humans of the village. But the nights too were full of danger, for the black slope was full of swarming, nattering rats, which, like me, came there only in darkness.

The pickings of the slope were meager—only the contents of wooden slop buckets and the most inedible and disgusting of scraps and refuse were thrown down the slope—and first painstakingly processed by the pigs. I ate whatever seemed to me to offer any promise of nourishment. Then I would wait for a moment to see if I would retch it up—which usually I did.

For these loathsome meals I had inevitably to fight with the rats. I soon lost a piece of my ear to them and had an aching wound on my muzzle that never seemed to heal. And there was hardly a spot on my flanks or legs that did not have either a fresh rat bite or the memory of one. For my part, I found that when I seized them by the neck and shook them from side to side with all

DON PHILLIPS

my might they would grow limp. I would have tried to eat them too but the excitement of my kills always generated an enormous uproar among the rats. They would come scurrying across the slope, squealing and biting at me, but then their attention would focus on the limp rat, and after it was well torn up, a huge quarrel would erupt among them, and while I crept back into the marsh, they would fall on each other and only a few would emerge from this great, squirming, writhing mass with anything more than a bloody stump for a tail.

Besides the refuse of the black slope, my hopes for food centered on the rare kill of a frog and on the berries that grew in the brambles about my lair, which I found I could pluck without injury from the thorns if I raised myself up on my hind legs. I had great difficulty in swallowing the frogs and even greater difficulty in keeping them on my stomach – for their texture, at once rubbery and mushy, was repellent to me. And, after one of them loosed on me a vile spray that covered my muzzle in a suffocating foam, I no longer pursued them. The berries did little to quell my hunger and, in any case, dissolved into mush, and then disappeared, as the summer grew hotter. But then I began to find nuts littering the floor of the swamp near the few scraggly trees that grew there. And though my belly always ached after I ate them, their thin shells were easy to crack and they seemed to better subdue my hunger and to give me strength.

There was no time, day or night, during my life in the swamp when I did not feel pangs of hunger and stirrings of fear. I had many enemies—the hogs, the rats, the skulking dogs of the village, and the knobby-cheeked villagers themselves. Of friends, I had none. Sometimes I would try to think of Uncle Stupid, Splendid Moon and Precious Wisdom, and old Li Huan but I could not make these reveries vivid. They dissolved before the bleakness of my life and I was left with only a vague, dull feeling of sadness and loss. Sometimes, too, just to relieve my solitude, I would suddenly let out a few crisp barks and a kind of howl and just as suddenly silence myself, fearful that these sounds would bring on some calamity. I began to bring sticks and pieces of wood, which had never before interested me, back into my tunnel and to chew them incessantly. And sometimes in the full heat of the afternoon sun when all was still about me, I would run around in circles in the small clear space just outside my tunnel and leap into air as though trying to snatch some treat dangling above me, repeating this again and again until, panting and exhausted, I crept back into the shade of the lair, unable to continue.

I had a special enemy in the village, a crippled boy whom I often spied

180

peering at me just before the hogs came out at dawn from behind a bush along the rim of the slope. While the other villagers seemed to stay in their huts and cower at night and would on no account come down the slope, he began, late at night and early in the morning, to creep farther and farther down the slope, balancing himself uncertainly with the forked stick he used as a crutch and had to pull again and again from the muck.

Sometimes when I came out of the swamp and started up the slope, he would be crouched down behind a sparse bush or stunted tree and would jump up and throw stones at me. But as these fell nowhere near me, I paid little heed to him and continued my foraging, taking care only that he did not come closer to me. Then, he began to use a slingshot and of this I had to pay heed, for on one occasion he actually did hit me—right on the wound in my haunch—and I fled yelping back into the swamp. Each night after that I found him hiding ever farther down the slope but, as I took care to stay well away from him, he was not able to do me any harm and his stones plopped uselessly in the muck before me.

Late one morning, however, before the hogs had come out, when the sky had just begun to lighten, I found to my surprise that he had positioned himself behind a stunted broken tree at the base of the hill between me and the marsh. As I came down the slope towards the trail that led into the swamp, he loosed a few stones from his sling at me, which came so close that they splashed muck onto my whiskers. I ran back up the slope only to hear the first grunts and snorts of the hogs making their way through the village. I ran far to one side of the slope, then reversed course and ran far to the other side. Heavy rains had fallen over the past few days and there was deep black mire on both sides of the trail.

The boy, his sling now tucked into a sash about his waist, leaned on his crutch and waved a long sharpened stick at me. The hogs snorted and grunted, much closer now. I burst into a run down the hill straight at the boy. Then, with a quick twist of my body I dodged to the left of him and raced through the broken branches of a tree, scraping myself badly on their jagged points. The boy spun round, losing his balance in the effort to thrust his spear at me. But he soon picked himself out of the branches, whining and cursing, and began to pursue me, his left arm draped over the front of his crutch, the crude spear balanced in his right hand. I hurried along the trail, which became ever narrower and more treacherous as the squishy, deep black mire closed about it. Finally, I came to a point where no trail was visible. As I hesitated, making sure to get my bearings—for I knew there was a thin line of solid ground meandering under the muck, the boy came at me with a great rush, moving quickly despite his crutch. With a wild yell, he hurled the spear at me. It stuck a glancing blow on my brow, just in front of my ear.

My vision blurred and I felt for a moment as though I could not run forward and needed to fall down. I looked back: the force of his throw had carried him off the path and his crutch was sinking ever deeper into the mire. He swung round on it and fell over backward into the mud. I shook off the tremor in my legs and tread unsteadily atop the mire until I reached a stand of marsh grass, then wriggled deep into it. The boy was waist deep in the mud now, struggling and filling the whole marsh with his wails. Soon a crowd formed at the top of the slope and I could hear them bickering amongst themselves and shouting down into the swamp.

"Cheegee, have I not told you never to go there?" A woman's voice shrieked above the rest. "Come up, come up here. Obey me at once." But the boy had ceased struggling now and only wailed louder.

"Ai-ya, the demons will surely get him," another woman shouted.

"Yes, I can hear them creeping through the reeds," another woman screamed, as a gust of wind blew through the swamp.

"Cheegee, come here this moment," the first one shrieked again. "Misbegotten wretch! What crime have I committed to have such a stupid, disloyal son? Demons take me now for I do not want to live with such a son!" And she continued to shriek for a long time, cursing Cheegee and herself and crying out to the demons as, all about her, the villagers echoed her plaints. But none would come down into the swamp.

Finally, when the sun was well up in the sky, I heard the splash of feet in the swamp itself and shrill, fearful voices cursing Cheegee and imploring the demons to spare them. I raised up, ready to flee, as three old women, spattered with mud and shaking with terror came down the trail. The boy had ceased wailing now and stared at them wide-eyed, with his arms stretched out on top of the mud.

For a long while they stayed on the trail, continuing to curse him and to plead with the demons, one of them shaking over their heads a slender stick with tiny bells as they did so. Finally, they waded into the mire and amidst much cursing and shrieking and slipping and falling, they managed to drag Cheegee to the trail and began to make their way hastily out of the swamp, one of them pulling the boy, the other pushing and beating him with a stick, the third ringing her tiny bells above them—while Cheegee alternated between yelps of pain and resentful, weakly defiant cries of "I have wounded it!"

That night, although my head hurt badly and my ribs and ever-sore haunch ached from the scraping of the branches, I made my way up the slope again. I had another fight with the rats and, when I left them, my neck and muzzle were smarting from three fresh bites. As I slunk back to my tunnel, despite the cool of the morning, I found myself panting and snorting as though trapped in the glare of the summer sun. And then a terrible shivering came over me. Barely able to crawl to my lair, I plopped over on my side and fell into a dull half-sleep, my body wracked again and again with gusts of burning heat followed by shivering cold.

I heard Uncle Stupid calling "Xiao Ji Long." But I could neither bark nor move in response to his cries. Gradually, his voice died away and I filled with fear—of the rats, the hogs, the skulking dogs, the crippled boy, and the villagers with their knobby cheekbones and strangely-tilted heads and swollen throats. I tried to summon up the memory of those palace days full of play and carefree wanderings, but I could not—for all I knew now was a misery and constant hunger that no longer came just from my belly but danced always before me. And fear—not the fear I had known at the Palace, which was like a sudden and ever-so-short storm in an endless sunny day of kindness and indulgence. But an ever-present, ceaselessly gnawing fear of everything about me, with never a pause for play or affection.

11
Life Begins Again

I gripped the nipple tight in my mouth, sucking hard as I tried to snuggle in closer to the warm darkness of my mother. But the chill that traveled along my spine would not go away. I tugged harder, snorting and mewing with impatience but still no milk would come. A feathery dampness touched my muzzle and I opened my eyes. The roof of my tunnel was covered with white and here and there a spray of snow fell through. I got up and stretched, my legs stiff with the cold of the morning. But the shivering and fever were gone and in their place the ache of hunger throbbed.

Far above in the village, I could hear shouts, drums, and the clatter of sticks beaten together and, for the first time, peals of laughter and delight rang out of its dusty misery. I crept out of my tunnel. The clean, fresh snow had transformed the swamp about me, burying its odors and muffling its sounds. Only a few big flakes of snow fell now and I leaped into the air and bit at them, as I remembered doing one time on the path that ran by Sea-Like Lake while Uncle Stupid and Precious Wisdom laughed at me.

Although it was daylight, I made my way through the swamp and up the slope. A few hogs rooted in the snow-covered refuse but paid no attention to me. I continued all the way to the top of the slope, heedless of the danger. The villagers were far away, gathered about a line of wagons interspersed with horses and donkeys and strangers in bright-colored woolen coats and hats. The skulking dogs were nowhere to be seen. The drumbeats were louder now and the shouts and laughter of the villagers, and the echoing shouts and laughter of the strangers, rang out crisply against the stillness of the snow-covered paths and huts. I stopped and watched them anxiously. Then, abandoning myself to the throbbing of my hunger, I left the slope and walked into the village.

I had taken only a few steps when a great on-rushing flood of odors burst over me, sweeping aside all other smells and sensations. At the other end of the village, well away from the other wagons, a cart stood tilted forward, its long wooden shafts leaning into the snow, untethered. It was from there that the smells came. I headed toward it, breaking into a trot, and despite the danger I knew to be all about me, I could not keep myself from uttering a faint, quivering whimper such as I used to make at the Palace in expectation of some treat. A cage of thick wooden poles held a cargo of bones of all shapes and sizes within the cart, with here and there the long line of the jaw of a cow or horse still lined with teeth. A layer of hides covered the top of the wagon and just behind it, a ledge jutted out from hillside.

I ran up the hill, the snow slipping under my feet, and leaped on the hides. As they were only loosely tied, I dug easily through them, and suddenly I dropped into the midst of the bones, drinking in the dizzying power of the smells all about me. The wind blew up and howled as it raced through the village, carrying off one of the hides, and snow swirled about the wagon. But I paid no heed to this and only burrowed deeper into the bones, biting and sniffing at every one I could get at, ignoring the jar and bump of their sharp, hard edges against my wounds. Though they had been scraped, there were still bits of flesh and fat and grizzle to be had.

Voices came closer to the cart. I became still and smelt the approach of men and, with them, a donkey. I could barely see them in the swirling snow as they tethered the donkey to the cart. Then one of them began to curse and I felt him climb onto the top of the cart. Still cursing, he moved the hides about while the other pulled them far down the side of the cart and tied them to the poles. Shouts of command rang out from the other end of the village. The one on top of the wagon climbed down and sat himself on the donkey. As the bone wagon began to creak and jostle along the path, my paws slipped from bone to bone as I struggled to balance myself in the jumble of pointed and irregular shapes. At last I settled into the spacious curve of the hip bone of some cow or water buffalo, gripping the leg bone of some smaller animal tight between my teeth.

I peeped out into the swirling snow. The villagers waved and shouted, turning their faces away from the wind, as the wagons passed by them. Then all trace of the village was gone and the wagon descended a long, low hill and entered onto a broad, level plain. Soon the wind and snow ceased and a deep stillness engulfed us, interrupted only by the creak of the wagons and the muffled roll of their wheels. I thought only of the bone in my jaws, gnawing it with unwearying determination as the clouds first brightened and then grew dark again. Gnawing it until a sweet paste began to ooze through its cracks, until long after it had began to buckle and break and had lost all flavor. Finally, I let it drop.

I looked out from under the hides. The white of the snow seemed to stretch out forever. Above it, the sky was clear and black and, just above the horizon, a thin slice of moon hung. I was aware again of the aching in my haunch and the soreness of the bites that covered my body flamed up each time a bone jolted against them. Although I was glad to leave the harsh, miserable life of the swamp, a shudder of fear and anxiety ran through me—for I was all alone now and did not know what next awaited me. I began to howl but, realizing my error, stopped short. The driver slowed his donkey and rose up on it. Then he let out an anxious shout and hurried the donkey toward the wagon in front of him.

* * *

The sun was high and hot, easing my aches and sores with its warmth and stirring up to their fullest the intoxicating odors of the bone wagon. There was no longer any sign of snow. Bare brown hills lay on both sides of the dusty road before us with here and there a tree hung with patches of dry leaves. Ahead I could see the walls of a city. But the wagons veered off before we reached it and turned into a vast dusty field, teeming with donkeys and horses, with bunches of sheep and goats running across and beside us, with wagons and tents and tables and rugs covered with food, pots, and ironwork, bolts of cloth, and other things beyond number. And everywhere, men and women and children ran and shouted and bumped against each other. I watched them intensely, for I had not been this close to humans in a very long time and was, as always, exceedingly curious about their doings, which might lead to the bestowal of a morsel of food—or a kick. Here and there I saw the wooly, outstretched neck of a camel and, though my chest filled up with the urge to bark—for these ungainly, foul-smelling beasts had always enraged me when they were paraded in front of the Son of Heaven—I kept my silence.

The bone wagon stayed well behind the other wagons as it wended its way through this confusion. Men and women moved aside and averted their faces as it passed while dirty-faced children held their noses and scrunched up their faces, shouting and waving their hands as if fanning away the stench, their comrades laughing and jumping up and down beside them.

Then I was seen! First by one child, who ran screaming and pointing alongside the wagon, turning in circles with excitement, then by another, and another. Soon a pack of children surrounded and chased after the bone wagon, screaming and shouting, waving their arms, holding their noses, bumping against and pushing and fighting with each other, knocking each other down and picking themselves out of the dust—seeming every bit as ungoverned and dangerous as the rats who had assailed me on the black slope. They began to beat on the sides of the wagon with sticks and to poke the sticks between the poles, trying to wound me, laughing so hard as I growled and yelped, and bared my teeth, as I twisted and turned to avoid the sticks, that many fell to the ground.

The bone wagon stopped and the driver dismounted and came round to the cart. He looked, not like the brightly-clad strangers that had stood beside the other wagons, but like a villager, his clothing a jumble of rags, his eyes dull and hollow behind his knobby, burnished cheek bones. The children hushed for a moment and pulled back from the wagon as the driver approached, shouting and swearing at them. When he saw me his jaw dropped, and he leaned back as though struck dumb. And the children rushed again to the side of the wagon, screaming and pushing and laughing as before. Their sticks began to find their mark now and I yelped in pain as one of them struck a rat bite on my neck and another stuck deep in my ribs. But my cries only excited them all the more as they bumped and jostled against each other, frantic to secure the best position from which to wound me.

Suddenly, the sticks fell away as two children, bigger than the others, forced their way to the front of the mob, knocking the sticks to the side as they did so. With pale, long faces and black, fiery eyes, they looked and smelt very much the same. But the hair of one was fixed in a long braid while that of the other was wound into a topknot and, when they pressed against the poles to look at me, I could smell a trace of maleness in the braided one.

"Leave it alone," they said, turning and facing the others, speaking at almost the same time in a strange, broken Chinese. But in response the crowd grew louder, re-gathering its strength. One boy stepped forward, waving his stick and shouting angrily. The braided one knocked the stick away with one hand and struck him in the nose with the other and he fell to the ground wailing. Another boy stepped forward, swearing at them, and the top-knotted one stuck her leg behind him and pushed him to the ground.

The crowd fell back and grew quieter but still they milled uncertainly about the wagon, undecided as to what to do next. The girl-child turned to me, "Shushee," she said in a soft voice and she pushed her hand through the poles as if to pet me but could not reach me.

A deep, booming voice then sounded and the driver woke from his daze and began chasing the children away. A crowd of adults began to approach the wagon, a man with thick black hair falling to his shoulders and a flowing black beard such as I had never seen before, towering over them. He wore a padded silk jacket embroidered with ropes of blue and gold threads and loose blue trousers of wool. He had the same close-set, intensely black eyes as those of my two rescuers and his face was just as pale above his beard. He grasped each of the twins by the shoulder and began to lead them away but the girl-child jumped up and down, pointing at me and calling out "Shushee, Shushee" again and again. The tall man turned and looked at me, then threw off a deep laugh like the beating of a drum.

"What curious beast is this you have found, Ayaru?" he said and laughed again. "Something the vultures forgot to pick clean?"

He summoned the driver with a crisp twist of his fingers and walked him to the side of the wagon. The tall man leaned over him, waving his arms in forceful yet graceful movements while the driver stooped below him, his face and manner at once fearful and stubborn. The crowd moved away from the bone wagon, forming a circle around them. They began to join in the discussion, laughing when the tall man wiggled his outstretched finger at me and laughed, sighing when the driver sighed with a weary shake of his head. Finally, the tall man pulled a sack from within his jacket, took three dried figs from it and pressed them into the hand of the driver.

There was a flicker of excitement in the eyes of the driver but still he shook his head, slowly and sadly. The tall man tossed his hands in the air and rolled his eyes heavenward. With a thundering grunt he pulled another fig from his sack, pressed it into the palm of the driver and folded his hand shut over the figs. Still, the driver shook his head, a little more slowly and sadly this time. The tall man snatched the figs from the driver's hand and began to walk away in huge strides, grabbing the twins by the back of their coats and dragging them on tiptoe alongside him. A look of terror seized the driver and he chased after him and the crowd ran after both of them, reforming a circle around them.

As I watched the hands of the tall man fly up and down above the cringing driver and the heads of the crowd, the ache in my haunch welled up again and a chill ran through me—for the sunshine no longer fell on the wagon. After a very long time, the tall man rushed back to the cage. He stared at me disgustedly, scrunching his face and shaking his head. With a slow, climactic movement, he pulled first one fig from his sack, then another, and another... and placed them in the hand of the driver. Finally he produced a fourth fig and, taking a knife from round his waist, cut it in half and placed it on top the other three.

The driver looked down blankly at his hand and nodded in assent and the crowd sent up a cheer. Then he climbed on top the wagon and, with great difficulty and much cursing and yowling whenever the bones pinched his shins or ankles, he extricated me from the wagon. He leaned over the top of the wagon and dangled me before the tall man by the scruff of my neck.

But the tall man wrinkled his face in disgust and would not take me until Ayaru found an old cloth with which to wrap me. I hung there for a few moments, squirming and wriggling in the driver's bony grip, as the crowd pressed closer so as to better stare at me. Then the tall man snatched me roughly, and rolled me up in the cloth and tucked me under his arm. He raised the remaining half-fig high above him and sweeping it through the air in a series of spirals, he pressed it into my mouth. At this, the crowd around us erupted, dancing with laughter as we plowed through it. So stunned was I by his wild behavior and all that had gone before, that I let the fig rest in my mouth and did not begin to chew it until we were far away from the wagon and the tall man had let Ayaru pull me away from him and fold her arms around the bundle of cloth that held me.

* * *

I had become very afraid. The booming voice and heavy bold stride of the Father frightened me. [In all the contacts I experienced involving this merchant family, the "Father" and "Mother" were inevitably referred to as Hayar and Majiar, even by other adults. Originally, I believed these to be their actual names but Professor Komodorovich has persuaded me that it is more likely that they are corrupted forms of the words for "father" and "mother" in an ancient, now extinct, dialect (somewhat akin to Armenian) and, in all likelihood, used with honorific intent. "Shushee," he believes, was almost certainly a term of endearment, but he can offer no insight into the etymology of the word—S.D.]

Although the twins, Ayaru and Kaidan, spoke to me in high, sweet voices as if I were a baby, I stayed on guard whenever they came near me and watched them carefully out of the sides of my eyes. "Shushee, Shushee," they would say again and again and, although this sound meant nothing to me, I learned that it foretold that something was expected of me and my stomach would tense whenever I heard it. Although I did not protest when they picked me up, and they always rushed to do so, it caused me to tremble—for I could not be sure of their intentions. They had, in their smell and demeanor, a trace of that savage, chaotic quality that I had found all children to have—and which made them the most unpredictable and unsettling of all humans.

There were mice in the campsite, and smallish rats, frantic, pathetic creatures, not one-third the size of the monsters with which I fought on the black slope. But even these scared me. I had only to hear one of their loathsome squeaks or see one rush across a carpet and my whole body would shake and my teeth commence to chatter.

But most of all, I feared the Mother. From the first, she did not like me. Always, she carried a horsehair flapper with which to swat flies and whenever she saw me, she would smack it in her hand and, her eyes flashing and the coins she wore round her wrists and ankles jangling and glistening, she would say with a snort, "Three and one-half figs wasted!"

When I was carried into their campsite from the bone wagon, the Mother had rushed up to us and stripped the cloth off me. With one hand she grabbed her nose and thrusting the other hand over her head and twisting her fingers as the Father had done by the bone wagon, she shouted, "Clean that thing. Not one step further until that vile beast is cleansed."

Kaidan and Ayaru had rushed me off to a nearby stream, rubbing my flanks and belly and scrubbing my head with a harsh-smelling, gray substance that badly stung my wounds. But I did not bite at them, as I had always done half-playfully with Splendid Moon, who bathed me in the same fragrant water in which she herself bathed. Instead, I stood rigid and trembling before them, trying to shrink away each time they reached out to touch me.

When we returned from my bath, the Mother looked at me with wide eyes. "It looks even worse clean than filthy!" she yelled, grasping her forehead. "Look at those dripping sores. And such ribs! I have seen skeletons with more flesh. What are we to do with such a miserable creature?"

"It is an unusual beast, "the Father replied confidently. "I have never before seen anything like it. And one can always find some way to profit from that which is unusual."

"Like your barbarian powder?" the Mother said with a snort.

"It cost me but three and a half figs," the Father said in an aggrieved voice.

"Three and a half figs I would rather have eaten myself!"

"The twins were very keen to have it." With that, Ayaru and Kaidan began to cry out "Shushee, Shushee."

"It is cute as a little monkey, Mother," they shouted in unison.

"Cute?" sneered the Mother, "I have seen scorpions I would rather have in my home."

The Mother complained always about my strange ways. Although I was very hungry, I no longer cared to eat in front of others. Most of the time, I would carry off the mushy meal they gave me mouthful by mouthful from the bowl into some dark passageway between the sacks of cloth and dried fruit and grain. Other times, I would eat so fast that I retched it up immediately and when I would try to eat it again, the Mother would scream and rush at me with the horsehair flapper.

When the twins beckoned to me to sit with them, I would not come but instead would seek out some passageway among the sacks. But if they chanced upon me, while I was asleep, I would leap to my feet immediately, snarling and snapping. When they called out "Shushee", though I would tense inside, I would not show any sign that I heard them. Instead I would curl up more tightly and lay there with half-shut eyes and hope they would forget about me.

Sometimes when I would have a fit of trembling, the Mother would imitate me, shimmying her head and shoulders, sending the twins into giggling laughter.

"Gods of the Earth and Sky and you gods who rule over domestic animals which are useful," she would say, emphasizing the last word and grasping some amulet or small statue, "rid me of this creature who is infected with demons and ghosts."

* * *

Many days passed at the campsite and, as they did, my spirits revived and my strange ways began to fade.

Each day the twins rubbed me with a sweet-smelling ointment, pressing it delicately into my wounds. I was given two big bowls of mush a day, and in the morning, a dollop of thick, pungent fat was thrown in. "To make its coat shine!" beamed the Father. Although the Mother disapproved, the twins also would sneak bits of dried fat and meat to me.

My wounds healed steadily, though the straight line of my ears was forever ruined by the tear in my right ear and the ache in my rear haunch would sometimes come upon me suddenly and cause me to stumble or even fall. The flesh began to thicken and spread over my body and no longer could my ribs be seen through my coat. I roamed freely about the campsite now and felt less and less the need to seek out the dark passageways among the sacks. I began also to regain my sense of fun and play and spent many happy moments chasing and being chased by the twins and play-biting at the hands they were forever jabbing into my face.

In the center of our campsite stood a long wooden wagon with a top of canvas, lined with felt on the inside. Mud-spattered carpets and makeshift huts with no walls, their thin roofs of dry, brittle leaves supported by crooked sticks, spread out on all sides. Strewn about the carpets or bunched under the huts were open sacks of grain, and dried fruits and nuts, great bolts of silk and piles of fur, and grouped under one hut, bright stones and chains that sparkled when the sun hit them. Horses and donkeys stood all about the perimeter of the campsite, tethered by wooden stakes driven into the ground, and two goats were tied to the back of the wagon. Beyond our campsite a hundred others stretched out on the brown plain.

The wagon was cramped with sacks and cloths, chests and jars, and filled with the tickling scents of incense and spices. Now that the nights had become cool, it was here that the Father and Mother and the twins slept and, although the Mother disapproved, I was invited to sleep with the twins who said I warmed their bellies—for they always lay face to face on their mats at night and, now that my strange ways had faded, I was very fond of working my way in between them.

At the rear of the wagon, set off from the rest of it by hanging strips of silk cloth, was a tiny room filled with small statues and hung with amulets and charms and glittering stones of all sorts. After I had begun to lose my fear, I sometimes wandered into this room, which contained many curious smells.

The statues, which stood atop the many chests crammed into the room or on shelves wedged in between them, were made of stone or metal and I loved the cooling touch they lent to my tongue. One day I pulled from their midst a small statue of a naked man who sat cross-legged, with his hands pressed flat together in front of his chest and an old curled cap full of folds atop his head. I carried it in my mouth to the thick rug of lambskin in the center of the room, and, as I sat there licking it, the Mother threw back the silk hanging and saw me. I knew immediately that I was in great danger and, as I heard the smack of the flapper, I dashed past her and leapt out of the wagon. She came quickly after me, the flapper striking the floor, then the frame of the wagon, then the ground just behind me.

"This monster would eat the Great Buddha himself!" she yelled as I dodged through carpets and huts, leaping across sacks and stools to avoid her. "And lying," she yelled even louder, "like a queen—on the very rug on which I render my prayers!"

Finally, she stopped chasing me and stood by the hut with the bright stones, breathing heavily, watching me with keen angry eyes and smacking the flapper against her palm as I stretched out, panting, a safe distance away from her.

The Father rose up from a stool and came toward me, wagging his finger. "I cannot save you, Shushee, if you are to be irreligious," he said, looking at the twins out of the corner of his eye. "For you must understand that we are the most devout of all families. We honor the gods of sun and moon and fire and earth and sky, of rain and wind and mist, and the gods of both sweet waters and salt waters. We honor the gods that bring fertility to the soil and those who govern love and war and wisdom and industry and crafts. And we honor not just general gods but those that are specific to a certain place. For one cannot neglect these local gods and spirits. And just now we are especially reverent to the Lord of the Yellow River because we must soon cross him."

"We worship too the Supreme God, for there is always one who bests the rest of them in cleverness and power—and not just the One from the lands from which we come but those from the lands in which we are soon to go. We worship this god Buddha, whom you tried, blasphemously, to eat, because more and more there are those who favor him in the West and among the Hindus, though from what they tell me I am not sure he is a god. But we do not limit ourselves to full-blown gods but pay reverence to half-gods and heroes and spirits of all sorts."

The Mother fixed an angry glance on him.

"And this is as it should be!" He boomed even louder. "For one must not neglect the gods, though there are so many of them that one must take care not to exhaust or impoverish oneself in trying to please all of them but must pick and choose and, like a sharp trader, determine which god offers the greatest benefit or poses the greatest risk."

"It is true they are capricious and their ways are hard to understand. One might very well wish that they were more straightforward and would strike a clean bargain rather than leaving one always uncertain as to whether they have been appeased or not. But that is not their way. Still, one must always remember that hidden among their tricks is the power to avert disaster, to keep those profits we have made, and to turn our losses into profit." The Father seemed pleased with this thought and fell silent for a moment.

"See if you can teach this Shushee to jump upon command as he has just done in fleeing the Mother," he said to the twins as he walked back to his stool.

* * *

So far did my fears fade that I soon became quite intrepid and tireless in protecting the campsite and in maintaining propriety within its borders. The horses and donkeys I had gotten used to and generally ignored unless they failed to maintain their correct places. And when they did so, sometimes breaking loose from their tethers, I would race upon them, barking and lunging at their legs, taking care to avoid a kick, until I was satisfied that the new positions they had taken up were acceptable—or I was driven off by the flapper.

However, the sight or smell or sound of another dog approaching the campsite or loitering near it infuriated me. I would charge towards these intruders, usually stopping at the edge of the campsite, though, sometimes, going well beyond it in my zest—and there I would brace myself and send forth a kind of yodeling bark, the fur on my back raised up, my whole body bouncing up and down. Many large dogs wandered among the campsites, though nearly all of them were gaunt and ill-kempt, with the cowed look of the village dogs, and most would saunter off at my approach. But there were a few, with hard and steady eyes, who would come relentlessly at me—even into the campsite—and when I realized their overwhelming size and that they would not take proper notice of my warnings, I would flee to the center of our campsite, where the twins would ward them off with clubs or stones or the Father would dismiss them with his booming voice and the shake of his fist.

Humans I would allow to enter the campsite. But I would march alongside them, turning my head over my shoulder at them, keeping up a steady bark so as to properly warn the family of their approach. I was behaving thusly when Chung the Contrary first came into the campsite. He seemed almost as old as Li Huan, but there was no stiffness in his movements. He walked onto the campsite as though he were floating, graceful and unhurried—and entirely undisturbed by my barks. Unlike other visitors who ignored me or cursed me under their breath, he slowed his walk and looked down on me with mild and serene eyes. This strange behavior provoked me and I barked at him even more loudly and vigorously, turning in circles and doing half-leaps in the air.

"I do not believe a word of your protests," he said finally, resuming his walk, and I tagged behind him, able to manage only an occasional snorting bark—for he had quite unsettled me.

The Father greeted him warmly, grasping Chung's thin, delicate shoulders with both his large, hairy hands. Then he turned and pretended to speak to me as he often did to amuse the twins, glancing at them or the Mother whenever he finished a sentence. "So now you have met my dearest friend, Shushee. A man so close and dear to me that he will tell me nothing of himself and says that his name is…only…what is the name you claim?"

"Chung."

"But Chung what? Chung Fu? Chung Ting? Chung Wang? Chung Shih? For no Chinese man has but one name."

"Chung is enough."

"Ah, how maddening he is, Shushee. But perhaps he is not Chinese. For I have never seen such a nose on a Chinese man." The Father took his finger and drew a hook across the bridge of his own nose. "And no Chinese man goes as far west as you and I have gone—unless he is mad or on some devilish mission of the Emperor's."

Looking at me, with sideways glances at the Mother and the twins, the Father asked Chung many other questions—where was he born and where had he lived and why had he left, what was his prior profession and that of his father, whether he had brothers and sisters, and many more but Chung said only "it is not important" or did not answer at all.

"Let us sit down, Chung. You have wearied me with your long, roundabout answers. But still I am discontented with the name Chung alone. It does not express the friendship I feel for you. It has a flat, dispiriting sound to it—like a rock dropping into mud. No, I must call you something more. Chung the Contrary, that is what I shall call you."

"As you wish."

"Ayura, bring Chung the Contrary and me some tea. And Kaidan, stoke up this fire for us. You will dine with us, I insist upon it. For you eat nothing anyway and yet become, by virtue of my generous hospitality, indebted to me."

"So it is. And thus have I been willing to purchase the barbarian powder

195

from you."

"Yes, at a pittance. One-hundredth of what I paid for it."

"I do not want it. I only offered to buy it so that you would no longer smear the faces of Kaidan and Ayura with it. No one wishes to buy it. The women fear it will harm their complexions. But I may perhaps be able to persuade someone that it is suitable to mix with paint or mortar—but only at a very low price."

"See, Shushee," the Father glanced at me. "He becomes talkative only when trying to steal from me."

Chung the Contrary and the Father each sat down on low stools. I sat down between them, but close to the Father, watching Chung intently. There was almost no smell about him except for a thin, dry scent that stirred my memory but which I could not place. He turned his soft gaze on me, looking at me until I turned my eyes away from him, still continuing to stare at me long after that. The Father noticed his interest in me.

"What do you think of the Shushee? I dare say you have never seen such a curious creature."

"She is of the Lo-sze Breed."

"What? I suppose you know of many such creatures?" the Father sneered.

"Such dogs are bred for the Imperial House alone and are select favorites of the Imperial Family. They are thought—foolishly—to bring or take away luck. Their very existence is little known outside the Palace."

"How do you come to know this?"

"I have known emperors and palaces."

"But of course, you are a king perhaps or a marquis? Or a Minister?" Chung did not respond but stretched his hands slowly and gracefully towards the rich-smelling fire, which began to flare up and smoke as Kaidan added new bricks of dung.

* * *

Each evening before the meal was served, the Mother would unroll a small carpet covered with designs in brilliant gold and red and black and place it just beyond the fire, in the direction in which the sun had set. She and the Father would talk for a long time about which gods and spirits it would be best to honor on that day and then she would bring from her tiny room an armful of statues, amulets, and charms and place them carefully about the carpet.

196

When the meal was simmering in the pots, almost ready to be eaten, the Father would stand, raise his silver cup and fling wine high into the air so that it fell to the ground on the far side of the carpet. Then he would pour the remainder of the wine into the dusty brown earth on the other side. Next he would toss into the air a ladleful of the choicest dish to be served that night— perhaps a spicy mutton or goat's head soup—and pour what remained in the ladle on the other side of the carpet. The sight of this food being thrown about so freely always caused me to stand and let out a strangled whine, at once hopeful and worried. But the Father would fix a stern and angry look on me and I would lie back down immediately.

The Father would first address the Supreme Gods, sometimes calling upon Buddha, sometimes Pangu, sometimes Vishnu.

"Supreme Ones, or whichever of you is now Supreme, I ask that you protect this family, and not put unnecessary obstacles in our path—for the way is hard enough as it is. That you make our journey a profitable one—or at least not undercut the bargains we strike with unexpected developments. That you keep far from us the demons of the desert and all those other demons that infest the mountains and valleys and flatlands of the road west—as thick as fleas in the summer heat of Turpan."

The Father would then address the Earth Mother asking that the soil be fertile, the rain or sweetwaters flowing from the mountains be ample, the wind not too strong and that the harvests be bountiful so that prosperity would fill the land, thus facilitating brisk trade at excellent prices.

Then he would turn to those gods and spirits who could be most immediately helpful or whom he and the Mother had a sudden whim to solicit. The Lord of the Yellow River was always praised since we were close to its banks and would soon cross it. And those who governed all rivers as well as those gods and spirits who looked after travelers and promoted industry. Great attention was also paid to Goddesses of Beauty in the hope that they would awaken an interest in the barbarian powder which sat unsold in a huge sack outside the wagon.

After his first visit, Chung the Contrary always attended our dinners. Often, when the Father was offering his prayers, I would climb into his lap, much preferring it to that of the twins, who would fidget about and annoy me by pulling my ears and grabbing handfuls of the flesh on my back and sides. He gave off no more smell than before but he now wore always about his waist a cloth belt with many pouches in which one could sometimes catch a glimpse of dark brown, waxen cakes. And these cakes gave off a very curious

197

and powerful smell, at once repellent and entrancing. Chung, however, would never allow me to press my nose close to his belt but would always rearrange me so that I faced away from it.

Chung sat always very serene and still during these speeches, his eyes half-closed and his breathing hardly noticeable and so comfortable was his lap that I would soon doze off. I would be awakened by a sudden boom in the Father's voice.

"And let fly your curses, O Highest of the High and all lesser gods and spirits, and all the malevolence in your command, against those who have wronged and betrayed me. To the fiends of my native Ghoatchee [probably a tribe or village southeast of the Caspian Sea—S.D.], so vile they dare not call themselves men, who conspired with the King of Bokhara to rob me of my lands and wealth, who enslaved my other wives and children, and who would, had it not been for your beneficence, have killed me and enslaved as well the Mother and Kaidan and Ayaru who remain with me. To those, I ask that you bring unrelieved death and destruction, that their crops be scorched with heat and made rotten with torrents of rain, that they and their animals be afflicted with plague and die in torment, that fierce tribes from the north descend upon them and kill or enslave them all …and that they be unspeakably and unbearably tortured before they are killed."

"And to those in Samarkand and Bokhara, in Merv and Barkh and in Suniga and anywhere else who have sought to cheat me out of bargains justly made and then have persecuted and hounded me because I have sought to remedy or avenge such transgressions (for being an honorable man I cannot but act in the face of such outrage unless the opposing force is overwhelming; and no one who would perpetrate such a deed deserves to live anyway). I ask that their women become barren, that demons invade their minds and drive them mad, that insects enter into their bellies and torment them into insufferable anguish, that their children turn against them and slay them."

The Father would become very excited during this part of his speech and Chung and I would watch him as he strode around the fire.

"And if there are any other punishments I have not mentioned that you deem appropriate, please inflict them as well," he would say at last and then after a pause, he would conclude: "Our offerings are humble, but if you wish more to eat or drink, speak to us or send us a sign. For all we have is yours."

"Chung does not approve of offerings to the gods," the Father would sometimes say as, squirming with impatience and envy, I watched them eat their meal, "although all others in the world rely on them."

"I do not approve or disapprove. I do not think it matters."

"And this is because, as you say: Heaven does not have a mouth, or if it did, it would be too huge to fill; and that it does not have ears, or if it did, it could no more hear a man than a man can hear an ant?"

"No, it is because gods and spirits do not exist except in the mind of man. All events, both natural and those which defy that which we think of as natural, can be explained by the activity of ying and yang and the five processes of nature—such as the cooling of water or the warming of fire."

"And you know this to be true, though all the world thinks otherwise."

"Yes."

"But what of the appearance of ghosts, and omens that foretell the future, of animals who have turned into humans and men who have been changed into beasts, of dragons and unicorns, of those who can bring drought to an end or forestall floods, of all these marvels which occur and have been witnessed by many and recorded again and again? How can these be explained without gods?"

"I do not deny these occurrences, but all can be explained without gods and spirits. And though sometimes our explanation is faulty, gods add nothing to it."

"I cannot accept such a strange way of thinking. For if gods do not exist or cannot be affected by the actions or pleas of men, then I have wasted a fortune in trying to placate and win them over—and years of time and effort. But I would rather that they not exist at all than that they are indifferent to our offerings and prayers—for in that case, what good are they?"

After the meal, the talk would turn to shrewd purchases, sales made and bargains struck that day; to those remembered from trips and towns and markets far to the West; and to those that would be made in the future. The Father and Mother and the twins joined eagerly in these conversations and would rise from their places and walk about excitedly, demonstrating how they had haggled and bargained a deal to conclusion that very day—or years ago. How they had brushed aside an inadequate offer with a shrug and a wave of the hand and an unblinking look of utter disdain. How they had walked away from a purchase with such firmness that the seeker had chased after them. They criticized each other for sales lost or made too cheaply or purchases made too dearly and play acted how it might be done better. Chung sat silent and content throughout their talks, sipping his tea.

"Profit," the Father would say, when at last it seemed they might exhaust the telling of their experiences. "Profit," he would pronounce again, savoring the word, with the full attention of the twins and the Mother now upon him. Profit and the hope of wealth lay behind every human action and pretense; all else was foolishness and fraud. Without profit and wealth, he stressed, a man or a family, no matter what their situation in life, would come to a dismal end. And to those not born kings or nobles, or plundering warriors, profit could come only through steadfast devotion to trade and to the practice and perfection of the skills of bargaining. It was these skills which had enabled them to survive the betrayals and ill-luck that had beset them and which would cause them to rise again to their destined place in the world. Nothing should be undertaken without the prospect of gain, the Father would conclude. No rewards would be won except by those who excelled in the skills of bargaining.

"And yet there are some who do nothing and yet earn profit," the Father said one evening, sitting down and cradling his chin in his hands. "Such as they merely sit and offer no argument and look for all the world as though they are in a dream until the price rises or falls to their satisfaction. From that I deduce that there is a god or spirit watching over and favoring them."

He thrust his face forward towards Chung: "So admit, Chung the Contrary, that you have beguiled some god or spirit into favoring your transactions."

But Chung did not answer him.

* * *

Each day, the twins would prod me to jump the low stools and sacks that sat about the campsite and would seek to teach me other tricks as well. But, after Chung had spoken of my origin, they were careful to hide me whenever a wave of murmurings swept across the campsite, signaling the approach of soldiers and officials. The tricks that, long ago, Uncle Stupid and Cheng Sung had taught me—to sit, to roll over, to play dead, to leap through hoops, to crawl through a sack as I had once crawled through the hollow logs that Cheng Sung had placed before me—these quickly came back to me. They also tried to make me talk, as Precious Wisdom and Splendid Moon had done, and I would respond to their chatter, much to their delight, with a long, thoughtful hum or a querulous gurgle, or, when annoyed, draw in my breath and make a raspy, menacing sound—which they said was like the hiss of a demon.

One day, they discovered me as I stood on my hind legs, peering into a sack of figs. I quickly dropped to the ground as they came upon me, for I feared they would punish me for trying to steal the figs. But they urged me again and again to rear up on my hind legs, rewarding me with a fig when I did so. Then, in the hope of getting another fig, I stood up—as I used to do when plucking berries from the thorn bushes—and, peering first into the sack of figs, I walked a few steps more to peer into the sack of walnuts. The twins turned somersaults around me, overcome with delight, and soon had me walking the full length of the wagon, a fig held enticingly before me. They called for the Father and Mother, who were greatly impressed by my accomplishments. The Father rubbed his hands gleefully and even the Mother smiled at me, not even once smacking the ever-present flapper into the palm of her hand.

From then on, my two-legged stroll became a regular part of our exercises and a performance of some of my tricks became part of our evening ritual. The twins encouraged me to turn in circles on two legs and to walk ever farther—sometimes as though I was taking a leisurely stroll, carefully examining the sacks about me; other times, to hop and complete my walk as quickly as possible. The longer and more intricate my walk, the more richly I was rewarded.

* * *

All day, the campsite was a buzz of activity. The bulging piles of silk, which had grown larger and larger, were rearranged, rolled up tightly and stuffed into huge bags of canvas. Only a few furs remained and they were thrown into the wagon to warm us. The few remaining sparkling stones and chains were removed from the hut, placed carefully in tiny bags and taken into the wagon. The twins took the sacks of dried figs and other fruits and nuts, already nearly empty of contents, on wooden platters to other campsites or dumped them into smaller sacks, stuffing handfuls of these foods into their mouths as they did this and tossing odd bits to me. Coins and bits of gold and silver were secreted throughout the wagon and in the packs that lay scattered about the campsite.

The Father cursed as we did this work, for he said that he had at last sold the barbarian powder to Chung for a paltry sum and that Chung had sold it but hours later for ten times that price. Angrily, he tethered two donkeys to a small cart and rode off. When later he returned, the cart creaked and rattled with pieces of ironwork that the twins and the Mother rushed to cover with coarse hempen cloths. Then they began to roll up the carpets and dismantle the huts and move all their belongings to the wagons and carts, where each thing had its special place, leaving outside only that which was needed to prepare the evening meal.

All of this filled me with anxiety. I was very happy with the ordered life of our campsite—the clearly established border that I must protect, the two meals I was given at the very same time each day, the many opportunities for additional treats, the tricks that I practiced everyday and performed each evening, the gathering around the fire with the Father, the Mother the twins and Chung … each evening much the same as another. And everything I saw and smelled and heard told me that this was to be disrupted.

The evening meal came and I settled into Chung's lap, resting my head glumly between his knees.

"Do not look so morose, Shushee. You must acquire the bold spirit of a traveler if you are to live with us," the Father said before he commenced the prayers and offerings. "You must learn to welcome new sights and sounds, new hardships, for though it is the lust for profit that drives us on, it is the love of novelty that enables us to endure it.

"But what drives you on, Chung? For you seem to care little about profit or wealth—though it always comes to you—and to have no zest for adventure—though that too always comes your way."

"I have given up all loves and lusts but one," Chung answered. "And that one fills up my nights and enables me to endure all else as though it were the dream of another in which I have no more part to play than a rock or stone."

"And will you tell us of this one love?"

"No."

"I did not think so," the Father said and, filling his cup, rose to his feet to begin the prayers.

"What do you think of this Buddha?" the Father asked Chung after the meal was finished.

"His teachings are nothing more than those of Laozi, though they carry one less far, and are not so intelligent, and are led astray by fundamental errors."

"And is this Laozi also a god?"

"One cannot be what does not exist. He was a minor official who somehow learned that the way to act and think is not to act and think."

"He sounds to me just as perplexing as this Buddha. You know him, of course, since you have known everyone and seen everything?"

"No, but I have studied his thinking and have learned some useful things. You would call them 'tricks,' I am sure. But I do not think he is a suitable subject of interest to you."

"Because I am not intelligent enough?"

"No, because you cannot bear inactivity."

"For once I agree with you. Let us leave him, then, and come back to this Buddha. For there is one thing that most perturbs me. I am told that he says that men are reborn again and again in different bodies, or even as animals or insects; in fact, I am told that all the Hindus believe this. I am attracted to this idea—though only as it concerns being reborn as a man, not a sheep or a lizard or a fly. It would seem to me an excellent opportunity to better one's position and to avenge oneself against enemies. But I feel in my heart that it cannot be true. This, however, is not what most perturbs me. What I find most strange is that these Buddhists say that one must direct one's life towards ending this cycle of rebirth. What sense does this make, since men desire immortality as much as they desire wealth and profits."

"I will not argue in favor of this belief since I do not believe any of it myself. If each man is but a reborn version of a previous one, there could be no increase in population—yet we have records that show a five-fold increase in the population of the Central Kingdom alone. It does not seem to me possible that these new men are those who have died in other parts of the world."

Chung looked into the fire and gently rubbed one of the pouches in his belt and brought his forefinger to his lips before speaking again. "But of what account is a dead man anyway? A man who has died is but ice that has melted, a sack of rice from which all the rice has been eaten. He is no more. He is without form."

"You and this Buddha may take comfort in that. I do not. These problems of religion are vexing. Why can I not find a god that I can speak to straightforwardly? I tell him what I want; he tells me—not through signs, or omens, or oracles that one can interpret in 100 different ways, but directly, in clear speech—what he wants. Directly, I stress—not through some magician or priest who spouts gibberish and pretends to be a darling of the gods but ends up, despite this favored status, killed or tortured—or worse yet, runs off with your money. I want profit, wealth, an untroubled journey, revenge on my enemies, many wives and children. Let him tell me his wants. Then, perhaps a bargain can be struck."

"What men want most is to talk all night about useless things," said the

Mother, suddenly and unexplainedly angry. "It is better to pray to the gods and make our offerings and leave it at that. This constant fretting and questioning can only make them angry."

"You speak always of profit," she continued, unconsciously smacking the flapper against her palm—and I rose from Chung's lap and crawled away from her to the other side of the fire. "What of this little monkey who sashays about like a lord, who sleeps all day when she is not stealing our figs and eating our grain, annoying our horses and donkeys, or bringing into our camp snarling and snapping dogs that she has provoked. What has this creature to do with your dreams of profits?"

"Ah," said the Father, winking at the twins. "But the Shushee will someday return a profit, three, perhaps five or even ten figs for every one eaten. And when it does we shall call it 'Lord Shushee'".

The Father's laugh was taken up by the twins who began to repeat "Lord Shushee" in giggling delight. A faint smile flickered on Chung's face and even the Mother laughed. But she quickly became angry again and marched into the wagon without saying anymore.

Just as I always did, I lingered by the fire as Chung retired to his own campsite and the twins and the Father made their way to the wagon, hoping they would forget about me so that I could eat the food that had been thrown to the gods and lay now in the dust alongside the carpet. With the huts dismantled, the carpets rolled up, and so few things left scattered about, the look and smell of the campsite seemed no longer familiar and this filled me with distress. When I returned to the wagon, the air was thick with the smell of incense and the Mother was in her tiny room, kneeling on her fluffy rug before her statues and amulets and charms and smoking candles and imploring the gods in piteous tones.

The next morning, all that remained in the campsite was loaded into the wagons and carts. A great crowd of horses, donkeys, oxen, wagons, carts, and people awaited us at the river. After much screaming, we were all loaded onto rafts of wood and round boats of inflated animal hides and pushed out into the Yellow River. It was the first time I had ever seen the rushing, muddy torrents of a real river—for I had known only the tiny, gently lapping waves of Sea-Like Lake. I leaned far over the edge of the raft, so far that Kaidan grasped my rear legs, as I strained in fear and fascination to get closer to this curious being, forever changing its shape, that rushed ceaselessly past me, heedless of my barks and squeals.

12
Lord Shushee

The nights have become cold and we sleep all in a jumble in the wagon—the Father and Mother and the twins and I, with furs and cloths twisted all about us. The Mother no longer complains about my presence in the wagon, and sometimes at night when it is very chilly she presses me to her bosom. Although the Father has invited Chung to sleep with us, he says he must keep his two oxen company and every night after we are done huddling together over the meal and talking of profits and gods, he goes off by himself to his wagon.

The days, however, are still very pleasant—though all we do is walk, ever in the same direction. The sun warms us but the air is so cool that it does not make us hot. There are few clouds to chill us and the wind is very mild. But the Father says that this will change. I spend much of my day walking alongside our caravan of horses and donkeys and carts and wagons. And also camels, for the Father, who sold two each of our horses and donkeys before we crossed the river, purchased five camels after we crossed it. The goats are no longer with us. We killed and cooked them while in the campsite, and what we could not eat, we salted for the journey. Though I do not like the camels and raised a great ruckus when the Father first led them to us, I have become reconciled to them and bother them no more than I do the horses or the donkeys. And these I bark and nip at only when they stray or slow their pace.

The twins urge on the donkeys by making a noise that sounds as though they are gagging while the camels are hurried by a cry of "Zhoo-Zhoo." The Father whistles one way to speed his horse and another way to slow or turn it. All day long the caravan reverberates with these sounds.

The road and all the land about us is made of clay and covered with a soft dust, and thus is not difficult to walk on. Because of this, and because the air is so cool and pleasant, I do not tire easily and all have praised me for my stamina. But when they see that I am wearying, the twins are careful to put me in the wagon or to let me sleep on a bolt of cloth they place in front of them across the necks of their donkeys.

The first evenings of our journey were very agreeable and much the same as those spent around the fire at the camp, though each and every evening our belongings must be taken out of the wagons and carts and set up anew—and I must explore the terrain and determine the boundaries of our new campsite. But the Father says that now I must earn my title and he now invites visitors to our campfire each night from the wagons in our caravan or, every so often, from those caravans heading east which have stopped beside us. I can now walk on my hind legs the whole length of the wagon and turn in place five times before my front paws fall to the ground. Or turn about in circles as though chasing my tail until everyone says they have become dizzy watching me. Since we began our journey, the twins have taught me a new trick as well: I can now jump from the ground to the wagon and leap onto the back of the horse tethered before it. There I stand, stretching myself to my full height, enjoying their shouts of approval before leaping to the ground. Sometimes I end the trick by bounding against the hump of a kneeling camel and bouncing away before he can turn to snap at me.

The Mother also performs on these occasions, playing a narrow, one-stringed instrument, from which red balls of yarn dangle, that they call a geezhik, and shouting out songs in great, sorrowful wails. Only when she sings and plays in this manner does she wear her coat of bright red and yellow and her fur hat embedded with a huge red stone and decorated with feathers of every sort.

There are even more visitors in the sprawling courtyards of the inns where we rest every few days. And all the visitors are very impressed with my performances and shout their approval, calling me Lord Shushee the dancing dog, though some say I look more like a monkey than a dog. As they leave, they drop coins or pieces of stone or small sacks of figs—for everyone knows I am very fond of figs—or some other food in the bowls the twins place around the fire.

The Father says that we must go to the town of Liqian, even though it is not on our route, and that we will rest there for a few days. Chung has told him that there are strange men who live there, who once were soldiers for the

Xiongnu but now are all very old. They wear their hair very short and remove their beards each day and many have bright eyes such as only barbarians from distant lands have. There are few of them left now, Chung says, and when they drink, they become quite mad and shout chants in a strange tongue that no one has ever heard before and tell everyone that their Emperor, who is an eagle, is even greater than the Son of Heaven and that some day his legions will conquer the Central Kingdom. [Chung's comments would seem to be strong evidence in favor of a fascinating historical theory that holds that a small, displaced band of Roman soldiers, originally defeated and captured by the Parthians, later impressed into the service of the Xiongnu, and, finally, captured in the Chinese seige of a Xiongnu town, settled at last near the ancient town of Liqian (now called Jielu) where they intermarried with local women—S.D.]

The Father says that he is curious to see them, but that he is even more eager to see the marvelous, ferocious monster, kept outside the town that looks as though it has been painted black and white, that passing caravans have talked about.

* * *

The Father says that he was disappointed in the strange old men, who spoke only in bad Chinese and would not get drunk. And he is annoyed that few visitors have come to see me, but instead rush to see the monster.

A small man with red teeth and a large peaked hat that swoops down far over his brows sits in front of the wooden enclosure in which the monster is kept. The Father argues with him for a long time before giving him a coin so that we can enter the enclosure. The monster is a most peculiar beast. He is as large as a horse but has a smell like that of a dog (though sweeter). He is colored bright white and black, with broad black circles around his eyes. He sits on his rump like a child playing with toys, picking up one and then another of the bamboo stalks that are piled all about him, a strip of leather dangling uselessly from one hind leg. Although his presence enrages me, I cannot get at him, being held fast on a leash. In any case, he does not pay the slightest attention to me or anything else but the stalks of bamboo, which he ceaselessly picks up, strips of their leaves, and then chews on.

The Father speaks for a long time with the man with the peaked hat and the next few evenings, I am placed in the enclosure with the monster—always before a large, approving crowd, for everyone wants to see the Ferocious

Spotted Monster and Lord Shushee, the monkey dog. I walk about on my hind legs on one side of the enclosure and then race in circles around the monster, growling and barking, while it ignores me and chews its stalks—always to great applause and approval. But my most appreciated trick is a new one the twins taught me: I snatch a small piece of stalk from the pile beside the monster and, balancing it in my jaws, rear up on my hind legs and walk away from the monster as though I am seeking to tiptoe out of the enclosure.

* * *

My tricks have earned many coins and other offerings, and when we leave Liqian, all are in high spirits—except for Chung. The Father says he is behaving strangely; in Liqian he sold a great many of his goods—at shamefully low prices—though he well knows the market there is poor!

One night, after the visitors have gone, as we sit around the smoking fire, the Father says, "How shall we deal with the desert demons? We must come up with a plan to outwit them."

"I address this question not to you, Chung the Contrary," he continues, "for I know you will only tell me that such exists only in the imagination of men or through the workings of your infernal yin and yang and five processes. But I know better. I have heard them howling and crying out, sometimes in sweet voices, sometimes with awful, piteous wails, beckoning us into the desert. I have seen them bewitch and entrance men, changing themselves and the desert into an army marching along a broad unbroken highway or a group of travelers sauntering over a grassy field."

"No, I ask Lord Shushee for his advice." When I hear my name I look up at him and cock my head to hear him better.

"Yes, come here. You need not say it aloud. Whisper it in my ear." He leans his head toward me and I lift myself up and lick his ear, as the twins and even the Mother giggle. "Quite so. But we will not tell Chung. We will leave him to his five processes."

"I will not pass again through the Gate of Conciliation," Chung says abruptly, as though speaking to himself. "I fear that my love will not follow me to the West. I will go only to Jiayuguan and stay there."

"Perhaps you are a Chinese man after all." says the Father. "For do not all Chinese believe that life ceases at the border of the Central Kingdom?...And who is this love that makes you ardent, old man?" he asks.

But Chung will say no more.

* * *

The road is no longer soft, but full of gravel and stones. My paws have become sore and each night I lick them until I fall asleep. When the Father sees that I am limping, he commands that I be put in the wagon for the rest of the day. That night, he cuts some pieces of leather from a hide and ties them around my paws. The Mother says that I am the most pampered dog that has ever lived and that I am treated better than her. She complains also about the way I drink water and says that I waste half of it. We have plenty of water now, she says, but the way I slobber it about on the ground will one day cost us dearly.

To the left of our road, there are high mountains, capped with snow. Each day they become larger and the white stretches further down their slopes. To the right we sometimes see ranges of black mountains and sometimes great mounds of earth with watchtowers at the top. When it is very clear, we can see tiny black dots moving about the towers, which the Father says are soldiers. More and more often, we walk on stony trails alongside dried up river beds with great, black fissured cliffs rising straight above us. All around us are rocks and dirt and stone, with nothing green and only here and there the dried husk of a bush.

Chung is acting more and more strangely, the Father says. At the last inn, he sold more goods at poor prices. He offered the Father some bolts of silk at half their value, but the Father told the twins that this insulted him and he would not take them—besides, he feared it was a trick. The Father says he will be glad to get to Zhangye. He believes Chung should sit by a fire for several days as he fears Chung's brain has become frozen from going off by himself at night.

He has heard from an eastbound caravan that V.J. is in Zhangye! [V.J. is an approximation. "The Father" claimed that the name of the merchant— something like Vijnanabhikshu Jayatirthakrishnu was unpronounceable and used two symbols from his own (now extinct) language which do not easily translate—S.D.] This very much excites the Father. V.J. is the greatest teller of tales in the world, he says. There is nothing he has not seen or heard—and whereas Chung believes nothing that is said and not even that which he sees with his own eyes, there is nothing V.J. does not believe or claim to believe.

The Mother only scoffs at this and calls him a Hindoo windbag and a weasel and says that he has no sense. But the Father says he shows sense enough in matters of trade and profit, and in concerns of business is as keen and sober as any man.

* * *

We wander along high walls of plastered mud and straw for a long time until it is nearly dark. Here and there the walls open into lakes and ponds that sit perfectly still in the setting sun with brown reeds stuck in their skim of ice and bare trees all around them. When we find V.J. he is sitting in the center of a room dense with smoke and the rich odors of the dung fire, speaking in high-pitched, sing-songy Chinese, surrounded by many men, both Chinese and barbarians. He wears a cloth wrapped many times round the top of his head and the skin of his face and hands are of a darkness I have never seen before on a human.

He does not at first see us enter, so engrossed is he in his talking. His eyes shimmer with excitement and when he pauses, he stretches his neck forward and his eyes dart from one listener to another. When finally he hears the booming voice of the Father, he rises to his feet, a look of great joy on his face.

And then he sees me. He lets out a great laugh and then stomps his feet, waving his hands and yelling as though challenging me, and all the while laughing as though he is having great fun. But I can smell that he is terrified of me and his jerky movements frighten and incense me. I run at him, stopping just before his stomping feet, barking with all my might, bouncing up and down from the force of my fury, my hackles starting to rise up. Even the threats of the Father will not quiet me and finally he tires of the commotion and orders the twins to take me away.

* * *

V.J. has joined our westward caravan. I have become reconciled to him for he always brings me little treats of fried, sweetened dough. At first, I would continue barking at him as soon as I gobbled them down, but now I have become used to him.

At night, V.J. and his three servants huddle with us around the fire—for it is now too cold for my performances—and he and the Father talk of gods and profits and strange occurrences. Chung the Contrary says less and less and seems as though he is always dreaming. He sits nearly motionless except for the slow and almost imperceptible rub of his forefinger against the pouch on his belt and the graceful arc of this finger to his mouth. I no longer prefer his lap because it is not warm enough, but instead nestle between the twins, who hold to each other in a hug.

V.J. has brought special night-glowing wine cups of black and green jade that sit on three legs, which he purchased in Zhangye. "Hold them up to the moonlight," he says, when the Father says that he cannot see them glow. But still only V.J. can see them glow.

"It is very far to the south that I encountered these people." All evening, V.J. has been telling stories. "They go about naked just like savages. And they worship the first thing they see in the morning. If a gull flies overheard, they worship gulls. If a cockroach runs across their toes in the morning as they wake, they worship cockroaches that day."

"So if they were here, they would worship Lord Shushee," says the Father, "since he is the first thing I see every morning, staring into my eyes, wanting something to eat."

"But there is another group even stranger and they live just beyond the mountains. They worship rats. They will not tolerate anyone harming rats and they have built a shrine for the king of these rats, a great, huge rat, who has grown enormously fat, so many offerings have they brought it."

"Ugh," says the Mother, "that is even worse than worshipping a dog."

"At one shrine I visited, the priest wore round his neck two hundred stones. So heavy were these stones that the priest was stooped far over, resembling a fish hook. They found that after the priest died, even after the necklace of stones were removed, they could not straighten him. But, anyway, each hour of the day, such priests as these say a prayer for each of these stones—200 prayers per hour. Most of them do not live long because they hardly have time to eat—and, in any case, they disapprove of eating." V.J. pauses and sticks out his neck expectantly towards the Father, then the Mother, and then towards Chung, who takes no notice of him.

"Do they just say these prayers during the day? Or at night too?" asks the Father.

"Oh, all day and night. For they hate sleep too, calling it a dark demon, and fear it will take possessions of their souls."

"I have no use for such religions. They are unreasonable and would allow no time for trade or profit or any useful activity," the Father says dismissively, then asks: "and what do you think of this Buddha?"

"He is the holiest of the holy," V.J. says with a grave and dramatic air, lacing his fingers together. "He is to be revered above all other gods. For only he has shown us how to surmount the terrible cycle of endless rebirth and bring our torment to an end."

"But are you so tormented? What is it that torments you?"

"Well, I am not tormented now except sometimes by cold, heat, hunger and indigestion, and fear of death. But I am not yet enlightened."

"I myself am tormented by thoughts of priests," says the Father, "who claim always to seek poverty and simplicity but wind up always surrounded by wealth. While I, who seek only wealth, have wound up poor. For that reason, I pay close attention to priests and other religios. There is some secret in them that I have yet to uncover."

"You must find yourself a true Bodhisattva as I have done. Mine is called Analokitesvara and dwells at the Temple of Rapturous Emptiness. When first I saw him it was as though I was struck by lightning, and for days afterwards I wept uncontrollably. He sat with the solidity of a mountain and no rock could match his gaze in steadiness. When he rose, he seemed a mighty tree. But he moved swift as a gazelle and when he walked it was as though he was in the center of a whirlwind!"

"How far can he fly?" Chung, whom everyone thought was sleeping, says sharply. V.J. jerks his head so as to focus on him.

"I did not see him fly, though I am sure he could if he chose to do so. But he does not follow the path of vulgar tricks. I know that many lesser men have been reliably reported to have flown, though it is possible that they were gods in disguise."

Chung says something about 'feathers', but then falls back into his dream and cannot be persuaded to repeat his sentence.

* * *

It has become colder still and a fierce wind blows through us all day long. The twins, the Mother and Father, V.J. and his servants, and even Chung are wrapped in furs and padded cloths and wear great hats of fur pulled over their ears. They have tied a thick, padded cloth around my body which drapes over my head. Still, if I stay out very long, I become so numb that I begin to stumble. So they let me walk only a little while at a time and keep me most of the time in the wagon with the Mother. But no one stays too long in the cold; instead, they take turns sheltering themselves in the wagon.

Despite the cold, each night we still huddle together and discuss gods and profits and strange occurrences. V.J. and his servants now sleep together with us in the wagon amidst a multitude of cloths and furs. The Mother has pulled many bolts of silk out of the bags and lays them over top of us as well. But Chung still goes off to his wagon by himself. Chung has sold all of his belongings now except for his wagon and two oxen.

"They say that the king of the country west of here is truly a god," says V.J., "for he was abandoned as a baby and raised by a she-wolf and brought meat by a blackbird and . . .

"All kings are descended from gods," says Chung in dull, flat voice, "and their forebears reared by wolves, tigers, eagles, or elephants. They apparently do not thrive on mother's milk."

V.J. begins again: "The people of this city believe that god has chosen them—"

"All cities are the center of the universe and each one has been chosen by god as his earthly home," Chung interrupts again.

"In the land of Ferghana," says V.J., "if the king sees a beautiful woman, he immediately makes her his wife or concubine, even if she is already married. So the men hide…"

"That is standard practice among kings. I have never heard of a king anywhere who did not hog all the beautiful women—unless he preferred boys," the Father says.

"Far to the south, in an island in the great ocean, there are men with tails."

"And you have seen them?" asks the Father.

"Yes, but only from a distance. For they run when they see foreigners. But the native men on that island say that they mix with them freely and trade with them, and sometimes even marry them—though this is discouraged and the better class of people never do it."

"I would not care if they had tails if I could get a good price for my wares out of them, but I do not believe I could abide having a wife with a tail. Though I might wish to lie with one of them just to see what it was like." The Father pauses for a moment and looks thoughtful. "To me the strangest belief of all is that there is but one god who is all powerful. I do not see how people can observe all the uncertainty and confusion and unfairness of life—and argue that there is but one god."

"I must agree with you, it seems implausible," says V.J. "Although some of these gods may take on a multitude of forms—which, of course, just makes things all the more confusing."

"I can accept that there might be a chief god who has somehow wrested control from all the others and has, by struggling and plotting constantly, maintained this power for a while. But one god only? How can people believe such things?" says the Father. "What do you believe, Chung?—for you have been unusually talkative tonight, having already said two, or was it three, sentences."

"There is perhaps some unifying principle that underlies yin and yang and the five processes. . ."

"The five processes again?" interrupts the Father.

"—But to call this principle a god puts it in bad company," Chung concludes.

"But some gods may take many forms," V.J. repeats. "A soothsayer once told me that I was an earthly form of Vishnu, though not one of his most important earthly forms. Of course, one can never be certain of these things. But I confess that I have strange dreams in which I have marched forward in battle with Hanuman, the monkey-god."

Chung stands up, dumping me from his lap, for since he has been sitting very close to the fire this evening I have returned to his lap, and walks away to his wagon without speaking.

* * *

The Father says that Chung has now sold nearly all his belongings or given them to the Father, expressing the wish that he use the sale of them to attend to Chung's meager needs. He has kept only one ox to which he says he has become attached, and he rides it like a horse beside our wagon. Bundles of furs and a few sacks hang over its sides. At night he sleeps alongside his ox, wrapped in his furs and sacks. The Father says he cannot understand why Chung has not died.

We do not mind the cold so much now, for we can see the fort of Jiayuquan in the distance and alongside it the huts and walls of the settlement. Huge snow-capped mountains glisten against a deep blue sky to our left and black mountains swell up to our right. The Father says that we will take some rest there and sit before a stove all day and sleep on a dung-warmed kang [an earthen or masonary platform heated by fires underneath—S.D.] at night. Chung says he will stay there and never again go through the Gate of Conciliation, the west gate that leads into the great desert.

Everyone converges on the road into Jiayuquan because the pass between the mountains is so narrow. A man on horseback rides up beside us and stares very hard at Chung and then takes off his cap and waves it over his head, yelling in great excitement. Then he rides towards the settlement at full gallop.

Before we reach the walls of the fort, we find a large crowd waiting for us, many with bare, shaven heads despite the cold. They are all very happy. "Master, you have returned," they shout, jumping and laughing and singing.

The Father asks what they are talking about. A man with a shaven head replies: "He is Laozi, returned on his black bull after hundreds of years." The crowd swarms around Chung. He is surrounded by outstretched hands, which seek to touch him, to pull him from his ox.

"Are you Laozi?" the Father shouts at the top of his lungs.

Chung looks like he has just awakened from a dream but is still half in it. "I do not believe so," he says as they carry him away, "I have no recollection of it."

* * *

We have not seen Chung for several days. Whenever we go outside, we hear chanting and singing, drums beating, flutes playing, and horns blowing. But we do not go out for very long except in the middle of the day when the sun is at its fullest. The rest of the day and night we stay within the room, which is crammed with other travelers, and push as close as we can get to the stoves or lie beside or atop the kang the Father has secured for us. Anyone who comes near our kang he threatens with his knife.

I have become very fond of this warm room with its walls of dried mud from which wisps of straw stick out and its rich, permeating odors of smoking dung and weary, toasted humans. The twins and the Mother say they love this room and do not wish ever to leave it. But the Father says we must leave tomorrow and march with all our might so that we get to Dunhuang before the deep snow falls. Then we will travel no more till spring.

* * *

As we move toward the Gate of Conciliation, all who see us turn away their heads. The Father says it is the custom never to look at those who travel into the desolate lands of the west for it will bring bad luck. He says also that he has heard nothing from Chung though he has tried several times to send a message to him. As the caravan passes through the Gate, each party comes to a halt and several men walk to the wall and throw stones at it. The Father and V.J. lead our party to the wall. The walls are covered with lettering. V.J. says they are poems which express the sorrow and despair of those who have left the Central Kingdom for the savage lands of the west. But V.J. can read very little of these poems and wishes Chung were here to tell us what they say.

"As though, there were nothing more to life than to live among

Chinesemen," the Father sneers.

V.J. and the Father both throw their stones against the wall at the same time. They bounce back towards us and I start and growl as their echo travels along the ridge of stone that runs perpendicular to the wall. Both V.J. and the Father are delighted: a rebounding stone means they will return home; an echo means the trip will be prosperous—and there were many echoes. The Father says he does not wish to return home, for he no longer desires to live amongst villains and betrayers, but he interprets the stones as meaning that he and his family will all survive the journey in good health and that his dealings will be so prosperous that he can make his home wherever he chooses.

It is a glorious sunny day. We fall back into the caravan and head west. After days in the dark and smoky room, the mountains seem more full of snow than before and are so bright they hurt our eyes. In front of us stretch endless, scalloped ridges of dirt and sand. Suddenly, we hear a great commotion behind us. The caravan halts to see what is happening and we dismount and run back towards the wall.

Chung is riding his black ox through the Gate of Conciliation in the midst of a great throng. Many have shaven heads, but there are merchants and peasants and peddlers and women in the crowd, too. Even soldiers and officials have joined the dancing, cheering, singing mob. The Father picks me up hastily, covers me with a piece of cloth and slings me under his arm.

The crowd pulls Chung from the ox and carries him to the wall so that he may throw his stone. Since he is so thin and feeble, they place him very close to the wall. An enormous roaring cheer rises from the crowd and echoes along the ridge of stone. I squirm and bark from under my cloth but the Father squeezes my neck and silences me. From the tunnel of my cloth, I see people flood by us, their faces bright with joy.

"The stone did not fall nor did it bound back! But flew straight up into the sky and disappeared into the heavens!" they shout to each other.

The crowd carries Chung away from the wall and places him back on his ox. They stay just outside the Gate of Conciliation, joyfully dancing and singing and waving their hands. As the noise of the drums and flutes and horns start up again, Chung rides his ox off alone into the West.

For a long time, he rides his ox far to the side of the caravan, struggling in the loose sand and dirt, ignoring the shouts of the Father. I am still covered with the cloth but the Father has handed me to Kaidan and we ride behind the Father and V.J on a donkey. Finally, however, Chung turns his ox towards us. The Father and V.J. bring us to a halt, letting the rest of the caravan go past us, and wait until Chung reaches the hard-packed earth of the road west. He rides his ox in the middle of the horses of the Father and V.J. Never before has he been so talkative.

"I would rather die in the desert or even to risk living without that one thing I love than to live among such fools and lunatics," Chung says. "All day long they look at me with adoring eyes. If I stumble, all around me walk with a stumble. If I go out in the night, covered in furs, and sit and light my small fire in the courtyard, all follow me and soon the courtyard is as full of glowing fires as the black sky is full of stars."

"No matter what I say—even if I say I wish to relieve myself—their eyes light up with joy. And scribes write it down and then immediately all begin to speculate about its meaning."

"I tell them I am not Laozi, thinking this to be a straightforward statement. And a great argument breaks out. Some say I mean that Laozi is merely a discarded earthly form and thus an inappropriate name since I am now among the immortals. Others say as life and death are but parts of the same boundary-less universe; I cannot just be Laozi, but must be Laozi and non-Laozi at the same time. A third and fourth school then spring up—arguing some nonsense that I could no longer stand to listen to."

"It was only by telling them that I must go back to the West as I had done centuries ago—and that I must go All Alone (I emphasized)—that I could escape. For I had come to Jiayuquan to see if the Daodejing had taught yielding to man, I told them. [The Taoist "Classic of the Way and its Power." Supposedly, Laozi gave this text to a frontier guard before heading into the western regions on his bull and disappearing—S.D.]

"I had seen that their understanding was imperfect and that even those who had started on the way were too full of striving. I must retrace my steps—In Solitude, (I emphasized), and rethink, without thinking, but through effortless, Undisturbed (I emphasized) contemplation, all that I had said before. They must reflect on my visit and learn, without learning, the great letting go. And to one who did so I would appear, unbidden and through no will of my own, and reveal new teachings."

"And when they cried 'How long will you leave us this time, Master', I wished to shout 'at least another 500 years!' But I said only that the Way cannot be measured or enfolded by time."

"What about the rock?" the Father asks.

"It was difficult to see with so many jumping about but I am certain it fell to the ground," Chung replies.

V.J. clears his throat. "Shall we now call you Laozi, or Chung the

Contrary as before?" he asks in a very timid voice.

Chung does not respond but somehow speeds his tired, old ox into a gallop and moves out in front of us, where he stays until night comes.

* * *

We no longer stop but continue all through the day and night. The road is covered with a thin layer of snow now, which crunches as we move over it, and always, it seems, is blown about by an icy wind. Beneath the snow the ground is hard as rock. But I spend little time outside; instead I stay in the wagon, which is always full of smoke now from the pot which sits in the middle of the wagon and hardly burns enough to warm us—for the Father say we have little dung left and that, besides, he fears we will catch the wagon on fire. Our bags of water freeze each night and each day we warm them on the stove until they become slushy enough to drink from. The camels, however, do not wait for the ice to become soft but immediately chew and gobble down the chunks of ice that are given to them.

The Mother and Ayaru, who has become ill, stay always in the wagon and the Mother goes often to her tiny room of statues and amulets now. But only for a few moments. Then she rushes back, rubbing her arms and putting furs about her, and crowding close to the smoking pot.

The others—the Father, Kaidan, V.J. and his servants, come into the wagon in spells and climb under the furs and cloths and huddle together with us around the smoking pot. But hardly anyone speaks. Their hands and faces are red and raw despite the furs they cover themselves with—except for V.J. whose dark color does not redden but drains away in the cold. Chung stays in the wagon all day, too. The Father says that he has sold all his few remaining possessions except for the belt that he wears always about his waist, the pouches of which are now stained a deep brown. In Anxi, he ordered that his ox be slaughtered, saying he did not wish such a noble creature to live any longer in a world of fools and lunatics, and gave us a great feast. All ate as much as they could—except for Chung, who ate only a taste of its heart—and the remainder we stuffed in bags of hide and tied to the wagon. It no longer has any smell and, when walking one day in the snow, I reach up and paw at it, it is hard as stone.

In the middle of the night, Chung leaves the wagon and, tying as many furs as he can around him, he untethers a donkey from the wagon and rides it far to the side of us. We look out sometimes to see if he is still with us and watch the glow of his small fire in the black night. At the first light of dawn, Kaidan and Ayaru–for she has recovered from her sickness–rush out and load Chung onto the donkey , then lead it back to us. Then they pull Chung down, stiff as a board, and carry him to the wagon. V.J. and the Father agree that he is indeed an immortal, favored and protected by some god or many gods, for no mere man could live as he does and not die.

The flakes of snow fly thickly on us now, covering the wagons and carts, and the backs of the horses and donkeys and camels, and the furs in which we are all covered. But everyone is very happy. The Father calls to us to come from the wagon and Kaidan carries me out with him. V.J. and his servants rush to join us. The Father points ahead of us at dim shadows far beyond the snow. They are the city walls of Dunhuang, he says. Everyone—except Chung—jumps about, shouting and laughing. Then they join hands and run in a circle, stopping now and then to pick up snow and throw it at each other as they do so. Ayaru pulls up my front paws and tries to make me walk on my hind legs, but I am too cold and will not do so.

"Come, let us hurry," shouts the Father, "for, when we get there, I will buy us such a batch of wood as will fuel a bonfire—so sick am I of these dung fires. And then I will buy a wagonload of dung and wood as big as a palace. We shall not leave Dunhuang till spring, but shall sit day and night by our fire until we are cooked as black as V.J."

13
We Cross the Desert

Everyone says they are happy to leave Dunhuang. They say they are sick of sitting in foul, smoky rooms. They yearn too for the sweet figs and fresh melons and dates and grapes that only spring and summer can bring. The Father says there was no good business to be done in Dunhuang and our profits have seeped away like water through sand. He blames the soldiers most of all, for they have nothing to do in Dunhuang in the winter and again and again they came to inspect our wares. And each time it costs something to get rid of them. Whenever they came, Ayaru or Kaidan would roll me in a cloth and hide me in the wagon or carry me to another inn. But one time a soldier spied me before they could rush me away and he threw himself flat on his back on the floor and began screaming like a madman that I was his dog. The Father had to give him a sackful of copper coins before he would quiet down.

We move in a long straight line out of Dunhuang. Before us, waves of sand stretch out in some places; in others, flat plains of yellow and brown dirt extend. There is no life in front of us but that of the caravan. Still, the air seems fresh and clean after Dunhuang. The sun warms us nicely but is not too hot. Everyone says they do not regret leaving Dunhuang, but the Mother carries an armful of statues and charms and fidgets with them as we pass beyond the patchy green of the valley fields and enter into the wilderness of stone and sand and dirt.

"Though it seemed all dull and gray while we were there, it seems now full of color and variety," says V.J. wistfully as he looks back at Dunhuang and then forward into the desert.

We have sold the long wagon and all but two of the smaller wagons and carts. Of our horses and donkeys, only the four donkeys that pull our two small carts remain. And only two horses. The Father rides these, and he keeps whichever one he is not riding on a rope behind him. However, we have now a great many camels, which the Father purchased fresh in Dunhuang (for he sold all the old ones when we arrived), piled high with sacks and bags of all sizes. The Mother rides almost always in one of the carts and, rarely, on one of the camels. The twins sit sometimes on the donkeys before us, and sometimes they walk alongside the wagon. But mostly they ride the camels. They are very restless and get first on this camel, then that one, and the Father keeps scolding them for prodding the camels to run faster than the pace of the caravan.

The Mother has crammed her statues and charms and amulets all over the back of the cart amidst the sacks and implements and many of them dangle as well from the wooden ribs or canvas top of the cart. She often crawls back with them, but it is difficult for her to pray because the sacks are piled so high. I hear her grunting as she struggles against the rocking of the cart.

In the cool of the morning and in the late afternoon and early evening, when the cart can shield me from the sun, I walk for long stretches alongside the wagon. Much of the day, however, I spend sleeping alongside the Mother or curled up among the sacks in the back of the cart. But I no longer bother the Buddha or any of the other statues or charms.

We have traveled only a few days from Dunhuang when we see a square of tall mud walls rising before us, standing oddly alone in the midst of the desert. "The Jade Gate!" says V.J., who has ridden his horse back to the Father.

"More soldiers!" sneers the Father.

"Very soon, you will long for soldiers such as these and such as we have seen in Dunhuang. For they are modest in their demands and still fearful of doing too much wrong. Beyond this point, what few soldiers of the Son of Heaven there are have become insolent and reckless in their demands. Bandits swoop down at their leisure knowing the soldiers will not bestir themselves to prevent their raids. And we must go through the lands of many great kings, whose intentions cannot be relied on."

"Great Kings!" the Father sneers. "Kings aplenty there are. That, I grant you. A young camel cannot break free and have a good romp before it has entered a new kingdom. With new fees and taxes and bribes required! They may consider themselves great, and certainly I, and everyone else, will call them great to their face and pretend that the light of their greatness hurts our eyes. But they are not great. They are pissant kings—lackeys of the Son of

Heaven. Except for the Hsiung-nu, may the gods protect us from them."

"It does not seem reasonable to me that there can be more than a few great kings." The Father says and turns his horse towards Chung, who is lolling on a camel behind him. "Tell us Chung, for you have not spoken since we left Dunhuang, how many great kings are there?"

"I know of two very great kings. By which I mean that their kingdoms are very great in extent and power. I do not speak of their character. The Son of Heaven and that king who rules the lands beyond the great mountains west of Kashgar all the way to the rich, ancient lands that sit upon the three great rivers that flow into the sea. Many lesser kings pay tribute to him. There may also be another great king far to the west. There are tales of such a great kingdom, which some call Da Qin [believed to be the Chinese name for Rome—S.D.]. But that may be just a story for children—like the Queen Mother of the West."

"There are also truly great kings south of the mountains in India," says V.J.

"I have not been there and know nothing of them—and do not care to know more," replies Chung.

"Well, anyway, three or four great kings—one for each corner of the world—that would be plenty," the Father says. "If there were only three or four kings, I would not mind them so much. I see no reason why there should be so many. But I do not agree with you, V.J., about the intentions of kings. They are not like gods who do things for all kinds of strange reasons or for no reason at all. Their intentions can always be relied on—for it is always to steal from us as much as possible. But we must distinguish between good kings and bad kings. A good king is wise and clever and he steals in a reasonable way so as to maximize his thefts. Merchants will say 'He is not such a bad king; I can live with that amount of thievery' and pass through his land. But a bad king becomes mad with greed and power and steals everything, or too much, in any event, and may murder or imprison you to boot. And thus, in the end, he dries up the business that feeds his desires."

"There is much in what you say," agrees V.J. "and that is why we go to Hami rather than Loulan, which, were it not for the madness of their king, would be a shorter and more pleasant route."

"They say that when the walls of Loulan were being rebuilt," adds V.J., "that, if a slave or workman died during the work, they let him lie where he fell and packed the mud about him—so that he is built into the wall!"

"That is just the sort of ridiculous thing mad kings do—for I am certain that having such bodies in the wall only weakens the foundation," snorts the

Father.

As we approach the gate, Kaidan throws a cloth on me and pulls me into the back of the cart. He gives me a piece of dried donkey meat and tells me to shush. It seems as though we no sooner enter the gate than we are on our way out another gate. I hear V.J. laugh a high-pitched, hollow, friendly laugh and, over the Mother's shoulder, I can see him toss a sack of coins to a brocaded soldier. As we go out the gate, a crowd of beggars swarms around us. The Father tosses copper coins to them. They throw the coins over the heads of the donkeys and yell "Happy Journey!" Kaidan peeps through a tear in the canvas at the back of the cart. "They have gathered them up and given half to a soldier," he calls out to the Mother.

Each night, our cart is untied from the donkeys and put alongside the road; and our tent and carpets and implements and other necessary belongings are taken from the carts or camels and arranged always in the same way. The Mother takes a few of her statues and charms and sets them in the western corner of the tent. While this is done, I explore and determine our boundaries. Then the fire is started and the meal is prepared. And after the offerings and the talks, I am called on to perform. There are many in the caravan who have not seen me before; moreover, eastward caravans sometimes pull alongside us in the night. Interest in my performances is very keen, and many gifts of figs and other foods, and coins and stones, are bestowed on us.

V.J. has his own tent, but Chung shares our tent, though he does not stay in it very much. In the middle of the night, he leaves the tent. Sometimes Kaidan and Ayaru slip out of the tent after he leaves and carry me with them. We can see his slight dark figure, wrapped in furs, against the glow of the small fire on which he cooks brown, sticky cakes. Sometimes he leans well over the fire, and, closing his eyes, breathes in its fumes. We crawl close to him and the twins try to annoy him by making strange sounds, but he never moves or gives any sign that he hears us.

The unvaried pace and predictable rhythms of this life are very pleasing to me. Food is generously provided and much attention and companionship is lavished on me. I sleep easily wherever I am put, disturbed neither by the roll and bounce of the cart nor the swaying of the camels. I feel very content.

V.J. and the Father are apprehensive about our passage through Xing Xingxia. Each time they say the word, I look up to see if they are trying to shush me, but they are not concerned about me. The soldiers there are very greedy and arrogant, they say. One must be very careful with them: if you give too much, they will think you are very rich and detain you so as to get more money from you; if you give them too little, they become scornful and detain you for spite. Chung, as usual, is indifferent to these concerns.

The soldiers do not let us pass through Xing Xingxia. Instead, they make us pull along the slope of the ravine. It is very steep and full of large rocks, and only with great difficulty can we set up our tent. The whole slope of the ravine is covered with camels and tents, with horses and donkeys and the carts of other caravans. At night, it has begun to rain and water, mud and rock wash under the side of our tent, fouling our belongings. It is said that bandits have crept down through the rocks the last two nights and robbed and murdered travelers. The Father and V.J. argue all the time: the Father says we gave too much; V.J. that we gave to little. Each day the soldiers stride into our campsite in a very haughty manner and poke our sacks and bags with sticks. They have seen me many times now, but seem to have no interest in me. The Father and V.J. rush up to them when they appear, arguing and pleading, and when they leave our campsite, they follow after them, still arguing and pleading.

* * *

At last we are free of Xing Xingxia. The sun is very bright when we leave. The rains stopped several days ago and the camels and horses and donkeys kick up great clouds of yellow dust. Bells have now been tied around the necks of the camels and everyone has replaced their cloth caps with broad straw hats that encircle their heads. The jangling of the bells and the ways in which the straw hats have altered everyone's appearance keep me growling and on edge as we first go into the desert. But soon I grow used to it and begin to doze on Ayaru's lap and when the sun gets too hot I leap back into the cart and fall asleep on a sack.

The Father is not happy. He mutters all day about the unreasonable bribes the soldiers extorted from him. At night, he calls down curses on them along with his betrayers when he performs his offering and prayers. He is very concerned about the time lost in Xing Xingxia. Also, that it is already so hot. It should not be so hot this early in the year, he says.

The heat has begun to bother me. I sleep most of the day now, lying on my side panting, and no longer like to walk in the shade of the cart in the late afternoon. The mornings, however, are still pleasant. Fascinating bones of all sorts—camels, cattle, horses, donkeys, goats, and sheep—litter the sides of the roads. I cannot resist dallying with them, sniffing and pawing, and must constantly run to catch up with the cart.

Shouts pass from the front of the caravan to the back. Hami, or Ximu, as V.J. calls it, is near. It is Kaidan who first sees, across the stony, dusty plain, a long green line on the horizon.

"Hami!" Chung says and his eyes briefly light up.

"You have been here?" asks the Father.

"A most agreeable lot of barbarians," says Chung, "who care for nothing but singing and dancing, and making music and versifying in their own strange tongue. They do not complain about the Red Dust—as your Buddha does. Before I found my true love, I came here as a young man. They are very kind to strangers and fond of having them sleep with their wives, while they go off and occupy themselves otherwise. They say that this pleases their local god. Though this god looks like nothing so much as a grasshopper with a human head, I consider him to be among the most benevolent of imaginary gods."

Chung pauses and strokes his sparse beard. "I slept with many of them; they were very obliging."

"Well, it must indeed be a wonderful place to pry so many words from you," the Father says. "I myself have always gone through Loulan in the past. Tell us more." But Chung's eyes are no longer bright and he has nothing more to say.

The road leads us through green fields crossed by ditches of water that sparkle in the sun. Clumps of red and blue and gold flowers line the ditches. I can hear the croaking of hundreds of frogs as we pass and, submerged beneath this sound, the slow trickle of water. We enter Hami through a huge bronze gate pressed into the white of the city walls and pass into the cool shade of its broad avenues. I am let down to walk between Kaidan and Ayaru in the soft and pleasant dust alongside the cart. High mud walls bound the side of the road and above them we see pink and white blossoms flutter and blow across the road. Gusts of perfume, from the blossoms and from the fruit and berries ripening behind the walls, blow with them. Above us, sky and sunlight flit harmlessly through a canopy of broad green leaves.

Suddenly, pandemonium breaks out all about us. We are surrounded by stalls and tables of fruits and nuts, dyed cloths, rice and wheat, tweeting birds in small round cages, knives and axes and pots and jars. Men and women and children are everywhere, screaming and chanting. Some of them thrust bright-colored partridges and ducks and geese hanging upside down at us. Flocks of black and white sheep run across our paths with tiny lambs hurrying to keep up with them. Goats hurry along behind children as though they are anxious to get home. Everywhere there are donkeys braying, staggering under enormous loads three times their size—and boys waving switches, shouting at them incessantly. We pass through a long line of stalls on which there are nothing but melons, dozens of different kinds of melons. The Father says they are not fresh, but have been stored in the sand all winter. Until the fresh ones come, he prefers the dried melons. He buys several long strips of dried melon and passes them to the twins and the Mother. Ayaru gives me a piece. It is very sweet and I whine for more.

At night, huge crowds attend my performances. They do not stay for long, but rush to other parts of the market place to see jugglers, musicians and dancing girls, dwarfs who jump and spin in the air, and groups of singers who make faces as though they are in great pain. As soon as one crowd leaves, another takes its place and when we return to our tent, our bowls are full of food and coins and stones. I am given so many figs that I throw up each night, but that does not deter me in the least from eating as many as I can the next day.

* * *

Though he looks very tired, V.J. does not wish to leave Hami. He says the women here are fascinated by his dark skin and he does not want to insult his hosts by a short visit. But the Father says we cannot afford a long stay because of our delay in Xing Xingxia.

"We cannot, must not, will not get stuck in Huizhou [modern name: Turpan—S.D.] in the summer," the Father says, his voice rising with each syllable.

But officials of the king, whom the Father says is not a real king but just a lackey of the Son of Heaven, have pulled the bags of silk from our cart and discovered the ironwork. They say that it is illegal to export iron from the Central Kingdom and they must report this crime to officials of the Son of Heaven. The Father argues that the presence of the ironwork was known to the Son of Heaven's soldiers at Xing Xingxia and they raised no objections. He produces a stick with a wax seal on it, but the officials pay no attention to it. V.J. can hardly contain his delight as the officials keep us in Hami for many days. Each night he goes off to accommodate our hosts.

Finally, we leave Hami. The wind blows up when we pass through the city gates and sand swirls about the legs of the donkeys and camels. The

Father and the Mother and V.J. look at each other, their brows furrowing with concern. The Father begins cursing the officials for their unwarranted thievery.

Soon, however, his mood lightens, for the wind dies away and high white clouds fill the sky and shield us from the sun. And he is very proud of a device he has invented to protect us from desert demons. A sheet of canvas has been strung between the two camels that march in front of our party. Chinese letters have been painted on it upside down. The Father had to hire a Chinese man in Hami to paint them, since Chung refused to do so. This will act to thwart demons in the same way as the walls that wealthy people put before the gateway to their courtyards, he says.

"They must indeed be frightful and ingenious demons who have neither the strength to leap over these barriers nor the sense to walk around them," says Chung.

"In the Kingdom to the south of Huizhou," says V.J., ignoring Chung, for he too is impressed by the Father's device. "The people say that their king is not born of humans, but comes from a sort of tuber that is nourished by the roots of bushes."

"A kind of royal turnip," says Chung flatly and everyone except Chung laughs.

* * *

Each day it seems to get hotter, and my sufferings increase. The Father has placed the leather boots on me again but I no longer like to walk, not even in the mornings. The bones which litter the road no longer interest me and I do not walk for more than a few moments before I am ready to be put back in the wagon—for even in the shade of the cart, the heat is ferocious and I feel it rise up through my paws into my body. I lie all the day in the cart on my stomach or side, panting furiously, my parched and quivering tongue sticking far out. I think of nothing but how hot and uncomfortable I am. Not even the mush they give me kindles enthusiasm. It is only water that I crave—and they never give me enough in my bowl, though Ayaru and Kaidan sometimes smuggle secret mouthfuls of water that they spit into my bowl or into the cup of their hands. It should not be so hot this early in the year, the Father says again and again.

I regain some of my strength and appetite during the cool of the night, although I have not felt well enough to perform the last few nights. There is, in any case, not much interest in my performances. The travelers do not seem to want to walk about, but sit dull-eyed around their fires. Although the camps are mostly quiet now, quarrels sometimes break out, for tempers have become short. The Father quickly becomes angry if the twins do not obey his commands immediately, and their ears are red from the rough tugs of his fingers. The Mother spends more and more time in the back of the cart, clutching one statue or another to her bosom or pressing one of the charms to her lips. When she comes out, her face is red and swollen.

The Father still performs his prayers and offerings each night—and he now includes the officials of Hami with the soldiers of Xing Xingxia and the betrayers as those who should be cursed. But he has shortened the prayers and only throws a bit of food to the gods as an offering—for wine is no longer drunk at night and water cannot be wasted. What little talk there is around the fire is seldom of gods and profits and strange occurrences, but of the unseasonable heat, sandstorms and bandits, and desert demons. V.J. says the Father's device must be working because we have neither seen nor heard any desert demons since we left Hami.

But V.J. still talks sometimes of the Buddhas. He says there are those who believe that there are many Buddhas who dwell in other universes—universes much purer than ours. The Father and V.J. agree that makes sense and there should be many Buddhas—rather than just one—which would be like there being only one god, though the Father is less convinced of these other universes. V.J. says that through performing acts of piety, in particular, giving much of one's wealth to the temples which subscribe to this belief in many universes, one can be reborn in one of those other, purer universes and take a sort of shortcut to Enlightenment—achieving this without so much discipline and meditation, for which he has little talent or inclination. V.J. says that the trader Patanjali, whom both he and the Father know, has given all of his wealth to such a temple—for the priest assured him that in this way he will certainly be reborn in a purer universe—and thereby shorten by many lives the path to Enlightenment.

"That is the sort of clever idea that make me admire religios and priests," says the Father. "But I wish I had met Patanjali before he did this for he was very cunning and stole me blind on more than one occasion. Perhaps his first act of piety might have been returning to me that which he cheated from me."

* * *

The sun glows all day in the sky like an oven. The cool of night no longer restores me. I do not willingly leave the cart in the day or the tent at night and must be carried out. All thoughts of play and companionship and territory have been boiled out of me. Not even food interests me, although sometimes I swallow a bit of mush or a piece of fig if it is pressed into my mouth. But often I cannot do even that and I let it dribble down my chin to the ground. Also, nearly every day and sometimes at night as well, I have begun to have a kind of seizure, where I cannot catch my breath and I make a horrible honking noise. When this occurs, Kaidan or Ayaru or sometimes even the Mother will rush to me and rub my head and ears and the bottoms of my paws with a damp cloth and fan me with a piece of silk they have strung between two sticks. If the honking persists, they thrust my head into a small bowl of water. After this is done, they pour the water carefully back into the jar that has been set aside for my seizures.

"Lord Shushee did poorly in the cold," the Father says every time he sees me lying on my side, panting and snorting. "But in the heat he is hopeless." Then he holds the slender tip of my ear between his thumbs and forefinger. "It is burning hot," he says, then adds, careless of who hears him, "Lord Shushee is dying."

"Everything must die," he says, when the twins look at him accusingly, "except maybe V.J., who worries about having too many lives, or Chung, whom nothing can kill."

But after he says this, before I can die, we arrive at an oasis. It is a shabby affair, with its mud walls half buried in sand. Only a few patches of dust-swept green fields and a line of scraggly trees set it off from the surrounding waves of sand. Before we reach the walls of the houses, the twins rush me from the cart and throw me in one of the tiny pools of water that lie in the fields. The water is greenish and very salty and the twins hold my mouth shut to keep me from drinking any of it. They place me in it up to my haunches and pour water from their cupped hands over my head and back and tail, splash it into my face and rub my belly with it. The water near the houses is better and I can drink as much of that as I want. After I drink my fill and lay all day under shade trees near a pool of water, I feel much better and am able to eat some mush.

The Father bends over, feels my ears, and says, "Maybe Lord Shushee will live after all."

* * *

The thin island of green standing out from the endless grit and sand that Kaidan spotted when the air was still cool and the sun was still low in the sky now surrounds us. Bright green trees with broad leaves line the dusty road and fields of green, criss-crossed with ditches of still water (brown except when the sun flashes on them) and dotted with wells, stretch out to the horizon on both sides of us.

But these sights do not generate much enthusiasm. The sun is directly overhead and boiling hot. A parching wind blows directly in our faces, carrying off all traces of moisture with it.

"Huizhou," says V.J., "The Land of Fire!"

"Yes," the Father says. He wipes his forehead and looks at his fingers. There is no sweat on them, only dust. Then he points to the hills beyond the golden brown walls of the city to the red mountains, which seem to sizzle and flare. "The mountains themselves are aflame."

"Chung the Contrary," the Father yells at Chung, who is rocking along on the oldest camel, "did you sleep with wives or maidens here?"

"Neither," replies Chung, "for when I visited here it was many years later and I had already been to the land of the drooping, white flowers and found my one true love."

When V.J. and the Father are alone, the Father says that Chung is behaving more and more strangely. His eyes seem without life and his lips now have a blackish tint, they agree. Had Chung not given him so much gold and so many preciosities for his maintenance, the Father says, he would leave him behind.

We pass through the gates of the city and travel along its leafy well-shaded paths. The shade and greenery that is everywhere around us cannot dispel the heat, however, and when we come into the market place, everyone dismounts or climbs down from their carts and rushes to the large walled enclosure of water that sits in its middle. Everyone drinks the water from their cupped hands, splashes it into their faces, and rubs it onto their arms and their hair and the back of their necks. It is cold as ice. I am thrown into the pool and sink below the surface, then rise paddling wildly and snorting and gasping. I begin to make my honking sound and Ayaru pulls me from the water, slaps me on the back, and holds me over the side so I can drink my fill. I drink for a very long time, then gag and throw up the water. Then drink again and throw up. And this continues till I am full of water and wish only to sleep.

There is almost no one else in the marketplace or alongside the roads.

"All are underground waiting for the cool of evening," V.J. says and rides off on his horse while we stay in the shade of the trellis of grapevines close by the fountain. Within moments, everyone is completely dry again and my panting resumes.

"I have procured the use of an underground chamber for us," V.J. says when he returns. "There we can wait out the sun as does the rest of the city."

We walk down steep, dimly lit stairs to a narrow corridor so dark we can barely see each other. A single torch is lit. The corridor is bordered by huge earthenware vessels cool to the touch. Some are of wine and some of water, says V.J. Chung unrolls a thin cloth on the stone floor and lies down on it and goes immediately to sleep. V.J. commands his servants to prepare a place for him and leans back against one of the vessels. The rest march up and down the stairs carrying bed rolls and other necessary belongings and the statues and charms of the Mother, who arranges them in the far corner of the corridor. Someone must guard the camels and horses and carts and all our possessions, the Father says, and goes up the steps. He seems anxious to leave the underground chamber.

The air is damp and close in the chamber. It is so still that you can hear the flickering of the torch and the rustle of cloth each time someone moves in their sleep. The sounds are hollow and quickly swallowed up by the darkness. After we are well-settled, I begin to hear scratching noises along the floor. Scorpions emerge from the corners and crannies. I bark and growl until the twins kill them with their sticks or drive them back into their retreats, but they do not stay there long and advance whenever they believe us to be fast asleep.

When we leave the chamber, there is—just as in Hami—a bedlam of shouting and yelling, braying donkeys, drums and flutes and chanting singers, but all is done by the light of torches and the moon; the tumult begins to melt away as soon as the sun rises and by mid-morning all is still again. When we return to our chamber, there is a pungent smokiness in the air for, day or night, Chung almost never leaves the chamber.

There are melons here and the Father says that some are already fresh, and each day we eat several of the fresh ones. Raisins, black and white, and wine are sold everywhere here. The Father says that trading is good. He sells off all of his ironware, which has become a great nuisance to him, and, with his earnings, buys wine, raisins, gold, and bronze knives and implements. He is very pleased that he has been able to make a profit, even if not as great as he had originally anticipated. I am allowed two days rest and am put to performing again. Although I do not seem able to run so well on two legs as before, my performances are, as in Hami, a great success and profits are excellent.

The Father, however, is determined to leave Huizhou, for he detests the chamber with its close air, the scraping and skittering of the scorpions, and, even more, the hairy black spiders which noiselessly snuggle up to us. He does not spear or chase the scorpions and spiders with a stick as do Kaidan and Ayaru, but, awakening everyone with a stream of curses, he smashes them again and again with a club he carries until they smear the floor. He cannot abide staying long in the chamber, but rushes again and again upstairs, only to return moments later with his face boiled red. As soon as he reaches us, the sweat begins to pour out of him.

V.J. does not wish to leave: in Huizhou the talk is all of the heat, which is the worst anyone can remember at this time of year; of the bandits who are worse than ever; of sandstorms, which have sorely tested every caravan—for it is said that those who wander off the trail into the desert never come out again. A westbound caravan is said to have disappeared completely in a black hurricane before it even reached Yarkhoto. V.J. says that Huizhou cannot be that unhealthy, because the people here live to be hundreds of years old. The Father says that probably they just imagine themselves to be so old—for a day spent in these underground chambers is an eternity.

At last it is decided: we will prepare to leave Huizhou as soon as the sun goes down. The Father says that the heat that we have experienced must recede, for it is too early in the year to stay this hot day after day. In any case we shall travel only by night and save our strength during the heat of day. As for bandits, there are always bandits; one would never go anywhere if ruled by fear of bandits. Besides, the parties to the caravan have combined their funds to hire twenty imperial soldiers (or ex-soldiers; being so far from Chang 'An, their status is not clear) to accompany the caravan to Korla.

* * *

The moon is full and brilliant when we pass through the city gates of Huizhou. The streets are choked with people, but their sounds fade quickly. Soon, too, the shadows of the trees and the dark stain of the fields are far behind us and we see only rolling waves of sand—white in the moonlight— on both sides of us. Far to our right are the dim gray shadows of those mountains which had sizzled with flames when we entered Huizhou. Everywhere we look we see the glowing bones of pack animals. They lead into the desert like stepping stones, becoming smaller and smaller until they disappear.

We march until the daylight has been with us for some time and the cool of the night has dissipated. Then we set up our tents and lie still until the sun is almost to the horizon, when preparations begin for the evening meal, the only meal we eat now. A haze covers the sky the first few days and the heat is not too harsh. The Father is very happy about this. "We were wise to leave Huizhou," he says.

But then the haze clears away, and the sun is hotter than ever. Far beyond the hills of sand which sweep up far into the sky, we can see white-capped mountains. They look small and unsubstantial against the towering mountains of sand. Sometimes, from under the flaps of our tents, we stare at them, but they do nothing to cool us. Immediately, I am ill again, for lying in the tent under the boiling sun seems even more agonizing than traveling in the cart all day. I lie on my side, panting and snorting. My honking and wheezing are worse than ever. Ayaru has become weary of hovering over me with the fan.

"What is the matter with you, Lord Shushee?" she says. "It is only a few days since we left Huizhou and already you are like an old, crumpled beggar lying half-dead in the street. I cannot keep fanning you. I am tired myself. Nor can we keep sneaking water to you all the time!"

"Do not look at me with those sad eyes, Lord Shushee—as if you are about to rise into Heaven," she says, repenting a bit when I lift my head and give a weak wag of my tail. But as soon as my honking ceases, she goes to the other side of the tent and, with a groan, lies down and sleeps.

* * *

Sunlight has just begun to stream over the horizon, quickly chasing the cool of the night away. There is a commotion at the rear of the caravan and it is brought to a halt. Kaidan carries me out of the cart under his arm to join the others who have gathered to see what is happening. A long line of dots, black against the light of the rising sun, extends from the sandhills to the left, crosses the road, and runs far into the sandhills on the right.

We watch them for a long time before we can tell that they are moving towards us. Then V.J. and the Father and all the other headmen of the caravan rush excitedly to the leader of our troops, a short, squat man who wears a peaked cap and says he is a general—though the Father and everyone else scoffs at this. Despite my weakness, I feel excited and apprehensive, for I smell currents of raw fear arising out of the dust and fatigue of the caravan. When the Father returns, he says that "the general" will send his second-in-command out to meet with the bandits. For, though many hold different views, it is hoped that the slow approach of the bandits signals that they want to negotiate.

We watch as the "general" and the second-in-command argue for a long time. Then the second-in-command mounts his camel, but quickly dismounts and begins to arrange his saddle. Then he mounts again only to dismount to go into a tent. When he leaves the tent, the general and other soldiers march along beside him, brandishing knives and spears. Finally, he rides off towards the bandits. In one hand, he carries a long pole topped by the yellow pennant of the House of Han; below it, a yak's tail waves to show that his authority comes from the Son of Heaven. The black figures of bandits are larger now, but very hard to see as the sun behind them dazzles our eyes.

Though the second-in-command moves very slowly towards the line of the bandits, his pennant and yak's tail flutter boldly, for the wind has suddenly become very strong and plumes of sand spiral and dance all along the hills.

When he has gotten half-way to the bandits, they let out a great yell and five of their number charge at him, waving their swords above their heads. The second-in-command turns his camel from the road and races it, slipping badly, along the slope of a sandhill. The bandits are quickly upon him. The blade of one sword cuts the staff of the pennant in two, and the flat of another knocks the second-in-command from his camel, and he goes tumbling and running, pulling his legs heavily from the sand, tumbling and running again down the slope.

There is suddenly a deafening roar from the front of the caravan and darkness begins to fly across the sky. For just an instant, the bandits appear as though they are nearly on top of us, then their image is flung far away. In the next moment, we are flailed by stinging, wind-blown sand and pebbles. Chung, who has been standing idly at our side since the bandits first appeared, moves his lips but we cannot hear him. The second-in-command and the bandits are forgotten. Chung grabs the shoulder of Kaidan, who grabs the arm of Ayaru with his free hand and we run toward the cart. But all becomes a whirling black of sand and stones and we can no longer see it.

Ayaru feels the shaggy neck of a kneeling camel and pulls us down behind it, but Chung is lost to us, blown off somewhere in the black whirlwind. Kaidan and Ayaru struggle to loose the edge of a blanket of rough cloth from the camel and finally succeed in pulling it over us. They push me between them and wrap their arms around each other and wriggle close to the camel.

There is nothing to do but lie there and listen to the roar and howl of the wind. Sand and stone beat against the blanket. The camel winces and groans from their sting and smack. The weight of sand atop the blanket becomes heavier and then lightens, then heavier and lighter, again and again.

* * *

V.J. is still with us, as are two of the other parties of the caravan, but we have not been able to find one of V.J.'s servants. And our party is intact—except for the horse that the Father was not fond of, which we cannot find anywhere, and a camel that carried much of our water supply. Chung we did not find until almost nightfall—sitting half-naked, for his clothing has been reduced to tatters, buried to his waist in the sand. His thin, bony body is covered with sores and scratches, but all that he cares about is his belt and its pouches, which the wind stripped from him and carried off. But we can find no trace of the rest of the caravan, nor of the soldiers or bandits. Nor can we find any sign of the road, but are surrounded on all sides by hills of sand, the tops of which are hidden by clouds of drift sand.

The Father says that for all we know the other parties of the caravan may be marching along beside us, so choked is the air with dust and sand. There is little difference between day and night. The dim light we see sometimes behind the dark veil of haze might be the sun or it might be the moon.

The Father and V.J. have picked a direction they judge to be northwest, which they believe to be the best course to follow, for they fear above all wandering southwards into the heart of the desert. We have left our carts behind, for we cannot move them in the deep sand. The loads have been reapportioned among the camels and donkeys, but all are very heavily laden now even though the Father has left behind most of the raisins and wines, which have less value in the west than in the East, and many other things of low value. V.J. has done the same and, in addition, has left his tent behind and will share ours henceforth. But the Mother has insisted that all of her statues and charms be saved and they have been packed tightly, except for a few she carries with her in a sack, and loaded onto a camel.

* * *

The air has suddenly cleared and the sun bears down on us from a cloudless blue sky. But this clearing does us no good. All we see about us are towering hills of sand. When the Father climbs to the top of one hill, he can see only waves of sand stretching out forever. He cannot even see the white-topped mountains far off and cannot understand this. We have begun to travel only by night again. We can move only very slowly in the deep sand, struggling up the slope of the hills and sliding down the other side. Each hill is a tremendous effort and accomplishment that leaves everyone exhausted. Sometimes the camels lose their footing and must be rolled back to the bottom of the hill before they can right themselves. Kaidan and Ayaru and I, who all ride the same camel, have now been thrown twice. I have become ill again and am now afflicted by my seizures several times a day. But the Father says I cannot have water each time I throw a fit, and when he finds Kaidan trying to smuggle water to me in his mouth, he strikes him so hard that Kaidan falls to the ground and the water is lost in the sand. So now when my honking begins they pat me hard on the back until it ceases.

Each time the Father looks at me he says that I am sure to die. He reaches down and squeezes the top of my ear, seeming annoyed that I have so far defied his prediction. Lord Shushee will not last much longer, he says. Chung is very ill as well and spends the day yawning and shivering, though it is boiling hot within the tent. He will take neither food nor water (which the Father says is a blessing.) But water runs continuously from his eyes and nose.

We hear a shout of joy ahead of us. "The road has been found?" the Father asks hopefully. But it is not a road, but a dried up riverbed that has been found. One of the headmen is certain, however, that a waterhole will be found to the west. So all night we follow the river bed westwards. The bed is hard-packed and level and much easier on the camels and donkeys, but we find no sign of water. We continue marching even after the sun comes up, stumbling along the shimmering riverbed that writhes and wriggles before us in the heat. We stop only for a little while when the heat is at its very harshest. Then we start again down the riverbed—for our water supply has become very low and it is essential that we soon find water.

One of V.J.'s servants shouts and races his camel ahead of us. He flings himself off the camel and plunges his face into a puddle of brown water no bigger around than a melon. I smell a horrible bitterness rising up from the water as we rush forward and, before we reach the puddle, the servant has rolled onto his back, writhing in pain. We tie him to his camel and march forward again. All through the night the servant groans and vomits and his body rears up with sudden twists and spasms of pain. When finally we stop, V.J. says the servant is dead.

The Father says his horse can go no further and is also near death. He and V.J. pull the legs of the horse so as to situate its rump up the slope of an embankment and the Father cuts the throat of the horse, careful that all the blood flows into a bowl. We all share in drinking the blood of the horse and feel somewhat better.

"Should we drink the blood of the servant too?" the headman of one of the other parties asks. But all agree that this would surely offend one god or another.

* * *

There is a dark spot in the riverbed before us; alongside it are dried-up reeds and the bleached and broken branches of stunted dead trees.

"The sand is damp," Ayaru and Kaidan shout, for they are the first to reach it. They began to dig in the sand of the dark spot with their hands. I totter beside them. The moist coolness on my paws makes me forget my illness, and I also began to dig. Soon everyone is at the dark spot, digging with their hands or with the spades that each headman carries. The sand becomes ever damper. The Father has dug a hole so deep that the top of it reaches to his waist. He pulls clumps of sand from the bottom and holds them happily over his head, squeezing them to show that they form into balls. But when he digs further there is only dry sand. We keep digging until all of the dark spot is churned up but nowhere does the dampness turn into water.

"It is here that the waterhole should have been," the headman who led us eastward says wearily. Everyone lies down on the churned-up sand through the rest of the night. No one speaks.

* * *

The wind has begun to blow hard again. Swirls of sand dance all along the riverbed and a yellow-red haze veils the sandhills surrounding us. We can hear strange howlings and creakings coming from beyond the riverbed.

237

"Desert demons," the Father says. "They are calling to us but we must not heed them." He regrets that his device was destroyed by the black hurricane, because it seemed to be working well. Its destruction, he believes, was also the work of desert demons, enlisting the aid of the spirit of the black wind.

The other headman says that he is certain that there is a small oasis due north of the dried-up water hole where we now rest—no farther than a full day and night's march. It is decided that he and the Father and V.J. will go there and bring water back. The rest of us will stay behind for they do not believe that many of us can survive another day's journey without water. A tent is staked out to cover the dark spot, its sides left open so that the wind can blow through. Kaidan and Ayaru bury me up to my neck in the moist sand, which the night air has made cool again; then they bury the Mother and themselves in the moist sand. All others in the caravan do the same. But Chung will not be buried. Shivering and twitching, he says he will not stay behind. He is skilled in reading the stars, he says, and, besides, has become as light as dust; it will be no burden at all for a camel to carry him.

Chung must be lifted onto the camel and the Father and V.J. and the headman totter and stagger alongside their camels before they are able to mount them. The Father's camel will not get up. He beats it with a stick. Still it will not move; instead, it stretches out its neck and legs in the sand. "It wants only to die," says the Father, and he stumbles to another camel and seizes its bit.

The camels carry them off with tired, deliberate steps, as though fearful one misstep will cause them to crumple. I can hear their bronze bells jingling for a long time as they go into the desert. Then the wind blows up again and I hear only its creaking and howling and the labored breathing of the dying camel. Though it lies well away from us, the stench of its breath fills the air under the tent.

* * *

Before the sun sets, the camel is dead. Kaidan and the headman who remains and another man crawl out and slit its throat. Kaidan brings back a bowl of blood for us to drink. It suits me fine, though it is very thick and does nothing to quench my thirst. But Kaidan and Ayaru and the Mother cannot swallow it and gag when they put it to their lips.

Just before sunrise, we hear the jingling of bells again and then joyful shouts. The camels of the Father and V.J. and Chung and the headman appear before us—in the same place as where they left us. But when they see us, the Father, V.J. and the headman throw themselves onto the dry, salt-crusted bed of the river, sobbing and groaning. They have spent the day and the night traveling in a long circle and are back where they started! Chung slides from his camel and falls onto his back in the sand. He remains in that spot, shivering, water again pouring from his eyes and mouth, wracked by yawns that seem as though they will twist his face apart and sudden, violent twitches and kicks.

The Father and V.J. stagger to the bank of the riverbed and tumble into the stones and pebbles and will not move.

Gray-blue clouds spread over the sky, protecting us from the sun. Everyone hopes they will bring rain, but they do not.

V.J. tries to speak, but at first his mouth is so dry and his tongue so swollen that he cannot make words. "I wish to give all my wealth to the same temple as did Patanjali," he says, finally managing to push the words through his blue lips. "I ask only to live long enough to do this. For I care no more for this life. Once I have disposed of my wealth, I wish only to go quickly so that I may be reborn into a more pure universe."

No one else speaks and V.J. falls silent. Though we call to them from the dark spot, they will not move. Kaidan and the Mother crawl out from under the tent and pull at the Father's arm, but he waves them away.

The wind begins to blow hard again, thinning the gray-blue clouds and driving them to the east. Sand begins to drift over the clothing of the Father and Chung and V.J. but still they will not move. V.J.'s body begins to shake with hiccups. The wind begins to howl now and above us a dark haze moves across the sky to replace the blue clouds.

The Father stands up suddenly and brushes the sand from him with a brisk, vigorous motion.

"Do you not hear them?" he shouts. "These are not demons, but angels. No, not angels, even, but a caravan sent by angels. Hear their bells and drums! They are beating drums so that we will hear them and come to them."

No one else hears anything but the howling and creaking of the wind.

"See, they are just to the left of that giant sand hill," the Father points across the riverbed into the south. "Surely you can see them. It is a caravan as big as an army." No one can see anything but a towering sand hill with plumes and sprays of sand running up and down its slope.

"Do not just lie there!" the Father shouts angrily, "they will pass us by!" He runs across the riverbed and starts up the slope of the hill on the other side.

V.J. struggles to his feet but falls when he moves towards the Father and cannot get up. Kaidan and Ayaru and the headman who stayed behind run across the riverbed after him. We watch them as they struggle up the hill far behind the Father, who gets ever farther ahead of them. He reaches the top of the hill and disappears. It takes them much longer to get to the top, and then they too disappear.

The haze has cleared and the sun is low in the western sky when first Ayaru, then the headman, then Kaidan and finally the Father reappear at the top of the hill. They run and tumble and slide down the hill as though they are playing.

Water, we hear them shouting when they get closer to us. A river runs behind these hills, they shout. There is no caravan, but a river. Broad and flat with water cold as ice and clear as crystal, and green rushes and tamarisk trees about it.

Everyone in the caravan except Chung, who remains in the sand, shivering and twitching, rises up and rushes to them. Everyone wants to touch them because despite the hot sun, their clothing is still damp. We are saved! Everyone begins to shout. We are saved!

* * *

Neither Chung nor I have recovered from our sufferings in the desert. We lie all day and night, side by side in the cart, for the Father and V.J. have purchased new carts and fresh horses and camels and donkeys and V.J. has bought two slaves to replace his servants.

Chung no longer shivers and twitches, but lies as though dead, unable to raise his head. He will eat nothing, and when they try to pour water into his mouth most of it runs down the side of his face. The Father says that all flesh is gone from his body and that he weighs no more than a feather. I lie on my side, panting furiously, seized more and more frequently by fits of snorting and honking when I cannot catch my breath.

The Father is certain that I will die and mentions it often. He believes, however, that Chung will live—despite his agonies. Chung, however, insists that he will die. It was foretold, Chung says, when he is able to speak, that he would be sick but one time in his life and then die. The Father tells him that he should take heart, that we will be in Kumchuk [probably a lost oasis town between Korla and Kucha—S.D.] in only a few days. Chung says it is not death he fears, but when the Father asks him, he will not say what he fears.

The Father says we will stay in Kumchuk until the summer heat is gone, for everyone is worn out from traveling in the harsh, unrelenting heat. There are said to be excellent physicians in Kumchuk, he adds, and others who can cure illnesses.

* * *

Kumchuk. We are laid out in a tiny room with whitened walls of mud. Chung lies on a thin mat of woven rope in the center while I am laid on my side on the bare floor in the corner, though later Ayaru slides a mat under me. The room is the same as the wagon: insufferably hot in the day; only the cool of night brings relief. But water is plentiful. I can drink as much as I want and Ayaru and Kaidan come in often to bathe me and apply a cool, wet cloth to my muzzle and ears and paws.

A short, stout man of grave bearing in a black robe and cap comes in to examine Chung. He has a thin, wispy beard like the officials of the Palace, but a long face and beaked nose. After much poking and thoughtful sighs, he says that Chung's illness lies in a secret cavity just above the midriff. Needles cannot reach this place, nor can any drug or the smoke of curative plants find its way there. Nothing can be done, he concludes: Chung will die. But he takes a gold coin from the Father anyway.

He will not examine me and says haughtily that he is not such as to look after the health of dogs.

Later, the Father leads two gnarled and stooped old men into the room. They are wrapped in white rags from which their bone-thin legs and arms and bald heads stick out, brown and leathery from the sun. "They are saints and ascetics," the Father says proudly, "their breath has the faculty of curing illness." They squat down on their haunches and begin to walk like ducks about Chung, puffing hard on him. Chung writhes and groans. The Father is encouraged by this. "Perhaps it is beginning to take effect already," he muses.

The Father gives them a few extra copper coins and they squat down over me. Since I am small, they do not need to walk, but only to bounce their heads about to ensure that their puffing covers me entirely. I feel the wind of their breath ruffle my fur, but it is empty of smell.

Hot days and cool nights pass. Neither Chung nor I seem to improve.

I hear drums beating outside. It is evening and the air is pleasant. Today

241

the heat has not been so severe. I feel better and lay on my belly instead of my side. Three tall bearded men carrying drums of calfskin enter the room, accompanied by V.J. and the Father. They arrange themselves around Chung and begin beating the drums with their fingers, fists, and palms. Every so often they rise up, throw their drums in the air, catch them, and while still beating on them, rearrange themselves around Chung. I bark weakly at them at first but the effort exhausts me and I roll onto my side, panting.

While the other two beat softly on the drums, one of them stands and talks to the Father and V.J. about Chung and his condition, for Chung cannot, or will not, talk to him. Suddenly, he falls to the floor, groaning and writhing, his tongue thrashing from side to side. When at last he lies still, the others ask him what the nature of Chung's malady is.

"He has sinned against many gods—nay, all gods!" the fallen one says. His eyes are closed tight and his mouth seems to move of its own accord. His voice is very deep—much different than it was before.

V.J. and the Father nod their heads in agreement. "Can he be saved?" the Father and V.J. and the other drummers ask in unison.

"Much must be done to propitiate the offended gods," the fallen man says in his strange voice. "Sacrifices must be made to them and a great feast prepared in their honor. Two dozen jugs of good quality wine must be gotten," he says, his eyes still closed, "two sheep and two lambs, one of each with a black head and a white head; grapes, figs, and melons in abundance."

The Father snorts.

"Two more magicians must be brought, who have in their special care idols that they will bring with them to the feast," the fallen man says.

"I can furnish the idols myself," says the Father, "for my wife has a wagonful of them."

"Young women of the sort who can dance and leap and tumble, and whose flesh clings tautly to their bodies must be brought," the fallen man says finally. The Father and V.J. confer and agree to begin preparations for the feast.

When the fallen man has awakened, the Father points to me. He rises and comes alongside me and then sits himself carefully on the ground, rolls over on his back, closes his eyes and shakes his body a few times. "It has sinned against the goddess of domestic animals," he says in his strange voice, "but its sins are minor and can easily be remedied."

All through the evening the magicians beat their drums alongside Chung. V.J. and the Father arrange a makeshift tent outside the room; carpets are unrolled and two tables are set under it, laden with fruit and dishes and jars of wine. The Mother and the twins carry all the statues and charms and amulets to us and arrange them on each side of the door to the room. But their presence is not desired by the gods and they must leave. Fires are lit and I begin to smell mutton and lamb roasting. For the first time in many days I feel pangs of hunger.

I hear the sweet voices of young women and the magicians cease their drumming. But before they leave the room, they place me up to my neck in a bag of powdered cow dung and hang it from the wall. The Father looks in the doorway. "This will cure its illness," they explain. Although I do not much like hanging from the wall, the dry powder is soft and soothing to my skin and its smell is dense and pleasant.

All through the night, I hear the beating of drums, the clink of jars and cups, giggling and laughter, the rustle and swoosh of the women as they dance and leap about. Then the drums cease. Flutes play and there is shouting and singing. The light of the torches goes out and the flute-playing and shouting and singing die away. I hear grunts and sighs and anguished cries calling out thanks to the gods.

Just before dawn, the Father stumbles into the room. "Rise up, Chung!" he shouts, weaving unsteadily from side to side. "Do not be contrary, rise up!" He leans over and pours wine from his cup into Chung's mouth. Chung coughs and then turns his head to the side and the wine drips onto the mat. The Father spies me looking at him. He pulls me from my bag of powdered dung and brushes me off, then leaves and returns with a huge leg bone of sheep to which much meat still clings. He tosses it into the corner for me. "Perhaps you will live after all, Lord Shushee," he says.

The day is at its hottest, and the young women are gone, when the Father and V.J. and the magicians wake. They come into the room and I growl at them for I fear they will take my bone. But they pay no attention and gather again around Chung and begin beating their drums. The Father asks if Chung has been forgiven and will recover. The magicians beat harder on their drums. Then the one who speaks in the strange voice rises and twirls around. He falls to the floor, shakes a few times, and sticks his tongue out and wiggles it.

"No. The gods are still angry," he says in his strange voice, his eyes closed. "A goat must be sacrificed. A spotted goat of black and white and brown, and two more sheep. Two dozen jugs of wine—better quality than the last. And fruit, of course. Incense must be brought and showered about. And honeyed cakes."

"And young women?" V.J. asks.

"Yes. New ones," says the fallen man.

When night comes, I am again placed in a bag of fresh dung powder and hung from the wall. The night passes as before—with singing and dancing, grunting and sighing.

The next day the Father asks again about Chung. The magician falls down "No," he says, after writhing about for some time, "the gods are still not ready—"

"I ask you to reconsider, spirit," says the Father sternly, his fingers playing at his knife. "For Chung has not provided me with enough money for a third feast."

"The gods are not yet propitiated. But you need only give the magicians one jug of wine each to offer at the great temple," says the fallen man. "Then Chung will recover."

* * *

Chung sits on his mat. The room is full of a powerful smell like that which had clung to his belt. I am in my corner. I feel very much recovered and very happy, for many huge bones were left from the feast and have been given to me.

The Father and V.J. stand before him. "Do you not now admit, Chung the Contrary, that there are gods and spirits? Who first saved us in the desert and then brought you back to life?" the Father asks smugly.

Chung does not at first answer.

"I would have much preferred to die," he says finally," for it would have been timely. But I feared those imbeciles that you assembled would have sought to revive me by baking me in a pie or burying me in cow dung in their mad longing for some proof of their powers. I had no choice but to obtain that one thing that I love and that sustains me and bring myself back to life."

* * *

Though it is midday there is a chill in the air. A gray mist hangs above and all about us. We see only the salt-encrusted track on which we travel, which crumbles under the weight of our donkeys and camels and carts. And here and there a glimpse of swamp impaled with brownish reeds or the yellow-green of a patch of field. "Kashgar should be very close," the Father says. "If it were not for this damnable fog, I am sure we could see it.

I rise up from Ayaru's lap and stretch, pressing my front paws against the shaggy hump of the camel to balance myself. An unfamiliar smell wafts across the road and I raise my head and sniff.

"Ah, do you smell Kashgar, Lord Shushee?" says the Father pulling his horse close to us. "What do you smell? Cunning and stinginess, no doubt. For the people of Kashgar are so tight-fisted that they make me out a spendthrift and V.J. a saint in his generosity. Chung, of course, they would judge mad. But he is mad by any standard."

"In Kashgar, there are but two sins: buying too dear or selling too cheap," he says as we see V.J. riding back to us.

"The outline of the city walls of Kashgar can be seen ahead," V.J. shouts. "We should rejoice and be thankful!" But he sounds neither joyful nor thankful. Nor is anyone else excited by the news. No shouts of exultation ring up and down the caravan. All are thoroughly sick of our endless journeying

* * *

Early each morning, when it is barely light, we awake to the boom of firecrackers and the blowing of horns that announce the opening of the gates to Kashgar. At once, a thousand donkeys—V.J. calls them the 'nightingales of Kashgar'—bray. And two thousand boys yell at them. Shouts and singing and the music of horns, sitars, flutes and tambourines break out from each part of the city and seem to grow with each moment.

The narrow streets are jammed with men, women and children of every dress and complexion. With donkeys, yaks, horses, camels, goats, sheep, lean, dirty, pointy-nosed dogs, birds, and chained monkeys and bears. With long tables and stalls on which lie every sort of fruit and meat and fowl and grain and cloth and tool and jar and pot. Whenever a small space opens up, a young boy races his horse or pony into it, heedless of any danger, then brings it up short when the crowd again closes round him. On those days when there is no mist or dusty haze, you can see vast fields and orchards lined with watercourses that spread out into the plains all about Kashgar. And beyond them, bunched brown hills rising quickly into a forest of snow-capped peaks shining so brightly that you must turn away your eyes. But it has been a long time since we have seen this. It has rained for many days now and the narrow streets are awash in mud and the river has turned dark brown.

Though I am not able to run and leap so spryly as before, the crowds that come to see me grow even bigger. So huge have they become that we must move several times to a larger area in which to perform. Those at the rear can hardly see me and sometimes they climb onto each others' backs and arguments break out.

The donkeys are braying and V.J. and the Father and Chung are drinking their morning tea. The Father curses the niggardliness of the people of Kashgar as he does each morning. For the prices offered for that which we wish to sell, and for the donkeys and camels that we have brought through the desert (which the Father says are nonetheless in excellent condition), are very poor. While those for that which we wish to buy are so outrageously high as to be nothing but thievery!

Then, his face brightening, he says, "It is arranged that the Council of Elders will come tonight to settle the dispute about Lord Shushee."

"Yes, everyone in Kashgar speaks of this controversy," V.J. says and he and the Father look at each other with twinkling eyes. "Everyone has bet on it—from slaves to the wealthiest merchants."

"Yes, the people in Kashgar love gambling more than any pleasure—and are far more willing to pay for it," says the Father.

"Well, you two have done your utmost to stir them up," says the Mother, and everyone laughs.

* * *

My audience is noisier and more quarrelsome than ever. They jostle against each other, surge forward and are pushed back. Suddenly, as I am walking on two legs with a long bamboo rod in my mouth, they hush and fall to the side. The Council of Elders enters into the circle. There are at least a dozen of them, flanked by an even larger number of attendants, and the crowd must be pushed back to widen the circle and accommodate them.

The Elders are old and stooped and wear long white robes and white skullcaps on which black symbols are embroidered. Except for the oldest, who is the greatest of the Elders and wears a skullcap of pure black, and must be helped into the circle. They are followed by three younger men in red and blue robes with conical hats of bright red. The Father whispers to the twins that these are advocates.

A stool is provided for the greatest Elder and, after he settles down on it, uttering a whine of discomfort, he claps his hands feebly. The others seat themselves on both sides of him on carpets that have been laid across the muddy earth. "Let the inquisition begin," he says in a warbling voice and one of those with a red hat rises and walks close to me.

"Look how it stands on its four legs," he says. "There is no doubt it is a dog." He has long bony fingers and he traces the circle in the air with them. "Run!" he commands. But I see no reason to obey his commands and, besides, this interruption of my performance has unsettled and confused me.

"Run!" he commands again but still I do not move. The Father and twins surround me and, after much coaxing, I trot slowly around the circle, my tail hanging limply in protest.

Kaidan holds me up to the advocate and he pokes disagreeably at my haunches and forelegs, my paws and ears. The structure of the body is clearly that of a dog, he says, and tugs painfully at my ears. He says that, although they are strangely folded, no monkey has ever been seen with such ears.

Next he drops his shoulders and, doing an imitation monkey walk, he ambles around the circle. Observe the difference between this monkey walk and the gait of Lord Shushee, he urges the crowd.

"Bark!" he commands but I refuse. Suddenly he rushes at me, throwing his arms about clumsily and growling like a bear. This strange behavior startles me greatly and I let out a sound more like a scream than a bark and dash behind Kaidan's legs. But then I recover and lunge at him, yapping and growling as he returns to his place. There is much murmuring in the crowd; many do not feel he has been persuasive.

Another advocate rises. His face is very round and reddish and he gives off a strong scent of sweat and apprehension.

"It is a monkey," he declares. "An unusual monkey, no doubt, unlike any we have ever seen, but a monkey nonetheless. The flatness of face—which bears no resemblance to any dog; the wrinkled, upraised nose like that of an ape; the luminous, childlike eyes, which betray an intelligence beyond the reach of a dog; the tightly-curled tail, clearly designed to enable it to hang or swing from a tree branch; and of course, the ability to walk on two legs. A monkey may choose to run on two legs or four legs but a dog can run only on four legs," he says in a tone of absolute certainty.

Having said this, the round-faced elder then says it again, though a bit differently, pacing back and forth with his hands folded behind his back. Then again, though in somewhat different order. The crowd grows restless and the black skullcap of the chief elder wags slightly and his eyelids flicker. Suddenly, the round-faced one snatches me up and, despite my squirming, pulls a piece of silk around my head like a scarf and parades me around the circle. He urges the crowd to look deeply into my "monkey-like" face.

Then he gestures toward the crowd and a small, gangly monkey is led into the circle on a rawhide leash. But before he can resume his argument, the monkey lets out a horrible shriek and runs about in great agitation, winding the leash around both the advocate's leg and that of the man who had brought him forward. When he can move no further, the monkey sinks his teeth into the thigh of the advocate and a tremendous struggle ensues before they can disentangle the monkey and lead it, shrieking, back through the crowd.

His face red to the point of bursting, the advocate hops around the circle shaking his leg and squeezing his thigh with both hands. Ignoring the roars of laughter and merriment all about him, he signals again into the crowd. Three men enter the circle, one of them with a bamboo pole. When they reached the advocate, two of them place it on their shoulders and lock it there with their hands. I hide behind the twins, but the Father pulls me out and hands me to the advocate. Taking great care to keep his fingers clear of my jaws, he in turn hands me quickly to the third assistant, who turns me upside down and twists my tail around the bamboo pole. The advocate then repeats, very loudly, his argument about my "monkey-tail." At his signal, the assistant pulls both hands away from me.

There is a gasp from the crowd as I fall with a plop into the mud. Then another roar of laughter, as I race around the circle, dripping with mud, growling and snorting in protest at this treatment. Loud jeers ring out from the crowd and some began to throw clumps of mud and the shells of the nuts they are chewing at the red-faced advocate.

The Elder in the black skullcap must rise to his feet to restore order. Only then does the third advocate rise to speak. He has a rolling, soothing voice that calms me—for I am still much upset by my fall—and seems to placate the crowd as well. The face is clearly not that of a dog, he says agreeably, nor could a dog walk on two legs like the creature before us. The strange noises and screams it made were not those of a dog. But! Its gait and sniffing and barking, it's four-legged run, its body structure are just as clearly not those of a monkey.

"As for its tail. . ." He points to the ground and another wave of laughter shakes the crowd.

The advocate holds his right hand near the side of his face and opens his palm "Dog?" he says. "An indefensible proposition." He then holds up his left hand and opens his palm. "Monkey?" he says. "A ridiculous proposition." Then his demeanor suddenly changes, he rolls his shoulders forward, his face hardens and his eyes become bright and intense.

Involuntarily, I growl at his transformation.

"Such a creature could only be cobbled together by desert demons," he declares in a dramatic, ominous voice. It is known, he says, that this creature, this self-proclaimed Lord, this Lord Shushee, first appeared to the caravan without warning on top of a giant sandhill. That, as it stood in the midst of the black hurricane, the winds parted around it, with not a grain of sand or a pebble striking it. It is known that, after the storm passed and the way was completely lost, that this creature, this self-proclaimed Lord, this Lord Shushee, marched in front of the caravan for seven days without food or water, that he stopped to rest only when those of the caravan could no longer…"

"Known by whom," shouts one of the headmen from our old caravan. "For I was with it in the desert and the thing did naught but lay on its furry back panting from the day we left Huizhou." There is much muttering and snickering and others join in the jeering.

"No, it appeared not on a sandhill," says another from our caravan "but atop a giant pile of bones for it had eaten every horse, sheep and goat within 100 li of Dunhuang."

"No!" another shouts, "it floated from heaven in a flaming gold pisspot."

The tumult of jeers and laughter is so great that the advocate cannot continue his argument. "Such a creature could only be cobbled together by desert demons," he shouts one last time and returns to his place.

The Elder in the black skullcap must stand for a long time, while all the other Elders and their attendants motion to the crowd to be silent. Finally, they are hushed.

"We must go and reflect on this difficult matter," the greatest of the Elders croaks. But the crowd will not tolerate this irresolution. They hoot and shout and stomp their feet for a decision right now. Finally, the Elders agree to this; they huddle together on their mud-specked carpets and begin their deliberations.

It is not until rain begins to sprinkle us that they can reach a decision.

"The Council finds that the creature in question is indeed a dog—though a very strange one," the greatest of the Elders says. He speaks as loudly as he can, but his weak voice cannot be heard by many. The decision must be picked up and shouted back and forth across the crowd many times. There is much shouting and groaning, rejoicing and cursing as the elders and the advocates file out. The advocate with the bony fingers is surrounded by admirers who grab at him and slap at his back and arms; some try to lift him above them but they are so jostled by others in the crowd that they cannot do it. V.J. and the Father go from one person to another in the crowd, looking very happy. The twins run through the crowd with their bowls, thrusting them at those who seek to sneak away without contributing coins or other gifts.

Late that night, after the crowd has long departed, V.J. and the Father sit side by side in the tent, arranging the coins and stones on the thick new carpet the Father has just purchased, then placing them in sacks. Although they are very happy, they say little and we can hear the patter of a light rain on the tent.

The twins announce a visitor and V.J. and the Father rise and greet him at the entrance. It is one of the Elders, not as old as the rest. He walks easily and does not stoop at all. They offer him tea but he does not wish to linger. The Father hands him a large sack and all bow to him.

After the Elder leaves, the Father sees that I am watching him—as I always do when he moves, curious, worried as to what he will do next.

"All things have their cost," he says, "one cannot expect even the truth to show itself without the help of money."

* * *

V.J. says he must leave and travel south to his own country. He says that he very much regrets parting with the Father and the twins and the Mother who have been such dear friends to him. Also, though Kashgar is wallowing in mud and the traders are difficult, his stay here has not been disagreeable. The women here are very comely, he says, and tell him that they find his dark skin fascinating. Though they do not seem to charge him any less because of it, he adds with a laugh. V.J. speaks less now about the new universes and giving away his wealth. He says that he has concluded that it would be unwise to give up all his wealth at once. It is surely more efficient to give up just some of his wealth—a goodly amount to be sure—and use the rest to earn more wealth. In that way, he can make even greater gifts in the future and accumulate a greater and greater inventory of acts of piety to benefit him in future lives. This may enable him to skip several universes and go directly to a very much purer universe than if he were to give up all his wealth now.

When he is ready to depart, he and the Father grab each other—so tightly that they stumble about in front of the cart for a few moments. Their faces are wet with tears. He bows politely to the Mother and the twins, folding his hands together. They are weeping also and return his bow.

Then he glances at me. He is, I can smell, still afraid of me though he has learned to hide it much better now. Still, by way of saying goodbye to me, he makes a great show of stamping his feet, and jerking his arms about as though he were going to strike me, laughing wildly, though his face is still wet with tears as he does so. I have grown used to him and very fond of the sugary treats he gives me whenever he can get them, and I no longer have any wish to bother him. But his peculiar behavior riles me and I leap to my feet, throwing back my head and barking full force.

Everyone is made very happy by this. The Father even picks me up, which he almost never does, and dances around with me.

In the next few days, everyone is very busy, rushing this way and that through the market, buying new wares and supplies and selling off old, packing our wares and belongings in bags of hide and stuffing them into the carts, tending to the new animals the Father has purchased. Our camels have all been sold now and in their place are small, shaggy-haired, brown and white ponies and yaks covered with brown, black, or gray hair. The yaks are even more foul-smelling and objectionable than the camels and it takes many days before I can reconcile myself to their presence in our camp.

Chung and I have little to do, however. In the evenings, as the others rush about the campsite, we sit on the edge of a low cliff above the river and look across the city into the mountains far beyond. Chung ties me to the thin, twisted trunk of a nearby tree, for my wanderings have led to many run-ins with the slinking, mud-flecked, pointy-nosed dogs of Kashgar, who have sometimes pursued me all the way back into our camp. Though the twins enjoy the battles with these dogs, the Mother and the Father have declared them to be a great nuisance and ordered that my wanderings be brought to an end.

Chung sits cross-legged on his carpet, pinching bits of the brownish cakes he carries in his pouches and placing them in his mouth, as we watch the sunset. The rain has ceased now for two days, though broken gray clouds are scattered about the sky.

"These are the most beautiful sunsets in the world," Chung says. "Look, see how the world is now bathed in yellow, orange-tinged light. That is the effect of the particles of red grit that forever blow about here. And now the clouds begin to pick up touches of pink and rose, even far behind us in the east. There, there to our right a streak of purple settles below the roof of clouds. Now look how the rose and pink begin to climb little by little above us, moving from one gray band to another, reaching out now to those delicate wisps and curls and fluffs. Even that mud soup of a river picks up the color and becomes beautiful."

"In my youth, I might have had the boldness to render such a scene in poetry. But I could not then have seen it as I do now. For I yearned only for kings and intrigues, powers and pleasures. And I had not yet found my love."

"Look," Chung says more urgently, and he sticks a thin finger far in front of him. When I do not respond, he picks me up and tries to point my head toward the sunset.

"See those dense bunches of crimson and deepest red gathering where the sun has gone down. See how they now flare up." Then, as though wearied by his effort, he sets me back down.

Excited and confused by Chung's insistent manner, I move close to him and wave my head up and down, following his finger as it traces the sky. Then I look beyond his finger, thinking that perhaps there is an intruder or a bit of food to which he wishes to alert me.

"Here," he says, pushing a tiny bit of the brownish, waxen cake toward me. "This may enable you to see it as I do." The powerful smell of the cake both repels and attracts me. I am uncertain as to what to do. I turn my head and curl my lips but at the same time snap my jaws as though I am biting at it. Chung laughs softly, places it in his mouth, and looks again at the sky.

"Now the gray gathers strength," he says after a few moments. "It seeps back, determined, as always, to regain control. And a colorless pale rushes in between the clouds.

"Such is life," Chung says pleasantly, "but that which I love has the power to drive away the gray."

When later the twins come to get me, it is dark and I am fast asleep, Chung is gone, though the smell of his brown cakes lingers on the carpet and in the air. The twins call him but he does not respond.

* * *

Chung is missing. The yaks and ponies and carts are packed and we are ready to leave Kashgar. The bustle and confusion of our departure as always unsettles me and I run aimlessly about the campsite, distressed that the rhythm of our life is being once again broken, fearful of the new patterns that await us, fearful that I may be left behind. The Father and the twins have searched through the markets, the streets and alleys of Kashgar, and down by the river, but still they cannot find Chung.

Finally, we can wait no longer. I am called and put into the cart with the

Mother and we begin to march through the narrow streets of Kashgar. The branches interlaced above our heads are bare of leaves now and the gray mist has returned.

"Even after allowing for a reasonable profit," says the Father, "which I would not have taken anyway, since Chung is my friend, there is still much left over from the gold and preciosities that Chung gave me to sustain him.

"I do not understand such a man!"

14
Across the Mountains and into the Steppes

My screams have unnerved the whole caravan. The Father says that if I do not stop, he will skin me and make a fine hat out of me. But the higher we go up the rock-strewn, zigzag path, criss-crossed by banks of soggy snow, the more frequently the lop-sided feeling pours into my ears and I cannot repress my screams. Others in the caravan sense something as well. They raise their heads and sniff the heavy, still air as though they were dogs. The feel of the air is eerie, they say, and bodes no good.

In the beginning everyone was concerned that the weather was too warm. Each heap of bones, thrusting out of the melting snow, was seen as fresh proof that the snow ahead would be too rotten to navigate easily. That the hooves of the yaks and ponies and the feet of those walking alongside the caravan would break through the snow and be mangled by unseen boulders and soaked with running water. But now eastward travelers have been encountered who say there is already fresh snow in the passes. Now everyone is worried that snowstorms will bog us down and close the passes before we get through them.

* * *

The trail has become very steep and rugged, covered with ice and loose stone. Above us, a towering expanse of unbroken white reaches down ever closer towards us. The cart jerks back and forth continuously and it is impossible for me to settle myself in one place very long. The ponies slip more and more often; several of them have injured themselves so badly that we have had to slit their throats and hastily butcher them. Only the yaks seem never to lose their footing. They plod forward at the same slow pace without worry or difficulty, punctuating their walk with that never-changing monotonous grunt they make.

The cold has seeped into everything. Even at night when we sleep in a huddle of furs and cloth, the chill never goes away. Often I have pains in my head and it does not seem as if I can get enough air to breath. All my old wounds have begun to ache—most painfully, my haunch.

The jolt of the wheel against a boulder throws me against the back of the cart. Then the path is almost smooth and an engulfing stillness settles down on us. It becomes thicker with each moment and fills my head with the lop-sided feeling and I can do nothing but turn in circles and let out my scream.

A blast of wind strikes us head on as we round a narrow bend and we are all at once submerged in an ocean of white. Men, yaks, and ponies—all stand still for a moment as though the wind has been knocked out of them. Then the men recover and try to force the ponies and yaks forward into the snow that is already deepening on the trail. They do not want to move—even the yaks resist—and have to be struck with whips and switches. The men grab the bridles of the ponies and the ropes that run through the noses of the yaks and pull them forward. At last we begin to move again. But we cannot move more than a few feet at a time before we must stop, as the whirling snow confuses us and ponies and carts are forever slipping to the side of the trail. Each foot we advance must be won with curses and whips, with neighing and grunting and the gnashing of teeth. But we continue this agonizing, slow march through the day and night and into the next day—for all are certain that to stop on the trail means disaster.

* * *

The winds have stopped now. The sky is a clear, cloudless blue and the sun is painfully bright—though it does nothing to lessen the cold. The trail has turned downward now and the snow is not so deep. It is easier to move forward but, at the same time, more dangerous. Several ponies have slid to the side of the trail, kicking and neighing, and pitched into the huge rocks below. Carts too have fallen and broken. And men, with ropes tied about their waists, climb down to free up the ponies and yaks and salvage the cargo when this can be done.

The Father has rags tied around his eyes—as do many other men—and

Kaidan must lead him by the arm down the trail, warning him where the snow is deep or where treacherous boulders lie underneath. His face and the faces of the twins are swollen and burnt red and flakes of skin hang from them. But the Father says that these ailments will not last and that the worst is over. We will be all right, he says.

* * *

"There is Zozz," the Father says, pointing to the mud walls, hardly higher than a man, surrounded by fields of faded green and furrowed brown earth—and beyond them sandy plains dotted with coarse, yellow-brown grass. It does not seem that he is talking to the Mother but it is not clear who he is talking to. The twins lag far behind us and there is no one else around for we no longer travel with the caravan.

"Zozz!" echoes the Mother, her voice an equal mixture of contempt and despair. "Zozz!"

Each night when we camped along the broad pebble-strewn riverbed, the Mother and Father argued and they continue these arguments now that we have settled into the marketplace at Zozz.

[One or two bits of information garnered from my sometimes sketchy contacts with "Lord Shushee" suggest to me that "the Father" ran afoul of his old enemies, probably at or near the modern city of Tashkent, and reluctant altered his course northward. I believe that it is likely that he traveled along the Syr-Darya River, possibly part of the way by boat, toward the Aral Sea. But these hypotheses cannot be regarded as much more than speculation. As in the case of Kumchuk, I have been unable to find any record of Zozz, which seems to have been a quasi-independent kingdom (albeit a "pissant" one by the Father's standards) located very near the Aral Sea—S.D.]

"I would rather be dead than in these barren northern wastes," she says to the Father and, "Pride has turned you into a nincompoop. You have no more sense than Chung" and many other such things.

When he says he will beat her, she turns her back to him and bends forward and says, "Go ahead, strike me, powerful and courageous man that you are. Strike a poor, weak woman." When he says he will kill her, she sticks her neck out and says, "Go ahead cut my throat, brave man. Cut the throat of a helpless woman." And when once he did strike her, she spewed out such a torrent of curses and screams and wails that even the yaks started and all of us—the twins, the Father, and I—fled from the tent because we could not bear it.

Now that we are in Zozz, the Father goes off every night. When he returns, he smells of wine and pretends to be merry. "Zozz is truly a wonderful place," he says with a laugh in his voice, but his eyes are hard and the scent he gives off is one of anger. Then they begin to argue again and the twins and I crawl as far away as we can to the other side of the tent.

* * *

The Father has made many new friends in town, all merchants like himself. Each night after my performance, they sit round a smoking fire in one of the squat, flat roofed dwellings near the marketplace and drink wine and discuss the rumors of war that are on everyone's lips. Armies of barbarian horsemen are said to be very near Zozz. They are not mere bandits, it is said, but armies such as no one can withstand. Ever since summer, they have been active all along the borders of the Neotene Sea [Aral Sea—S.D.]. The Father says maybe they are Hsiung-Nu whom he believes can be dealt with reasonably. But the other merchants say they are neither Hsiung-Nu nor Wu-Sun, though they live much like them, tending huge herds of sheep and cattle and horses on the great grass-covered plains and having no cities or towns. And like the Hsiung-Nu they are superb horseman and ferocious in battle but such is their barbarism that they can hardly be said to be human.

One merchant says that they eat human flesh and drink the blood of their horses. Most dispute that they eat human flesh except perhaps in special rituals and they do not find the drinking of horses' blood to be objectionable—anyone would do it in extreme circumstances.

"Yes," says the merchant, "but they drink it in preference to all other foods and drinks."

Another merchant says that the warriors of one of the tribes are said all to have red hair and blue eyes. Very odd, says another, for in my entire life I have seen but three people with red hair though many with bluish eyes. It is also said that the women fight alongside the men and that their right breasts are destroyed as infants so that all the strength will go into their right arm and shoulder.

"I do not believe that a woman can defeat a man in battle," says a merchant.

"You have not met his wife," says another merchant, pointing at the Father, and everyone laughs. Even the Father laughs grudgingly.

Where do they come from, someone asks, for they were not in this region before this year. It is said that they came from far to the north, says another eagerly, beyond even those regions where men turn into wolves and those where men sleep a full six months out of every year. They are dripping with gold, he adds, so it is believed they have some truck with the griffins that guard vast stores of gold in those northern regions.

That is nonsense, a tall merchant says with great assurance, they are not one tribe but many and some hail from the plains above the Great Sea [presumably the Black Sea—S.D.] far to the west on the shores of which the Greeks live. A hundred years ago they were hurled eastward by defeats they suffered at the hands of the Parthians. Others have lived forever to the west and north of the region. But all are the same in their love of horses and killing.

* * *

The horsemen are all over the city, sauntering unconcernedly through the marketplace, where everyone makes way for them, and through all the streets leading into it and even idling in front of the big houses where the king lives that they call the Palace. Their passage through the gates of the city was not opposed, for no one dared to do so. The horsemen wear trousers and boots and tunics of leather and felt that are covered with patterns of bright green and red and blue and sometimes yellow. And peaked caps of felt with the same bright colors, from which their beards and wind-gnarled hair protrudes. Their faces are weathered and stern and they do not smile, but look down on those about them with an air of vague and contemptuous curiosity that causes everyone to avert their eyes. Most are dark-haired, though a few have red or yellow hair.

Each wears a breastplate of leather armor and carries along his left leg a leather bow case in which he keeps his bow and arrows. On his right leg, he carries a long knife or short sword. All wear gold earrings and their breastplates and tunics and trousers are decorated with emblems and plaques of gold. Some wear armbands or gold necklaces as well. Their horses, most of them colored in shades of reddish brown though a few are white, are also decorated with bright colored felt and leather and sometimes even with gold plaques. Though their horses, which they never seem to dismount, are no larger than those the Father and V.J. rode on the desert, the horsemen all appear huge to us—and invincible.

When the merchants gather round the fire that night, I smell, and see by the haste and awkwardness of their gestures, that everyone is full of fear and anxiety. The cups of wine are poured quickly.

"What do they want?" a merchant asks as everyone drinks thirstily.

"What do they all want?" replies the Father. "Treasure and to humiliate a king or two in the bargain."

"I am told that they demand that a portion of the taxes collected on all trade and travelers passing through Zozz be granted them," says one of the merchants and the Father tosses up his hands with a knowing air, "and that King Sosylon make gestures of submission to their king, whose name I am not sure of, and accept him as his Lord."

"Which so far," says another, "Sosylon has refused to do since he says he is already pledged to the King of Bactria and that his honor will not allow him make such an oath to another. And also he seeks to haggle with them over the amount of the tax."

"His honor! Haggling over taxes is to be expected! But since when does a king make only one such oath. I have known far greater kings than this pissant king who have taken five such oaths!" the Father says amidst a scattering of laughter.

"And what do these barbarians say to this?"

"I am told that if by tomorrow he still balks at their demands, they will behead all the men of the town—except for the king to whom they will not be so merciful—and makes slaves of the women and children!"

"And what of the merchants? It is only by chance that we are here."

"You should not expect that beasts like these barbarians will concern themselves with such niceties. I am told that when they take a dead king about in his funeral procession (for it is their custom to drag them around from tribe to tribe for months, they say.) If anyone chances across the path of this procession, they kill them and add their bodies to the concubines and attendants who are to be buried along with the king!"

"Even merchants?"

"What sense does that make? The concubines and attendants would be of use in an afterlife. But what good would a bunch of strangers be?"

"They are not to be trifled with! In Talkhus, to the south and east of the Aral Sea, the King sought to play with them, saying that his fealty was to the King of Parthia, though I am not sure which one (there are so many who now claim the kingship), and that should they seek to harm him, they would call down on themselves the wrath of Parthia."

"What a dolt! Talkhus is an even more miserable kingdom than Zozz!"

"What was the result?"

"They cut him up into pieces, cooked him in delicious spices, and along with a generous amount of mutton, served him at a huge banquet, which all the nobles and headmen of Talkhus attended—and then they cut off their heads too!" There was much laughter at this result—and calls for more wine.

"They kept the king's head, scoured it out, and gilded it—so as to make a drinking cup of it."

"I saw such a cup. I could not make out what it was at the time, dangling from the saddles of that big one on the white horse with the nasty scar that dents his forehead."

"But what of the merchants, why should they harm those who are merely passing through Talkhus or Zozz and have no say in the foolishness of kings?"

"Let us hope King Sosylon has seen the skull cup and is reflecting on it."

More wine was drunk and a special liquor brought out that was said to be the pride of Zozz—that many spit out when first they tasted it. And, as always happened when they drank this liquor, they began to joke about the peculiar, square-shaped heads of the common people of Zozz. Some pretended to be worried that it was this liquor that made their heads square. But others argued decisively that it was a contraption of boards that they placed on the heads of their infants that accounted for the strange shape of local heads and several said they had actually seen such contraptions. The smell of fear evaporated and the merchants turned to eager and merry talk of what should be done. Finally, the Father stood up, and I stood up with him, for I wished to return to the comfort and familiarity of our tent.

"It is agreed," he said in his booming voice of domination. "We shall send a delegation to King Sosylon and give him a sack of gold as a token of our esteem and urge him to accept the oath. And we will then go to see the scar-faced one, who appears to be the leader of these barbarians, and offer any services that might be useful to them and any oaths they desire and give him a sack of gold as well."

But then the Father sat back down and musicians with flutes and drums were brought in and songs sparked up and died just as suddenly. Many rounds of wine were drunk and all shouted their agreement to what the Father had said—although they quibbled for a long time about the sacks of gold, agreeing in the end that they should be half the amount originally proposed.

* * *

The next day word spread of a great ceremony and, by afternoon, the square that led from the palace to the marketplace was filled with people. A platform covered with woolen carpets had been set up at that end of the square closest to the Palace and on it was a throne of camel's hair with a canopy of blue tasseled silk. The Father pushed in close to it and the twins and I followed in his wake.

Kaidan persisted in holding me close to his face so that I could see through the crowd as he did, though I had no interest in these proceedings and wished only to be let down. Barbarian horsemen ranged about the platform and the borders of the square. All were, as before, stern and unsmiling and looked about them with blank, contemptuous stares. All but one—for near to us, a barbarian fidgeted about on a white horse, laughing and joking, looking around the square with bright and playful blue eyes. He wore no cap to cover his long hair, which was burnt red in color, and had removed his tunic, baring the lean, taut muscles of his arms and neck. His arms were painted with writhing, entwined animals, partly hidden by golden armbands.

When he caught the eye of a man glancing at him, he drew his forefinger across his neck as though slitting a throat. When a woman looked briefly and timidly at him, he flexed and wriggled the biceps of the arm nearest to her and, raising his eyebrows, poked the muscle with his forefinger. When he spied me in the crowd, leaning against Kaidan's shoulder, he thrust his face forward and forced his eyes wide open in amazement, then pulled out his long knife and whetted it with his thumb. Though fearful of offending him or attracting his attention, the crowd watched his antics with sidelong glances and the tittering of suppressed laughter followed wherever he moved about the square.

Horns were blown and everyone, except the barbarian horsemen, fell to their knees. At last, King Sosylon came out from his palace, wrapped in a red gown trimmed with fur and carried on a litter. Attendants walked before him sweeping the earth and sprinkling the ground with incense. The nobles and officials of the city marched behind him and barbarian horsemen rode at the sides of the procession. The litter was carried onto the platform and the attendants assisted King Sosylon, who looked very fat beneath his robe of silk and fur, in walking the two or three steps from the litter to the throne.

Horns were blown again, as the nobles and officials marched in front of the platform and arrayed themselves in proper order of rank on each side of the king. When the horns ceased, the crowd was allowed to rise and a tall, white-bearded man, holding a big pole from which a dozen or so ribbons and furs and animal tails hung, positioned himself directly below the king and began to speak. He stood on a low stool so that he was higher than the others but still much lower than the king.

He shouted first of the exalted lineage of King Sosylon and traced his ancestry, generation by generation, back to the first king who had been left on the earth (in those ancient days when Earth and Heaven first separated) as punishment to his parents who were, of course, gods themselves but had displeased the other gods by lingering too long on the earth. So that when at last his parents answered the summons of Heaven and returned, they were not allowed to take him with them and he was left to fend for himself. Alone and abandoned, he would have perished had not the god of the north wind taken pity on him and blown him into a herd of yak. Sensing his divine origin, the yaks formed a circle around him, providing protection from the harsh cold with their shaggy bodies and nourishment from their bushy teats.

"Disgusting thought," whispered a merchant to the Father.

"What a blowhard!" the Father whispered back.

The white-haired man talked for a long time about the heroic adventures of this king, who was also called Sosylon, who wandered the plains for 200 years with no companions but a lioness, a wolf, and, of course, his yak-mother. A titter shook the crowd to our left where the red-haired one pretended to fall asleep on his horse and let it scamper a few steps forward, scattering people before him.

Shouting louder and louder as his voice grew raspier and raspier, the white-haired one drew attention to the ancient sacred bond between the Kingdom of Zozz and the people of the plains, in urging the gods, all of whom he enumerated, to bless the friendship between these two peoples. He praised the divine mission of these warriors of the plains, whom he called Sauratae, and of their king whom he called Atea. He spoke of the delight of King Sosylon and the people of Zozz that their wanderings had brought these warriors here. He invoked once again the blessing of the gods on Zozz and the Sauratae, and on King Sosylon and King Atea.

There was a moment of silence and confusion after he had finished, which was broken when another barbarian on a white horse, the one with the huge scar that dented his forehead, rode to the front of the platform. Then the king rose slowly and, alternately looking pained and relieved, he took from an attendant first a bowl of the earth of Zozz and then a vessel of water from the Sacred Spring that flows from the rock near the palace and presented them to the scar-faced one. Then another attendant brought to King Sosylon a bronze ornament, also adorned with ribbons and furs and animal tails, which the king also gave to him.

After the scar-faced one had received these tokens of submission and handed them to a slave at his side, he pulled his long knife from his sheath (at which the king involuntarily drew back) and, with a mighty inarticulate roar, in which only the words Zozz and Atea could be understood, he waved it around in a circle above his head. All the other barbarians did the same, shouting and waving their knives, and the red-haired one did a handstand on his saddle. The crowd too cheered, and hopped and stamped, grateful to relieve the stiffness and numbness in the legs and feet. And everyone returned to their own affairs very happy.

* * *

That night, there was great merriment and rejoicing in the marketplace. Large crowds gathered for my performances, easy to please and generous. Just as I was finishing one of my two-legged walks, all the noise and frivolity emptied from the audience and the scent of fear suddenly filled the air. The red-haired one walked his white horse slowly though the parting crowd and into my circle. He stared down at me and, without turning his eyes from me, tossed a small gold coin that flashed briefly when the firelight struck it. Ayaru ran out from behind me and caught it. Although I did not understand what was happening, I had the sense that some wrong was to befall me. The red-haired one pointed at me. Neither the Father nor anyone else moved or spoke. Then he pointed again and twisted his finger with impatience. The Father looked and smelt strangely small and weak to me as he moved across the circle and picked me up and handed me to the horseman.

The red-haired one pulled me against the hard, scaled leather of his breast plate, and then he bundled me into a leather sling that barely left my head exposed. He pressed his knees into the white horse, and it turned and charged forward, careless of the crowd, which had to run and jump from its path. In a moment, we were gone from the marketplace and racing along the street that led to the North Gate of Zozz. My life on the caravan, my life as Lord Shushee, was over.

—To be continued—
in
I, Tutus: Citizen of Rome

Printed in the United States
36565LVS00003B/82-255